BETWEEN THE DEVIL AND DEEP BLUE SEA

by
Emil Steinberger

1663 Liberty Drive, Suite 200
Bloomington, Indiana 47403
(800) 839-8640
www.AuthorHouse.com

This book is a work of non-fiction. Unless otherwise noted, the author and the publisher make no explicit guarantees as to the accuracy of the information contained in this book and in some cases, names of people and places have been altered to protect their privacy.

First published by AuthorHouse 11/02/05

ISBN: 1-4208-8048-9 (sc)

Library of Congress Control Number: 2005907817

Printed in the United States of America
Bloomington, Indiana

This book is printed on acid-free paper.

Dr. Steinberger, when it became known by readers of the Jewish Herald-Voice that you would be releasing, in a book form, the chilling Holocaust survival story of you and your family surviving the dangerous trek from Germany through Poland and the Soviet Union – before coming to America – it is interesting to report the unusual number of "where can I find it?" telephone requests.

Joseph W. Samuels
Publisher

Dedication

This volume is dedicated first and foremost to ANIA, the backbone and the purpose of my adult life.

However, without the loving care and survival skills of my Parents and of Uncle Leon, I probably wouldn't have survived for ANIA.

Houston, Texas 2004

Authors Note:

This is the first volume of a trilogy entitled: *The Journey*

Table of Contents

PREFACE

Voluminous literature has appeared since the end of the Holocaust dealing with its political, psychological and philosophical background. The unspeakable, inhumane, barbaric behavior of the perpetrators has been described, analyzed and roundly condemned by countless writers, politicians, philosophers, dignitaries and statesmen. Hundreds of individual memoirs have been published describing the details of murder, torture and suffering of the hapless victims of this infamous episode in mankind's history. Numerous accounts of individual survival in concentration camps have been detailed in books and formal oral history interviews.

This book illuminates a different facet of the results of Nazi persecution. This tale chronicles a young boy's view of the world around him prior to and during the time of Hitler's march to "glory" and ultimately to his oblivion. It also deals, from a teenager's perspective, with some aspects of the war's aftermath. The story is not meant to dwell on horrors and inhumanities afflicted on man by men. It addresses the issues of survival after Hitler's attack on Poland; it deals with life under Soviet occupation; and it discusses the survival of a young teenager in a Soviet Gulag (Labor Camp). Despite the complexities of the struggle for life in a war-torn Soviet Central Asia, the boy retains a positive view of life around him, obviously tinged by youthful optimism. At the end of the war, an opportunity presents itself and he returns to Poland. Here he witnesses the physical devastation of the country and learns about the loss of most of his family. He faces, but poorly assimilates the enormity of the Holocaust and is forced to witness the smoldering animosity of the native Polish population against his people. His parents consider Poland a "cemetery of our people" and refuse to remain there.

Despite the fact that he is able to enroll at a university and is trying hard to look toward the future through rose-colored glasses, the reality of his environment and the persistence of his parents, force him leave Poland via an underground organization. They smuggle him and his immediate family through Czechoslovakia and Austria into Germany where he becomes a "Displaced Person." In the postwar Germany he pursues three goals: 1. Survival 2.Education and 3.An opportunity to immigrate to America.

CHAPTER 1. The Bullet.

Something was tickling my nose but I was scared to move. The aircraft engines were wining and their sound was coming closer. The stutter of the machine guns was interrupted only by the characteristic sound of falling bombs, a whistling prelude followed by the "boom" of an explosion as the bombs were hitting the road, the wheat fields and the potato fields in which I, my parents, my sister and the rest of the family were trying to hide.. I finally realized that a huge, green grasshopper crawling on my nose was the cause of the tickle. The fear, however, was paralyzing and I wasn't about to move a finger to remove it, fearing that any motion may call the pilot's attention. The Stucka bombers were diving and strafing people huddled on the ground, some in bushes, others in potato fields, in seas of wheat, hugging the ground melting into it and praying that the pilots will not zero in and use the machine guns on them. Suddenly I felt as if a horse had kicked me in the left upper arm, but there were no horses around.

The Stucka's disappeared over the horizon as fast as they came. People started to get up to return to their carriages, to their horses or simply to get back on the road and continue their treks east. I was still on the ground to scared to move, fearing the fighter planes may return. With a startle I felt something warm running down my left arm. It was blood. A bullet ripped through the upper arm muscle and exited from the side of the arm. There was more and more pain, more blood, then everything went black. I must have fainted.

****

My friend Tulek's father was lifting the perfectly round pieces of marzipan from a bowl of melted chocolate with a three-pronged wire fork and placing them upside down on a sheet of cold wax paper. The chocolate solidified rapidly. This quick hardening of the chocolate allowed for the formation of candies with three little ridges on the upper portion formed by the three pronged wire forks. I was thrilled to finally figure out how the ridges on the candy's chocolate surface are created! Within minutes, dozens of chocolates were made and pretty soon the large pot of molten chocolate was empty. Duvid, Tulek's father, knew exactly why we were standing there, ostensibly looking for work to help him and to act as his apprentices in making the marzipan candies. We hoped that the imperfect pieces would remain for us to feast on. Sure enough, we found a few rejects in no time and got what we were waiting for. During our free time, we almost lived in the room where chocolates were made--the idea of stuffing ourselves with chocolates was always irresistible. The sweet fog of the chocolate aroma in the air, the delicious taste of almonds in marzipan made us lazy and unusually docile for ten-year-olds.

"Where are you, guys?" a voice sounded from outside the window. "It's time to get going with the rehearsal." Although the entire gang was sold on the idea of putting on a show this summer, a show that required a great deal of work and of time to rehearse, the sweet nothingness was stronger and we didn't budge.

Finally Anciek, our show's "impresario" came in, grabbed me by the ear, grabbed Tulek by the back of his shirt collar and dragged us outside to the improvised stage on the fourth floor terrace of Tulek's apartment house. All the participants in this venture assembled. Anciek was two years older than both of us. He was already getting ready for his Bar Mitzvah, and it didn't take a great deal of effort for him to drag us out--particularly since we didn't really offer much resistance.

On the terrace, the noise was unbearable, everyone was talking at the same time. Mendek, our "director" was in our eyes essentially an adult. He was fifteen. Rumor had it that he knew all about girls and was willing to share his erudite knowledge with those of us who really put their heart and soul into the play. The play was another rendition of *Tevyeh the Dairyman*, a highly modern and progressive rendition of this Shalom Aleichem play. The Hassidic idiosyncrasies, expressed in the play, resonated perfectly with the pre-Second World War socialist bend of the adolescent Hassidic imagination. The play was an interpretation written for us by our role model, Mendek, a Yeshiva "bocher," who was also a student at the Hebrew Gymnasium in Krakow. His rendition of the play was fundamentally an expression of his rebellion directed towards his Jewish teachers in the *Chedar* and partly towards his parents. The plot and the lines were his responsibility, but most of us, in addition to plying our parts in the play, took interest in other aspects of this enormous enterprise.

As we scattered through the terrace, which at this moment served as the stage for our theatrical endeavors, the opening lines of the play sounded clearly in the early evening air. Tevyeh, played by Anciek, was loudly opening up his discussion with God. He was making a logical argument to God using all the dialectic techniques that Mendek had command of and was able to incorporate into the play. Tevyah endeavored, with a great deal of emotional involvement, to sway God towards a quasi-socialistic solution to the problems facing Jews in a tiny Russian village in the late part of the 19th century.

This rendition of the play was not a musical; it was a hard-hitting critique, written by a young, idealistic teenager. "Oh God, where is your fairness?" the voice cried.

Anciek, however, was suddenly interrupted by an adult voice. It was that of a neighbor, Pan Sztolc, an orthodox Jew who operated large soft goods wholesale business. "Can't you kids be quieter, I am trying to pray." "Your voices are much too loud. The gentile neighbors may hear you and create problems, you sound almost like the revolutionary leftists."

The absolute condition we had agreed to when getting the permission to use the terrace was not to antagonize the neighbors. We quitted down several octaves and the rehearsal went on. It was a balmy summer evening. When the rehearsal came to an end, and most of the kids went home, I returned with Tulek to his apartment. It was vacation time. I had the permission to stay with Tulek and have supper with his parents and his sister, a girl of seven.

Having arrived with my family only a few years back to Trzebinia - a small town that could be considered a suburb of Krakow - I was delighted to make friends and be able to interact with their families this closely. Both of my parents were professionals and because of their professional responsibilities had suppers much later in the evening than most. Thus, I usually had supper with my much younger sister and our governess. On some occasions I was given an opportunity to spend an evening with Tulek and his family. This was great.

During dinnertime, we discussed almost everything, from making chocolates with Tulek's father, to Haile Selasie fighting the Italians in Abyssinia; from the mysterious ways of Mr. Roosevelt in the distant paradise (America) to the increasing hostility of Hitler's Germany. Tulek and I felt like adults in the company of his parents. Indeed, I felt that we were quite well informed. My origins in Germany, with vague recollections of being thrown out from there, made me quite an expert on the German issue. Tulek's parents, however, had a great deal of fun with me whenever I tried to suggest that the real intentions of Germany were to conquer Poland and then all of eastern Europe. They were convinced that the Germans didn't have the slightest chance to progress militarily, for any substantial distance into Poland and the Polish army with the help of the British would destroy the German military machine in no time. Tulek's father, who served under Marshal Josef Pilsudski during the Polish war of independence, would put the finishing touch to this discussion: "Polish cavalry is the best in the world, and I served in it as a corporal. Germans essentially have no cavalry, thus we will overpower them instantly and the war will be over." I managed to squeeze in a weak "but," however, it didn't go over very well and as usual I lost my argument.

The life of a young boy in the second half of the thirties in a small town in Poland was not all that bad. I remember the three stories "kamienica" (an apartment house which belonged to my Grandfather) where we lived for the first year. It also housed, in addition to the apartments for grandparents, two aunts and two uncles, a soda water factory, and a grocery store ran by my grandmother. There were also horses and wagons used to deliver the soda water and an icehouse located on the grounds belonging to my great uncle, some distance from grandfather's house.

It was fun in the summer to frolic in the icehouse on a huge ice cube covered with sawdust to prevent the ice from melting. It was great to play in the cold icehouse, particularly when it was hot outside. The real fun, however, came in wintertime when the ice was "harvested."

My uncle would "buy" a small lake; actually he would not buy the lake but only the rights to the ice on the lake! When the ice got thick, usually about one to one half feet, a crew went to the lake, cut the ice into large squares and took it by sleds driven by horses to the icehouse. There it was stocked up solidly and sparkled generously with sawdust. I would never miss this activity.

Usually, I would get all my friends and we would go to the lake to do some skating. The "ice crew" would first clean the snow off the ice and the next day start cutting. That gave us all the time to skate on a "private" lake and on "virgin" ice. This was a real treat because there were no commercial ice rings where the ice would be maintained and cleaned from snow. We used to skate where ever there was a bit of frozen water, as long as the snow was not too heavy on it and the surface not to rough.

Thus, skating on a frozen lake where the surface was cleaned was a real treat. The following day, when the workers started cutting the ice, we were there to watch and when my uncle was not around, we would skate on the intact areas of ice. When he was there, he would not let us do it since this was really quite dangerous. One could easily slide right into the water in areas where the ice was already removed.

While this episode sticks in my mind, the rest of the memories when we lived in Grandfather's house are quite hazy, with short flashes of memories related to visits of relatives, holy days and excursions with my aunts and parents to the forest and to a stream called Chechlo. This I enjoyed although I do not have clear memories of what we were doing there. I also remember attending a prayer house, a "schtibl," located in the backyard of Grandfather's house. It was very small, having only a few dozen members. Nevertheless, this was the place my grandfather attended every morning and evening and all of us on the Sabbath.

I spend quite a bit of time playing in the soda water factory or in Grandmother's grocery store. This was very convenient since both were in Grandfather's apartment house.

I recall visits of various aunts, primarily fathers' sisters, who lived all over the world--Hungary, Austria, Yugoslavia and mother's sisters from Germany and America. There were also visits of my cousins. The two I remember best were my cousin Kitty who now lives in Australia and my cousin Harry who now lives in Princeton, New Jersey.

I had one "best" friend, Tulek, and a group of four boys who were my "close" friends; their sisters and cousins completed the group. All in all, we were about ten to twelve kids spending a great deal of time together, particularly during the summer vacations.

I felt ambivalent about leaving for two months for the mountains because none of my close friends were coming along. Friends I made in the mountains during the vacations in the past couple years were a totally different group and in many ways actually different. The mountains were vacations, pure "fun." our interactions were games; problems were of temporary nature and usually considered on a much lighter level.

The interactions with friends in Trzebinia were frequently more serious; the issues we addressed were more important, more "adult" in nature. Today, we were getting the entire group together, going to a mountain near Trzebinia were we were to build a big fire and prepare our favorite food.

This was to be part of a serious discussion regarding rumors concerning a possible war with Germany. Tulek was charged with getting the huge black iron pot from his mother's kitchen. I was getting the potatoes; Anciek was getting the herring; and someone else was getting the onions, butter, salt and pepper. The responsibilities for the provisions were organized with great precision since the place we were going to was quite remote and once we got there the chances of getting supplies were slim.

We started walking early in the afternoon and arrived at the mountain by six o'clock. Quickly, we gathered firewood and started the fire. The potatoes were peeled, onions sliced, herrings cleaned and cut into narrow sections. A layer of potatoes was placed on the bottom of the black pot, followed by a layer of onions, then herring followed by potatoes again. This was repeated until the pot was full. No water was added. A round piece of iron was placed on top of the pot and a large stone on top of it.

All of us found a place around the fire; some sitting on huge boulders, others stretched out on the grass. The girls tended to be close to each other. The fire was burning merrily shooting high into the sky and occasionally erupting into fiery showers of sparks. We waited for the fire to burn out so that we could place the pot on the hot red coals to allow the food to cook. The sun was setting on the horizon in a cloudless sky.

Mendek, who was the oldest and a student in the Gymnasium in Chszanow, was the first to speak. He was our Guru and we listened to him with great attention. In a slow sleepy voice he commenced, "What do you thing of the rumors making rounds everywhere concerning the war?" It obviously was a rhetorical question. Mendek was setting the stage for a monologue he was to deliver. We knew it, he knew it--but it was a traditional way of interacting and we all happily went along with it.

"There is a great deal of apprehension among the European powers concerning Hitler and Mussolini. Actually, many are concerned about Mussolini more than about Hitler. The affair in Abyssinia didn't sit well with most. But Hitler's excursion in Czechoslovakia and now into Austria has been worrying every one.

I feel strongly that all this is of no consequence for us. Those were fundamentally Germanic countries that actually hoped that Hitler would annex them. The situation in Czechoslovakia is somewhat schizoid since it is a Slav country. However, there is a large Germanic population there, particularly in the Sudetenland. It is a little surprising that there was so little resistance to its take over. Austria on the other hand had a strong Germanic influence and they obviously were only waiting for the annexation.

We are a different story. We don't have a large segment of German population looking towards German occupation, except at the western borders. Furthermore, Poland is a country well prepared for war. Hitler will think twice before attacking us."

As Mendek continued to expound, the fire was dying out and the hot coals were flickering red with little blue flames dancing on the top. Most of the kids were sprawled around the fire listening eagerly to what Mendek had to say and ready to enter into a lively discussion with him.

I was also rearing to say my "piece." However, the aroma emanating from the black pot was overpowering and the issue of breaking up the discussion in favor of the "black pot" became quickly a non-issue.

Anciek, who was unanimously accepted as the head chef, dragged the black pot out of the fire, took off the iron plate from its top and after a bit of digging into its content and tasting, declared that food was ready.

We have brought with us in our backpacks genuine army issue aluminum bowls and aluminum fork and spoon combinations. These were put quickly to use. As the food was being dished out from the pot, the aroma was even more overpowering. The fundamental principle in preparation of this dish was to let it cook long enough so that the first layer composed of potatoes would get burned. This would allow a smoky taste to penetrate all the other layers of food in the pot, blending the different flavors into the potato base.

The long hike, then the wait and now the aroma, all have contributed to ravenous appetites. For a while there was a complete silence interrupted only occasionally by clanking of the utensils on the aluminum bowls. The coals in the fire were glowing through the layer of white ashes. The sun had set and the western sky had turned blood red.

We realized that we were not solving the problems dealing with the war issue tonight. It was getting late and slowly the darkness would overcome us. It was time to pack up and go home. The food, the fire, the talk, the slowly descending darkness made us very lethargic. No one was ready to get up and start the trek back home, but the authoritative voice of Mendek, while soft and at the same time quite persuasive, sounded again. This time it was not to stimulate a discussion, but to make us move and start on the way back home.

CHAPTER 2. On the Road to Lwow

"The bleeding stopped. Don't worry, he will be all right." I could hear my grandfather's voice coming from a great distance, from behind a great blue cloud. But it was not a blue cloud; it was the sky I saw when lying on my back. I opened my eyes. I could hear my mother's voice saying: "I am finished bandaging his arm, we must get going to find a safe place for the night."

After realizing where I was and what was happening, I also began to feel a dull ache in the arm. "Can you drink?" asked my mother, offering some water. I was parched. "Yes, but let's get going. The arm hurts more and more, maybe we can find a place for the night," I said. Unceremoniously they loaded me on the buggy and we joined the throng of people on the road.

Soon a large car, full of army officers, came down the road scattering the people, horses and buggies as well as the life stock crowding the highway; it was followed by a detachment of cavalry.

The horseman noted beards on some of the people. "This is a bunch of dirty Jews," one of them cried. "Get off the road 'Zydy,' get off the road!" I heard their screams.

Soon the cavalry horses were put into action, pushing people, carriages, buggies, bundles, and sacks, all into the ravine by the road. People were confused. "This is our cavalry," they exclaimed. "Why are they trying to destroy us," was the cry.

Obviously, the only answer was to get off the road and hide. My uncle who was running the horses and the buggy refused to budge. He, like my father, was tall, blond and blue eyed. He screamed back to the cavalrymen. "Stop acting stupid, we are one of you!" and the pushing slowed down. He continued waving an identification card. "I am an officer in a tank division trying to get to my section." (This incidentally was only partly the truth.) "These people are my family," he went on screaming.

At this point, the planes returned and commenced again the diving and strafing. They must have noticed a concentration of military personnel on the highway. I could hear the staccato of the machine guns. As I was being dragged off the carriage into the bushes, the pain in my arm become excruciating and I passed out again.

It was dark. I could hear voices. I could smell the animals. It obviously was a barn. Again, as if from a great distance I could hear my mother's voice: "He must have lost a great deal of blood to pass out this easily." "Probably he is simply scared," my uncle volunteered.

I had no idea what was happening except for the sound of the bombers and the pain in my arm. However, I was getting hungry. "Is there anything to eat?" I asked. This question provoked a chorus of answers. "He is up." "He feels better." "Get him some food." Everyone was happy to see me coming back to the living. There was plenty of food. We had taken a lot before leaving home, and although this was the third day on the road, there was still plenty. In addition, my uncle Josef "organized" in a village a couple loafs of bread, some sausage and "sour" (i.e. cultured) milk. "Eat, eat," he cried, shoving a half of a loaf of bread and a foot of sausage at me. I was starved and in no time consumed most of it. "It was great," I thanked Josef. "The arm hurts much less," I said to all present. This immediately put an end to my problem and attention then turned to the issue of where to go. We could hear the German artillery and see a totally disorganized segment of the Polish Army running with us on the road towards the east. The wisdom of the eldest was to head towards Przemysl, cross the Bug River there and see if the Polish Army could finally stop the Germans at the river and start chasing them back west so we could return to Krakow.

As we approached Przemysl, the roads were getting more and more crowded. It felt as if the entire country decided to run east and plug up the roads. The dust was unbearable. We stayed in a reddish brown cloud all of the time. Probably the worse harassment was matted out to us by small, former military detachments. Sadly, these detachments were what was left of branches of the Polish Army, now walking east on foot. They were dressed only in remnants of what remained of their uniforms. On their backs, they carried gas masks and parts of what was left of their original arms—moving on with the masses of dislocated people, just like us.

The cavalry detachments, however, played havoc with people on the road, simply riding over those who didn't have the time to scuttle away. The worst were cars with officers trying to get through.

Ultimately we got off the highway onto small country roads where we were dependent entirely on the instincts of my uncle Leon, who was quite clever about these things. On this route, our progress was much less stressful and more rapid.

By next evening, we could see Przemysl and soon approached the River Bug. The bridge over the river was solid with people, horses and an occasional truck or car. The river was also full of people in all types of watercraft. Locals were making good profit faring people in small boats and rafts.

It was daunting to note that the traffic moving exclusively east included entire military units. Josef remarked, "It looks as if the army is not thinking about stopping the Germans. Let's find a way to cross the Bug and move on to Lwow."

Here my uncle Leon was the master. He could talk anyone into doing his bidding, and he was the epitome of a "fixer." Sure enough, in an hour or so, we drove the carriage with the horse and all of us on a huge raft made of rough logs and nothing else.

It seemed as if the contraption had only been built in the last few days for the explicit purpose of making a quick buck from people streaming in great panic across the river to the east. Blocks were placed under the wheels to prevent the buggy from rolling off the raft.

Suddenly a whine in the air drowned out all other sounds. The horse reared. "Oh, oh, whoa," my uncle Josef screamed, trying to quiet down the horse, however the staccato of the machine gun bullets fired by and the diving bombers had drown out the whinnying of the horse. Before we realized it, the horse was struck dead by several bullets and so was the owner of the raft. After letting out a shriek, he fell dead next to the fallen horse.

The raft was drifting rapidly down the stream. Nevertheless, in response to a few powerful strokes of the oars by Uncle Leon, it started moving slowly towards the opposite shore. Josef was screaming, "Cut the horse off, and push it off the raft." My father tried but was unable to cut through the harnesses and ropes.

Mercifully, the current kept pushing us both down the stream and towards the eastern shore. My mother held on tight to my sister Stella and to me. "Hold on kids," she intoned coolly, "hold on."

There was remarkably little panic. My grandfather, Leopold, didn't utter a word throughout this episode. He just sat there. Once we reached the opposite shore, my uncle turned around to mother and said, "You know he changed his mind, he doubled the price and informed me that if we don't pay, his friends will simply cut our throats as we go through the forest."

Mother reached into her bottomless purse and handed the money. "Thank him," she said, "don't make him angry, we simply need to get going." She didn't realize that the peasant was already dead!

This ordeal took most of the strength from all of us. Uncle Josef was in the woods trying to find a way to get horses to pull our carriage. Uncle Leon found a small farmhouse near the river and led us there to rest. The owners left the house in a hurry. There were chickens running around in the yard. In no time, a fire was going and Mother had a chicken cooking on the stove.

A dental surgeon like my mother always finds a way to get things done, I thought. As we were ready to sit down to our meal, Uncle Josef showed up on horseback, leading two additional horses behind on a long rope. "Where did you get them?" all of us yelled in unison. Everyone was surprised, excited and happy. We badly needed at least one horse and here Josef showed up with three! "I found them wandering in the woods," he said. "They must have gotten loose from a barn during the bombardment." We were not particularly concerned how they got loose, or whose they were. We badly needed these horses and were grateful to have them.

Everyone was tired and sleepy and wanted to stay overnight in the farmhouse. "No, we must go on, the Germans are getting close to the river," said Josef. He learned about a country road leading to the east through the forests. A road that may not be bombed and may not have the kind of traffic we battled all along since Krakow. Reluctantly, we piled out of the farmhouse. Grandfather and the two children climbed on the wagon, and the rest trotted alongside the wagon pulled by the three magnificent horses. I was dozing, hearing only snatches of conversation, "If all goes well and we find a place to rest during the day, we will be able to move on tomorrow night and the following day we should be in Lwow," Uncle Leon said.

"The Germans will be stopped ultimately," my father said as I dozed off again. The next thing I knew we were in a forest. The sun was up. The horses were grazing under a thick canopy of tree branches. It was quiet; we were alone in this big dark forest. I could smell the blueberry plants. It felt like the usual summer vacation camping trip. I was confused--why was everyone here? What are both my parents doing on this camping trip? Why are my uncles here? Usually my parents didn't join me on camping trips!

Suddenly, I heard dozens of aircraft engines, whining high in the sky. Soon I saw the sky turning dark as the planes went over us swiftly. They didn't see us. We stayed frozen still. Now, I remembered. We were running away from the Germans, a war was on. The Germans were after us. I could again feel the pain in the arm where the machine-gun bullet hit me a couple days ago. War, war! Suddenly I felt scared. I started to cry. I felt deceived. Here I woke up thinking that I was still on my vacation; instead, I ended up in the midst of a war!

Under the canopy of the pine trees, it seemed almost like evening. Uncle Josef suggested that we keep on moving. With the respect to the transportation, we felt very comfortable. Three horses gave us some extra slack. Matter of fact, one of the horses was always running behind the carriage as a spare. We have not encountered a single soul on the road. The conversation around the wagon ceased and I fell asleep.

During the night, we passed through several villages, but everything was quiet, people were apparently asleep. I woke up as the rose-colored light started seeping through the forest. We faced a new day, new problems and new challenges. Everyone was awake. A quiet discussion was in progress. Father wondered whether we should again stop for the day and continue the next night. Both uncles, Josef and Leon, felt that we should continue.

The German Army must have been fairly close behind us since we could hear occasional explosions that sounded like cannon fire. This convinced us that we should keep on moving. Josef, who was an Army officer, showed a great deal of concern in respect to our situation.

Daylight was filtering through the branches of pines over our heads. The road was narrow and full of ruts. To sit in the carriage was very uncomfortable, since it swayed and tossed like a ship in rough seas. My sister Stella was awake; we both jumped off the carriage and walked at the side of the horses. Although there was daylight, the forest was very dark, thick and foreboding. We felt scared and intimidated.

Everyone was engrossed in his or her own thoughts. Suddenly we could hear, on the road behind us, sounds of a motorcycle engine. A cloud of fear passed over everyone's faces. We stopped the horses and looked back at the road from where we just came. We could see a cloud of dust enveloping a figure on a motorcycle with a sidecar. It was a soldier wearing a strange uniform, not Polish, and a rifle slung over his shoulder. He stopped at a distance, took out what appeared to be a pair of binoculars and started inspecting us from a distance. He then removed his rifle strap from his shoulder, pointed the rifle at us and started walking slowly towards our little group.

Grandfather was sitting on the carriage. Uncle Leon was sitting on the front end of it holding the horse's reins. My parents were standing in front of the carriage, close to me and Stella. Josef stood in the back of the carriage and was partly hidden by it. The soldier approached us with his rifle still pointing in our direction. We immediately noticed his strange uniform. His sleeve had a white swastika on a round red field. It was a German soldier! My blood curled. There was a perplexed look on his face and an expression of uncertainty.

At this instant, a shot rang out. The expression on soldier's face changed to a pained surprise, as he fell face down into the road's dust. I looked up towards the back of the carriage were Uncle Josef stood. He was there all right, holding a small Browning in his right hand. He ran around the carriage towards the soldier with Uncle Leon on his heals. They both, almost simultaneously, pounced upon the soldier who was lying motionless, face down on the ground. Leon pinned the soldier's arms under his knees and they both twisted his face up. After a little while, Uncle Josef said, "He is dead!"

They ran to the motorcycle, bringing it back for thorough examination. Uncle Josef's training as an officer in the Polish Army paid off. Apparently, he knew a lot about why the soldier somehow had come upon us. After finishing an examination of the soldier's body and the motorcycle, he pronounced that the soldier must have been an army courier who got lost in the forests and found himself incidentally in the middle of nowhere, well ahead of the advancing German Army. Uncle Josef explained that he carried the automatic in his pocket, and when the soldier came over with his rifle pointing at us he felt that there was no choice but to pull his gun and fire.

The question was what to do next. Leon and Josef did not waste time to discuss this issue. They quickly pulled the motorcycle off the road deep into the forest where they covered it with pine branches. The soldier's body met the same fate. The entire episode didn't take more than fifteen to twenty minutes.

As soon as they were finished, they returned to the carriage very concerned. Josef said that "the Polish Army must be retreating in total disorder and the Germans are advancing very rapidly and on an uneven front. We will need a great deal of luck to escape the German Army. We will continue east but keep on going as rapidly as possible, during day and night to get to Lwow as soon as possible."

CHAPTER 3. The Siege

We entered Lwow's suburbs about one hour ago. The streets were deserted. The eastern sky was getting light. We saw fires as we approached the city. During the night, the Germans were bombing the city. As we entered everything was quiet. This was my first time in Lwow, a big city with huge houses. Here and there we saw Polish soldiers. No one, however, bothered us. We were moving swiftly to my aunt's house. When we arrived there, bombing resumed.

There was no one in my aunt's apartment. We found a neighbor who told us that my aunt's family was hiding in the cellars of the building that housed their import-export business. This building was several blocks away. My family knew the place and we got there in no time. My aunt, her husband and their two children were in the cellars. The reunion was subdued. My aunt's family went to their business building because steel reinforced beams held up the cellar ceilings. This, they thought, would give them better protection from the bombs.

It was quite obvious that members of our family were now in a state of confusion. They couldn't understand why the Polish Army failed to stop the Germans at the western borders. They couldn't comprehend why we ran away from home in Trzebinia, particularly since we left Grandmother, all the aunts with their families, and most of our belongings behind. Later in life I asked myself these questions many times, however, even today I would have difficulties to answer them clearly.

Mother and my sister Stella went directly to the cellars while I stayed behind with the adults to unload our baggage. We barely got the last piece off the buggy when again we could hear planes close by. My father grabbed me by the arm and dragged me down to the cellars. As we cleared the entrance to the first cellar, the entire building shook. The accompanying noise was hair raising, a deep rolling sound of an explosion that felt as if it could be coming from the inside of my stomach. Some cracked plaster came down on us from the arched ceiling, but the steel beams and the cement in the ceiling held well.

We listened anxiously but no further explosions could be heard. My father and my uncles cautiously crept out of the cellar with my cousin and me closely behind and climbed the stairs to the building's main hallway. The gate leading to the hallway was blown cleanly off the hinges and inwards by the explosion.

The street in front of us was littered with debris, and the apartment house across the way was burning. It must have suffered a direct hit by the bomb. Apparently, there were still some people in the basement. The fire was centered in the right wing of the apartment house; its main entrance, in the center of the building, was still accessible. My uncle Juzek ran through the main entrance into the burning and crumbling building. Soon he came out leading a queue of crying and screaming children and women who apparently were hiding in its cellars. The building continued to burn and parts started collapsing. The fire spread uncontrollably to the neighboring apartment houses.

Shortly thereafter, every one came out from our relative's cellars. We started to worry that the fire may jump across the street and ignite their building. There wasn't much we could do about it. No one had any experience in containing fires, and there were no hoses or water supply facilities. We just stood there, watched the fire burn and prayed.

The street was full of people, running and screaming, dragging bundles, clothing, and food, obviously trying to salvage all they could from the burning apartments. Some were unable to get down the staircases and were jumping out of the windows. There were no ambulances or fire trucks, just a wild mass of confused, screaming people. There were fatalities and many burned people. Finally, a military truck arrived and started collecting the burned victims. We didn't know where they were being taken. The family members who were well simply ran after the truck to learn where the truck was taking the injured.

Everyone on our side of the street that was spared took some of the people to their apartments for temporary shelter. We took a family of five into our cellars. My uncle apparently knew them well. Gradually the panic subsided, the dead bodies were removed and things quieted down. This was our introduction to Lwow.

As the days went by, life in the cellars wasn't that bad. We lit candles to read by. They had boxes full of candles among the other goods in the cellar. We slept on sacks full of raisins, exotic dried fruits, almonds and nuts, next to cases full of sardine cans, marinated fish and various canned meats from all over the world. We certainly wouldn't starve. Actually, every day we had a daylong feast. I could eat my most favored foods (raisins, nuts, almonds and canned fish) to my heart's desire. The only thing missing was bread. However, we had packaged crackers.

My two cousins were great fun. In the past, I barely knew them. They visited us rarely and I had never visited them in Lwow. The girl was my age, while Paul was two or three years older. He was thirteen or fourteen, essentially an adult in my eyes. We played, read and ate. My cousins were different from my friends in Trzebinia. They had no interest in current affairs and politics, an activity I so avidly pursued with my friends, an activity which could have flourished in these confined quarters. Paul's interests were limited to discussion of his first year in Gymnasium, the Secondary School, and after getting over with it, his joining father's import and export business.

Fundamentally, I was bored, but the days moved rapidly. The bombardment continued and we had no news, only rumors. The children were not allowed to go out of the cellar. The adults, who chanced excursions into the outside world whenever there was a lull in the bombardments, collected whatever little information was available.

Life assumed a steady routine. Our major goals were to pray hard enough so that a bomb would not hit our house, gather information and keep alive. We had quite a few people in the cellar—my aunt and her husband, my two little cousins, my parents and my sister, my paternal aunt, who was a single girl, two of my father's brothers and my grandfather.

To wash or to prepare hot food was difficult since there was no sink for washing or a stove to cook available. We used a small kerosene burner, "Prymus", to prepare anything that required heat. The ability to use the little burner was a salvation, although not an easy task. Preparation of cooked food for eleven people under these circumstances was a major undertaking.

The German Army was apparently encamped at the western and northern outskirts of the city; the Polish Army was engaged in these areas. I did not see many Polish soldiers, but I wasn't anywhere close to the battleground. We all however, could see and hear the bombs. The bombing was going on primarily at night, with some daytime activity as well. We were permitted to sneak out during the day into the backyard, whenever there was a lull in the bombing. We quickly got accustomed to the high pitched "wheeee" followed by deep base, low frequency "currrhum" sounds as the bombs were falling through the air and ultimately exploding on the ground and destroying some of the buildings in the vicinity. Several days went by. The war wasn't actually that bad! Suddenly, one morning it became quiet. No bombs. A leery, deafening quietness settled in.

CHAPTER 4. Intermezzo

People started crawling out of the cellars slowly and checking their apartments or what ever remained standing. Suddenly, we could hear singing in a distance. This was followed by the sound of hundreds of boots marching on the street pavement. In no time, we saw them. The Soviet Army was coming down the boulevards, with a song on their lips.

My parents, aunt, uncle, cousins and neighbors were standing on the sidewalk in front of the cellars from which we just crawled out, admiring this wonder. My father turned to us and said, "It's like during WWI when I was a war prisoner in Kiev."

My uncle, Leon, chimed in, saying "This is the first for me, and I don't trust the Soviets." We, the kids, however, were elated! People didn't know how to react. Was this our salvation? Were we being liberated by the Soviets? Were we being occupied? Whatever this act was, every one was happy—the war was over!

The soldiers of the Red Army were, to all practical purposes, our liberators. Finally, everyone could leave the cellars and start putting their lives together. We moved in temporarily with my aunt and uncle and soon started looking for an apartment. I was wild with anticipation of new things.

The Soviets made themselves very visible. There were constant parades and semi parades with the Soviet military showing itself in the best of light.

Large churches were slowly confiscated and many were remade into "Palaces of Culture" for the youth. By the end of 1939 one could see soldiers everywhere and soon pro-Communist youth "pioneers" wearing red neck kerchiefs, strolled up and down the streets, gathered in the parks and near the few stores that were open.

While these adjustments in lifestyle were occurring, the government promulgated other changes, changes to emphasize its positive attitudes towards people in a variety of ways. Not infrequently we would see a "spontaneous" performance by the Red Army entertainers on a large military truck stopped in one of the squares. The truck's sides would be taken down and the soldiers would start playing spontaneously ("?") the "garmoshka" (a form of an accordion) and to dance the "kozatchok". We, children (and adults?) were impressed. The Russians presented themselves as friendly, fun loving "culture" people.

The beautiful opera house was left essentially intact by the war at the foot of an enormous park near the center of the city. The Soviets took immediate advantage of it and restarted the opera performances and concerts almost instantly, having visiting performers from Moscow and Leningrad sing in lavishly produced operas within weeks after the war's end. .

In addition to classical music, the Soviet Army provided also a great deal of general entertainment. This included lavish parades showing off the military might of the Soviet Union. The soldiers marched smartly in the parades carrying the new models of automatic rifles; military music roared as did the hundreds of trucks and dozens of tanks. People lined the sidewalks watching the rolling trucks full of singing, "garmoshka" and balalaika-playing, soldiers; a state of festivity would emerge. Most people, particularly the youth, greatly appreciated these activities. The performing arts were a "natural" for the Russians.

Few weeks after the war, food and clothing shortages developed. One had to know someone to get bread, butter, shoes, underwear, etc. Soon a black market evolved which served as a safety valve for the shaky economy and as an easy technique for the authorities to pick up any one they wished to detain, when he or she happened to be on or near the black market. Such persons could be arrested and kept behind the bars until trial because trading at the market was formally illegal despite the fact that everyone did it.

By December, food could be obtained legally only in government stores. These, however, were empty by early morning, thus real shopping had to be done on the above mentioned and newly developed "black market". There, the prices were many times higher than in the government stores. Consequently, the money became "cheap" and since the government prices in the opera and philharmonic did not keep up with the black market one could easily afford tickets. This was a strong incentive to participate in this type of cultural entertainment.

On one occasion, an episode occurred that made me think a bit harder in respect to these various activities and specifically in respect to the Soviet military might. One day, as I watched a parade, while standing very close to the marching soldiers and vehicles, I became a witness to an unbelievable accident. The tanks were moving rapidly, when one stopped suddenly, the one behind continued and smashed into the rear of the tank ahead of him. Being very close to the collision site, I could observe the tanks very closely and to my horror, I realized that the body of the tank was made of thin plywood that collapsed upon the collision. These tanks were a mockup! A fake! Were these tanks a front to fool people with the alleged military might of the Soviet Army? This episode made me think hard about all the glowing statements about the Soviet Army made in the papers and in various official pronouncements. I realized that the Soviet Army might not be as powerful as it is being presented to us.

Later that evening, I approached Uncle Leon with my observations and doubts. It was clear that he was thinking about what I had to say and had difficulties responding. Finally he said, "You are probably right in your conclusions concerning the might of Soviet Army, however, when you go back to school do not discuss these ideas with your little friends and definitely not with your teachers." It was clear that something was bothering Uncle Leon greatly, but he didn't really want to talk about it. I decided not to press the issue any further and dropped the topic for now.

Soon rumors started that Stalin signed a non-aggression pact with Hitler and this pact allowed the Russian Army to annex a part of Poland. The official word was that the Russians fought the Germans to save the Poles. It soon became clear that these issues were not to be discussed. The feared NKVD had long ears and deep dungeons.

Within a couple weeks after cessation of military activity, schools were reorganized and reopened. Finally, I was able to enroll in a school, into the sixth grade. The school was an old private Jewish school, which became a government-run public school. It was attended primarily by Jewish kids. It should be noted that in Poland, before the war, there were no government supported public schools attended primarily by Jewish children

In the school, we were taught Russian, Ukrainian and Yiddish languages and literature! We did not study Polish, because this part of eastern Poland had become Ukraine. This was a major problem since all the children spoke Polish, some spoke Yiddish, but none knew any Russian or Ukrainian. We were made familiar with Russian, Ukrainian and Yiddish literature, but only with current authors, and in respect to Yiddish literature, only with those authors who expressed socialist or communist ideas. Shalom Aleichem was one of the favored authors we studied. There was, however, no mention of Jewish classic literature, Jewish religion or Jewish heritage. Neither the travesty nor the irony of this situation registered with me at that time. My concern was only with the fact that I had to study three new languages at the same time and all three were foreign to me. While Russian and Ukrainian literature were required, no mention of Polish literature was made. My Polish language was not helpful and the smattering of German definitely didn't assist me. I did learned how to read and write Yiddish, although, it was difficult for me to speak this language. I kept on confusing it with my fundamental knowledge of the German language. Since Ukrainian and Russian languages were "Greek" to me, I simply ignored them as much as possible. The other subjects were also to me of no consequence. I was much too interested in the various activities of the Palaces of Culture to pay serious attention to these subjects.

My cousins were my only friends since I did not make friends in school and fundamentally didn't interact much with my school peers. My two cousins and I spent a great deal of time roaming the city. With the advent of the "Youth Palaces of Culture," we spent time participating in various clubs, particularly the chess and the acting clubs.

However, there were certain peculiarities in the system and in its performance that created in me a schizophrenic attitude towards the Soviets. As an eleven-year-old boy, I enjoyed the government's positive and solicitous approach towards the youth and the various youth-oriented activities discussed above. I fully agreed with the principles of equality, education and fairness. Matter of fact, I realized that this propaganda was quite effective on me. I liked many things that were being said and the attempts made to implement them. However, there were certain issues of disturbing nature. These were numerous and serious, as for example the pervasive secret police, the NKVD, the failure of the economy, as manifested by the development of black market, the shortages in food and housing, the latter to be discussed shortly, and the general sensation of doom.

The city did not suffer severely from bombardment and artillery fire during the war, however, many building had been destroyed and more were damaged. The destroyed and severely damaged structures were left unattended; the less severely damaged houses were restored to a sufficient degree to enable people to live in them. Uncle Leon, who lived with us, was very clever and well versed in the art of "acquisition" during times of turmoil. He was a superb businessman, a magician in the art of negotiation, equipped with a caring and a brave soul. He was able to procure for us a "nice" apartment, formerly an office of an architect. It consisted of a single beautiful large room with a balcony, which became our living room, dining room, kitchen and a bedroom for Leon and a cousin, a tiny room where my parents and my little four-year-old sister slept; and a large storage closet, once used for office supplies and document storage, it became my residence.

It was not long before mother obtained a job as a dental surgeon and my father as a dentist with a Soviet military hospital. That gave us a chance to obtain the necessities of life a bit easier. Food, as mentioned above was generally scarce, but my parents' jobs with the military offered considerable connections giving us the opportunity to obtain extra food in special government stores. This alleviated the need to stand in a queue for food, or have to buy food on the black market at very high prices, essentially prohibitive for people with "normal" (not black market) income. My sister was still of preschool age and stayed home while I started back in school.

The usual conversation at supper would start with my father asking, "Any news from the front?" My uncle would answer, "The official Soviet word is that the Germans are experiencing little resistance in their drive to the west." My father would respond, "All this is propaganda. Allow the French and the British to organize a bit tighter, they will destroy the German Army when they are ready, and then they will move east to liberate us." My uncle tended to disagree "That is not what I hear," he would say. "My friends, who are crossing the Soviet-German border at night, are also a good source of information. They think that Germany is moving west with little difficulties and that the Germans are becoming stronger."

The various nightly discussions were simply a variation on this theme. No one knew what was really happening. Our family has registered with the Soviet government for an exit visa, hoping to be able to cross the Romanian border, then go south, ultimately ending in a Greek port where we could board a boat for England or the U.S.A., where my mother had sisters.

In our new apartment, I found a hidden closet with sacks of mail from all over the world, still in envelopes with stamps on them. This started me on a stamp collection and stimulated me to join the philatelist's club at the Palace. I dragged the stamp collection with me later on, through thick and thin, all over the world. Actually, 1939-1940, not counting the weeks of war, the living space crunch and the food shortages, were a lot of fun for a kid my age.

The reality that there was no adequate room to turn around in our apartment didn't bother me even though in the past we had lived in a very large spacious house. Similarly, the food shortage was of no great consequence to me since there always was enough basic food and I was not food oriented, in other words I could easily give up food for other needs or interests. On the other hand the clubs, the various facilities for children and 'teens, the ideas we were exposed to in school, all had a positive effect on me. Although materially we lived in squalor, I was quite excited and happy. The insidious effects of Soviet propaganda went unnoticed by me.

With so much happening, time moved on rapidly. Fall turned into a cold and snowy winter. The city slowly started returning from its "war" mentality towards a postwar status. Although now, looking back, it is clear that nothing was "returning." The food lines were becoming longer. The selection of goods, being it food or clothing, was becoming more and more restricted. The Russians were coming to Lwow from all over Soviet Union to buy whatever they could lay their hands on. Men were buying (when and where available) perfume and drinking it! Women were buying negligees and wearing them as fancy evening dresses to the opera.

The black market was growing larger and more important in daily life. Larger segments of the population derived a considerable portion of their sustenance from pilferage at work and dealing in the black market. Fundamental morals concerned with petty theft were being assailed daily and ultimately put aside as a "bourgeois" philosophy. Since official salaries were insufficient to allow survival, varieties of schemes and scams, primarily based on petty theft from the government or at the work place, were promulgated. The question being asked more and more frequently was: what next? How long will it take before we will be able to move on?

Since we had registered to leave Lwow and the Soviet Union, I felt that it was only a matter of time before the authorities would grant us permission to leave. Apparently, according to the discussions I overheard at home and information from my friends, there was a reasonably large number of people who registered for return to German-occupied territories. In our case, it was to leave for a foreign country, possibly Romania. There was actually very little we could do but wait patiently. We had a roof over our head, our stomachs were not complaining and I had an exciting time with my friends and the various activities we did.

Some new ideas advanced by the Soviets were quite captivating. In school, we had special time allocated to study "Political Sciences" in the 6th grade! That class was an introduction to Karl Marx's and Vladimir Lenin's writings. I was quite fascinated just by the ideas. To read Marx's and Lenin's writings would be a bit much, but to hear the material digested and put in a simple language by a teacher was fun.

While I pondered over these issues, the Sovietization of the city and, I assumed, the rest of the country continued. The fall turned into a cold winter. By January the morning trips to school in an overcrowded electric trolley car became a major chore because one had to hang on to an ice cold brass handle bar while standing on a step outside of the trolley car in freezing-cold weather, frequently in a snow storm. The school building wasn't well insulated nor was it adequately heated. Windows were broken and poorly patched, but the teachers were superb the camaraderie great. Despite the cold and hunger, we were learning and we were happy. As my mind roamed over the extraordinary events of the past several months, my thoughts returned back to the spring of the past year, the year of 1939—the year when the war broke out.

****

The school year was almost over. I had done quite well. I was elected president of the class. My major job at the end of the school year was to make sure that all school materials used by the class during the year were properly put away in the closets, the ink wells collected from all the student desks and locked up, all the maps rolled up and taken to the principal's office and an assortment of other little chores completed.

My mind, however, was too preoccupied to worry greatly about these mundane duties since I was already busy looking forward to the summer vacations. This year I was going again to the hotel Goplana in Szczyrk, where I spent the past summer, the summer of 1938 and where I made a great number of good friends. The hotel was reserved exclusively for preteens and young teenagers. It was staffed by a number of instructors who supervised the various sports and social activities and it employed a team of great cooks!

For a young boy, returning to the hotel was a very important issue. I must admit that I was looking forward to seeing again one of the girls who I had met the summer before. She had promised to return the following year. The only problem was that she was almost two years older and not particularly eager, I would think, to interact with a kid of my age.

I was also looking forward to seeing Erwin, a friend I made that year in Szczyrk. All in all, it was exciting time; time to pack, time to laugh, time to look forward towards great fun.

I couldn't, however, ignore totally the black clouds which seemed to gather in the past couple years and I realized now that I was sufficiently mature at the tender age of 11, to begin to understand the possible implications of the world situation and its political effects on our personal lives.

Actually, three years earlier, in 1936, my friends, who were a bit older than I and convinced of being politically quite sophisticated, were extremely concerned with the situation in Ethiopia and with Haile Selasie, the King of Ethiopia. He reigned from 1930 until 1936 when the Italians expanded their territory from Eritrea to annex Ethiopia. We kids were quite involved in the newspaper stories and the polemics at the League of Nations dealing with these issues. It is of interest to note that both Great Britain and France supported Italy's conquest of Ethiopia in the League of Nations, while the U.S. opposed it. Being quite liberal, we unanimously supported Emperor Selasie and U.S. against the Fascist government of Benito Mussolini. We followed with great interest what was considered at that time as "escapades" of Emperor Selasie, when he fled to French Somalia and later fought for recognition of Ethiopia at the League of Nations in Geneva. A great deal of this history was covered in the comics and we followed the comics published in the newspapers with great devotion.

In September 1938, Neville Chamberlain, the British Prime Minister, conceded to Hitler's demands. He agreed to annexation of a part of Czechoslovakia, the Sudetenland, and a part to Hungary to Germany. In November 1938, the League of Nations also approved annexation of a tiny part of Czechoslovakia, the Teschen district, to Poland. In March, the Anschluss, or the annexation of Austria to Germany, was also agreed upon. All this was done in the name of "Peace Now."

Thinking back to these days, I am still amazed that a group of kids between the ages of eight to ten years was so sophisticated, involved and sufficiently mature politically to spend time acquiring the knowledge, and more importantly, debating and discussing it.

However, no matter how sophisticated we were, we could not in our wildest imaginations conceive what the future held for us. All these happenings were actually exciting to watch and with "know it all" smile, conclude that the Germans have probably gone too far and it is time for them to feel the real power. It is time that they attack Poland so that our cavalry could teach them a lesson.

At this time, these considerations and discussions were, however, to take a second place in our lives. We were busy preparing for our vacations and fun, a much more real and important issue at this point. The usual preparations moved rapidly. New summer clothing was sewn and some ready-made clothing bought. The tutors were making quick summaries of the material I was supposed to study and review during the vacations. I was never given a long leash from the studies!

Finally, the day arrived. Mother took me to Szczyrk. The time on the train moved quickly, the green fields, dark forests and rolling hills were gliding fast by the windows. This year, only Mother came to accompany me to the hotel, the governess stayed behind to take care of my four-year-old sister. Father was to visit me later in the summer.

Upon arrival at the railroad station in Szczyrk, Mother hired a carriage, the driver loaded our luggage and we were off. The valley surrounded by forest-covered mountains was more beautiful than I remembered. The road wound itself alongside a beautiful mountain brook whose waters splashed rapidly over huge rocks polished smooth by the fast running stream. The air was full of fragrance composed of a mixture of aromas, pine needles, the fresh water, various flowers and cow dung.

Just after the railroad crossing came the hotel building, "Goplana," in all of its golden glory. The wooden siding was still like new; boards flashing the golden color of newly varnished fresh pine planks. The building looked as I remembered it from the last year, with high turrets and balconies running on each of its three floors around the entire building.

Seeing the windows of the rooms that overlooked the balconies triggered last year's memories. We would quietly climb out these windows, plotting some mischief, during the "quiet time" after lunch instead of taking a nap. I couldn't wait to see what new tricks my friends would come up with for the "quiet time" this year.

The arrival was noisy. Drivers argued with the porters as who is to carry our luggage to the rooms, and the staff screamed at each other. Kids were finding their friends from previous years, making new acquaintances or were simply being noisy overrunning the place. On top of all of this loud activity was the distinct presence of parents. We couldn't wait to see them depart and leave us in this paradise of paradise of paradises.

I was ushered to my room, and here came my first surprise. Standing there in all the glory of a thirteen-year-old was my old friend, Erwin! We were to share the room. My spirits soared even higher. Not only I had the good fortune to share a room with my best friend but also my best friend had changed.

Change is a much too insignificant word to describe the metamorphosis that has occurred. From a young boy, he has grown into a young man. Erwin, who already turned thirteen, was significantly taller than I, muscular, with a deep tan, wearing the most beautiful white velvet cap with silver *sznur*. This cap was part of a uniform of Gymnasium (secondary school) students. The fact that he has jumped the gun didn't bother me. (It wasn't until this fall that he would become a first year student in a gymnasium entitled to wear this cap.)

We just looked at each other and simply grinned with pleasure. He reserved the bed by the window for me, making me feel good and important, only later I learned what was behind this magnanimity. He also remarked quietly, under his breath, "I have a big surprise for you, will tell you later."

My mother came in and made a thorough inspection of the room and supervised the maids in unpacking my belongings and storing them in the closets. Slowly the afternoon was coming to the end. All of us, including some of the parents, were to have a supper together in the dining room on the ground floor. I still had to go through the ritual of getting weighed because it was the number of pounds that I was to gain during this vacation that would determine, according to my mother, the quality of the camp.

The din was getting louder as we descended into the dining room, culminating in an ear splitting noise. Some fifty kids, each shouting louder than the other, trying to greet old friends, making new friends or simply trying to tell in a voice that would carry over all the others the wonderful things they accomplished since last year. There was a great deal of bragging, posturing and putting out the best foot in order to make a smashing impact on the girls.

My mother, Erwin's older brother, Adam, who brought him to the camp, and I found space at one of the long tables and joined the general conversation. The hotel was only several years old, and the dining room was paneled just recently with golden-white pine planks that emitted a wonderful aroma. Great smells were also reaching us from the direction of the kitchen. I realized how hungry I was and couldn't wait for the meal to be served. The evening meal was usually composed of cold dishes because the main hot meal was served at noon. Thus, I was surprised to see mashed potatoes served with fat knockwurst and Sauerkraut! However, since this was a favorite of mine and since I was simply starved this peculiarity did not surprise me.

Mother was talking to Adam, Erwin's older brother, an "adult" of at least nineteen or twenty years. I was busy catching up with the stories told by Erwin. The past year was very good to him. Despite his varying interests, most of which did not include serious studies, and which occupied most of his time, he managed to finish the elementary school with flying colors, sufficiently high grades to be admitted to the Gymnasium in Bielsko with no entrance examinations.

I was amazed, impressed and a bit envious. Envious, not only of his achievements but also that he was going to be already a Gymnasium student while I will have to sweat another year in the grade school and probably suffer through rather rough examinations in order to get into the Gymnasium. While I was trying to pump him in respects to the exams and his school experience, he bend over and quickly whispered. "Nina, you remember, from the last year, the beautiful tall girl with the blond braids, she is back this year. You have to influence her to spend time with me. Last year she wanted to talk only with you. You are much too young for her!"

I remembered Nina, but never thought much of her. She was pretty, but for sure too old for me. She must have been Erwin's age, I thought at least thirteen years old. Bending over I quickly reassured Erwin that I will try to influence Nina to develop a positive attitude towards him.

The lights in the dining room were very bright, probably so the adults could easily keep a sharp eye on us. As the food arrived, the kids became busy and suddenly it got very quiet. Only the sounds of dishes clanking and food being chewed could be heard.

Mother, as usual, didn't eat much. She was busy interrogating Adam. After all, his brother, Erwin, was going to be my roommate for the entire summer. Mother had to become totally familiarized with Erwin's entire family in the greatest possible detail. She was leaving tomorrow and I felt that there would be plenty of time to attend to my personal business tomorrow. Today, I may as well spend my time primarily with mother and satisfy all of her whims.

After dinner, the chief counselor gave a brief introductory talk, all in general terms. Tomorrow, he said, we will be divided into teams and assigned to specific instructors. Tonight we still had one hour to spend with parents. Tomorrow we will also have breakfast with parents. But then, 'till the day we were to go back home, there would be no contact with the parents except by mail.

We were neither upset nor heart broken. Most of us welcomed this schedule. Despite the discipline that was to descend upon us from the camp's professional personnel, we felt quite mature and independent. The day was extremely full of activities and after dinner, when we were directed to say our goodbye's and return to our rooms. I was ready for sleep. Erwin was trying to talk some more, but I dropped off into a deep slumber.

****

My cousin Kitty, who was only seven, dragged me by the bottom of my shorts, repeating in German: "Let's go to the creek, let's go swimming in the creek." I was confused—how could I be with Kitty when I was in Goplana with Erwin? Something was wrong. But I remembered being in Szczyrk for an entire summer with Kitty, her mother Zosia and my other aunt Sala. We stayed there in a beautiful, newly constructed, log cabin on a mountainside overlooking the entire valley where Szczyrk was located.

I followed Kitty, who dragged me with her down the meadow extending in front of our cabin, to a ravine where a mountain stream was running. The water was rushing over huge boulders forming small waterfalls and pools. Early in the summer, we had partly dammed the creek; this created a perfect little swimming pool with a waterfall cascading into it with a great rush and music. The flowers and various grasses as well as the thick growth of pine trees surrounding the stream have scented the air heavily.

We changed into swimming suits quickly and jumped into the water. One had to jump quickly, otherwise common sense would have prevailed and we would not have had the nerve to do so. Water in the stream, which was coming from high in the mountains, was ice cold! But once we were in it, we just squealed with excitement and pleasure trying to swim the best we knew how.

I enjoyed the company of my little cousin although she was much younger, almost two years younger. I was already nine years old at this time. She not only was a beautiful girl, but also very kind and always willing to play, hike, swim, collect berries and mushrooms in the forest, build a fire on the side of the mountain where we could roast potatoes in the coals—in one word, she was a great companion.

As we swam, I could hear the voice of my aunt Zosia calling us for breakfast. Instead of having breakfast in the cabin where we lived this summer, we suddenly found ourselves in a fancy hotel in Szczyrk having lunch. Both of my aunts were dressed very formal; they were sitting by the table wearing fancy huge, white and black hats, and discussing with the waiter the appetizers.

Kitty and I joined them and sat at the table in our dripping bathing suits. Pretty soon a huge water puddle formed around us. We were sitting on the veranda of the hotel's restaurant and the water puddle, which was getting larger by the second, had overflowed the floor of the veranda and ran into the mountain stream running along side the hotel.

The entire situation was getting more and more unreal. The last thing I remembered was that the water was flooding the veranda. I tried to grab Kitty to swim with her out of the deep water when I awakened.

****

My friend Erwin stood over me shaking my shoulder: "Get up, get up, we are late for breakfast," he bellowed. He had shaving soap over his face and a safety razor in his hand.

My jaws dropped. Now I was totally confused. I was with Kitty, I was with Erwin, and now Erwin is shaving! Since when did little boys shave? Slowly I began to wake up and the reality dawned on me. I just had a dream about my vacation in Szczyrk two year's ago when my mother and my aunts rented a log cabin for the summer where we spent the vacation and Kitty was there also.

Now I am in Goplana, and Erwin is not a little boy anymore but a precocious teenager who is trying to grow up rapidly and who has indeed some beginning of beard growth which, only by a significant stretch of imagination, could be shaven, may be occasionally.

I didn't expect it, but target shooting became a good sport for me. This afternoon I again got the best score. This was good for me since I was getting tired of the derisive comments constantly made by Erwin, who was an excellent tennis player and a superb swimmer. But all the ribbing was good-natured.

We were having a great summer. Every morning we would wake up at 6:30 a.m. to the sounds of a trumpet sounding the Taps. By 6:45, we gathered at the back of the hotel at a gurgling mountain stream for calisthenics followed by a dip in the ice-cold waters of a creek flowing down over a bunch of rocks. Breakfast was served at 7:30 and we were ready to face the world by 8:30 every morning.

On this particular day, we were to go hiking in the mountains and have lunch on the way. We filled the backpacks not only with personal items but also with lunch food and other items necessary to spend a day in the mountains for a group of about fifty boys and girls. No tents were needed, but a lot of food, drinks and variety of pieces of equipment were at hand to be used during the hike.

It was 9:00 a.m. as we turned off the main road and entered the forest covering the slopes of the mountains surrounding the valley in which Szczyrk was located. The cool air, heavily scented by the pine tree sap, literally hit us and surrounded us with a feeling of exuberance, a desire to run, jump and sing.

As we walked on a soft, springy carpet of pine needles, the sun was finding its way between the branches of the stately pine trees. Large islands of thick soft moss were dispersed between the trees and small clumps of raspberry plants covered with a bountiful of gleaming red raspberries grew in the clearings.

It was as if God knew what will drive us crazy! We literally attacked the bushes, forgetting the fact that raspberry bushes carry heavy complements of vicious thorns, and in no time red blood mixed with red raspberries, was flowing abundantly.

But nothing deterred this army of kids who gorged themselves on the sweet, juicy and incredibly fragrant berries.

As I was picking the berries standing next to Erwin, he suddenly elbowed me and pointed his face toward the right. "Do you see her?" he asked. I was too preoccupied with the berries to pay much attention to him. "Emil," he whispered, "did you get a chance to meet Nina and talk to her?"

I had to admit that I had not run into her since we came to Goplana. "Go to her, say hello and then introduce her to me," he said.

I turned and faced Nina. She was bending to pick a berry and had not seen me. She wore a loose-fitting white dress. Obviously, she had cut off her braids. Her blond-golden hair reached the shoulders in total disarray. She looked far more beautiful than I remembered from last year. Something funny stirred inside me. I really liked what I saw. I wanted to talk to her, touch her, be with her, a feeling I have never experienced before. My heart, however, fell. She not only was painfully beautiful, but she also looked so mature. I actually thought that I could make out developing breasts under her shimmering white dress. On the other hand, I still felt like a little boy.

I'd better get Erwin in a position to meet her, I thought to myself. He had also grown up, like her. It will only be the proper thing for me to do. "Nina," I exclaimed. She turned towards me and her face turned pink, actually acquiring a glow. She ran over, took my hand and exclaimed with obvious joy in her voice, "I was wondering if you will make it this year; it is so good to see you again!"

"You look so grown up," I replayed, but I couldn't make myself exclaim what I really wanted to add so much, "and so beautiful." Instead, I turned and quickly took Erwin by the hand and said, "Do you remember Erwin? I think you two met last year. Look at him, look how handsome he is, he has really grown up during the past year, like you."

Before finishing the sentence I realized how foolish I must have sounded, simply voicing what really bothered me. She, however, was not flustered. She shook hands with Erwin and then took me by my hand and started walking, following the rest of the kids up the mountain slope. We walked for a very long while without saying a single word to each other.

****

In Lwow, the spring was coming. Snows melted and school life became more frantic in light of the upcoming end-of-year examinations. I was somewhat worried because my knowledge of both, Russian and Ukrainian was worse than poor. In view of my other activities, the amount of time devoted to the study of these languages was minor. It was a peculiar year. I had not acquired new friends in school. Actually I was neither interested in making friends nor in making grades. I felt some interest towards the classes in Marxism and Leninism but none of the other subjects arose in me any passion or even moderate interest. I was happy to finish the year by making good grades but nothing outstanding.

Early summer was arriving, the weather was beautiful and the days were warm but still not hot. I was busy having a good time, vacation time. However, black clouds began to gather on the horizon.

My old friends from Trzebinia were only a memory. Neither my family nor I heard anything from them or about them. My uncle Leon found a way to visit western Poland once. He smuggled across the border illegally and has spent several weeks there in the spring of 1940.

Upon returning, he was not willing to tell us much about our relatives. His mother, my grandmother, remained in Krakow with Lola, one of her daughters; all of my mother's sisters and brothers who lived in Poland at the time when the WWII broke out remained there also. Similarly, all my friends apparently remained in Trzebinia. His stock statements were: "They are all OK; I didn't have time to find out much more." As a matter of fact, I heard very little discussions between him and the rest of the family concerning his trip until one night.

I was awakened from deep sleep by an argument. Leon was arguing with father. As he addressed my father, he cried out, raising his voice, "I told you over and again that it was difficult for me to get information in Trzebinia since everyone there knows me and they were afraid to speak to me. The trip was very dangerous. My Polish friends in Krakow told me that a few months after entering Trzebinia the Germans rounded up most of the local Jews on the market square and simply shot every other person. The rest were sent to some camp. They were looking specifically for the Steinbergers, particularly for our father [my grandfather], since he was a prominent citizen.

I couldn't tell who survived this episode and where the rest of the people were sent. There are rumors that in January the Germans started building some sort of a camp in Oswiecim (Auschwitz, a new German name for this town) and by March started deporting German Jews who were still living in Germany to this camp.

I tried to see if we could get mother and Lola across the border to join us here. They, however, were adamant in their decision to stay. It was heart breaking. I got a similar response from Julas' [my mother,] sisters and their families. I think that the Jews in western Poland are fooling themselves believing that they can survive under the Germans. I heard that there are plans to concentrate Jews soon in restricted areas with strictly limited access to the outside. In other words, rumors were floating around that "ghettos" of the kind existing in the Middle Ages, except much more restrictive, are to be established. Actually there are rumors that such a ghetto is being established in the section of Kazimierz in Krakow.

The really bad news is that the Germans are killing Jews randomly and with little, if any, pretext. Sometimes the Poles finger the Jews to the Germans. Taking all of this under consideration would you still want to return to western Poland?"

His voice was raised and I could sense the tremendous distress he was experiencing. Now I began to understand the scraps of conversations among the adults and the stories I heard in the school from some of the kids. The issue of registering for the return to western Poland, currently under German occupation, if we would have failed to get through the border to Romania, began to assume a new meaning.

****

The quiet discussions between my parents and uncles became more frequent; everyone was agitated. Juzek, my other uncle, also father's brother, who lived with his new wife nearby, came over one evening expressing signs of great distress. He heard from a friend who last week smuggled himself back from western Poland that Oswiecim was designated by the Germans as a concentration camp to be used to gather all the Jews. Apparently, no one knew what ultimately this would mean, but the possibilities were frightening.

Our plans to return to western Poland and try to go from there to Western Europe or England didn't look very plausible. Father, however, still had more faith in the idea that we would be able to leave Western Poland easier than Soviet Russia and would go there rather than accept the Soviet citizenship.

But, the suggestion by Uncle Leon that we again reexamine the possibility of crossing the border to Rumania was accepted unanimously. Leon was charged with the task of making a trip to Zaleszczyki, a town near the Romanian border to investigate the possibility of crossing the border there.

This was not a simple matter. Under the Soviet system one cannot just travel; one needs a special pass when traveling between towns. In addition, Zaleszczyki was near a foreign border, which called for additional passes and permissions.

Leon, as I mentioned before, was well adept to "fix" things. He, with the help of my mother, who was working in a military hospital, got to know some NKVD officers. Through them, Uncle Leon was able to get the necessary papers to make this trip. Unfortunately, the report he gave us upon return was very bad. The border was as tight as a drum. None of the locals were willing to even consider smuggling us across the border.

Apparently, the Russians would shoot anything suspicious that moved within ten miles of the border. Our only remaining chance was the hope that the Soviets will let us go back to German occupied Western Poland and then, from there, we may have a chance to smuggle abroad.

By now, the situation was becoming very tense and the elders spoke freely in my presence. My grandfather, my single aunt and Uncle Juzek lived near us. One evening we got together in our apartment to discuss this matter. First, the Soviets were exerting a great deal of pressure on those of us who registered for the trip back to western Poland. They strongly suggested that we apply for Soviet citizenship. My father, who was the oldest of the siblings, expressed adamant opposition to this. Under no circumstances was he willing to consider Soviet citizenship. Mother was not sure, but the rest of the family sided decisively with Father. Mother brought up the point that many from western Poland who escaped the Germans elected to accept Soviet citizenship and be resettled deep into Russia with assurances for a reasonable job. On the other hand, we knew of many Poles and Jews who were send to labor camps or prison camps because they were officers in the Polish Army or had expressed too loudly anti-Soviet ideas. However, the number of these individuals was still quite small.

After a long and exhausting discussion, the decision was made not to consider Soviet citizenship. Shortly after the relatives left, we went to sleep.

CHAPTER 5. A Trip to No Where

I was awaken by a violent pounding on the door. Father went to open it and three NKVD officers pushed their way into the apartment. "Poydiem, Poydiem," barked the senior officer. "We are taking you to a train that will take you west, to Germany."

By then everyone was awake. My five-year-old sister was crying. "You have exactly one hour to get ready. You can take one bag per person, the truck is waiting for you in front of the house, hurry up," he said, and turned on his heels. The other two NKVD men stayed behind, standing by the door with their gun holsters open, just looking at us.

Bedlam broke out. Now Mother started crying and everyone was speaking at the same time. On one hand, everyone was happy to finally be released from under the Soviets' control; on the other, we were very apprehensive--was it a right decision to return back to German-occupied territories?

Actually there was no time to think about these issues. We had to decide quickly what to pack since we were allowed only one satchel per person! Mother apparently prepared herself for this eventuality, at least to a point. I wasn't even aware of this aspect of preparations.

During the year that she worked for the Soviets as a dentist, she learned that one of the most coveted possessions for the Soviets was to have gold teeth! Many times, she was asked to place gold caps on perfectly healthy teeth. Matter of fact since this was not allowed officially and it could not be done formally in the clinic, mother would have the various officers come to our little apartment and have the work done there. She purchased a small amount of equipment to perform this work at home.

I also became aware that my parents were able to take with them from their laboratory in Trzebinia all the dental gold they had in stock. Here they were able to use it to great benefit. I also learned that in general the Soviets liked metal caps on their teeth, however, the lower echelon had no means to get gold caps so steel teeth and steel caps were the second best.

In view of this, mother had made for herself a large corset that she could wear under her garments to keep the gold hidden there. Thus, this was the first thing she did; she placed all the gold in the corset and the corset on her body. The rest of the preparations went by me as in a fog.

It was, therefore, a major difficulty to decide what to take with us because of the space limit. Exactly within an hour, the senior officer returned and intoned, "Poydiem, poydiem" as all three of them started pushing us gently but firmly, out of the door. Each one of us carried a single satchel.

A small army truck with a canvas cover was parked in the front of the house. As I looked around, I could see several similar trucks parked near by. It didn't take long to drive to the railroad station. The truck did not bring us right to the station, but to a siding where a very long cattle train was standing. "Poydiem, poydiem" was the refrain again. The cattle cars were old with holes all over. There was a huge sliding door at the center with two tiny windows on each side, close to the car's roof. We were told to get in.

By now, dawn has breaking and there was quite a bit of light developing in the sky. The day was to be beautiful, sunny and warm. However, inside the car it was dark, except near the sliding door.

The car was empty. At the center, there was a round hole cut in the floor, about one foot in diameter, surrounded by a little wooden balustrade. A small round iron stove connected with a pipe to the ceiling was standing near the center of the car. Both, the front and the aft of the car were divided by a wooden platform into a lower and upper compartment.

The NKVD hoarded us into the car and our family members were told to take the upper compartment in the aft part and place our belongings there. This also was the place where the six of us were supposed to sit daytime and sleep at night. By the time we got situated, the rest of the car had filled up. Another family was placed into our compartment making it extremely crowded, but there was no choice. The NKVD shut the huge door and we were left in semi-darkness. Actually, on the upper level there was considerable light because of the high placed window, but on the floor in the center of the car, there was very little light and in the lower compartments it was dark.

The people began to get acquainted and started talking to each other. The very first topic of conversation was that tonight, and at the latest tomorrow morning, we would cross the border and things would improve significantly.

As you might suppose, the second issue was the toilette. People needed it--now. But where was it? We were stealing side glances at the hole in the center of the car with dread and disbelief. Finally Leon stuck his head through the little window and ultimately got the attention of one of the NKVD personnel supervising the unloading of other trucks.

This soldier, although Russian, spoke some Polish. When Leon told him of the predicament, he only laughed, "What do you think is the hole in the floor is for? Use it!" It finally sunk in--this was the toilette.

Family members used pieces of cloth, found among peoples' belongings, to hold up around the hole when the need arose. While not the most elegant or convenient of procedures, it served its fundamental purpose.

By noon people started getting hungry. No one has brought food and obviously this issue became now quite acute. About 1p.m. the sliding doors opened and a Russian soldier appeared with a bucket of what looked like soup, a Russian soup, called "rosolnik." It was primarily warm water in which a few pieces of potatoes and pickles swam. There was also a huge container of clean hot water to brew tea. They also provided us with a brick of compressed green tea and two loafs of black bread.

The soldier also brought several dozen of aluminum bowls, forks and spoons and aluminum mugs. Although the menu was neither particularly exclusive nor very large, everyone was sufficiently hungry to attack his or her portions of the soup with vengeance.

In the afternoon, Leon gathered the family for a quiet talk. He said, “I have a peculiar feeling about this entire situation. If we are going to the west, then why are we getting this treatment? Why cattle cars, why NKVD? Why closed doors? Why such strict limits on luggage? We were not even given the opportunity to take with us the bare essentials for survival.” He whispered, “We must find a way to get some more things out of the apartment, particularly some food and utensils as soon as possible.”

“But how?” whispered my father. Leon answered, “We will have to wait until the next shift of guards comes on duty to give us enough time to get some of these things done.” My father looked very skeptical while asking, “But how will you get out from here and how will you bring things in?” “I really don’t know,” replied Leon, “but I have some ideas.”

“Maybe we should use the basic ‘human nature’ approach” while rubbing his index finger against the thumb. With this he crawled over to the window and started looking around.

As time went on we became better acquainted with the rest of the people in the car. My sister and I were the only children and I actually didn’t consider myself a child anymore. In December, I was turning thirteen. After the usual questions, the conversation turned immediately towards the issues dealing with the length of our trip and the prediction that probably by tomorrow we would reach our destination.

Most people didn’t bring up the horrible conditions we were exposed to: no bathroom, the abominable and insufficient food, the fact that we were being locked up, etc. All were certain that this was a very temporary situation which we should endure quietly.

I was curious to see what Leon was doing at the window and the only way to do it was to ask for access to the other window on the same side of the car. This I did and as I leaned out this window, I saw a NKVD officer talking with Leon. It was a quiet conversation. Ultimately, the officer extended his hand, quickly took something from Leon’s hand and briskly walked away.

Uncle Leon returned from the window and I could see him and both of my parents having a quiet talk. I walked over to the group sitting on the upper shelf and heard Leon concluding, “this was a stroke of luck, the guy was really after my signet ring, he loved it, it was the one with a huge ruby, this clinched the deal, I think."

Father asked: "how could you trust him? How can you be sure that he will return once he got the ring?"

"Well," Leon said, "there are three factors. One, I have a good feel when to trust a man, second I promised him that upon completion of this transaction, I would give him a lady's ring with a small ruby, and third, the most important factor, we really do not have any options."

Mother said, "I think that I may have a little ring with a small ruby that I was planning to give to Stella. You can have it to give to the NKVD man, but how will the entire process work?"

"Apparently we are not leaving until after midnight," said Leon, "he will let me out once it gets dark and let me use a NKVD truck to drive to the apartment. I will load up and return within one hour. He, then will help me unload.

My parents shook their heads and didn't say much. Ultimately my father spoke. "Do you think that I may be able to come with you? This would be of real help." Leon answered, "I will try to have you come with me but it may not be easy. The NKVD man is already sticking his neck out quite a bit."

As we were talking the door slid open and food arrived. This time it was cooked cereal with a side dish of, what looked like, rotten salted herring, two loafs of black bread and hot water for tea. We were expected to still have some green tea left from the lunch. Apparently, we were being indoctrinated into the intricacies of the Soviet culinary excellence. Although everyone was very hungry, this fare had not made a hit with us. Very few of us were ready for the Russian delicacy of rotten herrings.

It was getting dark. In another couple of hours, the door opened and a quiet voice called "poydiem tepier." Both Leon and my father quietly slid out from the railroad car and disappeared between the trains on the tracks. The remaining people in the car attacked us with questions about Father and Uncle Leon. How were they able to leave? Were did they go? Are they coming back?

Mother refused to answer. She was scared but stood her ground. She said, "If all works fine they will be back in couple of hours."

The time dragged on, every minute felt like an hour. Stella started crying, "Where is Father, where is Father?"

It was dark. We could hear the guards talking but couldn't see them. Then it all became quiet and the time hung over us like a huge black cloud. Suddenly, we heard scratching at the door. Someone was obviously doing something with the huge sliding door of our car. Slowly the door started sliding open. Uncle's head appeared in the opening. "Quickly, put out all the lights and be very quiet. We have only fifteen minutes before the guards will be making their rounds. We have to unload everything very fast." As he was talking he was already tossing pillows into the carriage. This was followed by four featherbeds, blankets and bundles of clothing.

Triumphantly, he handed Mother her beautiful Persian fur coat. At this point, Father appeared in the opening with a dozen of two-foot long salamis. Father did not outshine Leon, who handed bags of sugar, flour, a burlap bag filled with loaves of bread and several bottles of oil. Once the food got aboard Father handed us several packages containing dental tools, dental laboratory equipment and supplies. Both Father and Leon jumped into the car, slid the doors shut and joined the jubilation.

Everyone was shouting questions simultaneously, "How did you do it?" "Can we also go and get things?" asked the other people in the car. Well, "you can try," said my uncle. "You have to know how to bribe, how to select the right people who would accept the bribe. Some will not only refuse the bribe, but may get you in a great deal of trouble. Fortunately, the latter breed is quite rare among the Soviets. I've had a great deal of experience with these issues."

Actually, Uncle Leon had an uncanny ability to "read" people, and get the best possible deal in a nicest possible way; once all was said and done, everyone parted as friends. While the questions were pouring in and the excitement would not abate, Mother was distributing loaves of bread and salami to the rest of the people in the car.

Stella and I were already well into the second and third helpings of bread and salami. We were in seventh heaven. Not only was our starvation remedied - but also salami! It was always a delicacy for us.

The celebration continued. The emotional satisfaction and the ability to satisfy our hunger in this wonderful way made heroes of my father and uncle. We were temporarily suspended in time and place. We forgot where we were and what the situation was.

Suddenly someone shouted, "We are moving!"

I slid to the little window and indeed the few lights at the railroad siding where we were parked were moving slowly. Actually, it was our train rather than the lights that was moving. As the train gathered speed, we clearly could feel the motion and soon the sounds of a train in motion became quite obvious. Sometime around this time, the sounds, the train's motion and the wonderful meal put me into a very deep sleep, despite all the excitement.

I woke up to the sounds of excited voices. Everyone was talking at the same time. "But we are moving east," said a young man in a polo shirt who was, I noted before, always behaving very properly. "Yes," said my uncle, looking out of the little window. "We must be moving east, the sun as almost ahead of us, also, I do not recognize the landscape, it looks different from the usual Polish fields and peasant houses." "Wait," he said excitedly, "we are approaching a tiny railroad station."

The train slowed down slightly. Uncle said, "I can read some store signs, soon I will be able to read the name of the town as we pass the railroad station, "Wait," he shouted, "all the signs are written in Ukrainian language! We certainly are moving east, further into Ukraine, rather than west, towards Germany."

Total silence ensued. A middle age woman with three little children started screaming and hitting her head against the side of the car. "This can't be so," she intoned, "my husband crossed the border back to German-occupied Poland a month ago and we were to meet in our hometown after my return. What will I do now? He will be in German-occupied Poland and I somewhere in Soviet Union?" she asked.

No one listened to her. All were preoccupied with similar issues. How will this unexpected change affect them? Each experienced a different problem since each family had different plans. However, none of the plans included the Soviet Union. Gradually the exclamations, swearing, crying and screaming subsided, the discussion changed from expression of surprise and anger to those of uncertainty and worry.

My mother got up and announced loudly, "let's eat, and things will look rosier after a meal." The fabulous food brought by Uncle Leon, some of which was distributed by mother among the people in the car, supplemented significantly the extremely meager food rations received from the NKVD, and has made us forget our sorrows. Once the food was prepared and served in absolute silence, interrupted only by sounds of chewing, everyone settled in the car.

By noon we arrived at a larger town. The train was placed on a sidetrack; there we remained until evening. In the early evening the doors slid open, a pail of soup was handed to us, the doors were again shut closed, and locked. When the pail was retrieved later in the evening we were again given an old filthy metal milk container with hot water for tea. The train didn't start moving until almost midnight.

During the next day, the heat in the car was almost unbearable and the only ventilation was provided by the four tiny windows. Since we were not allowed off the train, the primitive provisions for bodily needs had to be used, and by the evening, the stench was becoming unbearable.

Due to the fact that we were given no facilities to wash up, and no water to clean the wooden seat and the hole in the floor utilized as a toilette, we were faced with an unprecedented situation. No one had any good suggestions how to remedy it. The night was spent in great discomfort; the air in the car was stifling.

The next day while we were in the middle of nowhere the train has stopped. Suddenly we could hear noises at the door and soon it slid open. A NKVD officer indicated that we could disembark, walk around and visit the bushes. We were also permitted to take the huge metal milk container to the locomotive where we could get some hot water from the boiler both for making the tea and for washing ourselves and cleaning up the facilities in the car.

Our captors felt quite secure in letting us roam around free since there was no place to escape, to run or to get away. Suddenly the locomotive's whistle blew and the NKVD man started hoarding us back into the carriages. This time the sliding doors were left open. A NKVD man came with a 2x6 inch board, long enough to fit into the open door space. There were metal brackets on both sides of the door's opening in which the board ends had fit. The train started moving slowly with the doors open. This was an incredible relief. We got some fresh air, less heat and the ability to look out without having to wait for one's next turn at the queue by the little window.

Thus, there were several new developments that were being discussed at great length by all the occupants of the carriage. Firstly, it was agreed that the Russians were not trying to kill us, matter of fact they tried to make our lives more bearable, when possible, under current circumstances. Secondly, from a practical point of view there was no fear that we may escape since the train was stopping always in a deserted area with no hamlets or living people around.

My father said with an air of authority, "Since I was a war prisoner during the First World War in Kiev, I have some ideas. Firstly, we must be somewhere northeast of Kiev; this means that we are being transported deep into Russia. They would not keep us in Ukraine. Usually the Russians sequester undesirables into northeast Russia or Siberia. Secondly, if this is the case we still have a long way to go. Thus, we may as well try to organize ourselves to make this journey as bearable as possible."

Gradually the trip became monotonous, the same routine. Our food supply was running very low. We were getting accustomed to the diet of watery soup, some black bread and hot water for tea. Our supply of salami and some of the other foods has dwindled to almost nothing despite Mother's progressively more and more stringent economizing.

Since we were totally isolated from contact with people outside the train, there was no opportunity to buy or barter. The only contact we had was with the NKVD personnel and at that time we still were not sufficiently experienced in dealing with them.

My family and the others in the railroad car were constantly discussing various schemas for getting some food, all to no avail. Whenever we would get near a town the train would speed up to prevent the possibility of someone jumping off or getting any information.

As a matter of fact, it was even difficult to read street signs or names of the towns we were passing. However, ultimately it became clear that we had passed Ukraine; the signs were now in Russian language.

We had been traveling for an entire week. But, we spent a great deal of time on various sidings waiting for trains to pass us. It was difficult to estimate how far we traveled. The conditions were getting more and more difficult. Not only we were hungry, but also we were unable to really take a bath or wash appropriately all this time. Occasionally, when the train stopped in the fields, we were able to run to the locomotive and beg for some extra hot water; it was used for washing, primarily by the women.

One night, we arrived at what appeared be a town. The train stopped at a remote siding. I could see reflections of lights in the clouds suggesting that we have stopped at a large city. It was dark and quiet around us. I kept on looking through the little window since the doors were closed and locked. Several shadows were moving close to the train.

I decided to use the few Russian words I knew. Cautiously and quietly, I asked, "Gdye my?" There was no answer. "Porzayustie, skarzytye, gdye my?" I asked again. This time I could hear a quiet reply, "w gorodye Kursk."

The figures disappeared like ghosts and all was quiet again. I pulled myself back into the car and announced to all, proud of being able to acquire this knowledge, "we are in Kursk".

Questions were tumbling from the mouths of all, "Where is Kursk? How far is it from home? What direction is it? Where are they taking us?"

My father, who was quite knowledgeable about Russia in general and in its geography in particular, responded, "Kursk is a city located not very far southwest from Moscow. We are moving east towards the river Volga."

This did not help much. Most people remained very anxious since this information had not clarified our fate. It was difficult to understand why the Soviets would spend the time and effort to move this many people, suddenly, without any inquiry concerning their wishes somewhere into the heart of Russia. This -twelve-year-old boy's curiosity was seriously challenged. I listened avidly to all the discussions among the adults. They, however, were in as much of a quandary as I was.

These were the times that I missed my friends most acutely, particularly Tulek. We were accustomed to spending a great deal of time discussing such political (?) issues. The adults and I would be even more perplexed and concerned if we would have known that a million people like us were taken like this, all almost at the same time, and moved east into the heart of the Soviet Union.

The other curiosity was the fact that all of us in the carriage were Jewish and I had the suspicion that most, if not all, the cars were filled with Jews. I was not only perplexed but also quite confused. In school we learned about fairness, about Communism, about catering to the will of the people, and here we were rudely torn away from normal life, lied to and taken against our will to who knows where. Slowly the discussion died down and I fell asleep.

In the morning, the train was still moving. Settlements were even sparser and we were given time, after the train stopped, to get off and move around in the middle of a prairie, taking care of the necessities and get some hot water from the locomotive.

We were, however, getting hungrier and unbelievably filthier. The food provided was, putting it mildly, extremely monotonous--black bread and cabbage soup. Finally, we arrived in a town full of churches. This time the train stopped at the railroad station. There was a great deal of activity; the railroad workers were running around counting the cars or simply gawking at the train.

Suddenly the train started moving slowly. We were taken to a railroad spur next to a large parking area filled with trucks. These were open, khaki-colored military trucks. Soon, the NKVD personnel slid open the doors and told us to take our belongings and disembark. Then they counted off about 400 people and loaded us on the trucks, which, once loaded, took off promptly.

We were driven through a town and reached a river; the shore was very high above the river's water level. We drove slowly down to the river's edge where several barges were tied down.

Everyone was in somewhat of a shock. Firstly, we were hungry; secondly this was totally unexpected. Our truck stopped by a good-sized barge. We got off the truck and were directed to embark. On the barge, we were directed to settle down on the decks. Below the decks were holds that were apparently used to transport merchandise;

primarily building materials, stone, etc. The holds were extremely filthy, unfit for human habitation.

All of us remained on the deck. It was quite warm, almost hot. Each family was trying to stake out the best spot. We found a spot at the bow. All the valises were placed side by side and the bedding on top. This way we could lie down and sleep on top of our belongings. Thus, the valises were protected and we could sleep on them somewhat elevated, away from the decks.

Once all 400 hundred souls got situated several questions loomed. First and foremost, we wanted to know where we could get something to eat; secondly, we wanted to find out where we were; and thirdly, where we were going.

Uncle Leon again showed his abilities. After learning that we will not be departing 'till next morning, he approached one of the crew and after a hefty bribe managed to get off the boat. It was particularly interesting that he was able to pull off this deed since his knowledge of the Russian language was miniscule.

Pretty soon, however, it became clear that the security was in general quite lax. I was able to get off the boat at will, walk around the docks and talk to the crewmen using my minimal and primitive knowledge of the Russian language.

Security was actually less stringent than it had been at the railroad station. Why? Were our captors not concerned that some of us may escape? This puzzled me from time to come, but the answer became quite clear in the next couple of months.

As I was walking along the docks I was amazed at the drabness of the surroundings. The docks were in disrepair. The people I encountered were poorly attired, looking at me with suspicion in their eyes. No one attempted to strike up a conversation. I was not about to do so either, primarily because my ability to speak Russian was almost non-existent.

Most of the people on the boat did not venture out. The food issue was on everyone's mind since the hunger level was only increasing. We had not eaten anything since yesterday.

Finally, Uncle Leon returned. He had a lot to tell us. First, he had brought a loaf of black bread, nothing else. He did not have any rubles and the stores would not take Polish currency. Finally, he bartered a small pocketknife for two loaves of bread.

He also had learned that we were in a town on the Volga River called Kazan. He couldn't tell us much more, except perhaps that there wasn't much food in the town and that there were many buildings looking like Russian Orthodox Churches.

By the time he finished relating his experiences, the day was coming to an end. Suddenly, we noted the boat crew carrying large metal containers towards us. They were full of hot soup, which consisted of water, cabbage and some barley. This, together with the bread brought by Leon from the city provided a welcome relief to the hunger we all suffered most of the day.

Gradually, it became dark and the mosquitoes made their entrance. I experienced mosquitoes in Poland but these were the large "economy size" bugs. In no time I was covered with bites and the only solution was to get under covers to eliminate exposed skin areas.

After the sunrise, the barge started moving. There was no food except for the one loaf of bread left from yesterday. Even worse was the lack of water.

While we were on the train, most mornings we could get off at some stops and get hot water from the locomotive. This wasn't so on the barge. It was somewhat ironic. Here we were in the midst of millions of gallons of what appeared to be crystal clear water and we suffered of thirst and lack of wash water.

Finally, Leon "organized" a length of rope and a wooden bucket to get some water from the river. Pretty soon most people got water from the river giving us the chance to wash and ultimately also drink when we realized that we would not be getting any water from our captors.

Actually, our current circumstances seemed somewhat leery; here we were several hundred, what amounts to, prisoners and we could barely see any Russians on the board. I could see no NKVD or military personnel. There were three or four, what appeared to be, civilians running the boat. There was no attempt to escape. I began to realize….. "escape…….. where?"

The day progressed slowly. Since the sun in the morning came up from our right side in was clear that we were moving in a more or less northerly direction. The river was a mighty body of water with heavily wooded shoreline. The western shores had high bluffs with an occasional village perched in the hills. The eastern shore was quite flat.

By early evening we tied up at the western shore near, what looked to be, a fairly large town. People were starved and the pails of soup brought aboard were extremely welcome. This time we were also given some black bread. The soup and bread brightened the mood considerably. The few children traveling with us stopped crying.

With strength from having a meal returning to the adults, they began talking to each other. Again, discussions concerning our whereabouts and our ultimate destination became heated. Since we concluded that we were on the Volga River, that we started sailing from Kazan in a general northeasterly direction, those knowledgeable in the geography of Russia (and I considered myself one of them having just finished the 6th grade in a Soviet school) tried to guess our ultimate destination.

Some, a minority, felt that we will end up in Moscow. Others were less optimistic and considered the possibility that we will end up in Gorky, a large city up the river, known for its industrial might, particularly car and other heavy industry. There they needed workers and it was felt that we might be brought in to engage in work at these factories. Obviously all of this was purest of speculations since we had no information what so ever concerning our destiny.

A few of the people on the barge spoke Russian and learned that the name of the town we docked in was Ceboksary. We stayed at the dock until sunrise when the journey resumed. Now, using the bucket and rope routine, we were able to obtain as much water as we wanted. The water was much more palatable and had no smell or oily residue like the water we used to get from the locomotive while on the train. This resulted in an orgy of washing ourselves and doing laundry. By noon we again got some black bread and cabbage soup. While not particularly satisfactory, the food, at least partially, diminished the hunger pangs.

That evening we arrived in a fairly large town, sitting high up on the left bank of the river. Here Leon was again able to get off the boat, get some food, primarily bread and learn that the name of the town was Koz'modem'jansk. The mood on the boat was not as depressing as before; it was expectant and quite optimistic, much more so than during the travel by the train.

Constantly under blue skies, there was the mystery as to our destination but only a partial mystery since we had already considerable information to use in making predictions. The boat was ripe with rumors. Firstly, we were absolutely certain that we are not going to western Poland since we were deep inside Russia, at the northern reaches of the Volga River. Matter of fact, we were close to Moscow. This stimulated a lively discussion of the possibility that we indeed are heading for Moscow. While tied up at Koz'modem'jansk everyone was trying to get additional information. The boat crew was extremely close-mouthed.

Uncle Leon, while roaming the town, was quite unsuccessful in trying to get any information from the locals. There was no way to predict our destination. Nevertheless, the mood on the boat was getting almost festive. It was impossible to tell whether it was a response of relief from the almost unbearable and severely constrained conditions on the cattle train, associated with hunger, oppressive heat and stench, or an irrational reaction preceding an inevitable tragedy.

We remained tied up at the dock for the entire day and following night. At dawn, as the river turned pink from the rising sun, we sailed away from the docks, continuing up the river. In a short while, I saw a great expanse of water off the starboard bow of the barge. We were approaching a mouth of a large tributary. The barge slowed down and turned into that river. Later I learned that the name of this river was Vetluga. After about a couple hours of sailing up the river, we saw a very tiny village and the barge nosed itself towards the shore, essentially running aground a few feet off the bank next to a tiny, rickety wooden dock.

We were told in Russian that we would be disembarking here and taken by trucks to our final destination. A scrutiny of the shore revealed that indeed there was a bunch of trucks parked there. The trucks were somewhat unusual; each had a huge vertical metal tank mounted on the outside close to the driver's door. I had never seen a truck of this type.

Uncle Leon, who owned a fleet of trucks before the war and was an accomplished car mechanic, explained to me that the engine on these trucks worked utilizing natural gas obtained from combustion occurring in these tanks. Later I learned that the gas was obtained by burning wood chips! Thus, theoretically if the truck would run out of fuel (wood chips), it could stop any place in the forest, the driver would find some dry branches, chop them up load them into the tank and take off! For me it was a novel idea.

As I stood on the deck of the barge I actually felt elated despite everyone's worries, the hunger pains, the mosquito bites and the squalor around me. It must have been a feeling of relief. First the war and the killings, then the uncertainty in Lwow, then even greater uncertainty, naked fear and incredible discomfort on the cattle train, the barge and now finally, it appeared that we were coming to the end of our journey. How mistaken I was!

There was a great deal of commotion associated with the disembarking process, which proceeded, however, in an orderly fashion. There were NKVD officers on the shore supervising the loading of the people (prisoners) on the trucks. The atmosphere was more expectant rather than laced with fear. The NKVD personnel was actually acting in a rather benevolent fashion and the truck drivers were outright friendly and helpful.

It wasn't until much later that I learned why these people didn't treat us in a nasty or hostile fashion. Our family and belongings were loaded on the trucks with several other families and few single people and we took off. The trucks drove in a very narrow lane cut into a virgin pine forest. The road was full of ruts and potholes, making the truck literally dance as it slowly moved ahead. We had to hold on tightly for our lives; otherwise we would have been thrown off the truck. We continued moving very slowly.

It was already afternoon and we were very getting hungry and tired while the truck was moving through the wildest of gyrations. Suddenly we came to a clearing on the shores of a lake. The lake was not very large and one could see in the far distance the other shore. There were several log cabins in the clearing.

CHAPTER 6. Nuzy Yary

We were all unloaded in a rather orderly fashion with the help of the truck drivers and the NKVD personnel. At this point, I counted the number of NKVD men, a total of six of them. Later, I learned that there were exactly 400 of us. We were obviously to be detained here, but there was no wall around the compound; there were no security towers or any other signs of structures designed with a purpose to keep an eye on us. That night we slept outdoors again on top of our belongings. I think this technique was becoming ingrained on us.

The next day, the remaining people arrived from the barge, and the weather continued to be sunny and warm. By noon, large pots of soup were prepared in one of the log buildings, which ultimately became our "stolovayia," a type of cafeteria. We were each given a wooden spoon, an aluminum container filled with cabbage and barley soup and we ate it together with some bread.

Subsequently, one of the NKVD men, a blond short fellow, spoke to us. It was a long speech delivered in Russian. Most of the people did not understand much of what he said. My knowledge of Russian, while quite rudimentary, was sufficient to get the gist of his talk.

First, he introduced himself. His name was Vladia [you go back and forth between spelling it Vladia and Vladek...are these two separate people?] and he wanted to be addressed Tovarisht Vladia. He actually clarified our situation and gave us an idea of what has been happening to us and what is expected of us in the future. We were inmates of a labor camp; we were to build houses to live in and later work in the forest as lumberjacks. He was the commandant of this camp.

As the commandant of this camp, he informed us that we had been relocated to this settlement (*posiolek*), a forced labor camp or "gulag," called Nuzy Yary, because we were considered "unreliable elements." We would remain in this camp for an indefinite period of time and were not to stray out of the *posiolek* or try to go to another village without a specific permit from him, the Commandant. "Further more," he said, "while the security measures in the camp will be lax, an attempt to escape will be futile." He continued, "You are surrounded by an ancient forest, there are scattered settlements and villages in it, but with your accent you will be instantly recognized by the villagers and we will come to pick you up.

He did not deliver his talk in a hostile manner, just the opposite; he put out some clear orders and indicated that a total compliance with the regulations and policies was expected. Any disobedience, he indicated, would result in a serious and prompt punishment. Then he reiterated that the nearest village was about thirty miles away and that we were in the middle of a huge virgin forest and trying to escape would be totally futile. We would either get lost in the forest or, upon reaching any type of settlement, be immediately arrested since we would not have any identification documents or would be picked up by his people.

"The first goal," Vladia continued, "is to cut some trees, make logs and build log cabins in which you shall live in. You will be instructed in these skills; there will be a crew consisting of a group of Russians who will to live permanently in the camp and help you. These will be people dealing with deliveries of food, supplies and truck drivers, and will be the stable and logging supervisors. There will also be some craftsman from nearby villages, whose primary knowledgeable is in logging, building cabins, stoves and chimneys for the cabins."

"Men over the age of 15 will ultimately be trained to do the logging, cutting and trimming of the trees and getting them from the forest to the staging area utilizing horses for this purpose. At the staging area, the logs will to be loaded on trucks and shipped out. The women were to function primarily in the food preparation areas, taking care of childcare and keeping house. No other specific duties will be assigned to them. I was not aware of it, but there were several dozen children in the camp. Each family will receive food allotment on the basis of the amount of work performed by the men in the family." Vladia also made a very strong point that "who does not work, does not eat". He also indicated that each individual would be given a "norma," or a quota assignment, for a specific amount of work per day; for example, the number of trees to be cut, the number of logs to be trimmed, etc. If the quota was not met, the food would be cut accordingly. Those who performed their tasks beyond the assigned quota would receive food bonuses. The food would consisting primarily of meals served in the stolovayia, which was open for breakfast from 6 to 8 a.m., and dinner, from 5 to 7 p.m. Each individual would receive daily 200 gm of black bread, some cereal and cooking oil weekly. Periodically, depending on supply, we may get some other food items, as for example, "Kilky," a tiny, two to three inch long salted fish and pickles.

The existing log houses were constructed just prior to our arrival. They were to house the NKVD personal and their families, and the Russian workers with families, who were to live permanently in the camp. The larger structures were a huge barn to house the horses, the stolovayia, a school house which was also to serve as a meeting place, a bathhouse (bania) built right on the shores of the lake, and "Comendatura," the building housing the NKVD offices.

When Vladia finished his talk, all adult males were taken to the school building. There they were divided into work groups and each group was assigned to a specific activity, actually specific "trades." Some were to be trained to fell trees, others to trim branches and the bark of trees, and the rest to cut the logs to proper sizes and bring them out from the forest --using horses to do this.

Since the initial task was to build houses, and since logs were needed for this purpose, the men had to be trained first in this trade. The training started immediately after lunch. Both, my father and Uncle Leon were assigned to a team (*brigada*) to be taught the art of felling trees.

Father's brother-in-law, Iziu, who by sheer coincidence was visiting us the night we were taken to the train by NKVD from Lwow and ended up with us in the Gulag, was also assigned to the "*horse brigade.*" He would be a danger to everyone when working with the trees in the forest because he was almost blind.

All of the men departed shortly after lunch for the forest, some riding in trucks, some leading horses and others just walking. I watched this wretched group of men in disbelief. Most of them were professional people – doctors, lawyers, accountants, artists or small business owners. There was also a substantial group of tradesman, shoemakers, tailors and blacksmiths. They all walked with axes on their shoulders or saws in their arms. I didn't think that any of them had ever in their life been exposed to this type of work. Most still wore their business suits since no other clothing was available.

Mother, my sister, who was about six years old at this time, and I were left behind.

The men were apparently quite capable and the instructors quite effective. In a matter of days, pine logs began to arrive to Nuzy Yary. Some of the men were taken out of the forest and brought back to the settlement. A number of Russians, who were obviously knowledgeable in the art of building log cabins, arrived and together with our people started building the cabins and out-houses. The latter were built out of boards, as well as the doors in the cabins and the roofs.

Trucks brought boards and material to build windows from a mill in a neighboring village. There was no sawmilling in Nuzy Yary, the work progressed rapidly. The settlement started taking shape. It was time to complete the work since it was already September and the weather was turning colder. Camping outdoors was getting more difficult. A number of the camp inmates were carpenters, or at least in the lumber business; they were assigned to build some crude furniture, tables, benches and beds. Now with the advent of colder weather, the work progressed even more rapidly and by the end of September we started moving into the log huts.

Each cabin consisted of four rooms, two on each side. The center area of each hut was for common use. Between the two rooms on each side of the hut was a large Russian style "pietchka" (oven). It opened on either side for use by the occupants. The fire was fed with wood placed in the unit's central compartment, providing heat in the winter and for preparing hot food. Each room housed a family or a group of single men. Our room housed our family of five people.

By October, the Gulag acquired a characteristic life rhythm. At 6 a.m. we all woke up, by 7 a.m., made our way to the cafeteria and at 8 a.m. the men departed for work. Women went to a distribution cabin for bread and what ever else was being distributed on that day.

By 6 p.m., or later in the day, the men returned from work and all of us went to the "stolovayia" for supper.

The amount of food, primarily bread, depended on the labor productivity of the men in the family. It was judged by work performed the day before and recorded by the "desiatnik," a person assigned to count and record the number of trees felled, cut, trimmed etc. The records were kept very carefully. The food was skimpy and we were always hungry.

Our cabin was next to the stables and close to the lake. Pretty soon I started visiting the stables and became acquainted with the men working there. Although I was only twelve years old and was not required to work, I spent so much time hanging around the stables that I started helping.

Soon I learned how to ride horses bareback since there were no saddles available. I would help with cleaning the stables, feeding the horses and most importantly riding the horses to the lake, a great privilege in my eyes. By then, I was entrusted to ride a horse into the forest to the lumber crews, whenever a horse was needed there. Returning by foot, I learned that there were mushrooms in the forest just for the taking, and early in the fall, there were also blackberries still there.

Later, as temperatures dropped below zero at night, there were red berries available. They were very sour but when cooked, very tasty.

These discoveries changed my routine activities. I would spend at least half of the day in the forest collecting mushrooms and berries. The NKVD did not interfere with these activities. The ability to supplement our formal food rations had changed our diet considerably. I would bring one or two buckets of mushrooms every day, part of it was cooked and eaten the same day, the rest was dried and saved for the winter.

Mother brought with her some dental tools and supplies. The word got around, and pretty soon Mother started seeing people with toothaches. She had tools for pulling teeth, doing root canal work, etc. All that work was done in our little room.

One night we were awakened by banging at the window. It was Vladia, one of the NKVD men. He came in complaining of excruciating toothache. He also indicated that he knew that Mother was a dentist. Mother indeed examined him and pulled the aching tooth right in the hut. What she did was a turning point of our lives in Nuzy Yary. Soon afterward, other NKVD men and their families with toothaches started coming to see Mother.

NKVD men could live with their wives in the Gulag, but not with their children. Some of the other Russians, like the various supervisory personnel, the "Natchalnik" (the chief civilian administrator), the director of the "Stolovyia," the supervisor of the lumber cutting activities, etc. were all Russian civilians. They lived in similar houses as we did, some with their families, including children, as long as the children were not of school age. This group of Russians also used Mother's dental services in emergencies like a toothache.

Work performed on inmates was in most instances free, unless someone brought something to eat or did us some favor. The Russians usually paid for the work with food they brought from the outside, and the special food they got in their rations.

Gradually I acquired more Russian language skills that on top of my theoretical knowledge acquired the year before in school enabled me to communicate with reasonable ease. This helped because the older generation had a major problem with the language. They spent the day in the forest talking to each other in either Polish or Yiddish; after coming home again, they were primarily in contact with their friends and families speaking the same language. On the other hand, I was constantly in contact with the Russians at the stables. This gave me a great opportunity to learn the new language.

One morning as I was marching to the stables to start my work, a number of NKVD came running calling for everyone to meet at the central square. As we gathered, we were informed that three of the inmates escaped the day before from the camp. They again reiterated that this is an offense punishable by being placed in a prison. Being an inmate in the Gulag was not considered to be the same as being in a formal jail.

We were admonished on numerous occasions not to attempt an escape because of its futility. However, the NKVD staff was somewhat *blasé* about the possibilities of escape; the entire procedure was handled at a low key.

Soon we found out why. The escapees were caught within two days. They actually returned to the Gulag on their own. They simply got lost in the endless *taiga* that stretched for thousands of miles. Upon return, they were taken away from the camp and sentenced for a long prison term, or so they told us. We never saw them or heard from them again. Subsequently there were no other escapes.

Later, the real reasons for the futility of this act became quite clear.

Time moved on rapidly, the weather was turning colder, and the lake started freezing. This created problems as far as watering of the horses was concerned. Initially I handled it by riding each horse partly into the water allowing the horse to break the ice with his huffs. However, when it got colder and the ice thicker, the horses could not break through it and I ended up having to cut holes in the ice with an axe. This turned out to be a bigger job that I originally envisioned. Since we had 25-30 horses, it would require hours when using one hole to water all the horses.

Gradually I started cutting more and more holes and as the temperature started dropping even more rapidly, many of the holes had to be re-cut. As the ice was getting thicker, it was more difficult to remove it. Early on there was no snow, but as the snow came, the job became almost impossible.

Since horses were needed in the forest early in the morning, I had to water them when it was still very dark. This made the job even more difficult, more dangerous and more time consuming.

I couldn't let an entire group of horses drink at once. Each horse had to be led to a hole in the ice carefully so he wouldn't slip, particularly when snow covered the ice.

Soon I got help. A boy, some three years older than I, was reassigned from a job in the forest to help me. This made my job much easier and much more enjoyable. Firstly, he lived in the same hut as we did. However, I had limited contact with him in the past because he was, in my opinion, much too old for me and kept very much to himself. Working together gave us the opportunity to become familiar with each other and to develop, what turned out to be, a very close friendship, despite the age difference.

David was an intellectual. Being older, he had the opportunity to finish three years of Gymnasium before the war broke out; this made him a fabulous mentor. I lived on his words.

We discussed all we remembered from before the war and then had major debates on topics I learned in school during 1939-1940. This was the year when Soviet propaganda was dished out to us in school, on the street, in the "Palaces of Culture," in the movies, everywhere. This propaganda had very definite and pronounced effect on me. It turned out that it had a similar effect on David.

We were essentially convinced that Communism was historically an evolutionary inevitability. Capitalism, the most recent form of governing and philosophical approach to life, was doomed to fail. The dictatorship of proletariat had to prevail. We spent countless hours, while working in the stables, engaged in discussions of dialectic materialism, Marxism, Leninism and Stalinism. Also, I learned that David played the violin. So did I. We both had our violins with us in the camp and soon we started playing duets. David was much more advanced and probably more talented and I enjoyed greatly listening to him play.

Winter was marching on with great strides. The lake was frozen solid and keeping the watering holes open was even a more demanding job. That brings back to my mind the situation with the "bania" (bathhouse) that was built by the lake in the summer. After it was constructed, we quickly learned the routine of taking a bath--Russian style. Inside the bathhouse, there were huge benches where the bathers sat reclined or rested laying down. There was a stove-like structure in the corner where a fire was lit to heat up huge stones. Lake water was stored in large wooden pails. The water was poured over the hot stones to create steam or poured over the bathers when they got too hot.

All over there were bunches of fresh twigs cut from bushes growing by the lake; these were used by the bather to periodically flagellate themselves. Soon we also learned this custom, however I never figured out its utility or pleasure.

Soap was in extremely limited supply, gotten basically by barter from the Russians who would bring small amounts of it from a village. Possibly swatting one's self with the branches substituted for the soap? At intervals of time, a bather would dart out of the bathhouse and jump into the lake for a brief period of time, only to return back to the bathhouse. Well, when the winter arrived and the lake froze, the same routine continued, except a hole had to be cut in the ice, large enough for a bather to jump in, to cool off?! Thus, from the super hot *bania,* the bather would run out and through the snow jump into ice water.

Surprisingly, a large number of the inmates took to this sport with great enthusiasm. Later when I talked about this with my parents, I learned that in Poland, before the war, a great number of Jews, particularly among the orthodox group, would regularly attend baths similar to the *bania*, they called them a *Schwitz*, a Yiddish word that translates to "sweat.".

December was approaching. A major happening had significantly affected our lives. Mother learned that in Russia to have a gold cap on a front tooth, a gold "crown" was extremely desirable. She smuggled into the Gulag in her specially-constructed under garment several dozen gold discs used normally to make "crowns" for the teeth. She also brought adequate, albeit quite primitive, equipment to produce such "crowns." One day she proposed to Vladia to make for him gold "crown." He was absolutely elated.

The procedure was a success and within a week, Vladek was sporting a gold "crown" on the upper left incisor. Not only did mother become a hero with the NKVD staff, but also Vladek was always walking around with a big grin on his face to show off his golden tooth.

Obviously there were numerous benefits to be had from this development. Pretty soon the other NKVD showed up hoping also to get a gold tooth. And they did.

Mother became a celebrity in their eyes. She was permitted to visit the neighboring villages, although she had to walk the 25-30 miles through thick virgin forests to the nearest one. This would usually take an entire day, so she would sleep over there and return on the third day.

Usually I was given permission to accompany her. By then she made quite a few friends in the villages and we were always welcomed guests in their houses. The village, which name I can't recall, was actually built in the same style as the Gulag. The log cabins were similar, but larger and each housed only one family. The interiors were usually furnished with professionally produced furniture; there were pretty, colorful bed spreads on the beds, nice curtains in the windows and a feel of relative well being when compared to our huts.

A huge contraption occupied the space of one half of a room. It was the *pietchka*, a large stove, a huge oven and a space on top of it where an entire family could sleep and stay warm there particularly during the winter.

This was the warmest place in the house. When in the winter a man came from outdoor work, he first jumped on the *pietchka* to thaw off and warm up before doing anything else. Unfortunately we did not have this contraption in our huts; this was a major deficiency.

On each of these visits Mother would see local villages suffering with toothaches and help them. There were always candidates for tooth pulling, a procedure she actually enjoyed and did extremely well, not only because she liked doing it but also being a dental surgeon, she was extremely well trained in this subspecialty. She always carried her tooth-pulling pliers of many different configurations with her as well as some that she designed herself.

After a day of visiting and seeing patients, we ended up provisioned with as much foodstuff as we could carry back home. The heaviest to carry was milk. Since it was winter, the milk was stored by freezing it in flat frying pans, *skovorodky*. In the process of freezing the cream, almost butter would separate on the top of the solid and one could scrape it off with a knife. The weight of the metal *skovorodky* and the milk added up to five pounds.

Thus, we were unable to transport more than one or two containers, if we were to take the other foodstuff with us also. Since milk and butter were priceless, valued at the weight of gold, we were still very happy, despite the fact that we had to drag the little sleds loaded to the maximum all the way to Nuzy Yary. This trip was a difficult one. Returning, we were caught in a horrible snowstorm. It wasn't 'till late that evening that we got back to Nuzy Yary. We were particularly grateful that we didn't encounter wolves, although we were repeatedly assured that in this part of tundra there were very few wolves.

It was getting close to my 13th birthday, the time for Bar Mitzvah at Nuzy Yary in the Soviet Gulag. We were to celebrate late in the month of December. Father made arrangement with a young man, a former *Yeshiva Bucher* (a student in a religious school), to come to our hut every day for one hour and prepare me for the event.

There were numerous Hebrew books available from the inmates. I was tutored in Jewish religion and in reading Hebrew before the war. Thus, the pre-Bar Mitzvah training was not a major task. Actually, I enjoyed getting together with the tutor since this was the only scheduled and formal educational activity. There was no formal school for kids in the Gulag.

The day of Bar Mitzvah came and in the evening we had a gathering of friends. There wasn't much food, however. There was no wine. But Mother "organized" (a Gulag expression that meant, to obtain by whatever means possible) through her connections with the food commissary *Natchalnik* (boss), the biggest herring I ever had seen. There was enough there for everyone to get a small piece in celebration of this important day for me.

In the middle of the party while everyone was relaxed and enjoying the celebration, a sharp knock on the door startled us. It was Vladek, the chief of NKVD. Everyone was petrified. We were not permitted to have any gatherings without a written permit (*pozvolenie*) from the NKVD. But Vladek did not come to punish us. He said, "I heard that you are celebrating your son's 'rights of passage,' I want to contribute to your celebration!" and he placed on the table a bottle of vodka.

Everyone was stunned. Vladek was actually feared by most of the inmates. Although he was quite fair, just being a NKVD chief made him a fearsome figure.

He, however, was not abashed at all. Actually he wanted to join the celebration and drink vodka with us. The first glass he poured was for me. We had a few chipped glasses, regular water size glasses, called in Russian a *stakanchik*. He poured a glass full of vodka and indicated that I should drink it up. I learned that drinking vodka in regular water-drinking glasses was a Russian toast! I, who never drank hard liquor, wouldn't even know how to take a tiny sip of this "fire water," much less a glassful. He was quite serious about my drinking the glass of vodka.

He said, “I like your custom of celebrating a boy’s passage to manhood, but in our country a man has to know how to drink vodka.” It took Mother’s entire store of diplomatic abilities to convince Vladek to give up on his idea that I should drink the entire glass of vodka. The major argument that won over Vladek was her point that one bottle will not be enough for the entire group of important guests to drink a toast for this occasion. Nevertheless, I had to drink a considerable amount of vodka to satisfy him. This actually made me feel very happy. Vladek also became happier and happier with each drink. Finally, he got up, ran out into the freezing cold evening, dressed only in his uniform, and returned in no time with another bottle of vodka. By then, most of the men also felt very happy and the party progressed with very little food, but with plenty of vodka.

The next day I woke up with a sensation of an “enlarged cranium” and a splitting headache. It was very cold, the men left for the forest and I was to go to the stables to take care of the horses. I reflected on the power of a gold tooth and the attitude of Vladek towards us. Actually, it became quite evident that the power of the “gold tooth” had been helping the entire community of the inmates in our Gulag.

As the New Year rolled in, the temperatures plummeted to below 30-35° C, and the work in the forest became brutal. People’s fingers and toes froze. They built huge fires in the forest trying to keep warm. The situation was critical.

I had major problems with the horses, particularly watering them, because the ice holes on the lake were difficult to keep open. I would cut the ice, and in few hours, it would freeze over. At least it was reasonably warm in the stable. The animals and the manure helped the matters. Finally, mother went to see Vladek to intercede for the inmates. Apparently, she had a long talk with Vladek. She tried to explain that the people were not accustomed to this degree of cold weather, particularly not to work outdoors at these temperatures.

Apparently, the “gold tooth” theory worked again! I am certain that her influence was primarily due to the fact that she had the capacity to make gold teeth. Matter of fact shortly after this episode Vladek sported a second gold front tooth. The “deal” she worked out consisted of an agreement that if temperatures dropped below 40° C in the morning, the work responsibilities for that day would be cancelled for those who worked in the forest. This was, I am certain, life saving for some. Those of us who worked around the *posiolek*, however, still had to discharge their respective duties.

I found it amusing that whenever the temperature dropped below 40° C, Vladek himself would run around the *posiolek* at 7 a.m. and bang on the windows to let us know of the temperature and reiterated that no one needed to go to the forest. Mother became somewhat of a local hero after this episode since everyone realized that she had influence with NKVD that could be very beneficial for all.

As winter progressed and the very low temperature became daily happenings, another unexpected problem arose. There, obviously, were no bathrooms (toilets) in the huts. We used outhouses. An outhouse was build for each two or three huts. The construction consisted of a hole in the ground with a hut made of rough boards around the hole and a board over the hole to sit on.

During the warm weather, as the hole filled up, a new hole was dogged nearby, the wooden hut was moved over the new hole and the old hole was topped off with fresh soil. Unfortunately, during the winter months the ground was frozen very hard and it was impossible to dig a new hole and move the outhouse. The excreta froze and became hard as cement. Gradually the heap of excreta became so high that it was impossible to squat on top of it. Thus, each time one needed to use the facility, one had to bring an axe and first chip off the top of the "pyramid" to make room for a new portion! Each morning, people with axes in their hands were running to the outhouses. Jokingly we called it, "lumbering in the outhouse."

The only benefit of the winter was the availability of *kilky* - tiny salted fish. They were usually delivered in huge wooden barrels packed in salt brine. I had never seen this many food-containing barrels. Something unusual had happened. The formal food available to us (except for the small amount of food gotten sporadically through black market type of activities with the Russians) consisted primarily of a small portion of black bread, cooked cereal or potatoes on some days, and soup. The fish, although tiny and very salty, was an unheard luxury, particularly since we were given as much fish as we asked for in the commissary. It was a holiday! It is true that the fish had a strong odor suggesting that it was probably semi-rotten, possibly kept on storage too long before delivery. Nevertheless, we were assured that it was quite edible.

Vladek himself arranged in the *stolotchnyia*, (the cafeteria) to have potatoes also served with the *kilky*. Apparently, *kilky* is an important and popular type of food in Russia and Vladek didn't know why we got this shipment and why we got this large amount. However, no one complained, particularly since, as the winter progressed, the food situation was getting worse. Large amounts of snow hindered food deliveries delaying shipments sometimes for up to two weeks. The horse-driven sleds had difficulties negotiating large, wind blown, snow drifts in the forests.

We, personally, felt the pinch. Mother obviously could not walk to the village to get the food. The Soviets had difficulties, even with a dental emergency, to make it to Nuzy Yary and I couldn't get any food supplements from the forest. There was nothing there except for snow and trees. People started dying from cold and malnutrition.

Everyone was looking forward to the spring. I however was actually busier than ever. Firstly, I still had to spend every day in the stables taking care of the horses. Fortunately, the stables were right next to our hut. My second job during the winter was to cut and chop the wood for the oven, particularly when the adults were working in the forest.

Actually enjoying this job, I "organized" several axes and a good two-man saw. Every week, Uncle Leon would deliver (pulled in by a horse from the forest) a large pine log and saw it with me into proper length pieces. Whenever I had time, I would then chop the wood into logs. It took a great deal of technique to do this job; however, I became quite proficient in it.

The supervisor of the stables, a Russian, for whom I worked, became my instructor. I had a large two bladed axe for the initial splitting of the log; the fragments were then chopped into small, ready to burn, logs using a much smaller single edge, very sharp axe with a relatively short handle. Usually, when the temperatures were very low, it took one hour a day to chop enough wood for a 24 hour period since we kept on heating the hut constantly.

The other job, which was also my responsibility, was to keep the floor clean and my mother was adamant that this be done regularly and appropriately. The issue was actually quite complicated. There were five of us living in one tiny room. Fall, winter and spring everyone would bring a great deal of mud from the outside and trample over the floor with their muddy feet. Mother insisted that the wooden floor be cleaned at least every other day. The floor surface was actually small but the technique of cleaning it was difficult and time consuming. I was instructed to use the "Russian" method. The method consisted in actually shaving the floor's wood surface with a huge and a very sharp knife. Millimeter after millimeter had to be shaved. One could not skip a single stroke because it would show up as a dark stripe on the floor. My sister was only six years old at the time, but I tried to teach her how to do it. Her hands, however, were too small and too weak to do it and I could not push this responsibility on her. Nevertheless, I had her assist me in whatever way I could to make my life easier in getting this chore, a task I hated, done as rapidly as possible.

By late January and early February of 1941, the cold became unbearable. On many days, the temperature dropped below 40° C. This allowed the men to stay home away from the forest. (Vladek kept his pledge to my mother). Since there was no shortage of wood, we could keep quite warm in the huts and except for the hunger-- the *kilky* were long gone and we were subsiding on 200g. of black bread, the norm when not working, cooked cereal in the morning and a watery soup in the evening-- there wasn't much to complain about. Matter of fact the forced inactivity stimulated a great deal of discussions concerning our fate, particularly the immediate resolution of the situation. We were never formally charged with any crime as a reason for the incarceration in a forced labor camp.

Whenever Mother, in a very delicate way, tried to steer towards this topic when talking with Vladek, she was always sidetracked with a huge smile and an off hand statement such as, "you know, you are a suspicious and unreliable element, also many of you were capitalists, we keep you here for your own protection." One couldn't get much more out of him. The discussions meandered over various topics and there were as many opinions as there were people.

During this winter, we became very close with the other three families in the hut. One family dealt with horses before the war, another had a small grocery store and the father of my teen-age friend, David, was an attorney.

As the adults occupied themselves with endless discussions, David and I would spend hours playing the violin and discussing Communism. As a "small" kid before the war, my friends and I, talked a great deal about Socialism. However, we were not introduced to Communism. The interest in Socialism was generated from a rather active participation in Zionist organizations, which at that time were quite socialist in nature. This was rooted in the agricultural idealism of those who wanted to immigrate to Palestine and become "Halutzim," members of an agricultural collective, a "Kibbutz."

Socialist ideas, particularly those related to the settling of new lands and turning a desert in Palestine into a lush agricultural paradise, held great appeal for the youngsters; Communism, however, was alien and threatening in its nature.

The Zionist groups did not present it to us as their ideology and we were quite ignorant of it. During the year in Lwow (1939-1940), I was in school where Communism was thought of as a formal class dealing with the philosophy of dialectic materialism, as well as parts of other classes, e.g. history, art, "Marxism and Leninism," "The Communist Party," geography, etc. The brainwashing never ceased. Ruminating on this topic and discussing it with David, who had one year of Soviet *Desiatiletka* (secondary school), it again became clear to me that the brainwashing had worked.

Despite the fact that the Soviets imprisoned us in a Gulag, despite of the inhumane handling, despite of the fact that we ended up in the Gulag because out parents refused to accept Soviet citizenships and still despite the fact that we were being starved and that some of us were dying of malnutrition, I felt quite ambivalent about Communism. Its apparent philosophy of fairness based on its theoretical foundations was particularly difficult to deal with. While in Lwow, the Soviet instructors in the school tried to explain Marx' teachings by emphasizing the dialectic materialism as one of the most fundamental aspects of the theory of Communism. It was very difficult to totally reject these teachings, particularly for us, so young, so inexperienced and well, so very naïve.

David and I spent many hours in discussions and arguments related to these issues. We were unable to reach conclusions. It wasn't until much later, several years later, that I could clarify this issue in my mind. I could clarify it only after studies conducted within a free society, one not slanted by Marxism, Leninism or Stalinism. Studies that opened my eyes to the philosophers who provided the Marxists' with the knowledge and philosophical foundations for utilizing dialectics and for giving them the opportunity to interpret political and historical issues using these foundations. This led them to an explanation and to predictions, based on their point of view, of the course of history and the economic factors leading to a successful struggle of the Proletariat.

In the meanwhile, we spent a great deal of time playing the violin and playing chess. Since David didn't have to go to the forest on many days, he would help me in the stable. While doing it, he also learned how to ride horses bareback and frequently, when horses were not needed in the forest we would ride them just for fun.

Slowly the extremely cold temperatures started to ease off. There were no more nights with temperatures below 40° C. Soon the tempo of work picked up, the road through the forest opened again and trucks started rolling in to pick up the timber. This also meant that some of the villagers were able to come in to see my mother with their dental problems. Obviously, it resulted in significant improvement in our diet, a very welcomed development.

As the snow started melting, Sergey, my boss at the stables and a friend, wondered if Mother could talk to Vladek about the possibility of letting us clear the land around the labor camp and use it for growing a garden. If so, he was willing to help us with it.

The very next day Mother went to see Vladek; he saw no problems with the request but had to check with his superiors. The following week he made an announcement to all of the inmates that the cleared land on the east side of the camp will be subdivided into small plots that will be assigned to the inmates to grow a garden. He will provide seeds in the next couple of weeks.

The response to this offer was lukewarm. Most people were not interested, probably very few, if any, had a garden before the war. They were too tired to participate. I was elated. The area where the lots would be staked out almost bordered on our hut and on the stables. In no time I had Sergey over. We marked off a small plot of land and he began the training of a new gardener - me!

Although we had a large garden before the war, primarily fruit trees, flowers and a small vegetable section, I was not very involved in dealing with it. Firstly, as a small kid I was never very interested in gardening. Furthermore, we had a full time gardener who took care of everything, I was permitted only to watch.

In the Gulag, however, things were different. Here the question was food! I indeed became very interested in gardening. First lesson from Sergey was to learn that the soil around the lake was very sandy and it will not support the growth of vegetables like cucumbers, beans or tomatoes. Secondly, he said that the spring is too cold to germinate the seeds on time and to grow the young seedlings. All that should be done in hot houses. We, however, did not have appropriate building supplies to build a hot house. Instead, he introduced me to a method of starting a vegetable garden that was totally new to me.

From the stables, we brought a large amount of horse manure and placed it on our garden plot where we spread it as a two foot layer. Then we built garden beds from it allowing for footpaths around each bed. In the meanwhile, we built some boxes from scraps of wood, filled them with the sandy soil mixed with a small amount of manure extract prepared with water and seeded them with the seeds given to us by Vladek.

The boxes were stored in the stables, kept warm by the horses' body heat and presence of the manure. I watered the boxes daily and couldn't wait to see the seeds germinate and the seedlings grow. Once the seedling reached two to three inches, they were planted in the manure beds.

The days were getting longer. The snow melted from most of the areas and the ice on the lake started thawing. The thaw started at the shoreline and progressed towards the center. This made the watering of the horses much easier and faster. Also, longer and warmer days made it more conducive for people to congregate outdoors in the evenings and, as usual, enter into speculations as to our future. The general consensus was very pessimistic. The indications we got from Vladek suggested that our status as inmates was that of a permanent labor force and probably we would live out our lives in this tundra felling lumber.

This was a dismal future for all. But, what about us, the younger generation? Were we also to grow older and ultimately join the lumberjack force with no other future available to us? To us it sounded preposterous. We simply couldn't believe it. However, there was nothing else to believe at this time. It was the daily toil, the daily needs, the daily worries that preoccupied us most of the time.

The mood in the camp was at its lowest. It was a hard winter during which a number of the inmates perished from malnutrition and many from various upper respiratory infections, probably pneumonia. I obviously was not either involved in or adequately informed to know the diagnoses, but in retrospect I think that tuberculosis could also have been an important factor in many of the fatalities.

There was no medical facility at the camp. In case of serious injury, the person was transported by truck to a hospital in a small town on the river. A number of inmates died as a result of such accidents at work in the forest. Most commonly, falling trees crashed them. After all, most had no experience to start. However, it was remarkable to observe how rapidly these inexperienced people learned the trades--particularly since most were physically unfit for this type of labor. Large segments were scrawny scholars who never in their lives did any menial work. They were grossly overweight. It is of interest to note that those who were initially obese had lost weight rapidly and within a couple months in the camp, they all started looking gaunt.

Personally, we were fortunate. Mother, even at this difficult juncture, was able to get some extra food through her dental work activities. Mother had also helped quite a few inmates with obtaining some food. This brought me closer to the entire group of inmates in the Gulag and it was at this time that it dawned on me that essentially all of the inmates in our Gulag were Jewish. This realization did not impress me at that time. However, as years went on and as the political situation changed throughout the world in totally unexpected directions, this and other observations altered my perception of the involvement of Polish Jewry in this entire historical episode.

As the spring progressed, the weather was turning gorgeous, sun was shining most of the time, the temperature has risen and the trees started budding and developing leaves. Sergey showed me how to make fish traps from reeds that grew at the edges of the lake. The traps were constructed in the shape of a conical basket in such a way that a fish could swim into the cone but was unable to swim out because of the trap's design.

The lake, during the spring, overflowed its shores and formed little areas in which the fish would spawn. We would place traps at the mouth of these areas and as the fish tried to swim in, they would get into the trap and be unable to swim out. We would set up the traps in the evening and check in the morning.

Many times there would be a fish or two in the trap, usually pikes. This had an enormous influence on our diet. Protein was the scarcest part of our diet. Fish not only was very palatable but also provided us with this scarce foodstuff. This food was apparently particularly important for pubertal children going through a growth spurt. I probably was a beneficiary. Unfortunately, this windfall lasted only several weeks, until the lake level returned to normal and the spawning period was over. By then, however, the beets started coming up and I would cut from several plants a single leaf and Mother would use it in cooking soups. It helped.

Work again moved into full swing. All the able men were in the forest logging and there was no end to this in sight. I still was too young for joining the inmates in the forest, but by then I was quite actively working in the stables.

With arrival of the spring our food situation has improved again. Mother was permitted to resume her visits to the villages to do some dental work there. Sometimes the villagers got the permission to come and see her for their dental needs in Nuzy Yary. All this activity was always associated with "gifts" of food

On June 23rd we were awakened to the news that Germany attacked Soviet Russia the day before. This was totally unexpected. We couldn't reconcile this information with memories of 1939 when escaping the Germans we ended up in Lwow and witnessed its occupation by the Soviet Army. At that time, we were barraged by the Soviets with propaganda that the Germans were the Soviet's greatest friends.

During the incarceration in the Gulag, we were almost totally isolated from news. The NKVD obviously provided no news from the outside. The villagers that we were in contact with were neither particularly interested nor knowledgeable of the world situation.

We had the feeling, however, that even the Russians were shocked by the news of the German attack. They kept repeating in disbelief: "why did they do it?" Apparently, the Russians considered the Germans as close friends. After all, Molotov signed a peace treaty with Ribbentrop, the German foreign minister, on August 23, 1939. This treaty resulted in the partition of Poland between Germany and Soviet Union. Indeed on the strength of this treaty, the Soviets invaded Poland on September 17th as Poland was reeling from the German onslaught from the west and trying to set up a line of defense in eastern Poland. As a further extension of this pact, on September 28th, an agreement dubbed as "the friendly borders," was developed between Germany and Soviet Union. It assigned specific lands in eastern Poland to the Soviet Union and was to be valid until 1949.

The Russians accepted the idea that Germans initiated this war as an unprovoked, sneak, attack on Soviet Union. A patriotic fervor was unanimous and very strong. Also, the population felt that the mighty Soviet Army would summarily defeat the scurrilous Germans and in no time, the Soviet People would be celebrating victory in Berlin.

Meanwhile, the mood in the Gulag had changed. The NKVD personnel became much friendlier; all the inmates were given permits to visit the neighboring villages. Each log cabin was given an audio speaker connected to a radio set in the NKVD offices and we could listen to music and news on a radio station tuned in by the NKVD. Later we learned that this was the system in all towns and cities in USSR Each house or an apartment had an access to a speaker connected to a central facility that transmitted the government station's programs.

Actually, I didn't see the need for this cumbersome system since there were no other radio stations in SSSR except for those owned by the government. This system however had a definite economic advantage. The minimum quality speakers provided--a simple paper cone with a tiny electromagnet at its apex and no enclosure--were much less expensive than the cheapest radio.

Soon we were able to listen to the war news and music. The music was superb, mostly classical and folk music. The news, on the other hand, although sweetened to prevent panic, was bad. The German Army was progressing very rapidly along the entire front that stretched from the Baltic for almost 1,200 miles towards the south. The Germans ran over the western provinces of Ukraine, Byelorussia and most of the Baltic States in a matter of very few weeks. The Germans started the offensive in June at the time of perfect weather for conducting a motorized war. The spring thaws were over with and the land was dry and easily traversed by motorized vehicles. There were several months of this weather in store as well as the onset of harvest time that would provide food for the advancing German Army. The Germans again, as in Poland, applied the techniques of "Blitz Krieg"; lightening armor units ("Panzers") led attacks using the "Pintzer" (claw-like) strategy. The latter involved a rapid advance of two narrow "Panzer" columns, followed by joining of the two heads of the columns resulting in pinching off and surrounding a large segment of the enemy's fighting force within the "Pintzers."

These techniques, in addition to the element of surprise, allowed the Germans to move very rapidly towards the heart of western Soviet Russia. By July, all of eastern Poland as well as parts of Ukraine, Byelorussia and most of the Baltic States were overrun by the Germans.

Within weeks after the German attack we heard rumors in the *posiolek* that a Polish "government in exile" was formed in England. There were numerous implications of this news. Since most of the inmates of the Nuzy Yary Gulag were Polish citizens, an entire new political environment had formed. The original premise for sending us to the Gulag rested on the supposition that we were an "undesirable" element. Soviet authorities defined the term "undesirable" in a totally arbitrary fashion. At the time, when we were labeled this way and taken to the Gulag, a Polish government could not object or intercede since it didn't exist. Now, with the establishment of a Polish government and the acceptance of it as one of the Allies, possibly a pressure could be exerted on the Soviets that could translate into a change in our status and our conditions.

The news from the fronts continued to be bad. The information obtained via the "grapevine" and the news on the radio was quite conflicting. Nevertheless, the bottom line seemed to indicate that the Red Army was in a massive retreat and the casualties were high.

Meanwhile, summer arrived in all of its glory. The days became warm. I took the horses to the lake not only to water them but also to wash them. That gave me the chance to swim with them. Although the water in the lake was cold, with some adjustments in thinking, it was possible to swim in it.

Also, in the forest I found huge patches of wild raspberries. This was a welcome addition to our diet that was already being supplemented by tomatoes, cucumbers and squash grown in our little garden. Although we were very short on meat and fat--it was actually almost non-existent except for the brief period in early spring when I was catching the fish--our need for vegetables and fruit was met quite satisfactorily. Matter of fact, I was able to help David's family in this respect.

I was particularly happy for the raspberries since they were my very favorite fruit. Soon the first variety of mushrooms also appeared in the forest. They were the tiny yellow kind growing in huge colonies on tree stumps. They were very tasty when fried on a skillet. Our food situation was certainly getting better! I interacted at this time a lot with David and although he was again assigned to work in the forest, we would get together in the evenings, play our violins and discuss our situation in great detail.

CHAPTER 7. Getting Out

Rumors were flying that the Polish Government may try to organize a Polish Army composed of former Polish subjects living now in the Soviet Union. That, we hopefully reasoned, would include those who, before the war lived in Polish territories but currently were dispersed in various types of camps and jails throughout the Soviet Union.

Indeed, in late August a delegation of Polish Army officials arrived in the *posiolek.* A meeting of all inmates was called. We were informed that indeed a Polish Army was being formed in Buzuluk near Kujbyszew under the immediate command of General W. Anders and the leadership of the Chief of Polish Armed Forces in Great Britain, General W. Sikorski.

This activity was based on discussions which commenced on July 5th (about four weeks after the German attack on the Soviet Union) between the Polish premier, the Chief of Army in exile, General W.E. Sikorski and Soviet ambassador, J.M. Majeski. This resulted in an agreement reached on July 30, 1941, between the Soviet Union and the Polish government in exile (in Great Britain). These agreements dealt with mutual military assistance, nullification of the Soviet-German pact dealing with annexation of parts of Poland by Soviet Russia and the establishment of a Polish Army on the territories of Soviet Union.

Kujbyszew (the name changed to Samara in 1991) is a major city and port on the Volga River. It is also an important railroad center for lines leading from Moscow to the Trans-Siberian Railroad. We were informed that those who could prove they were on the territories of pre-war Poland would be given an amnesty and would be liberated from the Gulag. Once liberated, they would be transported by ship on the Volga River to Kujbyszew

This news resulted in a flurry of activities. Although we were originally from Germany, some documentation had to be provided that we indeed were residents of Poland before the war. This was a problem since most documents we possessed clearly stated that we were from Germany and we didn't think that this would be a good recommendation for us. If only at least one member of the family had some document establishing that he or she lived on Polish territory before the war, the rest of the family could probably also be certified accordingly. A feverish activity ensued. Everyone was going with a "toothcomb" through their belongings looking for some documentation to support this claim. Mother had all our papers spread out on the bed. Uncle Leon walked in and looking at the papers asked mother: "What is this important looking pink slip of paper?" The paper indeed looked quite important. It was the size of a printed page, done in a fancy script with dates and stamps and our family names, all printed in large letters. "Well," she said, "I can't believe that I took this slip of paper with us. It is a receipt from one of the largest and most modern laundries in Krakow. The reason for all our names on it deals with the identification of the laundry according to the different members of the family whose clothing was included in this single large batch."

"This is it!" he cried, "This is your document, your *spravka* (statement of fact). It looks very official; it has the appropriate dates (August 1939), the place of issue (Krakow) and all of your names. Since Polish uses the Latin script and Russians use Cyrillic script they will not be able to really understand it except that it is Polish, with the appropriate date and appropriate names. Furthermore, the NKVD person in charge was Vladek an old friend of the family; we felt that there should be no trouble. And there was none.

The entire *posiolek* was in a nervous frenzy. All the men volunteered to join General Anders' army. This was the time that confirmed my suspicion that all the inmates were Jewish. Where were the gentiles? We wondered if the Russians had set up separate camps for gentile Poles and Jews and if so, why had they done it in this manner?

At that point, we were unable to get any answers although the question concerned us a lot and we spent a great amount of time discussing this issue. Actually many decades later, some of the answers started surfacing.

Obviously, we were given no details in Nuzy Yary in 1941. We were not apprised of the formal agreements reached between the Polish Government in Great Britain. We were not even aware of the Polish Government in exile in Great Britain.

The representatives of the newly formed Polish Army discussed the entire issue in very vague terms. Some of this could have been because they were not interested in having Poles of Jewish creed liberated from the Soviet camps to join the Polish Army. This was most likely true in light what has happened later. On the other hand they didn't want to create any "waves" that could hinder the release of Poles (not of Jewish creed) who at that time were also held in a variety of labor camps according to the Polish officials who came to Nuzy Yary to talk to us.

This information, and the fact that most of the inmates in our camp were Jews, made us wonder. Who made up the bulk of Gulag inmates brought from the eastern regions (occupied by the Soviets during the 1939 war) of Poland? Later in life, I sought out answers to these very questions. According to the official Polish statistics, 400,000 "Poles" living in the Polish territories annexed by the Soviets in September 1939 were deported to variety of labor camps. They were distributed in a total of 2,500 camps. There was a total of about 1.1 million people of all nationalities and creeds (Polish, Ukrainians, Byelorussians, Jewish and other) from the eastern Polish territories deported to Soviet Russia and sent to camps or jails after September 1939. This number included 336,000 people who escaped from western Poland in front of the advancing German armies and were caught by the Soviet Army as they occupied eastern Poland. This group, mostly Jews, was given the option to become Soviet citizens. Most rejected this offer and opted to return to the German occupied western part of Poland hoping to escape from there to some western country. Instead, they were incarcerated in labor camps deep in the Soviet Union. One of these camps was our camp, Nuzy Yary. (These statistics were obtained from a Polish Internet web page: WIEM 'Wielka Internetowa Encyclopedia Multimedialna').

Regardless of the politics and the staggering numbers that apparently were involved in this "happening," our immediate goal was to arrange for the trip out of Nuzy Yary. Leon, with help from Mother who had the contacts and local good will, started accumulating food that would not spoil and could be transported with us.

At this point, we had some experiences of life in Soviet Union. In the camp the life was difficult at best. However, we learned that outside the camp, in the nearby villages, life was not very good either and as the war progressed it was becoming more and more difficult. While before the war, under the best of conditions, food shortages were chronic and as the war progressed, they were becoming more and more acute.

In late August, we obtained papers from the NKVD. Actually, they were "orders" signed by the Polish military office and counter signed by our NKVD chief empowering us to proceed at the greatest haste to Kujbyszew and then to Buzuluk, the seat of the organized Polish Army-to-be. It was not entirely clear to us how this entire procedure would work.

The majority in our camp consisted of women, children and old people. What was to happen to this group once men, able to serve in the army, were selected? No one, however, was very concerned. The first and foremost thought to consider was the fact that we were to be liberated. Again, as in the 1939 Polish-German war, people believed that the war would not last but a few months; the time it would take to organize the great Soviet might and the time it would take to capture Berlin. Since the Russians were good at fighting wars during the winter, we estimated that by the New Year, Soviet forces would occupy Berlin and the war would be over.

Meanwhile the summer was progressing. Our garden brought fruit, primarily cucumbers, tomatoes and beans. The blue barriers and mushrooms were plentiful. Our food situation had definitely improved. People were scrounging for some form of luggage to pack their meager belongings when finally the day arrived. Vladek called us to the main square and announced that in a couple days trucks would arrive to take us to board a boat on the Vetluga River, which would sail to the Volga and then down the river to Kujbyszew.

The boat was not much different from the one that brought us from Kazan. We were placed either in the hold where we could sleep on the floor or we could stay on the decks. However, we knew where we were going, as well as why. This gave us a wonderful feeling of elation. People were excited. They were free again.

Every one was talking and making big plans for the future. The boat stopped in Kosmodemjansk and Ceboksary where we were able to get some food. Every family had some rubles; these were given to us upon departure from Nuzy Yary for purchasing food on the way to Anders' army.

In Kazan, Leon disembarked looking for food. Mother did not allow me to go along. When he returned, it became clear that availability of food was a problem.

Uncle Leon showed up with one loaf of black bread and a few tomatoes. The only food he could easily obtain were dried sunflower seeds. Indeed he brought a whole sack of the seeds. This was very welcome. We learned to appreciate the seeds while still on the *posiolek* where I grew sunflowers in my garden.

I developed a superb technique for eating the seeds. I could throw a handful of seeds into my mouth and then, very quickly, crack each seed separately, remove with the tongue the kernel and spit out the husks. We all looked like automatic spitting machines and the surroundings were always full of sunflower husks. Nevertheless, the seeds tasted divine and were very nutritious.

I asked Leon about Kazan. He said: "it is a very large town, a lot of buildings that look like Russian churches and few, if any, stores with food or clothing. Everyone is concerned about the war. Our ideas of a quick Soviet victory may be just a dream. It looks like the Germans are moving east very rapidly. The town is full of people and empty of food."

We departed Kazan early in the morning. The weather was good, the boat was crowded and there was very little to do. We spent most of the time talking; arguing about the future; since no one had any facts, everyone had strong opinions.

We arrived in Kujbyszew late afternoon. The port was on the west side of the river. The boat eased off slowly, being moved primarily by a slow current. As we got closer to the dock, a sailor tossed a rope to a man on shore. The rope was attached to heavy mooring line coiled on the foredeck. Once the rope was caught, the mooring line was slowly dragged to a huge cleat where it was belayed and made fast. The boat was attached securely in a rather lively current at the dock.

After a gangplank was lowered and secured on the dock, a short slim man in a khaki-green uniform addressed us. He was wearing a square military hat and a silver colored braid on his collar. We were told to assemble on the deck. "Friends," he said, "the leadership of the Polish Army in the Soviet Union decided to move its main activities and training camps to Central Asia, primarily Kazakhstan. This was prompted by the movements of German armies which have penetrated to a great extent towards the east.

"Unfortunately," he said "the Polish Army does not have the necessary number of train seats to transfer us in Kujbyszew to the Trans-Siberian Railroad and ship us to Kazakhstan. Other priorities do not allow this. Instead we are to continue on this boat to Astrakhan where we will have to find our way to Kazakhstan." He suggested that we find a boat in Astrakhan that may take us across the Caspian Sea to Krasnowodsk, a port in the Turkmen Soviet Republic. There we would be able to get a train all the way to Alma-Ata, the main city of southern Kazakhstan.

We were stunned, as we all were looking towards the end of this journey. Those of us who were able to serve in the military were looking forward to joining the Polish Army. The families hoped for some reasonable place to live and normalize their existence. All of us were very tired, undernourished, dirty and confused.

Questions were flying about. "Where do we get food? How do we pay for it during the journey that will take weeks? Who will help us in finding shelter during the trip? What documents will we use?"

The only answer we got from the Polish officer was: "the document you have indicating that you are on your way to join the Polish Army will be sufficient. Just explain that the Polish Army is evacuating from Kujbyszew to Kazakhstan. The entire country is running east.

No one will question you further." He turned on the heel and left the boat. He showed neither interest nor any concern about our well being, our needs or our future. He apparently discharged his duties fully.

After the officer left the boat's captain stood up and spoke to us. Unfortunately, he spoke Russian and many people had not understood what he said. But, some had gotten the meaning of his remarks. My friend David and I comprehended what he said. By now, we understood quite well a bit of the Russian language, although we couldn't speak it well. The rest of the family barely understood or spoke Russian. The gist of captain's speech was that the boat would continue to Astrakhan, and all who wished to remain on the boat were welcome to do so.

But bedlam broke out all around us. A group led by a redheaded middle-aged man started getting ready to disembark. The redheaded man announced that he wants to join Anders' army now and that he and those who felt like him should disembark here! Obviously most people were eager to join him and see some resolution to the problem now and with Polish authorities rather than go into a totally unknown future, unknown country and into a totally unknown situation.

Here the captain intervened. He declared, "I am planning to depart tomorrow at noon. Those who wish to investigate the possibility of staying in Kujbyszew are welcome to disembark, however if they will change their minds they are welcome to return by tomorrow noon."

The redheaded man thanked the captain and returned to the group that gathered around him. Uncle Leon joined them and I got close enough to hear what was being discussed. The arguments for disembarking were powerful: everyone was tired, hungry and unclean. Lice had appeared; people were trying to control this pestilence but not very successfully.

After a great deal of discussion it was decided that a group of men would be selected to find a way to Buzuluk and face the commanding officers of the Polish Army. The argument being that the men wanted to join the army now, not chase around Central Asia to find them, a difficult task by itself. The men actually did not have the slightest inkling as to the real difficulties they would be facing trying to make this journey, particularly on one's own. Four men were selected. It included the redheaded man and Leon among others. They did not have much time and had to depart forthwith.

All of us who were left behind tried to occupy ourselves as well as we knew how to shorten the wait. The time however crawled slower than a snail on a slick surface. Everyone was anxious and irritable. The goal was so close and at the same time so far.

A closure to the uncertainty of life in a labor camp, the new fear of an unknown equation, a new war and the unexpected news about Anders' army delivered in a cold and a threatening manner had unnerved everyone.

Suddenly a different issue came up that took our minds off the main problem. We all were aware that lice were gaining a foothold on the passengers of the boat. It started with children, moved to the youth and engulfed the adults. Searching for and killing them was a loosing proposition. They proliferated too fast. The lice infested clothing and bedding. Although attempts were made to wash clothing as frequently as we could get reasonably clean water, the soap supply was very limited. Furthermore, the infestation was becoming so severe that simple washing made only a minuscule dent.

It was clear that the only way to hold the onslaught of the infestation was to boil the clothing. This was very difficult. We had limited facilities to boil water aboard the vessel. Only those with a "Prymus," small portable kerosene-fueled burner could boil water and that in only small amounts, probably the largest volume being about a gallon. This however, was sufficient to boil some underwear and smaller shirts; a definite relief to the "lice problem."

The use of the Prymus for cooking water for tea and soup, and now the additional use for boiling underwear was rapidly depleting the miniscule supply of kerosene.

Those families blessed with kerosene-fueled burners that were still relics of pre-war Poland and survivors of the camp had to scrunch for kerosene to keep boiling water for these two principal purposes. Soon a third important use for kerosene was discovered. Treatment of the scalp with kerosene was quite effective in eradicating head lice. The issue of kerosene toxicity wasn't even considered probably because of the rapid and effective relief provided by the treatment.

So, the need for kerosene was great. Those who wandered the city were charged with the responsibility of finding and buying some kerosene. Soon information trickled in that there was no kerosene available in stores but one could purchase it on the *toltchok* or black market. This was a new reality that we encountered, a reality that followed us relentlessly throughout our stay in Communist countries. Regardless of where we lived, the black market allowed us to survive. The black market was a safety valve and lifeline. The entire commerce was conducted officially through government-owned and managed stores. To obtain food in these stores one had to present food coupons. The coupons were issued to the workers monthly in coupon ration books, *kartotchki*, according to the amount and type of work they accomplished each working day. The rations doled out were almost at starvation levels. One had to supplement it just to survive. The black market was the institution that allowed it. We were not issued any ration coupons— we obtained basic food, soup and bread on the boat.

Coming back to the immediate problems we had to make some decision concerning the kerosene. We had a Prymus but we were running out of kerosene.

Since Uncle Leon was gone, Father was elected to go to town and figure out how to get the kerosene. Sure enough, a couple hours later he was back carrying two one-liter containers full of kerosene. The joy was indescribable. The lice control would alleviate the most severe physical discomfort we suffered- itching all over.

First, we massaged the kerosene onto our scalps and all over those parts of the body covered with hair. We gladly suffered the burning sensation just to alleviate the maddening itch. Then we took off the underwear and began the process of boiling it one by one hoping to destroy not only the lice but also the nits (eggs) that were deposited in all the seams of the garments. The anticipation of being lice-free was foremost in our minds. Only after all these activities got underway did we turn to Father with awe and admiration. "How did you do it?" the question tumbled from all mouths. Not only were we excited to get the kerosene, but we also were amazed that Father accomplished it. We were amazed because Father was totally incapable of dealing in the world of deception, rough materialism and an environment where one had to use one's abilities to obtain items by whatever means.

He was a gentle soul, concerned with philosophies of life rather than with its practicalities. He was quite content to sit with a book or to engage a friend in a discussion of some theoretical issue than go out there and fight for a better piece of meat. Here, in a "dog eats dog" situation, he performed a miracle; at least in our minds it was a miracle.

"Well," he said, "it was rather easy. I was directed to the *toltchock* by people I met on the street. Once there I found the area where they were selling kerosene. I asked how much kerosene they would give me for my crocodile skin wallet. They offered me two liters for it and I took it." Apparently, he didn't bargain he didn't look for the best deal; he simply took what was offered to him. The wallet was worth probably many times the value of two liters of kerosene. Nevertheless we got the essential kerosene and he carried out the task admirably. The *toltchock* was a ubiquitous part of life in Soviet Union, and everyone participated in its activities. It was very much like the 'black market' in Lwow that has developed immediately after Soviet occupation.

People on the boat came alive. Once they learned that they could get kerosene on the black market everyone tried to get it and then make a deal with those on the boat who had a Prymus to use it for their needs, primarily for boiling the underwear.

David, my best friend from Nuzy Yary (whose family also ended up on the barge with ours), and I sneaked off the boat to investigate the port area. We didn't want to stray too far in fear of the unknown, but we made further and further forays as we became bolder and bolder.

Suddenly, on a small side street, we came upon a long queue. We were astonished and intrigued by the size of it. Upon inquiry, we learned that it was a soap queue. It would be a real lucky break to get some soap, since we had almost none on the boat. As we joined the queue, however, we quickly realized that we had no rubles. Soon we began talking with the people in the queue-- most were old women.

We told them that we were traveling on the boat coming from a Gulag. This wetted their interest and vivid conversations ensued. I think there was also a maternal instinct at work here since we were a pair of skinny kids, and I am certain, that we offered quite a sight.

As the conversation progressed, we indicated that we would be leaving the queue because we had no rubles to pay for the soap. They all started laughing, "Don't you worry about this," they said, "We will give you enough rubles to pay for the soap."

We looked at them, expressing thankfulness and astonishment. Seeing the astonishment on our faces for this generosity, they quickly came forth with an explanation. "You see," they said, "this is a government store with government prices. These prices are extremely low, matter of fact if you would want to buy the soap on the black market you would pay 50 to 100 times as much. Thus, the couple rubles it will cost to buy the soap will be inconsequential, we will be happy to pay for you."

Realizing that this was a great opportunity and since we had all the time to waste, we happily remained in the queue. This also gave us the opportunity to talk with the women more and learn about many things in Kujbyszew. Firstly, we learned that the Germans were moving rapidly into the heartland of Soviet Union. They actually invaded with a lightning speed.

I was somewhat surprised to hear rather positive emotions expressed by our Russian friends concerning the German's remarkable military feat. The positive feelings were mixed, however, with fear and concern.

Apparently, information from the front and from the occupied parts of the Soviet Union was contradictory and, as to be expected, very fragmented. According to the women in the queue, there were rumors of cruelty practiced by the Germans towards the Russian population, stories of wholesale murder of civilian populations, including children and women, by the German troops.

David and I were astonished by this news and by the attitude of the Russian women. Firstly, their rather free attitude toward us and lack of fear when talking to us was surprising. This was quickly explained. Since we were rather recent Gulag inmates, we could be trusted to have the correct mentality. They had no fear that we would go back to the NKVD and report them.

The second issue, dealing with their rather positive attitudes towards the German occupation and Germans in general, took a while to understand. The few hours spent in the queue were remarkably informative. We learned a great deal and acquired a great deal of insight.

The time with them, however, had flown by rapidly and we realized that our parents whom we left on the boat would be looking for us and would be worried about our whereabouts. It was decided that David shall return to the boat and explain the situation, while I was to remain to keep our place in the queue.

As time went on, the women in the queue became friendlier and more curious about us. Pretty soon, I learned the answer to the issue dealing with the positive attitude of these women to the Germans.

Apparently around this area of the Volga River, there was a large concentration of ethnic Germans. They were invited by Catherine the Great around 1763 – 1767 to immigrate to Russia and to settle around the Volga River. This immigration of Germans to Russia was stimulated primarily by the religious strife in Germany initiated by the Reformation movement in the 16th century. This was followed by the devastation of the Thirty Years War (1618-1648) felt primarily by the peasants who were also mercilessly exploited by the German nobility. The German peasants desired to leave Germany and it was this desire that Catherine the Great used to bring a well-trained peasant population into the steppes of the Volga region. The migration of Germans to the Volga region continued during the 18th century, fueled by the misery among the peasants aggravated by the Seven Years War. Interestingly the "Russianization" process unleashed by the Tsars in the late 19th century stimulated an exodus of Germans from Russia, primarily to the United States of America.

The 1917 Bolshevik Revolution closed the borders and stopped, for all practical purposes, all emigration to or from Russia. This explained to me, at least partly, the peculiar mentality of the population in Kujbyszew area with its strong German roots, towards the strides of the advancing German Army. I learned later that these feelings were not limited to the Russian population in Kujbyszew but also along the entire Volga basin and even in the city of Astrakhan.

David returned to join me in the queue. After several more hours of waiting, we learned, in addition to history and politics, some economics. It turned out that a number of women were in the queue primarily to get the soap for resale on the black market. They themselves were very short on soap, but getting it and selling it for profit was a means for getting a little extra money to buy even more essential items, like food. That was even in greater demand. This was the first time that I realized how the black market might operate to supplement one's fundamental needs.

Well, David and I felt that it was worthwhile to have stayed in line to get the soap. We hadn't had a decent soap bath for a long time. We thought that our families would be particularly appreciative of the soap after they got deloused with kerosene and could put on clean and lice-free underwear.

It was getting late and we had no food all day, but we were already at the head of the queue and soon we were the owners (after our Russian friends paid for us) of one kilogram of soap - each. The only problem was that the type of soap we received was nothing like we had seen before. The soap was given to us on a piece of newspaper. It was semi-solid, almost gelatinous. But as we learned later, it worked very well. We thanked our new Russian friends and ran back to he boat.

However, our achievement for getting the soap and the excitement of interactions with the Russians were totally overshadowed by the stories told by Leon and the other members of the group that went to see the officials of the Polish Army in Buzuluk.

The situation was quite confusing. Apparently, there were quite a number of Polish-origin people in Buzuluk. The army officials had nothing more to add to the statements the officers made on the boat. We were advised to find our way to Kazakhstan, anywhere we could get, preferably close to Alma-Ata.

They had been given copies of certificates to be distributed among all the families on the boat. The bumaschka (certificate) stated that the owners of the certificate are volunteers to the Polish Army and that the Polish Army requests any and all assistance that can be given to us in order to facilitate the trip to Kazakhstan.

Well, our fate was determined. Everyone took a deep breath of satisfaction. We had now a goal and a document making the goals legal and, from our point of view, appropriate.

The Polish Army officials also told our "delegation" that we could go to Kazakhstan by rail, and Kujbyszew had the rail connections for this direction; however, they tried to talk us out of this possibility. Apparently, the evacuation from western and central Russia was in full swing. Many people, government offices and entire factories were being evacuated via the rail.

Similarly, the early units of the Polish Army were transported via the rail to Kazakhstan. They didn't want us to compete for the limited space on the railroad trains. We were informed that once we got to Astrakhan, we should be able to find space on a ship going to the Caspian Sea and then to the port of Krasnovodsk in Turkmenia.

There, we possibly could get on a train going through the Central Asian Republics to Alma-Ata. The ship captain reiterated that he was taking the ship to Astrakhan and would be willing to take us along. Most if not all the people accepted his offer and the following morning we departed from Kujbyszew to sail down the Volga River to Astrakhan.

The captain apparently had sufficient stores of cereal to provide us once a day with soup made out of the cereal (thin millet porridge) and once a day with regular cereal (thick millet gruel, such where a spoon, when placed vertically, would stand up!). The river water was boiled and those of us who could obtain tea leaves somewhere made tea.

In Kujbyszew, Uncle Leon was able to obtain some sugar on the black market. It was in a form of a large, hard, yellowish-brown sphere. We would chip off a piece of it and use it to sweeten our tea. It tasted very sweet, exactly like sugar. The Russians called it "golowa sakhara," in translation a head of sugar.

The Volga at this point became a very large river. At times, we were unable to see the shores. The water was fairly clear and the western shores were usually high; the eastern, when we could see them, were fairly flat.

Life on the boat became monotonous. The food was marginal; barely to keep us away from frank hunger, but there was never enough to feel "full." In addition, it was extremely uniform and lacking of fundamental ingredients, fats and proteins.

We felt extremely fortunate that we were able to stem the lice invasion. Later I learned that this was important not only because of the discomfort that lice bites caused, but also that they were the primary transmitters, thus sources, of typhus.

One afternoon we noted some spires on the horizon. Soon we could discern buildings on the high shore. It was Stalingrad (now named

Volgograd). We tied in to a single long dock. Again we were given permission to visit the city. It was a rather large industrial city with many statues of Lenin and Stalin and large government buildings. I walked again with David; however, we were admonished to not stray too far since the boat was to depart that evening. Stalingrad apparently was also an important railroad center and an industrial-commercial center influenced by the proximity of the Don River.

The Russians we met were proud to tell us about the city, but again we felt peculiar reactions in respect of the advances made by the Germans. Was there a substantial segment of the population that was hoping for the Germans to reach and occupy Stalingrad?

Upon return, we found Uncle Leon already on the boat. He just arrived from the city in a horse driven cart, a cart loaded almost full with beautiful watermelons. I had not seen watermelons since before the war. He nonchalantly had a Russian boy help him unload and carry the melons on the boat and promptly started selling them or bartering for them with the passengers on the boat. Before the action really started, he called David and me, handed us two of the largest melons and told us to take them to the captain. We ran happily to the crew's quarters to deliver the melons. Uncle Leon created a great commotion with his melons among the former camp inmates. Everyone wanted one. He was very happy to oblige and obviously to make some profit on this activity. The melons disappeared within an hour. Everyone was happy but none as happy as Leon. Shortly after completing the melon episode, he disappeared again to return within an hour with several parcels. Their contents were to remain secret 'till the next day. In the meanwhile, the crew prepared the boat for departure. By dusk, we slowly departed from the dock.

The days were moving slowly. The weather was good. Some of us tried to catch fish from the boat. None, however, had proper hooks; proper bait or a fisherman's know-how. Thus the exercise, except for killing time, was fruitless. We played a great deal of chess. One could walk down the decks and participate in "kibitzing" dozens of games.

Our food situation had improved remarkably. The little adventure with the watermelons had earned Leon some money and items to sell on the black market, which is where he went after the melon selling activities. For all this he was able to acquire a lot of food. He bought primarily bread, but he also got some cheese and a slaughtered rabbit which mother used to prepare enough meat soup to last us for the next three days.

Since the basic needs were partly satisfied and the itching subsided to a great extent, people were fundamentally killing time, waiting for the journey to Astrakhan to end. We had a great deal of time on our hands; we spent it primarily predicting our future. However, we also spent a great deal of time on philosophical discussions centered primarily on political doctrines. I had an early taste of it while in school in Lwow. Although in Lwow I was only in the 6th grade, we had a daily class dealing with Communist party doctrines. The time was devoted, almost exclusively, to the study of Marx's *Das Kapital* with some added discussions dealing with the lives and philosophies of Lenin and Stalin. At the one-hour per day school-year long sessions, we covered a substantial part of *Das Kapital.* This made me somewhat of an expert in the theoretical aspect of Communism. Although my maturity level was grossly inadequate to fully comprehend Marx's philosophy, the age, however, made me more vulnerable to the teachings of Communism. The ideas appealed to young people with eagerness to support fairness and logic. Indeed, the fundamental theoretical concepts of Marxism were logical and appealing to me. However, the reality made the ideas confusing. The Gulag episode was particularly difficult to understand. Thus, I was very eager to participate in the discussions and my theoretical knowledge was actually appreciated by the adults.

The days began to run into each other. We were not stopping at any ports and the food supply again became a problem. Similarly, we were running out of kerosene and the lice problem returned gradually and became serious. We couldn't wait to reach Astrakhan. The discussions became less frequent but more aggressive. They centered now on the issues of the Polish Army, the brush off we got from the commanding staff, the uncertainty of our destination in relationship to the Army's location, the uncertainty of what would happen in Astrakhan, the enormity of the probable trip through the Caspian Sea and then through the deserts of Central Asia.

Slowly everyone was beginning to realize the impossibility of the entire enterprise. We had no money. Our knowledge of the Russian language was at best rudimentary; we didn't even have a map to get an idea of where we were going. Most people had only a minuscule idea of the geography of this region. In addition, we realized, observing the life styles in the few ports that we were able to visit, that the living conditions in the Soviet Union must have been very poor, even before the war. Thus, particularly now, with a war going on and the Germans moving rapidly into the heart of Russia, the chances of getting food and transportation during this journey appeared to be problematic.

While most people were becoming disheartened, I dreamed about Astrakhan as an exotic city, a springboard to the Caspian Sea and the gates to Central Asia; at the age of thirteen, my thoughts were adventurous in nature and preoccupied with the unknown and the exotic.

For those older and more mature, the German war was the main concern, the starvation was real and very unpleasant and the lice were, at best, annoying. However, in my long discussions with David, we stayed away from these topics, instead spinning fantasies of unknown future in Astrakhan, associated with many exotic adventures.

Just the name, Astrakhan, sounded alien and foreboding and exciting. I wish I would have known at that time the stories of Khazars who populated this part of Russia from 6th through 11th centuries AD. The historical writings and archeological data support the notion that the Khazars, a Turkic people originating in Central Asia, developed an independent political entity with the height of its economic and cultural power between the 7th and 10th centuries AD. They developed a stable government that was based on the characteristics of the Khazar nation--tolerance and justice.

The Khazar state was a glaring exception to the medieval-age states of the Western Europe. In the 7th or 8th centuries, they voluntarily selected and adapted Judaism that flourished in the Khazar kingdom with all of its Talmudic details and with total acceptance of the Torah. The Khazars were not only tolerant, allowing all religions to develop in their lands, including Christianity and Islam, but they were also very productive. They developed strong agriculture in the areas bordering the Volga River. The region was naturally arid, but artificial irrigation, using water from the river, made it very productive. Trade with both east and west had developed to a high degree and the Khazar tradesmen were highly respected throughout the ancient world. At its peak of power, their possessions included eastern Ukraine, northern Caucasus, Crimea, western Kazakhstan, northwestern Uzbekistan and southern Russia. The capital was in a town called Itil, in an area some sixty miles northwest of the present day Astrakhan, an area rich in archeological finds.

The Khazars used the Hebrew alphabet and adapted many cultural characteristics of the Jews. The conquest of the Khazars in the 11th century by the new nation of *Kievan Rus* established by Prince Oleg, spelled the end of the Khazar kingdom and its culture. Some of the historical and archeological data suggests that a segment of the Khazars migrated east, primarily to Hungary, but some also to Ukraine, Rumania and Poland. There, they intermixed probably with the existing Jewish population, thus the modern Ashkenazi Jews may have some of the genetic characteristics of the Khazars. With the advent of molecular genetics in the late twentieth century, this question should be settled in the near future. Nevertheless, I still wish that I had some of the story about Khazars at the time of our visit to Astrakhan. Despite the hunger, fear and anxiety about the immediate future, it would made this experience much more meaningful and possibly would set me on a search in Astrakhan for some clues as to this fantastic and extremely important part of my heritage.

CHAPTER 8. Astrakhan

One very early morning, we arrived in Astrakhan. Most of us didn't even realize that we arrived at our destination until the boat docked and was tied down. We were told to disembark immediately.

Everyone staked out a tiny area on the dock and stored up their belongings. There was a great deal of confusion and no one to tell us where to go or what to do. We had no food ration cards and it became obvious that, at least for the immediate future, some arrangements would have to be made on the black market to obtain the absolute necessities.

As expected Uncle Leon took over this responsibility. Father got busy to learn about the continuation of our trip. This entailed getting passage on a boat going to Krasnovodsk located at the southeastern shores of the Caspian Sea.

By evening, things had clarified somewhat. Uncle Leon managed to find few loaves of black bread and some milk. He also learned that the city was crowded, overrun with people, primarily from the Ukraine, who were escaping capture by the advancing German armies.

Father was told that at this time there were no ships going to Krasnovodsk. He added that no one knew of any temporary housing. In silence we ate what was left of the meager supplies. Then, we arranged our belongings in such a fashion that we could sleep on top of them. This was becoming a well-developed routine. We slept the same way on the deck of the boat that brought us to Astrakhan. Our belongings yielded themselves well for this purpose. We had few valises but numerous sacks with clothing, pillows, comforters and blankets. When properly arranged, this gave us reasonably good surfaces to sleep on. In addition, as we were to learn very soon, this arrangement provided at least partial protection from thieves. We quickly learned that we had to have at night one person awake to stay guard against thieves.

Gradually people started finding places to go and there were fewer and fewer remaining on the dock. David and his parents found a place to stay and left. This was the last time I saw David. In Soviet Russia, it was impossible to search for and find a person. There was no government service for this purpose. After the war ended, I tried but was unsuccessful in locating David. I never saw him again.

We had hoped to board a boat to continue our travel to Krasnovodsk. But it became apparent that this may not happen soon, and we were forced to start looking seriously for a place to stay. Since leaving the Gulag some weeks back, we had no chance to take a bath or even to wash up decently. Also, it was getting too cold to sleep outdoors.

One day, Mother came with great news; she met a man, Tovarisht Rainer, an engineer of German ancestry who was willing to sublet a room in his apartment. Apparently, he spoke some German and wanted to practice the language with us. It turned out that he and his wife were very nice people, particularly nice to us. Later I found out that we paid him for the room with a beautiful gold signet ring with a large sapphire that belonged to my father.

We were very fortunate to find a place to live. The room was about fourteen by seventeen feet. My parents, my sister, Uncle Leon and I--a total of five of us--moved in with all of our belongings. Again, we made our sleeping arrangements on top of our belongings; this left a bit of floor space for a couple benches and a small table.

The owners of the apartment had a bedroom and a large kitchen where we ate our meals together with our landlords. The landlords were absolutely great to us. My little sister, Stella, and I began to converse in Russian with reasonable facility, and my parents and uncle spoke German with our landlords. They were happy to practice the German language and my parents and uncle were happy because they could converse with them easily this way.

Our landlords introduced us to a Russian institution, the *samovar*. The *samovar* is a wood-burning machine to boil water for tea. It is usually quite elaborate; chromium plated, or it could be made of silver. We really enjoyed this convenience. We have not experienced in the past such luxury and the luxury of drinking tea made with water that did not have the odor of fuel or sewer. Our quality of life improved again. We slept indoors, there was food available and in the evenings we spent considerable time in the kitchen with our landlords. They were extremely interested in learning about pre-war Germany and Poland and once they got to know us better to tell about the life in pre-war Astrakhan and in general, the life in Soviet Russia.

While our index of suspicion, primed by the experiences in Lwow and those after the release from the camp, was high, we were not prepared for the stories we heard from the Rainers.

They told us that a food stamp program existed already before the war with Germany. The food was much easier to obtain than now but still it was rationed.

Similarly, clothing was in short supply, so was soap and other cleaning supplies. Vodka was available all the time. There was always a black market where everything was available.

Once we moved in with the Rainers, we established an address and obtained ration coupons. This was very handy because we were able to obtain at least some food at government stores. The rationed items were obtainable only in government stores, and long queues had to be braved (sometimes the wait would be all night, and by the time one got to the counter, everything was sold out). The price, however, paid at the stores was minimal.

There were a number of restrictions even prior to the war's outbreak. According to the Rainers travel between towns was restricted and a special permit was necessary to get a railroad ticket. Work was compulsory for both men and women. Absence from work (*progul*) could be severely punished, and depending on the circumstances, could even include a jail term. The simplest way to get a few days off work was to get a certificate from the doctor testifying of the presence of some disease or trauma. The granting of these "sickness certificates" was an important part of the functions of the health care providers and, as I will discuss later, an important source of income for the very poorly paid physicians. The physicians were paid less than factory workers.

Many evenings we sat drinking tea and listening to these unbelievable facts of life in the Soviet Union. While the constitution gave the citizen rights that were to be envied by anyone in the world, the reality was quite opposite.

Mister Rainer had a favorite joke to tell that summarized this issue in a nutshell: A man is awakened in the middle of the night by a knock on his door. When he opens it he sees a couple NKVD officers. He immediately asks them, "with or without," in other words with a satchel containing some clothing or without it. In the first case he is to be send to camp in Siberia, in the second he will be only questioned. He doesn't ask what or why, he doesn't expect to get any answers or to be judged by a court of law, he knows that he is to "go." Mister Rainer not only suggested, but also flatly stated, that no one had any personal rights when the political police was involved. He would hint at times that people were hoping that the German Army would get to Astrakhan and "liberate" the people from the yoke of "Sovietism."

Slowly, the weeks passed and it was getting colder. The German Army offensive was quite successful. We heard that they were approaching Rostov on the Don, a city about 400 miles northeast of Astrakhan, and were pushing hard towards Stalingrad (now Volgograd).

Some of the Russians in Astrakhan, possibly because of their German ancestry, were getting happier while we were getting more concerned. There were rumors that the German Army was committing horrendous atrocities on the occupied lands, atrocities in particular directed toward the Jews.

This information, however, was very vague and contradictory. The official press (quite scarce and poorly organized) emphasized the actions of the Germans against the general population. The specific action against the Jews was the topic of rumors and innuendos. No one knew what the situation really was. The reports concerning the atrocities were attributed at least partly to propaganda

Nevertheless, my parents and Uncle Leon felt strongly that we should get out of Astrakhan before winter and try to get as close as possible to Central Asia. At this point in time the only practical route was via the Caspian Sea. However, we did not have much time left. The river began to freeze up. If the water would freeze in Astrakhan harbor, we would be trapped. My parents and Leon redoubled their efforts to get space on a ship leaving Astrakhan for the Caspian Sea, preferably for Krasnovodsk.

Leon came up with information that the last ship to leave Astrakhan was to arrive within a couple days. It, however, was already almost totally filled by the wives of Soviet Air Corps fliers who were being evacuated from central Russia to Central Asia. In light of this information, Leon and Mother decided to see the person in power in order to do all that could be done to get on this ship. Leon was armed with the papers from the Polish Army directing us to go to Alma Ata as rapidly as possible and Mother accompanied him for moral support and possibly to add some other approaches to this issue. The decision to allow us to board the ship rested with the Commandant of the Port of Astrakhan.

Apparently, there were many who got this idea; there was a long queue to see him, actually to see anyone in his office. They waited in the queue for two days; actually only one stayed in the queue while the other would go home to rest and eat. They were disheartened. There were literally hundreds and hundreds of people trying to get on this boat. But the "luck?" or abilities and perseverance were with them.

On the third day, Mother and Leon both came running home with huge grins on their faces. The three days and two nights in the queue paid off. We got space on the boat and the boat was leaving in two days. We were really curious how they were able to get us on the boat and they were happy to tell. The Rainers were also intrigued and wanted to hear the story.

Their plan had two parts; neither act on its own would probably do the job. Firstly they had to get in, in other words be seen and considered for space allotment. Uncle Leon who brandished the traveling orders from the Polish Army Headquarters accomplished this part of the task. Once they got in to see the "*Natchalnik*" (commander), and had him review our documents he made it clear that while we were entitled to embark the boat, unfortunately there was no more space to accommodate us. The *Natchalnik* said that he was very sorry but there was nothing he could do under the circumstances. At this point Leon responded with a huge grin on his face and told him that he understood his position and would like to bring him a minor item as a token of appreciation for his attempts to help us. The *Natchalnik* expressed pleasure to this suggestion and gave Leon a *bumashku,* a piece of paper that entitled Leon to return to his office without having to wait in the queue.

I didn't understand why Leon wanted to give the N*atchalnik a* gift but this became clear shortly. Leon said, "The *Natchalnik* didn't need to see me personally to give a negative answer, he didn't need to apologize. He could simply instruct his assistants to tell us that there is no room for us." Father said: "Well, it appears to me that the *Natchalnik* wanted something." "Indeed," responded Leon. "In my opinion he clearly indicated that for an appropriate consideration he will be willing to get us on the boat. My response should have suggested to him that we are willing to negotiate the size of the "gift." However, I do not feel that at this time we are in any position to bargain with him." Leon continued, "We should offer a bribe that will be so far beyond anything others could offer that he will not be able to resist." "This is the last chance for us to get out of Astrakhan, we should not miss it," said Father. Mother added: "I fully agree and I think I have the right item that he will not be able to resist. We should offer him my Persian lamb coat." The coat was a possession Mother cherished greatly. It was a beautiful black "broad-tail" lamb fur coat. It was very expensive and she kept it for the occasion that would be one of life or death. Apparently, she felt that this indeed was the right time. After a brief discussion, Leon picked up the coat and left for the port. He returned that afternoon with documents for the entire family entitling us to board the ship and travel to Krasnovodsk, with a stop in Fort Schevtchenko.

CHAPTER 9. On the Caspian Sea

We were both elated and sad. Obviously we were absolutely happy to leave Astrakhan. But, the thought of leaving the Rainers behind made us sad because we became quite close during the few weeks that we stayed with them. But the Rainers, even if they could, were not at all interested in leaving. They actually looked forward towards the German occupation. We started packing our belongings and looking for a horse and buggy to get us to the port. Well, for a proper number of rubles, we got a buggy, but there were no horses to be had. It was decided that we will pull the buggy, but to do so we had to start early in the morning to get to the port before nightfall, particularly since the days were becoming very short.

We couldn't load up the buggy the day before, because everything would be stolen by morning, even if we would try to guard it. Thus, it was decided to load the buggy throughout the night and with down start pulling it to the port. As we started saying goodbyes to the Rainers, they insisted on helping pull the buggy.

It was quite a procession. Uncle Leon was harnessed at the lead of the buggy, followed by father, Mr. Rainer and then me. It was very difficult to pull the load; the buggy by itself was very heavy and when loaded it was almost impossible to move. It took us 'till evening to get to the boat. But once there, the boat crew helped to move our belongings and we were loaded on the boat in no time.

There were two upper decks with cabins that had windows; the families of the military pilots being evacuated occupied these. We were directed to a second level hold below the water line at the aft of the ship. There, on the floor, we placed our valises and bags. The area available to us was only about six by seven feet. When stocked up in this space, our bags reached almost the sealing of the hold. There was no way we could fit on top of our belongings; there simply wasn't enough space. We were given the opportunity to stock up our belongings deep in the third hold and sleep in the allotted area in the second hold.

Some of the bags containing bedding were unpacked and spread on the floor of the area designated for us and we went to sleep. It became clear that we couldn't sleep on our backs; there wasn't enough space. We had to stay on our side to fit in the allotted space. We were dead tired after a day of pulling the buggy, which helped us to survive that night. Two of the family members would stay up somewhere on the decks or passageways while the rest of the family slept in a more acceptable positions.

Upon awakening in the morning, we went to a huge dining area that distributed food in three shifts twice daily, in the morning and in the afternoon. We quickly learned that the food was a major problem. We were given the same food daily, 200 grams of black bread and potato soup for each person. Depending on luck and on the server's desires, one got a bowl of soup with several slices of potatoes in it or primarily the water in which the potatoes were cooked.

As time went on, the food situation became more and more acute since there was no way to get on shore and to the black market. To make things a bit worse, we soon realized all of us were full of lice. An incredible phenomenon occurred--at night the metal floor of the hold we were sleeping on became alive, alive with thousands of lice. Normally lice will not live on inanimate objects. But here, apparently the living bodies were on the metal floor in such density that the lice simply would fall off the bodies and quickly finds another body to inhabit. This was a disaster. It was essentially impossible to sleep because of the tormenting itch. We had a little kerosene left and this was used exclusively for the scalp. Unfortunately we had no facilities to boil the underwear.

To make things worse, the weather was cold and rainy. Most people were seasick. This made the survival even worse, the crowding, the lice and now the stench of vomit everywhere created a state of constant nausea so that even the scanty and bad food couldn't be consumed by most. Soon most of us developed chronic diarrhea and weakness. The water was essentially undrinkable because of its stench. However, one could get all day along with *Kipiatok* that is boiled water.

Before leaving Astrakhan, *Tovaristch* Rainer gave us a supply of tea. He said, "This is the most important ingredient to carry when you travel. Most of the time you will be able to get boiled water the tea will make everything bearable."

He was absolutely correct. The tea actually was quite different from the tea we were accustomed to. The tea I knew before the war was composed of black, tiny, dry, curled up leaves. The tea we got was a green brick. Apparently in Russia and Central Asia, the available tea was green and not dried little leaves but pressed bricks. To make it drinkable one broke off a piece and boiled it to make the tea. While the tea was a "life saver," the diarrhea did not abate. There was a constant queue at the toilettes. Those rooms had a steel floor in which six holes were cut out so that six people could use the facility simultaneously. The holes were open to the sea. One had to be very careful not to fall in. Actually just looking at the sea made one violently seasick.

In few days we docked at Port Schevtchenko. The weather was still very cold and windy, however, it didn't rain. The port was quite large with a number of fishing vessels and freighters moored or docked. We were permitted to disembark and walk around. There were no open stores. The streets were very dusty, with the wind driving the dust everywhere. There was nothing one could see or buy. The people living there, especially the men, were interesting. They were medium size or relatively small but very stocky with broad Mongolian faces. They wore beautiful fur coats. The fur was longhaired, golden yellow, looking a bit like the fox furs I had seen worn by women before the war. On their feet they wore prettily embroidered *Valenky*, felt knee-high boots.

Since there wasn't much to do or see ashore, I returned to the boat and found Uncle Leon there. He returned just before me. "What did you accomplish?" he asked me.

"Not much, I didn't find any food items, plus I had no money," I responded.

"I was lucky; although I couldn't find bread I did find some food stuff that will be helpful." He moved aside to show two good sized sacks placed under a cover in the middle of our sleeping area. One was filled with sunflower seeds and the other with pumpkin seeds. I was so hungry that I could eat anything, but this was an unbelievable treat. I always loved sunflower and pumpkin seeds!

I jumped to the sacks to fill my pockets with the seeds. Mother, however, had already taken over the management of this treasury. The seeds were to be rationed to every member of the family in an equitable way and husbanded carefully to last as long as possible since we had no idea where and when our next chance to get food would present itself.

The next morning we departed and life returned to the usual onboard routine, except for the fact that people were getting hungrier and sicker. In retrospect, I am amazed that we didn't develop typhus on the boat in view of the very heavy lice infestation. We were very lucky. While the seas were getting more and more boisterous, the temperature started rising. It became warm and the sun was out most of the time. This definitely helped the morale.

Most of us tried to spend most of the time on the decks, away from the holds that smelled and were full of lice. After a day and a night at sea, we saw mountains emerging on the horizon. My relatively well-developed sense of geography suggested that we were near a shoreline bordering the Caucasus Mountains. The boat did not get to the shore, but a tender was send out to the port and shortly after its return we departed. Later we learned that we were in a port called Machatchcala.

The boat continued on a southerly course. The seas quieted down and the weather got better and warmer. The passengers spent most of the time on the decks. The food consisted of two daily servings of warm cooked cereal and a quart of water. The lice infestation in the holds was unbearable. The constant itching from the bites drove us crazy. Ultimately we spied land. Soon we were entering a bay, the Krasnovodsk Bay, surrounded by high, barren mountains. At the head of the bay was the Port of Krasnovodsk. We had arrived in the Soviet Autonomous Republic of Turkmenia.

CHAPTER 10. The Deserts of Central Asia

At the time, I was not aware of the region's rich past and of the fact that the area was once called Turkistan (in Persian, the "Land of Turks"). While most people spoke Russian, their native language was a Turkish dialect. The region had changed hands many times during the history. Around 500 B.C., it was conquered by the Persians. Then, it was successively invaded by Alexander the Great, the Chinese, the Huns, the Arabs, the Turks, the Mongols and ultimately in 1867 by the Russians. Following the communist revolution in 1917, the area became a Soviet Autonomous Republic.

While I was only vaguely familiar with this history, I was excited to be there despite the severe physical discomfort associated with the passage and emotional stress of not knowing what the next day would bring. I was looking forward to, what appeared to be an exotic adventure.

The boat eased to a stop at the dock and soon was tied up. The weather was dry and very warm and as soon as we have arrived, we established a camp near the docks. Again the family set on, and during the night, slept on top of our bundles. This method was used to prevent theft, both during the day and at night, and to provide us with a place to sit during the day and sleep at night.

While we were establishing the camp, Mother and Uncle Leon went to town to look for food and to investigate the possibility of transport to Alma Ata.

My sister, Stella, who was six years old at that time, was really a good sport. Although hungry, dirty and very uncomfortably, she acted as a happy and content child, always looking to play with something rather than complain.

Father tried to reason things out, but under the circumstances he was essentially at a loss. There was nothing to do but wait. I was chaffing at the bit to go into town. It looked super exotic. Gaunt, brown-skinned men, some with turbaned heads were walking around leading skeleton-like obviously starved donkeys. There was an occasional, sad looking camel walking stately behind a barefooted man. All this was somewhat unreal and incongruous, since I had never seen a man with a turban or a camel, with the exception of at a zoo.

Nevertheless, despite the fear, the hunger and the obvious seriousness of the situation, I was excited and looking forward to, what looked like, a superb adventure. In my naiveté, I didn't even give a thought to the price we were about to pay for this "adventure."

Finally, Mother and Leon returned. Leon had his shirt off, using it to carry a load of cans. They turned out to be tins of preserved crabmeat!

"There is essentially no food in town; no bread, no fruits, no meat or vegetables, the stores are empty, and most are closed." he said. "However," Mother added, "there are a few shops full of these tins of crab meat, so there must be a major canning industry in Krasnovodsk and crab meat appears to be a major, possibly the only product canned. This provides, locally, for almost limitless supply of canned crab meat since none of it is exported to other parts of Soviet Union, for reasons that are not clear to me."

"What about transportation to Alma Ata?" I asked.

"Well, this is also a very complicated matter," Uncle Leon said, "There are several levels of difficulties."

"But," my father interrupted, "doesn't the document state that we are on our way to join Anders' Army?"

"Yes," Uncle Leon added, "but the paper on which the document is printed does not mention the word trains for travel! Thus, our first difficulty is the fact that there are only two trains departing east from Krasnovodsk weekly. The only direction to go on this train from here is indeed east, and the only place we will get to, as the first major city, will be Ash-Habad. We are now in the Soviet Socialistic Republic of Turkmenistan and I think that Ash-Habad is the capitol of this republic. The train will take us, over the great Kyzyl Kum desert, to Ash-Habad, then the train will continue eastward, and ultimately we should reach Alma Ata. However, the second, and under the circumstances, an even more serious difficulty, is the fact that at this time I see almost no chance for us to get aboard the train in the foreseeable future."

This statement was accompanied by an expression of bottomless glum. Father tried to bring up our spirits and cheer us up. "There are no impossible situations, I am sure," he said. "Something will come up to help us. In the meanwhile let's eat, I can't wait to try this crab meat. I don't remember when it was the last time I had some, it must have been in the fancy restaurant, Havelka, in Krakow."

We all agreed that this was a great idea. The only thing missing was something to go with the crabmeat. Crab meat was a super delicacy. I remembered having it only once or twice in my lifetime, some time before the war and only in tiny quantity, just to taste it. Here we had an unlimited supply of crab meat, but no bread or potatoes to go with it.

Mother opened a couple cans; all of us tasted the crabmeat and agreed that it was absolutely delicious. As we gorged ourselves on the meat, I thought I could smell something, something like baking bread or burning flour. Soon everyone agreed that there was a smell in the air resembling that of a bakery. It was an irresistible aroma and Mother volunteered to investigate.

She went, following her nose, in the direction of the source of the smell. I ran after her. After leaving the port area, the smell became more pronounced. Soon we learned where the source was located. Down the street, there was a large square crowded with people, camels, goats and donkeys. According to Mother, the square was empty before when she walked through it earlier on the way to the railroad station. Apparently a caravan arrived from somewhere in the past couple hours. We drew closer to them and struck up a conversation. They all spoke a foreign language that neither Mother nor I could place. Most of them, however, spoke also Russian, giving us a chance to communicate.

It turned out that indeed it was a large caravan having arrived from the east. They had fires going and were baking a form of bread, they called *lepioshky* in Russian. The dough was made of corn meal; it was flattened and placed on an iron support resting over fire made of twisted branches of very hard wood, which they called *Saksaul.* Later we learned that this plant was ubiquitous in the deserts--it also grew in the deserts of Kazakhstan and was a very sought after fuel wood because its hot coals burned for prolonged time and emitted a great deal of heat.

Mother in no time engaged in conversation with these native Turkmeni trying to find out where one could get flour to make bread. Our diet consisting at the moment exclusively of canned crabmeat would be greatly enhanced if we had some form of bread to eat with the meat. They clearly indicated that there was no source of flour in town.

Their caravan and other caravans were the major source of supply.They would be interested in bartering. We returned to the port and had a major family conference in respect to issue of getting flour. It obviously became Uncle Leon's task. He cherished this type of activity and initiated the process by first visiting the caravan and getting to know some of the facts of life there as well as striking up some conversations, primarily with the women. Upon return, he had his plan totally thought out. Mother had a beautiful French silk scarf, which she saved since the war started. It was white with red and blue flowers. Leon suggested that we trade this scarf for bread.

Off he went with the scarf in his pocket and in an hour, he was back with one of the Turkmen and a donkey. The donkey had on its back a huge gunnysack filled with what looked like round, flat, small plate-sized breads. The wonderful aroma of the bread was irresistible. We opened cans of crabmeat and attacked the meat and the bread with great enthusiasm. It was the best meal we had for years.

To complete our absolute luxury he pulled out from his other pocket a round dirty-yellow hard ball, which turned out to be a "head" of sugar. That apparently was the way the natives stored and transported sugar. The sugar certainly topped our incredibly luxurious meal.

After the meal, we all wanted to hear Leon's adventures and he was happy and eager to tell the story. First he learned who the leader of the caravan was and then learned which one was his wife. He approached the wife and showed her the scarf. The rest was easy. Leon had an unbelievable way with people. He knew how to make them like him and he knew how to excite their interest. Obviously the wife not only became enchanted by the scarf but also got to like Leon and introduced him to her husband. Leon offered the scarf to the husband, the caravan leader, as a gift for his wife. The gift was accepted and the husbands reciprocated by letting us have the bread, the tea and the sugar. In addition, the entire caravan became our friends.

In the evening we were invited to eat with them and it was our second great meal of the day. The meal consisted of *bizbermak* and *kumys*. *Bizbermak* was a very exotic and nutritious dish. It was prepared in a huge iron cauldron resting on several large stones under which a fire was lit. The cauldron was filled with water and large chunks of fat lamb meat were cooked in it. While the meat was cooking, huge sheets of dough made of corn flour were rolled out and when the meat was judged to be ready, sheets of dough were thrown on top of the boiling water. The boiling water ripped the dough into smaller pieces and the meal was ready. Once the boiling water cooled down sufficiently to be able to place one's fingers in it, the chunks of meat and the cooked dough were fished out and the soup was served in round deep dishes called *peealky*.

It was actually a pretty tasty dish and considering our starving state the dish was straight from paradise. *Kumys* was fermented mare's milk. It was prepared using a whole sheep's hide to form a sack, a container, with the fur inverted to line the lumen. The milk was placed into the sack and kept there until it soured and the fermentation process converted it into an alcoholic beverage. I tasted it but was unable to develop a desire to consume it. Matter of fact, I thought it tasted awful.

The next day we had a major family conference dealing with our chances to get on the train. Again, Mother and Leon were elected to further investigate this matter and they trotted off to the railroad station. Father, my sister and I remained on top of our belongings in the port.

There were several dozen families camping out; they all arrived with us on the same boat. It turned out that they were the wives and children of army and air force officers being evacuated from the lands taken over by the Germans. They were as bewildered and at a loss as we were. They were starving, but didn't have Uncle Leon to "arrange" things for them.

We talked with them but failed to learn anything new. They actually did not know which way to turn next. Krasnovodsk was as strange to them as it was to us.

Mother and Leon returned in several hours. They looked quite unhappy. Apparently there was no train leaving in the next couple days. They were unable to learn if or when a train would leave Krasnovodsk. There was no one at the railroad station willing to provide any information and we had no choice but to try to survive and hope to find another way to get out of Krasnovodsk.

As the day went on we realized that we had another problem--water. The water supply in Krasnovodsk was extremely limited. One needed special connections to get water in quantity. Fortunately, our water requirements were very small; nevertheless we needed some water.

Apparently, the city's water system was overtaxed, particularly when several caravans were in town, as was the case. Again, our newly acquired friends in the caravan were very helpful. They obtained water for the caravan and shared it with us.

The next day, Father was in the city and returned all excited. Firstly, he found a place where people met and played chess. Since he was an avid chess player and one of the former Europe Chess Masters, this was an unexpected and very welcomed pleasure. It also gave him the opportunity to become acquainted with many people, some of whom were quite influential in town. It was there that, through a connection, he also learned a bit of confidential information that indeed tomorrow evening a train was to depart for Ashkabad. This information was kept very quiet so there would be no rush for the train and only select passengers would be able to board it. That was the clue for Mother and Uncle Leon to spring into action. They left immediately for town.

The day went on. The sun had set and there was no sign of them. I suggested that I go to look for them, but Father restrained me.

He reasoned that if they were arrested, they would have told police about us and police would have come to get us. If something horrible would have happened probably one would have escaped and returned to us. Thus, he concluded, it was just taking them a long time to accomplish the task they were working on. Indeed he was correct.

As the dusk enveloped us, they both showed up, tired, hungry and very excited. Leon led the charge with a big grin on his face and the "pinky" of his left hand high in the air. "You see, you see!" he exclaimed.

I saw nothing except for his left hand. "Look carefully" he cried, "Look for what you can't see anymore," he demanded. I was flabbergasted; I had no idea what he was leading to. Finally Mother sat down and started to tell us the story. They were knocking on every door at the city government, the railroad station, and the military command, all to no avail. At each place, someone either refused to talk to them or told them that it was unclear at this time when a train would leave Krasnovodsk. They suggested that we watch the train schedule board at the railroad station and when we see a train being scheduled return to the office with the documents and our reasons for travel. At that point we could obtain a permit that would give us the possibility to purchase the tickets.

Obviously neither Mother nor Leon was placated by these "put offs." They kept on scouting around the area of the railroad station. The access to the inside of the station and to the boarding areas was restricted. Leon, however, sweet-talked his way to the inside of the station. While inside he found his way to the railroad tracks and the boarding areas.

There, to his amazement, he found a huge train with many cars obviously being readied for boarding. Railroad workers were checking the pressure in the brake lines between the cars; some were hitting the wheels with hammers checking for metal soundness. The car doors were opened. The train consisted of a large number of passenger cars and some cattle cars. Watching the activities, Uncle observed that there was one man who obviously was in charge. He was short and stocky, and Mother said that he had a "kind face." They both agreed to approach him. They decided to tell him that they know that this train is being readied for departure and that we must leave to join the army forming in Kazakhstan, and so on.

First he was ready to have them removed from the station forthwith. Uncle Leon, however, kept showing his left hand with the beautiful signed ring on his pinky finger, a ring with a huge ruby cut in a square design; a real "He-man" signet ring, obviously very expensive. After a bit of negotiating the station chief agreed that we could get a special *spravka* (a statement of permit) from him, giving us the privilege of travel to Kazakhstan without a ticket, as special passengers, so designated by him. He made it clear that this was not totally legal, but it had a good chance of succeeding. However, he said, we were to board the train that night, quietly, before the general boarding began the next day. Thus, it appeared that we might be able to leave Krasnovodsk within twenty-four hours, traveling on Leon's signet ring!

The station chief also assigned a couple of railroad workers to help us with the boarding. We were to arrive at the station at 11 p.m. With this great news, we approached the caravan leader for help in moving our belongings tonight to the railroad station. He was happy to assist and said that he would let us have a couple of donkeys and some of his men to help with boarding the train. By 10 p.m., we started loading the donkeys and then slowly moved towards the railroad station. The town was very quiet; it looked deserted. There was no one on the street. At 11 p.m., we arrived at the station.

The station chief was already waiting for us. Quickly he led us to the train, to the third car from the end. It was a very old car divided into compartments. Each compartment had a separate door to the outside as well as a door to a narrow corridor connecting the compartments inside the car. Each compartment was designed to hold six passengers; however, once we loaded up our belongings, there was scarcely enough room for the five of us.

The chief hung wooden signs on both of the compartment's doors stating: "Keep Off-Polish Army Personnel." He wished us a good trip and admonished us not to leave the compartment and always keep the doors closed until the arrival at a next station.

Once we got there, we could move freely and when questioned always refer to the signs and to our papers dealing with the trip to Alma Ata to join the Polish Army. He said at that point our chances of being kicked off the train would be very slim. We thanked him, thanked our friends from the caravan, closed the door to the compartment and tried to get some sleep.

I woke up when the sun was already high. The rest of the family was in various stages of waking up. We were still at the station in Krasnovodsk. There was noise everywhere. People were running up and down the railroad platform trying to board the train. There was confusion and arguments were erupting continuously. There were obviously many more people trying to board the train than there were available places. NKVD personnel were stationed everywhere, frequently asking for documents or leading some people away. We were very tense and worried that the NKVD people would start questioning us, and this could definitely lead to some difficulties. Father suggested that we stay away from the windows to attract less attention.

One thing we had no problem with was food. We brought with us a huge supply of canned crab and our friends made for us another sack of *lepioshki*. In addition, they provided us with a supply of dried goat cheese. A small piece of this cheese when chipped off a large cheese ball would supply enough nutrients to survive a day or two. Water was a problem but we had several bottles for immediate needs.

The day dragged on with the unceasing din of voices outside the car and constant attempt to pry open the doors of our compartment, both from the corridor and from the outside; we were nervous wrecks. We did not respond and kept the doors closed. When banging would get particularly aggressive, I, who spoke Russian best, would lower my voice as close to a bass as possible and respond. Since I was getting close to the age of 14, thus almost post pubertal, my voice was getting pretty low naturally and we hoped that I could get by as an adult.

As the day was moving on and we were not molested, the tension abated a bit. We had just started dozing off when there was a sudden noise and we almost fell off the seats. The train took off and in no time we were out of town. As far as we could see through the windows, a desert was stretching all the way to the horizon. We hugged and kissed; there was a great cause for celebration. We were on our way.

In the morning we learned rapidly that there were a number of difficulties to face. One was the bathroom. The bathroom in the railroad car was locked and we were unable to check the other cars because the doors between the cars were locked. Secondly, there was nothing to drink. The situation was getting critical when we sensed that the train was slowing down. Soon it stopped. People were running out of the train and hiding behind low desert bushes so they could relieve themselves. This sure was a relief. It was a bit embarrassing but essential. Since everyone was doing it, soon we also stopped feeling uncomfortable with this situation. We all walked around a bit before going back to the train and while doing so noted that many people went to the locomotive where a queue was forming. I ran over to investigate and found out that the train staff was dispensing hot water, *kipiatok*, from the locomotive tanks. This was an unexpected boon, so I ran back to our car where we had a large teapot and returned to fill it up with the boiling water. Mother made tea and this with the *lepioshki* was a treat, particularly since we had still most of the "head" of sugar.

As the train resumed its journey and built up speed, we looked out of the window to see a desert there. Although unaware of our exact location, we felt happy and content. We were moving, we were not thirsty, we were not hungry and our bodily functions were attended to. I kept on looking at the desert. It was awesome. There wasn't a tree, a building or a living body anywhere. Sand and areas of dry looking scrub extended on the left side. Through the windows on the right, I could see mountains in the distance; everything was yellowish-beige, looking quite forlorn.

I was always interested in geography and this helped me to become a bit more oriented. Calculating the elapsed time, the direction of our travel and the presence of mountains on the right side of the train while going almost due east, according to the sun position, I figured that we must have traveled fairly close to the Iranian (at that time it was still Persian) border. This should have moved us towards Ashkabad.

We slept through the night with no adventures and woke up in the morning actually in a good mood and feeling well. There was still plenty of food but we were again running out of water.

I ventured out of the compartment into the narrow passageway running up and down the length of the car hoping to visit the adjoining compartments and possibly learn more about the train, its destination and possibly get some water. The compartments were closed and one could not look in.

Almost at the end of the car the door of one of the compartments was open. Inside there was a young woman with a child and a man in a uniform. The various insignia on the uniform's shirt suggested that he was most likely a highly ranked officer in the Soviet Armed Forces.

I mounted all the courage I had and knocked on the frame of the compartments sliding door. The man looked up, flashed a friendly smile and invited me to come in. I told them that my mastery of the Russian language was very rudimentary, that we were on our way to Alma Ata and that I was trying to get information where to get some water. He asked me to sit down and explained that there is no drinking water on the train. But, he said, "by the evening we should get to Ashkabad and there we will be able to get some drinking water." He added, "This is an empty country with very few settlements on the way."

I asked if the train would take us all the way to Alma Ata. He responded: "The Trans-Caspian Railroad will get us to Tashkent via Bukhara. There we will probably have to change to another train that will take us to Alma Ata." He pulled out a map and showed me the train route. Presently we were crossing the Kara Kum Desert. I thanked him for the information and returned to share it with the family.

The journey continued in its monotony 'till the afternoon when the train slowed down and eventually stopped. Leon opened the compartment's outside door and stepped out on the running board to get a better view of the train. At the head of the train, by its locomotive, there was a group of camels, donkeys, people and some horsemen. Father, Leon and I got off the train and started walking towards the caravan. A caravan in the desert was quite a sight and we were curious to find out why the train stopped at the place where the caravan was camping.

The answer became obvious quickly. The caravan was selling camel and goat milk to the train passengers. They, however, had no water for sale. We all were thirsty and Father said milk is a fluid and better than nothing. We bought two quarts of camel milk. It was sold to us in a goatskin sack. Upon return to the train coach, Mother took over the management of the milk. She poured it into glasses (actually old glass jars we carried with us for this purpose) since there were no regular drinking glasses available. Matter of fact, we hadn't owned drinking glasses since we left Lwow.

I lifted the jar to my lips but stopped to look at it. The milk had a peculiar bluish color. When the jar got closer to my nose, I was assaulted by a strong odor. Unfortunately, the taste matched the odor. No matter how thirsty I was, it was virtually impossible for me to drink.

I looked at my parents and at Leon. All had the same expression on their faces--surprise mixed with disgust. No one could take it in his or her mouths. Finally, Mother said, "Let's save it 'till tomorrow. If we do not get any drinking water by tomorrow morning this may turn out to be our only source of fluids."

While we were busy with the camel milk, the train resumed its progress. Slowly I was lulled to sleep by the car's motions. It must have been the lack of motion that woke me.

A look through the window revealed that we had stopped at a railroad station. Although the station was fairly large, it was seedy and obviously neglected. It also was not very busy. There were only a small number of people on the platform. Leon was already outside trying to get some information. It became clear that we had finally arrived in Ashkabad.

I knew very little about this city. It was apparently the largest city in Turkmenistan, as I learned later from Sasha, my new friend on the train. It was an ancient city and the capital of the Turkmen Soviet Socialistic Republic. Uncle Leon had designs on going to the city and getting some food and water. This turned out to be impossible. The train stopped only to get water for the locomotive and coal. We were to leave within one hour.

Although we couldn't leave the station, we didn't miss the opportunity to get water. Indeed, we filled every container we could find and drank as much water at the station as we could. There was a spigot at the side of the station's building. Mother had a small pail with us, this was also filled with water and everyone got a chance to wash their faces in clean water. The time flew by rapidly and we departed before we knew it.

The monotony of the train travel overcame us again. I went to see my newly acquired friend, Sasha. He was a very likable fellow, obviously happy to talk to me. He indicated that he was with the intelligence service in the military and quite familiar with the geography and history of this region of the country. He told me that in 500 B.C., the Persians conquered Turkistan and were then chased out by Alexander the Great, only to be re-conquered again, after the death of Alexander the Great, by the Seleucid Dynasty, the rulers of Babylon. Sasha obviously was fascinated by the history of central Asia and was eager to tell me all the details but as he warmed up to the project, Father came and called me away.

When I returned to our compartment, everyone was engaged in a major discussion. Apparently, Mother, talking to some women, learned that from now on we would be traveling very close to the mountains and the Iranian border. In this area, bandits frequently board the trains and steal the personal possessions of the passengers. In view of this, it was decided to stand watch throughout the night.

I was considered sufficiently grown up to stand watch with the rest of the adults. I was assigned the first and abbreviated watch 'till 10 p.m., then Leon between 10 and 2 a.m., followed by father 'till 6 a.m. and Mother for an early morning watch between 6 and 8 a.m. I felt neither tired nor sleepy and this sounded like an adventure. I latched the compartment door and settled to watch clouds forming in the sky and running across an image of a full moon. I thought of our situation, the trip into the unknown, the war and the land we were crossing.

Although Sasha didn't get a chance to tell me more of the history of Turkistan, the little he did inflamed my imagination. I thought of Babylon, of Alexander the Great and I couldn't stop thinking about the fact that I was traveling over the land where such an exciting history has played itself out.

The time flew by fast and 10 o'clock arrived in no time. I woke up Uncle Leon, curled up and went to sleep. Sleep, however, didn't come. I kept on thinking about Alexander the Great, about Babylon and about us in these strange surroundings. I wanted to hear more from Sasha about the past of this region and get a look at his maps again.

Suddenly I heard something that sounded like metal scraping on metal. The moonlight flooding the compartment had clearly outlined all of us. Stella and both parents were deeply asleep. Leon was also dozing.

I looked at the sliding door and saw a piece of metal moving up and down in the area of the latch. Obviously an attempt was being made to dislodge it. I quietly picked up an ax, which we had resting next to the window for a variety of reasons, including one like this, and hit, with all my might, using the blunt end of the ax, the piece of metal being manipulated from the outside.

Someone outside let out a yell and dropped the metal strip. Everyone in the compartment woke up; Father opened the sliding door and ran out into the passageway. It was empty. This time we were lucky. Upon return, he was met by absolute bedlam. Stella was crying, Mother was taking stock of the items we had in the compartment and Leon looked dejected. He had missed his watch. I was proclaimed a hero.

The rest of the night was uneventful. I was much too excited to fall back to sleep. Everyone else, however, did.

The dawn was braking. The sky ahead of the train was turning pink. The landscape had changed remarkably. The mountains on the right side of the train disappeared and were replaced by sandy flats broken by small rocky outcrops and sparse, desert type brown vegetation.

I badly needed my friend Sasha's maps to get oriented. However, it was still too early to visit him and I was getting hungry and thirsty. While I knew where our food supplies were located, it would not have been proper for me to rummage in them while Mother was not around. She had total control of our food and water supply and I felt that I should wait until she woke up.

As I waited the motion of the train must have lulled me back to sleep, because when I woke up again the sun was high in the sky. Mother said, "I saved you some water. The only foods we have left are some cans with crabmeat and few *lepioshki*. The cheese is gone." I was famished and didn't care what I ate, as long as I had some food and water.

After eating I was anxious to see Sasha. He was in his compartment reading. I still couldn't figure out why he was given the opportunity to evacuate to Central Asia while his colleagues were fighting a war, a war that wasn't going well, according to the bits of information we had while still in Astrakhan.

He asked, "How was the night?" I related our experiences. He laughed. "This should teach you a lesson," he said. "You must recognize the realities of life and adjust accordingly."

I actually was not particularly interested in his philosophies. I wanted to hear more about the history of the land we were traversing and wanted to see his maps. "Where do you think we are right now?" I asked. "Well," he said, pulling out the map, "we crossed the Murghab River and stopped only for about one hour in Merv (now Mary, Turkmenistan). That was probably where the robbers, who tried to get to your compartment, boarded the train. They must have jumped off the train by now."

Pointing on the map with his finger, he said: "We are probably somewhere here; we must have turned a bit north because I barely see the mountains south of us. You know, before we were traveling close to Iran that was a few miles south of us; just where the mountains could be seen. Now, south of us is Afghanistan. Soon we will cross the Amu Daria River and enter the Uzbek Socialistic Republic, and then, on to Bukhara, one of the most ancient cities in Central Asia." He obviously enjoyed giving this lecture and I was more than happy to listen.

He continued: "The Amu Daria is probably the most important river in this area. It brings water to the Kara Kum Desert, making it possible for the cities to develop and grow, for the agriculture to survive and the oases to flourish. Archeological studies conducted by the Uzbek Academy of Sciences provided considerable evidence suggesting that Bukhara was established at least 500 years before Christ and that it had a very rich medieval past."

When relating these stories to me, Sasha was obviously very proud of these scientific accomplishments, especially of the achievements of the Uzbek Academy of Sciences. The young generation of Soviet men was proud of the system's achievements; a phenomenon which was in a stark contrast to the unhappiness and actual hatred towards the Soviet system expressed by the older generation, those brought up prior to the revolution, as exemplified by our landlords in Astrakhan.

"Unfortunately," he continued, "we won't be in Bukhara long, just a couple hours, and long enough to get some wood and water for the locomotive. Then, we will continue on to Samarkand, also a very ancient and great city and will travel through a relatively flat terrain, sandy and deserted, the Kyzyl Kum (Red Sands) Desert, except for the irrigated areas where cotton crop will predominate. The irrigation system," he continued the lecture, an activity that he obviously cherished, "is fed by the waters of Amu Daria, a river we crossed entering the Uzbekistan Republic, and in the eastern regions, near Tashkent, by the waters of Syr Daria."

I looked out the window; we were still in a desert, no vegetation, no settlements. The mountains receded from the view; I couldn't even see any hills. It was flat, sandy land, with a few rocky outcrops. Sasha looked at his wristwatch, a Soviet product the size of an onion! "Well," he said, "soon we shall arrive in Bukhara. We will spend the rest of the day and most of the night there."

I was amazed at his knowledge. He obviously must have been a high positioned man in the military intelligence service and very educated. I promised myself to get a bit more information in order to shed at least some light on this mystery that began to fascinate me. As I was ready to ask Sasha some more questions, my father came to call me. We returned to our compartment and it became clear that discussion there dealt with lunch. We had only two small tins of crabmeat left. No other food except for some green tea. It was very difficult to divide this amount of food among five people. It was already the afternoon and all of us were quite hungry.

I volunteered to see Sasha and find out when we would arrive in Bukhara with the idea that there we might be able to get some food. Leon walked up and down the train to see if there was anyone who may have some food and would be willing to sell some. I approached Sasha again and inquired about our arrival time. He didn't seem to have any difficulty to get this information. "See me in about one half of an hour. I should have this information for you." I thanked him and explained the reason for this request, namely that we had essentially ran out of food and hoped to get some in Bukhara.

Upon return to the compartment I heard Mother saying, "We will have to give the crabmeat to the children," I looked at Stella, she was crying from hunger. Mother brought out two tiny cans of crabmeat, and gave one to each of us.

Father opened Stella's can and was ready to open my can. However, I felt very adult and brave. I turned down the offer of crabmeat and announced that I would wait until we get enough food for all of us to eat.

On this note I returned to Sasha's compartment. He had a large grin on his broad Slavic face. "Firstly," he said, "I found out that we will be in Bukhara by 7 p.m., and there we will stay until midnight. Secondly," he said as he pulled out a large sack and handed it to me, "I got these for you." I opened the sack and to my astonishment, I found it filled with *lepioshki* and chunks of the white hard goat cheese.

Unable to restrain myself I jumped on Sasha's neck and started kissing him. "Now, now stop it" he cried while laughing. "At least this much I can do for the starving people." I couldn't stop thanking him and jumping around him. Finally, he showed me out of the compartment and admonished me, "they are all hungry, go, let them have the food."

I grabbed the sack and ran down the passageway leading to our compartment. The first thing I saw upon entering the compartment was the smiling face of Stella stuffing herself with the canned crabmeat. Leon was standing next to her holding proudly in his hand a cooked leg of lamb. Apparently he was also successful. However, that was all he could get and he paid a little fortune for it.

When I opened my sack full of food, pandemonium broke out. Everyone was asking, "Where, where did you get this, where did you get it?" When I explained that it came as gift from Sasha, they couldn't believe it. Before touching any of the food they all ran out to thank Sasha. Stella and I were left in the compartment and she grabbed a *lepioshki* to have with her crabmeat while I tore into the lamb. Upon return of the rest of the family, we had a real feast. I couldn't remember when was the last time that I could eat so much of such wonderful food. After the feast, most of us dozed off and it was already dark when I awoke.

The train stopped. We were at a station. It was a large railroad station; it had to be Bukhara. Both, Father and Leon were gone. Mother explained that they went out to see if they could get to the city and possibly find some food. I was very disappointed since I hoped to get a chance to visit the city.

Mother would not let me out, not even to visit the railroad station. I did consider the possibility of sneaking out, however by then, the evening became a dark night and I abandoned this idea. Instead, I went to visit Sasha. He wasn't in his compartment. I waited a bit, talked with his wife and left--still tempted to get off the train. As I got closer to our compartment, I could here the excited voices of my father and Leon who must have been detailing their experiences in town. When I walked in, I couldn't miss the pillowcase full of *lepioshki* and little chunks of dry cheese. They also brought back two good sized bags, one filled with dried sunflower and pumpkin seeds, the other filled with raisins. They had walked all over town, found the bazaar and got lucky, being able to barter for these provisions. The paper money, the rubles, were almost useless. Most of the food transactions were exchanges for jewelry or nice articles of clothing. The bazaar (*toltchock* or black market) was a very busy place. One could find almost anything there; however, food items were limited. We were lucky and very happy with their purchases.

I dove instantly into the bags of raisins and pumpkin seeds, and so did Stella. This, however, did not last very long. Mother put a stop to it and established a very strict rationing of these delicacies. She also placed some of the raisins into a bag and told me to take them to Sasha. I was very happy to do so since I liked Sasha and felt that this was a very nice gesture.

Sasha was touched; he came over to our compartment to thank my parents for the gift and tried to indicate that we shouldn't have done it because he had much better means to get food than we did. This interaction, however, was very good for me. It added to my friendship with Sasha and made it stronger. It gave me the chance to spend even more time in his compartment than ever before. Indeed, the same evening I was sitting with Sasha and listening in rapture, with an open mouth, to him telling the story of Samarkand.

As I enjoyed the story of Tamerlane, who according to Sasha was the greatest warrior of the 14th century and the force behind creating the splendors of medieval Samarkand, we were traveling through a relatively flat land. There were vast areas of desert covered by sand and scrub vegetation, but there were also huge cotton fields near the irrigation canals. Sasha explained that these were the *Kolkhoz* (collective farms) or *Sovkhoz* (state farms). The word *Kolkhoz* being an abbreviation of two Russian words: collective and management, while *Sovkhoz* is abbreviation of Soviet and management, the latter being a government organization while the former was theoretically under direct management by the farmers who were members of the "Collective."

All of this was new to me and I appreciated Sasha's explanations. He was proud of the *kolkhoz'.* He felt that these organizations reflected the great social achievements of the Soviet Union. They took advantage of the size of the economy while giving an individual farmer fair profit for his labors. As I listened to the details, I tended to agree with his analysis whole-heartedly. Listening to Sasha I felt that possibly Mr. Rainer, our landlord in Astrakhan, was a bit unfair in his constant anti-Soviet remarks. Maybe the Soviet system and Communism indeed were the ideal government structures for a fair deal in this world. Could I find all this to be acceptable despite having been unfairly incarcerated by this government in a Gulag? As I listened to Sasha I felt a bit confused in my reactions, particularly since the indoctrination to Marxism and Communism that I was exposed to while in school in Lwow was still firmly embedded in my mind. Sasha was a very knowledgeable storyteller, and I never had enough of listening and talking to him.

It was getting late and I had to return to our compartment, where I tried to go to sleep, but thoughts kept on crowding my head. I wondered why, despite the depravity, lack of minimum comfort, hunger and constant uncertainty as what tomorrow would bring, I looked forward to tomorrow and considered the entire experience a great adventure.

I perceived not only this trip, but the entire experience, ever since the first bombs fell on us September 1, 1939, as great adventure despite of having almost lost my life on several occasions, having being maimed and having suffered hunger, cold, lack of freedom and a tremendous sense of uncertainty of what tomorrow would bring. I obviously perceived the happenings differently than adults around me and actually felt quite happy most of the time. I felt somewhat immune, much more optimistic, possibly simply adventurous and not willing or possibly knowing how to look into the face of reality.

One of the reasons I couldn't sleep was the thought of Samarkand. I promised myself that no matter what I would try to get to the city. Sasha's words rang in my ears: "It is one of the oldest cities in the world, the oldest in Central Asia." I never had seen an oriental city and my adventurous soul yearned to see mosques, minarets, the medieval fortifications, the azure tiles covering the cupolas of the mosques and the colorful bazaars Sasha described. As I was falling asleep, I vaguely recognized that we stopped moving.

When I woke up the sun was up on the horizon and we were standing still. Father said: "We have been standing on this siding the entire night. Trains were passing us but we did not move."

The siding was in the middle of nowhere. There was an irrigation canal running parallel to the siding and in the distance, I could see few houses. People disembarked and were walking by the canal. It was quite warm, although not as warm as in Ashkabad, where the temperatures were reaching the 90s. Here, it must have been in the upper 70s or low 80s.

I thought that it would be fun to go swimming in the canal but I knew that Mother would not let me do so. However, I thought it would be great to at least undress partly and to wash up properly. Along the shores of the canal, there were bushes and some green vegetation. I snuck behind the bushes, took my clothing off and jumped in the water. I had no soap; all I could do was just wash as good as possible and enjoy the freshness and coolness of the water.

It felt great and I felt like moving away from the shore for a swim when the train, with no warning, started moving. I quickly got to the shore and into my pants, took the rest of my clothing and ran after the train. Luckily, the train started very slow and I had no difficulty catching up. After getting back to our compartment, I encountered the wrath of my mother. She was extremely angry. She asked, "Do you have any idea what could have happened if you were left behind in this desert? You could have died of thirst and starvation, you could have been picked up by someone but then the train would have been gone and how would you find us?" I felt horrible. How could I create this much anxiety with my thoughtless behavior? I apologized profusely and promised not to do such foolish things again.

As I was apologizing Sasha showed up. He was laughing. "I saw you running after the train holding up your pants. "That was quite a sight," he said. "I hope it taught you a lesson." Turning to Mother he continued, "Actually you didn't need to get all upset. About one half kilometer down the canal and the railroad track, there is a village he would have walked there and since train will stop in the village for couple hours he would have caught up with us." I was not this confident. Sasha probably was trying to relieve Mother's anxiety--for which I was grateful. He continued, "We are traveling now through the great Kyzyl Kum Desert. It extends from the river Amu Daria on the eastern border between Turkistan and Uzbekistan, a river that used to flow all the way from the Ala Tau mountain chain to the Aral Sea, to the river Syr Daria that flows in a parallel fashion also from the Ala Tau Mountains towards the Aral Sea in Kazakhstan. The rivers, however, are diverted throughout their paths into numerous irrigation canals so that now essentially no water reaches the Aral Sea. We will continue near canals in our journey to Samarkand where we should arrive by tomorrow morning."

Leon has hidden a bottle of vodka for emergencies, and this occasion, according to him, deserved an emergency treatment. He offered a drink of vodka to Sasha who was very happy to accept and they spent time together until late in the evening talking. I went to sleep.

We arrived to Samarkand in late morning and were told that the train would leave on its way to Tashkent some time at night or the next morning. No one knew for sure when the train would depart. I couldn't wait to get off and go into the city. It was obviously a large city.

The railroad station was apparently rebuilt in a modern way but was falling apart. It was filthy, the paint was peeling off the buildings, and people were sitting on the dirty floors, waiting. There was a general disorder even worse than in the other stations.

Last night was cold, about 40°F, however the temperature was rising rapidly since daybreak; yesterday, by noon, the temperature reached mid seventies. I decided not o wear a jacked. A short sleeve shirt should do.

While waiting for Father and Leon, I went looking for Sasha. He had already gone somewhere. I talked for a little while with his wife, but she had no idea where Sasha could be. While talking to her I noticed both Father and Leon walking down the station walk. Obviously, they decided not to take me with them. I ran out and despite their discouragement, I joined them. I wasn't about to miss this expedition.

As we walked out of the station, I was stricken by the incongruity in the appearance of the houses. Some were contemporary buildings, primarily offices. They were scratched up and the plaster was peeling off. Then some mud and plywood hovels stood next to ancient buildings, some were maintained reasonably well while others were falling apart. Many must have been mosques, converted to variety of uses, museums, schools, storehouses, etc. I was fascinated looking at these buildings. Some looked very exotic and very beautiful with blue tile covered cupolas.

Uncle Leon, however, was hurrying us. He wanted to get to the bazaar and find some food to buy. He was not interested in the buildings or the history. He kept on asking for directions, since we appeared to walk in circles.

As I looked across a tree-lined boulevard, I noticed Sasha walking in a fancy uniform and carrying two sacks full of goods. I ran over to him all excited, Leon and Father joined us shortly. He said laughing, "You are probably looking for the *toltchock*, let me show you the way, otherwise you will probably get lost." We were very happy to accept this offer because we were already lost. After about fifteen minutes of a brisk walk, we reached an edge of a huge plaza.

The din was unbelievable. There were literally thousands of people, and donkeys, horses and camels, all intermingled. The men around us were talking, screaming and obviously dealing very actively with each other. There were sections devoted to old copper products, candlesticks, utensils and ornaments. There were areas devoted to oriental silks, cotton products and oriental types of shoes. There was a section devoted exclusively to foods. Here one could get corn, dried sunflower and pumpkin seeds, jam and a local alcoholic drink, the *kumys*.

There were stands full of china, tea drinking cups with no handles (typical Russian style, or is it Asian style?), the *pialky*. We were amazed by the abundance of the various products. There were also camels, donkeys and horses for sale. There were bicycles, saddles, shoes, cigarettes and tea, literally anything one would wish.

"This is the largest bazaar in this part of the country," explained Sasha. We were absolutely amazed; we had not seen this amount of goods since the war began. The shock came when we looked at the prices. A loaf of bread that sold in a government store for 1 ruble was 500 rubles. A 500-gram slice of lamb was 1000 rubles; the official price was 3 rubles. We obviously couldn't afford to buy anything, however, we could barter. Soon Leon got two loafs of bread and some of the hard cheese. After looking at the various goods, we returned to the train station. I couldn't wait to get together with Sasha and ask him a lot of questions.

By the time we returned to the train, it was already dark. I had a bite of the *lepioshki* and some cheese. Mother and Stella talked to Sasha's wife who found water and *kipiatok* so that tea could be made.

I walked over to Sasha's compartment full of questions. He was also finishing his meal. With his usual grin on the face, he made a biting comment: "Well, so you did get back from town. Didn't you know that the train could have departed leaving you behind? The schedules, you know, are very, very flexible!" "But we were told that the train will not leave 'till late tonight or tomorrow morning," I said. As I was talking I could feel the train beginning to move, and in a few minutes we were moving quite well when suddenly the train slowed down, then stopped and reversed directions. We looked out the window and although it was dark we could make out the surroundings. We were being shuttled to a siding, where the train stopped. We were several kilometers from the railroad station.

Sasha continued grinning, "You see," he said, "You almost missed the train. You would not have found us easily." I was too impatient to start asking him questions and did not wish to pay much attention to his attempts to chastise me. I wanted an explanation for the *toltchock*, an explanation for the prices, an explanation for the total neglect of the city and of its historical sites, for the dirt and the wanton destructive tendencies of the people in respect to the buildings. The war was only a few months old! The *toltchock* must have been there before the war started and the neglect in the city was also there for years. How could this happen under Soviet government? I still felt that Communism was a fair and just political system that did everything justly and well.

Sasha was a bit taken aback by my somewhat aggressive questioning. He looked at me with a new expression in his eyes. "I didn't think," he said, "that you would be this serious about the political issues and the ideological aspects of our political system. Nor did I think that you would be this concerned about our cities while you are being physically deprived of basic needs after being released this recently from a Gulag."

I interrupted, "One has nothing to do with the other, and one should deal with each issue separately. The reason for us having been incarcerated in a Gulag has nothing to do with the presence of *toltchock* or with the horrible neglect of the city. Possibly I am out of order, but the picture of Samarkand, the beautiful city you described to me, was shocking; despite the empty stomach and other personal problems."

As I looked at Sasha, it was obvious to me that he was trying to make a decision which way to talk to me. He was clearly thorn in his thoughts. Finally, having decided, his face has changed. Before, it was always friendly with a hint of humor and some mischief. One never knew when he was serious, but now his face expressed concern, care and worry.

Finally he responded, "I am sure that by now you have realized that I learned to like you. I care for you and your family. I know a lot of things that you may not like to know, things that I am not at liberty to talk about. You should be aware that I am an officer in NKVD. The reason why I frequently have disappeared when the train would stop at a station was to visit the local NKVD offices and get interim directions and news."

"For example today I learned that our government has been evacuating ever since early October from Moscow to Kuibyshev; that German troops have captured Kiev and that the Rumanians captured Odessa. On the good side of the equation, the Americans offered to ship us the much-needed military equipment and the British have sent us a lot of tanks. I am pleased to be able to give you this information since none of it is classified and I am certain that you and your parents are eager to have it."

I was overwhelmed with the news and very pleased that Sasha had placed all this confidence in us. "If you will forgive me, I'd like to get back to our compartment and share this information with my family." With this I got up and ran back to our compartment. "You won't believe it," I cried, opening the door; and all the news Sasha gave me spilled out. Both my parents and Leon kept on interrupting, asking questions and making comments. Of particular interest to my father was the news concerning U.S. military help to USSR. "This," he said "is of particular interest to us since a good relationship between these two countries will be of major benefit to us personally."

My family continued its heated discussion late into the night. The remarkable advance of German forces was analyzed from every point of view and our narrow escape from Astrakhan was hailed as major luck. Since the port of Astrakhan was probably frozen by now, there would have been no chance for us to escape if the German Army would have advanced to Astrakhan.

The following day we arrived in Tashkent, according to Sasha, one of the oldest and probably largest cities in Central Asia. It was also the capital of Uzbekistan. Approaching Tashkent we were passing some irrigation canals and large cotton fields apparently belonging to huge *kolkhozes*. To the right of the train we could see the tall distant mountains. Sasha said that these were already the Tian Shan Mountains, part of the Himalayans. By the time the train pulled into the station it was getting dark. We were admonished not to get off to visit the city because the train was to leave at any time. Actually the train didn't really leave until early morning. Sasha started to pack up. He said that they will be leaving the train in Dzambul, a city almost half way to Alma Ata.

The temperatures plunged; it was getting cold on the train. The outside temperatures were in the 60ies. I was sad. In Sasha I found a friend, although age wise we were not compatible, emotionally and intellectually we resonated; it always felt good to be with him, to talk to him, to discuss ideas with him, to share our experiences with him. Actually it was a shock for me to learn that he was a NKVD officer. In retrospect I realized that many things I told him innocently, not realizing who he was, could have created problems for our entire family.

He understood our situation and I wondered, although he never expressed ideas supportive of my assumptions, whether he was positive towards our experiences and possibly supportive of some of my ideas. While the ideas were not very flattering towards the Soviet system, at that time I still was, at least in theory, convinced of the historical inevitability and fairness of the social evolution leading to a communist social system.

The enormity of this realization did not dawn on me at that time. A NKVD officer fundamentally agreeing on the rotten core of the Soviet system was not an idea that was easily acceptable.

When the train stopped at Dzambul's small and dilapidated station, Sasha and his family departed quickly and this was the last time I ever saw him in my life. I felt very sad when the train departed Dzambul.

The subsequent journey on the way to Alma Ata was through the Kazakhstan territories. It was a very slow trip with the train was stopping frequently. It was growing colder and each time the train stopped we ran to the locomotive to get some *kipiatok* to make hot tea.

The food was coming to an end. The cans of crabmeat we got in Krasnovodsk were long gone. We were subsisting on the remaining few *lepioshki,* that by then were covered with mold, and some of the hard goat cheese balls.

Finally we arrived to Alma Ata. This was a fairly large railroad station but quite primitive and much neglected. We disembarked, stocked up our belonging on the station's platform, by a fence, and went looking for some officials to help us with the next step. Both of my parents went while Leon stayed with us in case of some unforeseen difficulties.

It was getting dark and cold. Stella was sitting on top of our belongings all bundled up. We were hungry. I went inside the railroad station looking for some food. There was nothing available. There were people crowded on the floor with their bundles, obviously waiting for trains.

I tried to get some information, but my Russian language was not adequate to converse freely. Anyway, it appeared that the people didn't know much about the local situation or did not wish to get involved.

I walked out and returned to the spot by the fence where our belongings were piled up. The evening was clear and was turning into a very cold night. Leon was pacing in front of our bundles and valises trying to keep warm.

Walking out on the street to the other side of the fence, down the street in a distance, I could make out both of my parents. They were rushing to get back to us. Father, obviously quite agitated, said, "Finally we got to the militia, they informed us that no one is permitted to stay in Alma Ata, the city is overcrowded. However, in Kargaly, a tiny factory town in the mountains, some eighty miles south of Alma Ata, they need workers and we could be resettled there," he related this in one breath. "I immediately agreed." We can't stay here and the sooner we find a place to move in, the better it will be for us. We need shelter and food. The Commandant of the militia agreed to get us a truck, and first thing in the morning to take us to Kargaly. There, the local militia will find a place for us to stay and will arrange for work papers for the family," he said.

Mother began unpacking some bundles to reach our blankets. Our belongings were rearranged so that we could sleep on top of them to prevent stealing and again a watch schedule was worked out.

The immediate problem was food. It was late, there were no stores, and we had no food ration cards. We didn't even know the location of the *toltchock*. This was probably of no consequence since, most likely, it was too late in the day for the *toltchock*. We had no choice but to go to sleep with empty stomachs.

I created for myself a nest on top of the bundles and valises near the fence and ultimately fell asleep. Sometime in the middle of the night I was awakened by "something.." As I sat up, I noticed someone running on the other side of the fence with one of our pieces of luggage. I jumped over the fence and started after the thief.

Mother woke up, saw what happened and called out sharply to me, "Let him go, you stay here, it doesn't pay to chase him, you may get hurt."

The thief took an old hat box that I used to keep dirty laundry and the box really only had a few old rags. I returned back to the camp, and by then everyone was awake. Apparently, Mother was on the watch but did not notice the thief who removed some of the fence pilings and then pulled out the hatbox from among the various valises probably hoping that it contained money or other valuables. Well, after this episode no one could fall asleep. We were talking and wondering and feeling scared. We couldn't wait for dawn to brake. Ultimately a gray day set in. We kept on waiting for the militia to show up with a truck.

CHAPTER 11. Kargaly

At about 10 a.m., what appeared to be a small military truck pulled up to the station. A militiaman came over and indicated that we should load our belongings on the truck and get on top. We traveled 'till late afternoon over a severely rutted highway. The road turned towards the mountains towering very close to us on our left side, their white-capped peaks reaching to the skies.

Soon we came abreast a mountain stream flowing from a canyon opening at the mountain's foothills. From the canyon, on both shores of the creek, a settlement was spilling towards the flat lands. One could see a few industrial, multistoried buildings, and a group of smaller, obviously residential structures. As we approached the settlement, large cultivated fields appeared on both sides of the road. Some were probably state farm organizations, while others were most likely *kolkhoz* (cooperative farms). As we got closer to the settlement, individual farmhouses started popping up on the sides of the highway. The truck stopped about one mile before reaching the settlement in front of a small farmhouse. We were told to disembark.

The house was made of mud bricks and covered with a thatched roof. The side and backyard were fenced with a low, peculiar looking wall made of large brick-like structures. When we arrived the family came out of the house looking at us with great curiosity. There were two adults, of my parent's age, and a girl of my age. We were invited to enter the house. It was a clean, single room structure, with golden-yellow scrubbed wood floors and an enormous *pietchka.* I saw a *pietchka* like this one in the houses of rather "wealthy" peasant in the village near our Gulag in the Marian Republic. The *pietchka* was a huge structure dividing the house into two areas. One faced the door to the outside. The part of *pietchka* extending into this area housed a range covered by a black iron plate with three holes for pots or pans and an opening into the hearth that was used for baking and keeping food warm for hours. The other side of the *pietchka* faced the inner part of the room. Here the *pietchka* was relatively low with enough room on top of it for up to six people to sleep in reasonable (although somewhat crowded) comfort. This part of the *pietchka* had bedding on it; the family obviously has been sleeping there. In the wintertime, one could rely on the warmth maintained by the *pietchka* throughout the day and night. The winters here were very severe.

Some of our belongings that could withstand cold we stored in the loft of a small barn in the backyard. The barn housed two cows and a horse. The loft was used in the winter for the storage of hay; we found space there to store our empty valises and bundles.

Once we settled in and became acquainted with our landlords, the entire family of our hosts trotted with us to the tiny factory town, almost a mile down the road. There, we registered with the militia. Adults were told to see a personnel officer in the factory and, since we were foreigners, to also visit the NKVD office to obtain permits for living in Kargaly. The factory was to provide us with food ration cards. I was told to visit the school and find out what could be done with my further schooling.

It was late afternoon and we were starved. No one has eaten since the previous day. In the village, there was no place where one could buy a meal. Mother suggested that we go to the plant and see if we could register for work and possibly get the ration cards. The plant office was only a couple hundred yards away from the NKVD building. We were very fortunate to get there before the office closed for the day.

The plant must have needed workers, because once they saw our registration papers from the militia and the work permits from the NKVD, they gave jobs for the entire family. We also got food ration coupons, which entitled us to two hundred grams of black bread per day, a pound of meat per week and a pint of oil per month.

Unfortunately, the food store had already closed for the day. We were told that usually everything is sold by noon and that the store closes early; to get bread everyone has to show up early in the morning. Products other than bread also appeared in the store but only sporadically. One had to be there at an appropriate time to get them except, no one knew when was the appropriate time. That is unless one knew the store manager...

It was getting dark and very cold. Snow started falling and we hurried home. The road back was quite simple; it was the only road leading out of town. Soon we recognized the house and entered it with great relief. We had been walking in cold and in darkness and inside was pleasantly warm. A large kerosene lamp was hanging on the wall spreading a circle of yellow light. The Russian family was just finishing their meal consisting of a bowl of hot, thin corn meal with cooked pumpkin in it.

We were tired, cold and hungry. Stella immediately climbed on the *pietchka* and covered herself with some bedding that was thrown around there. Father started talking to the farmer and his wife. His knowledge of the Russian language was extremely limited and they were barely able to converse. The obvious pressing issue was food. Could they spare any? The farmer, Boris Ivanovitch, quickly understood our predicament, particularly when we showed him our food ration cards and tried to explain that we would get some food tomorrow. His wife, Natasha Michailovna, grinned and pulled out a huge black iron pot of a peculiar shape. It was round, with a narrow lower part flaring into a much larger top section. She put some water in it, placed it into one of the holes in the black iron plate on the stove, reached into a cupboard, where she had some corn meal stored, and started cooking it. The stove was still hot; there were many red, hot coals in it so that the meal was ready in no time.

Boris, with still a broad grin, invited us to sit down at the table. Once the corn meal was served, he brought a large, somewhat spherical yellowish thing that looked like a dirty piece of crystal and chopped off a small section of it with a huge knife. It was the typical Russian sugar ("head of sugar").

Natasha was very solicitous, making sure that we had enough to eat. While we ate, Boris started to boil water in the *samovar.* It was quite a beautiful contraption; it looked like a brass pot with ornate handles, with a foot, on which it stood, and an ornate tap. It was round, with a pipe running vertically through its center. One placed wood chips into this pipe and ignited them. The heat produced by the burning chips heated the water and brought it to boil. The burning coals kept the water hot.

When there was a need for making the tea, the *samovar* was placed outdoors while the wood chips were burning. Once the wood burned down to red coals, it was brought back inside of the house and placed in the center of the table. Natasha placed the tea leaves in a small brewing pot and added hot water to it. The tea was allowed to brew and form an extract that was then used to make tea by mixing it in a teacup with the hot water from the *samovar*. The *samovar* would keep the water hot for long periods of time because of the hot coals in the central pipe.

Since I was the one with the best knowledge of the Russian language, I was appointed to express our gratitude to the Russian family for their hospitality. That also gave me the chance to talk to their daughter whose name turned out to be Marusia. All the members of our family became mellow after having warmed up, having our hunger satisfied and having several cups of tea with sugar. Attempts for further conversation with our hosts were met with limited success. Our knowledge of the Russian language was still very poor. I had a somewhat better luck conversing with Marusia. We were both thirteen. Things, even language, were easier for us. Adults, however, simply could not converse with sufficient ease to allow for exchange of the simplest of ideas.

****

The winter days and nights were turning colder and colder. It was snowing almost every day. There were eight of us, five in our family and three in our host's family, all in the one room. No matter how cramped, we were getting along very well. The adults went to work six days a week from 8 a.m. to 6 p.m. It took them one hour to walk to the factory and when snow was deep, even longer. Thus, they left in the morning when it was still pitch black and returned in the evening when it was already dark.

There was a cafeteria at the plant where they got three meals a day. Breakfast consisted of tea and bread, the bread they had to buy on their ration cards. Lunch consisted of cooked cereal, sometimes corn meal, other times black porridge. The supper usually consisted of soup, mostly *rosolnik,* hot water with pieces of pickle floating in it. The food was very bad.

Soon we learned that there was a black market where one could purchase potatoes, corn, even meat and oil. Sometimes the farmers also sold milk and butter. The black market prices, however, were extremely high and we had already bartered most of our possessions that would be worth anything on the black market.

Stella and I had to subsist on the bread we got from the food ration coupons (200 gm/day each), the occasional few grams of meat, if one could catch the delivery in the store, and whatever my parents and uncle could bring from the factory cafeteria. We were always hungry.

Marusia would leave with the adults on her way to school. The school was in the village, thus all of them walked together. Stella and I would stay home.

My education, before being taken to the Gulag, terminated in Lwow with the 6th grade. Age wise I should have been in the 8th grade. The school's superintendent told me that I would have to wait until next year to matriculate because my Russian language was inadequate to start in the middle of the school year. By next September my language abilities should have improve sufficiently to continue with my education. However, at that point I would be placed into the 7th grade. Thus, two years behind. After a long discussion with the principal and some of the teachers, I was told that they would give me books to cover the material normally studied in 7th grade and if I pass special exams, they would consider placing me into 8th grade. I was elated.

One of the teachers, Nina Vasilevna, offered to help me in my studies. I immediately took her up on this offer. The negotiations and the selection of textbooks took a couple of weeks. However, I felt very good about it and couldn't wait to start the studies. I also learned, from talking to Nina Vasilevna, about the latest on the war. The battle for Moscow had been fierce. The Germans penetrated the western and southern outskirts of Moscow by early December. But the winter that year was particularly severe and the Germans were unable to neither supply the front lines nor maintain the morale of the troops at the front. The Russian Army, on the other hand, was making a physical and emotional stand at Moscow. With a super human effort, the army launched a counter offensive and by the middle of December the Germans abandoned the attack on Moscow and started retreating in disarray. However, the news from the southern front was unclear. The Germans were, in January of 1942, continuing their offensive.

Nina was always willing to talk to me not only about my schoolwork but also about the war and our prior experiences in Soviet Russia. She was very interested about my life in Poland before the war.

The winter was taking a cruel hold, bringing in a very severe weather. Fortunately, we had with us *Fufayki*, quilted jackets and pants, and *valenky*, felt boots. These were issued to us in the Gulag, and with mother's connections, all of us were able to keep warm having acquired reasonable winter garments. This type of clothing was absolutely essential to survive the bitter cold. Kargaly was located at the foothills of the Ala Tau chain of the Tien Shan Mountains in the northeastern part of the Himalayas. The factory town was located on a mountain stream flowing between two foothill ridges of the Ala Tau Mountains. While this tiny town or village was constructed on relatively flat grounds, adjacent to the buildings facing the mountains, the orchards around it climbed into the hills.

During winter, the ground was covered with snow and the swift mountain stream was partly frozen. It indeed was very cold. I spent most of my time immersed in my studies and when Marusia would return from school I would try to talk to her as much as possible to learn Russian. We became good friends and spent a great deal of time together. She told me about the school, the village, the factory and the *kyziak*. The latter were the mysterious bricks forming part of the border of the backyard. I learned quickly that these bricks were actually fuel for the oven. They burned after being ignited with a bundle of *Saksaul*, twisted, hard branches of shrubs growing in the desert outside the village. *Kyziak* burned with a very hot flame and most importantly formed long burning coal fires.

Soon I learned the mysteries of *kyziak*. It was a mixture of cow manure and straw. Not only was the manure, generated by one's own cow, carefully collected and stored, but in the morning when the cows were taken out to the pasture, the village kids would run after them with pails and collect the fresh produced manure. It was a social gathering and social activity for the kids; however, at times serious fights would erupt when more than one individual claimed ownership of the same pile.

The winter progressed brutally. The ice and snow slowed down transportation that was now possible only via horse driven sleighs. We walked to the town in deep snow; it made the walk difficult and long. I still visited school daily and read all I could find, in preparation for exams in the spring. I was not permitted to take books home; thus, the only study I could do was in the school building. However, Marusia had her books at home and this was very helpful.

As the winter roared on, so did the war. The information we received from the war theatre was very spotty, limited and sporadic. Occasionally a copy of a newspaper printed in Alma Ata would become available. Some people had a government radio and received the war news this way. The German siege of Leningrad continued. The defenders were determined and with the onset of severe winter weather, the German push had eased off. In the late fall and early winter, the Germans conquered Kharkov, Rostov and Kursk; the Germans pressed on a front extending from Leningrad all the way to the Black Sea; and Oddesa was conquered by the Rumanian troops. In the heart of the country, the German army had reached the outskirts of Moscow. The Russian front seemed to be on the verge of collapse. However, news was scarce and it was difficult to learn about the true situation.

Soon everyone was working full time in the fabric factory. The factory was producing cloth for military uniforms and was extremely busy. This called for overtime and increased the amount of food we were getting. In February we were given personal housing assignments. It was one small room with an oven, *pietchka,* in a two story wooden building, with easy walking distance from the factory and a mile from the school. Behind the building, there was an empty field that was divided into tiny lots distributed among the building tenants for their vegetable gardens.

After we moved in, Leon purchased a table and two wooden benches; this was all of our furniture. Leon, Father and I slept on the floor, which was lined with some of the bedding packed in sacks and our other soft belongings. Mother and Stella slept on the table, which for the night was moved against the oven so that they were able to sleep partly on the table and partly on the oven.

There was a major innovation in the room, a radio speaker. It was connected to a central radio station that broadcasted music and news into our speaker. Although we had no control over the input, the music was usually very nice, half and half classical and Russian folk music. The news, while only that which the government sanctioned and wished us to hear, was much better than what we had before, essentially nothing or only gossip.

Shortly after we moved in it became clear that the room, particularly the benches and table, were infested with bed bugs. Those of us who slept on the floor had fewer problems than Mother and Stella, who slept on the table. The table was full of bed bugs. We had some kerosene and used it to kill the bugs in the table. The rest of the room, however, had to wait as far as the kerosene treatment was concerned. While the treatment of the table with kerosene eased the problem temporarily, soon the bugs were climbing up the table legs from the floor creating further misery for Mother and Stella. At this point, I got the idea to place the table's legs into little saucers filled with water-- the bugs couldn't swim. This was effective, but only for a while. The bugs started parachuting from the ceiling.

In March, the winter was still with us but the temperatures started moderating. One day Leon came in with the news that he had talked to the political officer in the factory and discussed the possibility of going to Alma Ata to find out about joining the Polish Army organized by General Anders. After all we were released from the Gulag with the idea of joining the army.

After considerable deliberation, the officer agreed to give Leon a permit to go to Alma Ata for this purpose. He went on one of the factory delivery trucks and was gone almost for a week. Upon return, we had a major family gathering to discuss what he had learned.

Well, first, there was this tremendous news! Leon found Uncle Josef, (*Juzek),* in Alma Ata! The NKVD took him from Lwow to a special camp. It was actually a prisoner of war camp near Leningrad. He was there until the Germans attacked Leningrad. At that point, the camp was evacuated to an area near Archangels in the Arctic Circle. The inmates had to walk all the way to Archangels. Of the close to one thousand inmates, less than one hundred survived this exercise. Uncle Josef was over six feet tall, very strong and phlegmatic. I think that these characteristics were paramount in helping him survive. He was released from the camp under the same conditions that we had, to enlist in the Polish Anders Army. That is how he ultimately came to Alma Ata and there, at the Anders Army office, by chance met Leon.

Now the question was how to arrange for him to transfer to Kargaly. The reaction to this news was incredible. Mother was crying, Father was already planning the steps to get him to Kargaly, but Leon, also happy, was trying to tell us about the rest of the news.

The old issues of the past came up in stark outlines; the ancient issue of anti-Semitism has raised its ugly head again... The recruiting officer told them, in no uncertain terms, that Jews are not welcome in the Polish Army. When Josef pointed out that he was an officer in the prewar Polish Army, was in a POW camp for Polish officers in the Leningrad area and was one of the few survivors of the march, he was met with a derisive laughter.

Snooping around, the uncles got some answers for this attitude, expressed as an addition to the "normal" anti-Semitism that was to be expected. Apparently General Anders had been negotiating with the Soviet Government to evacuate the army, which was called the 2nd Corps at that time, to Persia and from there to Palestine. Palestine, at that time, was under British Mandate.

In Palestine, the Corps would be further trained, before being transported to a battle area, in a British controlled territory. At this point in time there were numerous Poles living in the Soviet Union. They lived there since before the outbreak of the German-Soviet war. Many were deported to Soviet Union after the Soviets occupied eastern Poland. However, even a large number probably included those, who emigrated from eastern Poland to Soviet Union searching for better life.

Now, on second thought, after experiencing fully the Soviet system, they decided that it would be better for them to leave Soviet Union with the Polish Army. Thus, the numbers that wanted to join the army or claim to be civilian dependants of army members became unwieldy. The Soviets were objecting to these large numbers, and obviously the easiest way to decrease these numbers was to eliminate the Jews from the army.

There was very little we could do at that time. However, we later learned that a number of Jews was able to become part of the army and ultimately leave Soviet Union. Under these circumstances, we concentrated on making every effort to get Josef to join us in Kargaly. By this time it became known among the plant management that Mother was a dentist and soon she started working in a little clinic associated with the plant. There she acquired patients among the plant management and an occasional gold crown in the mouth of one of the *natchalnicks* (managers) was an important diplomatic maneuver on her part.

These connections became particularly important when we tried to get Josef to move to Kargaly. It took only couple weeks with Mother's connections to get him moved. He was declared an "essential employee" and the move was assured. We celebrated Josef's arrival with a special dinner. Unfortunately, there was no room for permanent lodging in our quarters and he had to stay in the workers dormitory, even though he was at the house almost every evening.

By April the snow has mostly melted, and we were given a small plot of land next to the house to start a vegetable garden. The plot was about twice the size of our room. I made friends with a neighbor's son, Vasil. He was my age and very much into arts, primarily pencil drawing. This also became my obsession; the problem, however, was getting paper, a rare commodity. We helped each other and spent great deal of time together. He had a spade that I promptly borrowed and started digging up the parcel of land we were assigned to in the back of the house to prepare it for planting. At the same time, we were also assigned a parcel of land outside the village for more serious gardening. This parcel was almost one quarter of an acre. It was located in a rolling countryside; our lot was on a fairly steep slope, a characteristic I noted but had no idea what it meant, particularly what troubles it would create because of this location.

Since I did not attend school, gardening was my primary duty. I became a farmer. Uncle Leon accepted the responsibility for procuring some spades and rakes, a mean task since none were available. However, he learned that the farmers, for proper remuneration, could obtain these implements in the *kolkhoz* they worked in.

This was to be my first serious and practical lesson in the economics of the Soviet system. My personal reaction to all this was confusing. The initial contact with Soviets in Lwow was fairly positive. After all, they saved us from the Germans; they provided activities of direct interest to a pre-teenager. The school was full of communist propaganda, including introductions to the writings and philosophy of Marks, Engels and Lenin.

Lenin was of a great importance in shaping my beliefs; the discovery of inevitability of political evolution was very appealing to a naïve, young mind. The evolution to a communist-like system seemed fair and inevitable. However, subsequent experiences, particularly the detention on a Gulag, placed a sinister cast on this philosophy when practicalities turned out to be so ugly. Subsequent experiences, the escape from Astrakhan, the long trip through Central Asia spiked by extensive discussions with Vladia, a politically savvy military man, tipped my sympathies towards the system again. The war excused many of the glaring problems in the country, problems that I would have otherwise placed squarely on the shoulders of the system.

For me, the experience with procurement of garden tools, however, had placed a shadow on the system. This was petty theft. As such, it should not have serious reverberations on one's deep political beliefs. However, the constant occurrence of the petty theft appeared to be a fundamental characteristic of the system that was almost openly accepted by the society. I didn't realize that this experience would have such a profound effect on my belief in this system.

Coming back to gardening, I must say that Leon was exceedingly successful in procuring the gardening tools. He obtained three spades, two rakes and a pick. In the small garden near the house, I planted beets and potatoes. The beats I grew from seeds obtained by Leon from the *kolkhoz* farmers. I learned that planting a small portion of a potato, one that contains the "eye" would induce the growth of an entire potato plant. The remaining portions of the potatoes could then be eaten. This certainly had helped immensely since we were extremely strapped for money or anything to barter for potatoes. Once I planted the little garden, the time was ripe to start with the large piece of land.

The entire family went out to dig it up in preparation for planting. We were advised by the neighbors to place large rocks on the corners of the plot in order to prevent any problems later. This took the entire Sunday since the rocks were large and had to be carried from a great distance, near the foothills of the mountains. Since we had no wheelbarrow, the rocks were carried individually on our backs in burlap sacks. By the time this was accomplished, the skies turned dark red and it was evening and time to go back home.

I returned the following day to start digging up the soil. However, again a neighbor stopped me and explained that first I had to dig an extension of an irrigation ditch to my parcel of land. This was a major undertaking that took me the whole week. The following Sunday again the entire family showed up to help me dig up the parcel in preparation for planting. This time the task was accomplished since five of us were available to get the work done. Once the soil was prepared, we had to decide what to plant and how much of each crop. Here again we listened to the advice of our neighbors.

First, we were educated that the land had to be irrigated, since there would be no rainfall during the summer. This is why the irrigation ditch was so essential. Furthermore, we were advised that our parcel was probably the worst one since it was located primarily on a steep slope and this would make the irrigation procedure difficult. The water would be running off and would erode the field. To partly counteract this problem, they showed us how to sculpt the parcel to redistribute the water. They also told us that we would have to irrigate once a week and sometime twice.

Regarding what to plant their advice was very surprising. They suggested that the majority of the crop should be sunflowers. The oil of the sunflower seeds, they said, would provide the most important nutrient to supplement our diet during the next winter. Also, the sunflowers could be planted on the worst part of the parcel and they would still do well.

The second largest crop should be corn. It would provide the most compact nutrient. The third should be potatoes, an essential in Russian diet. The remaining land should be used to grow watermelons and cantaloupes. I labored mightily, from sunrise to sundown, to get everything planted. Stella kept me company and helped as much as she could at the age of seven.

At this time of the year, we were surviving essentially on small portions of corn meal that I cooked in the evenings. Both Stella and I were ravenously hungry all day long. The rest of the family who worked all day got some food at the factory cafeteria, but the amount was further decreased in the spring and they were not able to bring home much.

The week after planting the crops, I began to feel very weak and ultimately started fainting. Mother took me to the hospital where I was admitted with the diagnosis of malnutrition. I was hospitalized for three weeks and with some extra food, I was brought back to reasonable health.

Upon return from the hospital, I noted that the crops in our little garden started to develop leaves. Soon the leaves of the beets would be large enough to cut off and add to the corn meal; apparently, this was very nutritious since all of us, including me, started feeling much better.

At the same time, my friend Vasil took me to the mountains. It was late spring and the slopes were covered with wild rhubarb. The rhubarb was tart but also sweet. This was a welcomed addition to our diet. I would bring every day a sack full of rhubarb and we ate it with our meals, raw, like a fruit.

It was getting warm; May had arrived. On May 1, we had a big celebration, the Workers Day. Everyone was off work, there was a parade and the cafeteria at the plant was open all day; food could be gotten without food stamps. Everyone spent most of the day eating!

The time was coming closer to take the placement examination in the school. Everyone in the Soviet Union was required to attend ten years of school, the *Dzesietilatka.* After ten years, one received a diploma and could enter a University, which was optional. After seven years of schooling, one could matriculate in a trade school where one learned a trade (e.g. an electrician, plumber, metal worker, etc.)

Theoretically I should have been entering the 8th grade in September of 1942. However, I completed only six grades in Poland, and I was behind in the knowledge of the Russian language and Russian studies. Vasil was very helpful. So were the teachers in the school, providing me with books and helping me with the material. I decided to take an exam to place out of the 7th grade and start with the 8th grade. Thus, in September I entered the 8th grade. Well, I am getting ahead of myself now.

In May, while studying for the exams, I continued to take care of the crops. Since I was neither in the school nor working, I could manage the time better than those who had to work. I learned that irrigation was the most difficult of all the chores. Everyone wanted to water their parcels on Sundays, the only day off work. This, however, would drain too much water from the main supply ditch (*aryk*) leaving those down the line with dry feeder lines. Since our plot was very far from the main ditch, on weekends there was almost no water left in the ditch leading to our parcel.

On weekdays, the level of water in the main ditch was very low because it was diverted by the *kolkhozes* for irrigation of their fields. Thus, on weekdays, irrigation was essentially impossible. However, evenings, and particularly the nights provided a great opportunity. The *kolkhozes* didn't use any water in the evening or at night. I liked to come to the fields at about 10 o'clock at night after the other people finished their evening watering and usually by 3-4 o'clock in the morning, I had the entire parcel irrigated.

It was good to see the crops growing, particularly since the food was getting scarcer by the day. In June, the potato plants where already producing small potatoes. I got the idea to dig around the roots with my hands and pull out one or two small potatoes from under some of the plants. This apparently did not damage the plants and I learned later that the potato production from these plants was not diminished. Apparently as I removed some of the potatoes, the plant compensated by producing additional bulbs. This procedure turned out to be very important; it provided us with some supplement to our very meager diet.

The food supplies were getting further restricted as the Germans drove deep into the Soviet Union and occupied the agricultural lands of Ukraine. Also, a large number of people were evacuated to Central Asia placing much greater food demands on these areas. The situation was getting very serious.

My ability to use the Russian language had increased greatly. Vasil was particularly helpful in this respect. We spent a great deal of time together. He was a wonderful artist. I tried to draw also, however, only with a limited success; he was much better. On the other hand, I played the violin quite well. He was fascinated with the violin and made me teach him the rudiments of violin techniques. Thus, art had brought us even closer.

In early June, I spent a great deal of time in school. I was getting nervous and once the date for the exams was finally set in middle of June, I decided to study for at least ten hours every day. This definitely paid off since I indeed passed the examinations very well, although with the Russian language and literature I barely went over the top. By passing the exams, I was able to start in the 8th grade by September.

As the summer progressed, the garden started producing more potatoes, corn and ultimately sunflowers. Our food supplies improved dramatically although the general food picture was getting worse. The food store carried only the bread rations (200 gm black bread per day) although we had coupons for oil (one pint per month), meat (200 gm per week) and sugar (one pound per month), it was almost never available. In the interim, Uncle Leon was promoted at the factory. He was given a truck driver's job, which gave him the opportunity to travel to Alma Ata, a major city in Kazakhstan about 100 kilometers from Kargaly. The ability to travel to Alma Ata gave him the chance to get things (both buy and sell) at the very active Alma Ata black market. It also gave him the opportunity to contact the office of the General Anders Polish Army. Apparently, there were major changes according to some rumors among the people close to the army office. The emigration of the army out of Soviet Union was successful. Many thousands of members of the Polish Army and their dependants were transported by ship from Krasnovodsk on the Caspian Sea to Iran. The significant aspect of this was the fact that many Polish civilians were given the opportunity to evacuate with the army.

The issue of anti-Semitism still existed and actually became even more severe. There was a huge civilian population, including ourselves, who would like to leave the Soviet Union with the army. Since the available slots were limited, Jews were barred from even applying. Leon learned that there would be another group of ships leaving Krasnovodsk for Iran possibly in August and September;

this spured my parents and uncles to try even harder to get into Anders Army. However, all this was fruitless. Very few Jews were able to join.

The month of August was approaching and the heat was sizzling. I spent a great deal of time with Vasil. He showed me ravines in the mountains full of apricot trees loaded with juicy sweet apricots. We would leave early in the morning, when it was still cool, reached areas high in the mountains by noon, loaded a sack full of apricots and got home before evening. The apricots were a very special treat to everyone! Vasil showed me how to dry the apricots in the sun providing a remarkable fruit supply for the winter.

The corn we planted in our garden started ripening. The young corn was cooked directly on the cob. This provided a delicious meal. Once the corn matured, with the help of my uncles, I started harvesting it seriously, dragging it home in sacks on our backs every day. It had to be harvested rapidly to prevent pilfering.

Once we got it all home, we laid it out to dry in the hot summer sun. The dried corn cobs were trashed to get the corn cornels. We saved a sack full of dry corn cornels for cooking, but had to hang it in the corner of the room from the ceiling to prevent mice from attacking it. The rest of the corn was milled and the corn meal was stored in sacks for the use during the winter.

We were accumulating food for the winter to prevent the disaster of the last winter and spring when I almost died from starvation.

Slowly the sunflowers started ripening. Initially I would pick the ripe flowers and after roasting the seeds, distributed them to the family to be eaten as snacks. This, incidentally, was a major Russian pastime. Everywhere, if they could get it, people would crack and eat the seeds. The sunflower seeds were delicious and very nutritious. I suspect that the sunflower seeds were to a great degree responsible for the prevention of malnutrition deaths by providing the otherwise almost nonexistent fat nutrients to the body.

The entire family participated in this activity. It took about a week to complete, with me working all day, everyday, and the rest the family coming to the field every evening after work to transport the harvest on their backs to the apartment--a four kilometer trip.

Before we completed the harvesting that included also the digging up of the potatoes and the back braking exercise of transporting them from the fields to the house, school had started. This slowed down our harvesting substantially since I had to spend most of the day in school and had to carve out some time to do my homework.

I was, however, elated; finally, after a two year hiatus, I was back in school, in the 8th grade! I still had a bit of troubles with the Russian language, particularly with the Russian literature classes. The rest, however, was fun.

I immediately developed a crush on the Russian Literature teacher who was like a little toy bear, soft and always willing to help and explain. This was important for me because it was an area I had the least amount of background and experience. Furthermore, literature and languages were not my favorite and I actually began to develop liking for sciences. Except for the Russian language classes, I felt very comfortable with the other subjects and with the kids in the school. Several became good friends. I developed a friendship with Misha instantly. He was a very handsome and smart boy originally from Moscow. Later I learned that he was Jewish. Soon there was a group of us spending a great deal of time together.

Over time, we managed to bring the entire harvest home. There was not enough space, however, to store the potatoes. Finally, Father asked, "What is under the floor of our room? There may be a crawl space there."

"Let's find out," said Leon. That evening he returned with a chisel and saw. He cut into some of the floorboards, forming a square hole. Indeed there was a space under the floor but only a couple of feet deep. Leon looked at Father; Father looked at me and I instantly knew what was on their minds. They wanted me to climb in there and excavate essentially a cellar under the floor of the room. After some discussion, it was decided to excavate the space to the depth of four feet near the center and three feet in the periphery. I started immediately. Father and Uncle would move away the dirt and I kept on digging. The first evening I dug out barely four feet in depth under the hole we cut out in the floor. The digging of the shallow cellar became a major undertaking. It actually took us several weeks to complete the task. But the job was worth its effort. We were able to store a nice harvest of potatoes. My friends and I found some wild apple trees in the mountains. This gave us the opportunity to put away a large stock of apples in the cellar. The cellar was dry and cool in the summer and warm in the winter.

Gradually life had become routine. All adults worked at the factory ten to twelve hours a day. The factory was a short walking distance from the house we lived in. This was a major advantage, particularly as the weather turned cold in the winter. My schoolwork progressed well and the friendships I developed with the other students were very worthwhile. The friendship with Misha gave me the benefit of his experiences in the school and turned out to evolve into a very close relationship, particularly since he also was Jewish. Ilia, was a very serious boy a year ahead of me in school was from Moscow, while Misha was from Rostov. Ilia was much more serious than any of my other friends. With him I had a great deal of political discussions and learned more personal facts about the communist system. I spent most of my free time with Ilia, although he was two years older. I still spent a great deal of time with Vasil. Firstly, he lived in the next apartment and art as well as his knowledge of the local scene, kept us very close.

In school, I also became friendly with Katia, one of the local girls; she was a good soul. Her father operated the local mill where we had our corn crop ground into corn meal. The relationship with Katia gave me a first hand practical lesson of the value of close personal contacts in the Soviet Union. My friendship with the miller's daughter, who apparently must have liked me, and must have talked about me to her father resulted in him weighing out twenty pounds of corn meal after I handed him only ten pounds of corn kernels. This was a major help in our food bank.

It was the winter of 1942-43. The Germans were under Stalingrad since September; they captured most of southern Soviet Union. There was a famine throughout the land. Refugees from central and eastern Russian provinces were arriving by the trainloads. The food was becoming scarcer than last winter. If it were not for the stocks of potatoes, corn and sunflower seeds that we accumulated, we would most likely not have survived this winter.

Mother was extremely rigid doling out the food reserves; she maintained that this extreme economy was essential if we hoped to survive the winter. We were on a starvation diet. Everyone lost great deal of weight. The official food rations consisted primarily of soup and occasional cooked millet gruel at the factory cafeteria available only to the workers.

Thus we kids-- my sister and I-- had no formal access to food except for the 200 grams of black bread daily. The fruits of our gardening were our main food resources and a salvation. Despite this desperate situation, Stella and I were in school and an attempt was made to live as normal a life as possible. The ground was covered with snow but we kept most of the time warm in the house, burning strips cut from old, worn tires that Uncle Josef was able to "organize" at the factory by some obviously illegal means.

Occasionally we got a small supply of *Saksaul*, the fantastic desert plant that burned better than coal and gave off a great amount of heat. While the local situation was getting progressively worse, the news from the front was more and more encouraging. Earlier in the winter, Soviet troops in Stalingrad staged a counter offensive and gradually started to encircle the entire German Army that was focused on attacking Stalingrad and by the end of January the entire German Army in Stalingrad was surrounded. While this was a very important psychological stimulus, the economic situation was becoming critical.

As winter was coming to an end so did our food supply. We subsided essentially on the 200 grams of bread and watered down grits made of the dwindling supply of corn meal. I spent a great deal of time studying with Ilia and drawing with Vasil. Occasionally I saw Katia, but was embarrassed to be with her because she knew exactly of our desperate state, as far as the food supply was concerned. Whenever she saw me she tried to give me food. This was embarrassing and demeaning because it was so difficult to refuse these gifts.

As time went on, I found myself visiting Katia more often. It was very alluring. Each time I went there she had something good to eat in her house. I began to question my motives. Did I visit Katia because I liked her more as time went on, or was it the food that attracted me to her? She was on the heavy side with a pretty Russian, flat, round face and a pair of beautiful long tresses. Her hair and eyes were brown. She had the habit of placing her hands on me in a caressing fashion, in the way one touches a cat. My experiences with girls were miniscule, but I felt a great deal of positive feelings emanating from her. Nevertheless, I still couldn't decide in my mind whether it was the food or her company that influenced my visits to see her. It could be the schoolwork. She was in my class, or I could simply like her as a girl. Anyway, I was actually too busy to worry about these details.

****

In April, most of the snow had melted and I started cleaning up the ground near the house where we had our garden last year. This went fast, so did the tilling. In no time, I was ready to plant beets, potatoes, tomatoes and some corn. However, I kept on feeling weaker. The family looked also like skeletons, barely having enough strength to get up in the morning for work. My schoolwork suffered since I was unable to stay up and study.

Ilia's father was a highly placed administrator in the factory, so they had a special dispensary where they still could get some food. Occasionally Ilia would bring me corn bread, which was a great happening for the entire family.

This year the entire family helped to a great extent preparing the soil and then planting primarily corn, potatoes and sunflowers in our large garden outside the village. I was barely able to keep up with my little garden near our house and do some studying.

The first plants to come up from the earth in my garden were the beets. In no time, the leaves attained considerable height and I started pruning them as I had done the year before. I added them to the corn meal soup that by now was getting almost as thin as water. We were looking forward to the corn and potatoes that should be forthcoming soon from the garden. The official food rations, except for bread, were almost nonexistent.

Suddenly a disaster struck. The NKVD detained Uncle Josef. Apparently the Anders Army people in Alma Ata started spreading rumors that the only reason Jews are trying to join the Anders Army was to get out of Soviet Union. Since Josef was very outspoken with the Anders Army officials, demanding a commission in the Corps, they apparently submitted his name to some Russian office and this was the end result.

Mother, who by now had befriended the head of the dental clinic in Kargaly, started an inquiry and made attempts to find out where

Uncle was held. It turned out that they kept him in a detention center near Alma Ata.

After a great deal of "string pulling," Uncle Leon was able to get a permission to see him. He found Josef to be in good spirits; he was questioned about membership in a subversive group that tried to blacken Soviet Union by spreading malicious propaganda and then escaping to Iran with the army.

Soon, the entire family including myself, was taken to the NKVD offices for questioning. There wasn't much we could tell. We were not even aware of any subversive organizations. I was questioned intensively and admonished, not in uncertain terms, to refrain from talking to anyone about anything even remotely related to such organization, and to report to NKVD immediately any conversations between family members related to this topic. In other words I was to spy on my family for the NKVD.

At this time, Uncle Leon had gained a great deal of influence with the factory management. It was not clear to me on what basis this has occurred. Nevertheless, he was able to convince some high standing members of the plant's administration to intervene with NKVD on behalf of Josef. After several tense weeks, Josef returned to Kargaly. He was reluctant to talk about his detention time. He may have talked to my parents and Uncle; however, I was kept in darkness about this entire episode.

Our radio speaker was still working, transmitting music and news. The news was encouraging. There was a great deal of talk about a second front to be opened by the Allies in Europe. Indeed, in July the American forces landed in Sicily.

At the same time, the German forces again attempted a counter offensive, this time near Kursk, but not very successfully. The Soviet forces prevented any serious incursions of the Germans toward the east, and the front held steady. Matter of fact the Red Army had recaptured Kharkov. We listened to the radio news religiously twice a day. My friends and I were much more involved in listening to the radio news, discussing it in detail among ourselves, but not with the adults. They were exhausted and preoccupied with survival rather than with the war news.

One day Uncle Leon came with good news. He arranged for all of us to move to Alma Ata to work at our plant's sister factory, one that also was producing fabric for military coats. The factory was on Furmanova Street in the center of the city. Leon and Mother made an arrangement with the factory administration for jobs for everyone including Josef and Father. Mother was to set up a small dental office in a kiosk adjacent to the factory to service primarily factory managers. The management indicated that if we could fit in the remaining space in the kiosk we would be permitted to live there also. This was very good news. We didn't waste any time. The kiosk was abandoned and we could move into it any time. Leon, who by this time was already in charge of the trucking facility at the factory, made arrangements for a truck to move us to Alma Ata. Incidentally he was also appointed the Supervisor of the Transport Unit, in charge of the factory trucks, at the Alma Ata plant.

The move occurred during the following week. I was sorry to leave my friends, but to my surprise, Ilia's father was also transferred to the Alma Ata plant, thus Ilia was also coming to Alma Ata later in the fall. In addition, to my greatest surprise, Katia was moving to Alma Ata for the next year to live with her aunt and attend the school there. This was good news. I was happy to have some of my old friends in Alma Ata.

We loaded our belongings on a truck, and placed the table and chairs on top of the bundles and took off for Alma Ata.

We had already harvested many of our crops but there were some still ripening. I was to return with Leon in a few weeks to harvest the remaining potatoes and sunflowers. This was important because the famine was again getting worse and the winter was coming.

CHAPTER 12. Alma Ata

The Big City

Our new home, the former soda kiosk, was facing the sidewalk on Furmanova Street, a beautiful, straight and wide street lined by tall trees. The street ran through the entire city for many miles in the north-south direction. In the kiosk, facing the sidewalk, there were three huge windows originally designed for customer's easy access to the merchandise. We got carpenters who for a couple yards of cloth made them look more like conventional windows.

A Russian woman, whose husband was in the army and only had one daughter living with her, rented a nice room to Uncle Leon, Josef found a room at the factory in their single men housing units. Thus, only Stella, my parents and I stayed in the kiosk. However, most of the time, the two uncles would join us for suppers.

As fall progressed, food again became a major problem. Leon was developing connections within the factory administration as well as with administrative personnel at the other factories that interacted with our plant. Mother's dental practice was booming. She still had some gold discs to make gold crowns when necessary. Some of the factory directors were soon sporting gold teeth and this was extremely helpful to us.

Using a cloth curtain that Leon "organized" on the *toltchock* (black market) we divided the kiosk into two areas One was set up as an office where Mother spend most of the day seeing patients and working on their teeth. In addition to a chair in which patients sat while Mother worked with them, there was a low table covered by a thin mattress on which the patients would sit while waiting to be taken care of. I used the same table at night to sleep on. The only electrical outlet in the entire kiosk was in Mother's office area, under the window sill. For a little fortune, Uncle Josef was able to procure an electric hotplate. This was a real gem! Firstly, it was an almost unheard of luxury but also a very practical item, particularly since we didn't have to pay for the electricity. When the kiosk was built, its electrical circuit was integrated with the factory's system since originally the kiosk was an integral part of the factory. I used the hot plate to boil Mother's dental instruments for sterilization purpose. However I also used it for preparing meals, a chore that remained traditionally under my supervision.

When winter approached and the weather turned cold, the plate was used to supplement the heating function of an oven located in the "living" area of the kiosk. There, we placed our old table, the two benches and two chairs that we acquired on the black market to accommodate all six of us comfortably for meals. At night, the table was moved to the stove and used by Stella as a bed to sleep on.

Josef helped me to build a lean-to outside the back doors of the kiosk. It was located in the corner between the brick wall of the factory and the back wall of our kiosk. There we stored firewood and I also built a rough table and bench to do my schoolwork. During wintertime, it was much too cold to stay out there and anyways, in the winter, it was usually occupied by firewood. Outside the shed, in the back of the kiosk, using some stray rocks and bricks, I built a permanent fireplace to cook meals in the summer. By June, it was much too hot to fire up the indoor oven for cooking purposes, thus the outdoors open-fire cooking. When cooking outdoors I could look up and see the mountain peaks always covered with snow, while in the summer, the temperature in the city could soar into the nineties.

Soon I learned that the city of Alma Ata was founded at the edge of the foothills of the Ala Tau range of the Tian Shan chain of the northern part of the Himalayan Mountains. Furmanova Street ran due south so that looking southward along the street we could see the towering, snow covered peaks of the Ala Tau range. At the foot of the street, against the view of the mountains, was a grandiose opera house. All the streets were running parallel to each other with cross streets at 90-degree angles. This perfect chessboard arrangement of the streets was present throughout most of the city. It puzzled me. I was accustomed to the European cities with their ancient designs of street layouts, irregular and twisting. This extraordinarily regular pattern, resembling a layout of a modern American city, was surprising. I thought of Alma Ata as an ancient Kazakh city, currently the capital of Kazakhstan, which in my imagination had a design more like that of Ashkabad rather than of a modern city.

It wasn't until much later that I had the opportunity to learn the truth about Alma Ata; the city was actually built rather recently. Firstly, the name Alma Ata is derived from Kazakh words: Alma--an apple and Ata-- father. Thus, Alma Ata meant the "Father of Apples." Actually the derivation of this name is much more complex. One of the first travelers to this area of Central Asia, on his way to Mongolia, was an Italian monk, Giovanni Del Plano Carpini. He described a town named Almalyk, north of Dzhungarskyi Ala Tau mountain chain and south of the Lake Balkhash, in the general area of modern Alma Ata. There is essentially no information concerning the fate of this town during the subsequent centuries. It is believed that in 1855 the Russians established a fortress in this general area, Vernoi. In 1860, the Kokand Khaganate forces attempted unsuccessfully to dislodge the Russians. The area fell under total Russian control and Vernoi became a fortress-town. Subsequently the area experienced several devastating earthquakes resulting in major disasters associated with losses of hundreds of lives. During the period of the First World War, a number of rebellions and uprisings rocked the region and the town. Ultimately in 1918, with the end of the WWI, a communist government was established in Vernoi.

This, however, didn't last. There were fights between the Cossacks, Kazakhs and the communist rebels until ultimately the native Kazakh armies retreated to China and the rightist Cossacks were subdued by the communists.

In 1920, the Red Army took Vernoi and in 1921 the town's name was changed to Alma Ata. The Kazakhs who escaped to China were invited to return and thousands did. In 1929, Alma Ata was named the capital of Kazakhstan; however, no attempt was made to conduct any archeological excavations, although there were ruins in the vicinity of Alma Ata that could have determined the ancient origins of Vernoi. This was probably done to keep the Kazakh national impulses under control. Fast forwarding for an instant I like to share with the reader an interesting tidbit of irony. In 1991, upon dissolution of the Soviet Union, Kazakhstan became an independent nation. In 1994, the name of the city was changed to Almaty and in 1997 the capital of Kazakhstan was moved from Almaty to Astana.

Gradually we settled into our new living quarters on Furmanova Street in the converted soda kiosk. In comparison to the tiny room we had in Kargaly that we had to share with Uncle Leon, these were 'palatial quarters'. However, one of the more aggravating and actually difficult issues, at least for me, was the availability of water. We had to carry water from a public water pump located on the sidewalk. Unfortunately the pump was located on the Furmanova Street sidewalk five blocks south of us; thus, carrying water to the house was a major undertaking. It had to be hand carried for over five blocks crossing a number of streets and quickly evolved into my responsibility. This was a major job particularly in the winter when one had to walk over slippery snow and ice covered streets.

Shortly after moving to Alma Ata, I contacted Ilia. He had been admitted to a university in Swerdlowsk, Siberia and was planning to go there soon. We spent a great amount of time together. First, he talked to me of the importance of leaving the Soviet Union. He kept on saying that I had a golden opportunity to do so because ultimately the Soviets may let us go, particularly after the war will be over. Although the war situation was still precarious, Ilia pointed out to me that the July offense mounted by the Germans at Kursk was contained and the German army was defeated there. Recently the Soviet forces recaptured Kharkov. Ilia argued that the worse was over. I was sorry that he was leaving. He was like an older brother to me and like a guardian of my intellectual life. "In view of the war," he said, "and of my move to Swerdlowsk, the almost non existing postal services and essentially no facilities to search for people, we may not see each other again." I disagreed violently, he first waved his hand than placed his thin fingers on my shoulder, "don't argue, time will tell," he commented. How true were his predictions!

The New School

There was no trouble to matriculate into the 9th grade. My records from the Kargaly Desiatiletka were quite good and theadministration in the Alma Ata Desiatiletka # 14 for boys was quite happy to have me enroll. I was also glad to go back to school. During the very first days in school, I met a Jewish boy, Tolek, from Poland. He was in my grade. We became friends instantly. He lived only few blocks from us. Very soon we became inseparable; we were together in school or in each other's houses. Tolek was a thoughtful, but at the same time lighthearted friend. We immediately fell into a routine of studying together. We studied very hard but at the same time found ways to play.

In school, the only activities of importance were hard study to get good grades, sports and dancing parties, the latter we attended regularly. The dancing parties were organized with our sister schools that were exclusively female, while our school was a male-only institution. Apparently in the Soviet Union, in larger cities, coeducational secondary schools did not usually exist. The sexes were separated but a social contact between the students in these schools was encouraged as demonstrated by the frequent dancing parties. These parties brought the two sexes together and allowed for an easy social interaction and for a healthy social maturation process.

In addition to Tolek, I made friends with three local boys in my class; one was a tall, skinny blond Russian, Vania Lapschin. His father was the Secretary of the Communist Party for Kazakhstan. The other was a native Kazak, Ivan Abossobayev. His father was one of the government leaders of the Kazakh Socialistic Republic. The third boy was Igor Litvinov. His father was a professor of physics at the Kazakh State University in Alma Ata and his mother was a professor of chemistry at the medical school. Soon we became an inseparable bunch in school. After school, our interests separated us somewhat. With Vania, we went skiing, swimming or hiking in the mountains; with Ivan we went to parties and dances. Igor was the most serious in the group and with him we spent a great deal of time discussing the world and national politics, playing chess and just spending time together. Sometimes, I had the privilege to visit Igor's father in his laboratories at the university. I always looked forward to this experience. It gave me the first glimpse into the life of a scientist and work in a research laboratory.

At the time I didn't realize that I was actually witnessing research activity related to the most important scientific discoveries of the 20th century. Professor Litvinov was one of the leading scientists dealing with a nuclear physics and the splitting of the atom.

Looking back at our group's interaction, I realize that there was one "taboo" area between us. Although Tolek and I lived a marginal survival existence, as far as availability of food was concerned, while Ivan and Vania had all the access to food, this issue was never brought up between us. This is of particular interest since in 1943 and 1944 the food situation in Alma Ata was desperate. People were literally dying of starvation. Every morning horse-pulled carriages were picking up dead bodies off the streets; the bodies were swollen from lack of protein. Both Ivan and Vania's families had access to NKVD stores where one could still get a variety of foods. This, however, was never brought up.

Personally, we actually were better off in Alma Ata, food wise, than in Kargaly, where I was hospitalized with malnutrition secondary to starvation. In Alma Ata, Uncle Leon's job driving a truck at the factory opened various opportunities to him. Ultimately the director of the factory empowered him to barter with other plants using our factory's product, heavy cloth employed for making military winter coats. Every week he bartered some of the cloth with managers of various establishments for items produced there. These were then distributed among the workers after the upper management, including my uncle, got their share. Ultimately Leon developed connections with a plant making edible oil from sunflower seeds.

This became a major product of his bartering exercises. Thus, we were well supplied with edible fat, a crucial aspect of the minimally adequate diet; we not only had enough for ourselves, but we had enough to sell several bottles on the black market each week. This was a salvation for us because the money we got for the oil could be used to buy bread and sometimes even meat. I became the major oil trader for the family. At first, this was a problem since I had no experience with the black market and especially with the periodic raids by the militia.

These experiences, however, turned out to be very important to me, not only in providing us with basic food requirements but also in developing my appreciation of the practical aspects of Soviet economics and the Soviet regime as such. It made me open my eyes even wider and look at the Soviet society and its political structure through differently colored lenses.

It made me understand why at night so many people came to the outside walls surrounding the factory grounds to catch spools of thread pitched over the wall by the workers to their friends and relatives. This thread found its way to the black market.

Now I realized that the black market was actually a safety valve for the entire communist economic system, allowing the steam generated by anger, frustration, incompetence and confusion to be released. The anger was directed towards the Soviet market performance characterized by a chronic lack of minimum supply of necessities experienced by the great majority of the population.

This revelation disturbed me greatly and I had to discuss it with someone. Tolek, my new friend, was chosen to be the one. Actually we were spending great deal of time together; literally most of the day. During the early hours we were in school. Later in the afternoon, we studied together and in the evening we frequently studied together or went out together.

As the food situation was getting progressively worse, food shortages and its causes were a frequent topic of our conversations. As we became closer, I learned that the NKVD jailed his father for "anticommunist" propaganda. My friend and his entire family were born in Poland. Apparently his father has discussed the shortcomings of the system as compared with pre-war Poland. This landed him in jail for a long period of time. Tolek lived in a small, one room apartment with his mother and a former maid that reared him from infancy and who accompanied them to Soviet Union. The room was comfortable, under the circumstances, and since during the day my mother saw in our living quarter's patients with dental problems precluding any studying in my house, usually we studied at Tolek's house.

As the winter progressed we became involved in a wide variety of activities. In school, in addition to the standard academic subjects, we had a large number of hours devoted to "physical culture" that was combined with "military preparedness" classes involving weekly target shooting practice and a 2-3 hour cross country ski run three times a week. During the ski run, we carried a rifle strapped to our back and periodically had to fall into the snow, fire at a target and continue going. It was a hard exercise but it gave us a reason to compete and ultimately it became fun. This became a particularly sought after activity since upon return there was a good (large) lunch served.

The target shooting changed forever my class standing with my Russian peers. I was the only one in the class wearing eyeglasses, probably the only one in the entire school. This made me the butt of jokes and derision; sometimes not just verbal assaults. If it weren't for my friends Ivan and Vania, who wielded a great deal of power, my situation would have been very precarious. On the target shooting range, located in an abandoned stone quarry in the mountains, we were lined up in groups of five to shoot at a target located at 100 meters distance. I turned out to be a reasonably good sharpshooter. Usually I was the best in my group of five kids. This made them quite suspicious. Ultimately one asked to try my eyeglasses. His shooting performance improved remarkably. Soon others started asking me for my glasses and in no time, I became a celebrity. It turned out that a large number of kids in my class were nearsighted but either refused to admit it or hid it; it wouldn't be "manly" to wear eyeglasses.

The cross-country skiing also gave me access to skis in the school. This was a major benefit since in Alma Ata there were no skis to purchase. This gave us the freedom to use the skis on weekends and opened the opportunity of skiing outside the school hours and in the hills of our choosing. This access had actually influenced my entire future life; this will become clearer later.

As I settled down with school and friends, my parents and uncles settled into their jobs. Father became involved with the "Polish Sport Club" in Alma Ata and soon became the manager of their boxing group. This resulted in my joining the group and bringing Tolek into it the club as well. Looking back at this experience it is almost laughable to see young boys barely surviving on their food rations become involved in a sport activity like boxing in addition to all of the other physical activities. I surmise that this was the result of being young, foolish and undeterred by realities of life.

Soon, Tolek and I became actively engaged in boxing. Daily training and friendly matches with other youth clubs in Alma Ata kept us very busy, particularly since we had also other responsibilities. Dynamo, a national sport club had started preparing for their annual competitions to be held before the New Year's celebration in the main city arena. The Polish club was invited to participate.

At that time, our family and friends, almost all from Poland, began to feel much more positive about the outcome of the war. In December 1943, the Soviet Army launched a major offensive on the Ukrainian front and by January 1944 the Soviet troops entered Poland and on their march westward, relieved Leningrad after a 900-day long siege. With the successes of the Soviet Army, the meager but positive news concerning the military activities of the Allies, including successes in Africa, landing of Allied forces in Sicily and the intensification of the bombing of Germany, all resulted in a very positive attitudes and gave us a stimulus to do more than simply survive.

Thus, the boxing activity became one of the events that some of us embraced with great enthusiasm. The schoolwork became routine, so Tolek and I looked forward primarily to all of the extracurricular activities. With material successes of Uncle Leon, the black market activity increased. I became quite adroit in selling oil on the *Toltchok* and in return being able to buy many important foodstuffs. We actually could afford a pound of lamb, once or twice a week. I used it to prepare a delicious bean soup. This feast was not only for the four of us but also for both uncles who would usually join us for the meals. Thus, my cooking activities were usually of a rather grand magnitude.

One day Leon brought me a stunningly beautiful steel-gray color plaid suit that he "organized" in one of his black market "machinations." The suit fit me perfectly; I was "flying high." Finally I had something decent to wear when going to parties. At the parties, there wasn't much to eat, but the parties were fun, with a lot of dancing and a lot of girls. A new world, a world of girls, had opened up to me. The suit had definitely helped in making me more comfortable in their company.

The city had a large opera house and a great opera company. Its staff, singers and musicians, were primarily members of the Moscow Opera Company that was evacuated to Alma Ata. We had the benefit of having top Soviet performers in our city. Since the price of the tickets had not changed, while the actual cost of living had risen dramatically, the actual cost of tickets was literally inconsequential. For example, a ticket to the opera was three Rubles while the cost of a loaf of bread on the black market was 400 Rubles. Similar price disparity existed in respect to the price of tickets to movies, the Drama Theaters, etc. Thus, we could afford to attend various high quality performances several times a week. While starving and having essentially nothing to wear, we were pampered with cultural activities. We experienced a similar situation, although of a lesser magnitude, when the Soviets invaded and occupied Lwow in 1939. Prices skyrocketed on all essentials but the prices of tickets to theatres and opera remained at the pre war level.

One of Mother's friends was a conductor in the opera, so we were introduced to the opera choir and soon became its members. Actually, neither Tolek nor I had much of singing voices; however, we enjoyed the social interactions.

Here, on one faithful evening a friend of ours who also was a patient of my mother's and considerably older than I, about 18 years of age, took me by my hand and led me to a group of choir singers. There she turned to one of the girls, a pretty little blonde with big blue eyes, and said to me, "I want you to meet your future wife." The blue-eyed girl's face turned crimson. I also felt embarrassed and after shaking hands with the girl I had nothing much to say. We parted almost instantly. This episode was promptly forgotten. The choir practice sessions were soon interrupted by winter vacations and subsequently I did not come across this girl for some time.

It was the time of year for many parties. All the girls' schools organized parties and were inviting the boy's schools. Similarly our school had organized parties and invited girls from our "partner" school, "Desiatiletka #31."

Soon I met a girl that I liked very much, named Ada. Ada was an intelligent, slim, athletic girl of my age with a great deal of drive and love for fun. She wasn't exactly an intellectual, although her father was an engineer. We hit it off from the very beginning. Tolek also found a girl and the four of us became almost inseparable.

Between trying to find enough food for the family to survive on, , getting some business on the black market, getting time off to go skiing and keeping up with my school work, I had my hands full. The mood in the city was improving, despite an unbelievable hardship, essentially no food, clothing or fuel, since most of these items had to be "organized" on the black market... There was no food but the kids partied a lot; vodka was inexpensive and there was no age limit on drinking. A party commonly consisted of a group of kids, girls and boys, someone with a *garmoshka*, a primitive accordion, a few pickles, a bowl of sauerkraut and a bottle of vodka. The parties were held in someone's house, usually with one of the parents in attendance. The parent's presence, however, did not dampen the mood or interfer with a good party. We were careful to invite only school friends since the crime scene was becoming more violent as time went on. However, the availability of alcohol had not created any problems in our school age group of kids. Occasionally someone would get a little boisterous, but his peers would quickly control him. There were, however, "gangs" of hooligans and one had to be careful to avoid them. While their activity was primarily directed towards robbery, sometimes they would engage in hostile acts "for the fun of it."

Everyone had some form of protection on him for personal defense against the gang members. I made for myself a knife with a five inch long blade. A friend's father had forged the blade for me from a piece of steel at a plant he worked at. I did the final polishing of the blade by hand. The blade had a super keen double edge. I also made a handle for it from a set of plastic discs that were polished by hand to a perfect finish; whenever we went out in the evening to the opera, movies, dances or the theater, I carried this knife strapped to the back of my belt.

The city was full of young thugs and gangs. Anyone over the age of 17, in reasonable medical condition, was in the army. But those below this age frequently banded together, and once it got dark, preyed on pedestrians. Militia, the civilian police, were not particularly concerned with petty crime, thus one had to defend oneself the best one could.

The gang culture has developed to perfection. One had to either belong to a gang or arrange for "protection" by a gang. This was highly politicized. Everything, apparently not only in Alma Ata but also everywhere in the Soviet Union, was arranged "po blatu." To get things done "po blatu" meant to have it done on the strength of connections, acquaintances or bribes.

My friend, Ivan Abossobayev, having a father positioned very high in the political hierarchy, literally owned a huge and very powerful gang that also helped me personally on various occasions; I might have owed my life to their help. Obviously at the time I would have never admitted that, since I always felt that I was quite self-sufficient.

As spring progressed and the snows melted, we ventured for excursions into the foothills where we found fields of wild rhubarb, a very desirable find. Vegetables, at this time of the year, were almost nonexistent and this discovery added a desirable item to our meager diet.

About the same time, I was drafted for a work detail to be carried out on weekends. All citizens had to perform, in addition to the regular six-day a week job, a voluntary work duty called *voskresennik*. *Voskresenie* is the Russian word for Sunday. Thus, *voskresennik* was a government mandated labor detail performed "voluntarily" by the citizens on Sundays. If one refused to participate, one was enrolled into the *Trudovaia Armia ("work army")*. This was a paramilitary organization into which individuals that refused to 'volunteer' could be drafted. I and my best friend Tolek, had reached the age of being eligible for the "Voskresennik" duty. The very next Sunday we trudged away to join the work detail where we were assigned to a small dam project in the foothills of the Ala Tau Mountains. It should be noted that neither Ivan nor Vania were drafted for this duty. Obviously, their fathers arranged a deal "po blatu" to exclude them from it.

The weather that Sunday was abominable. Rain followed by snow, followed by hail, followed by rain again. We were transported to the dam by trucks, however we had to walk about one kilometer to the work place. The walk was through a sea of mud into which our feet sunk all the way to our ankles. Since the ground was not frozen, we couldn't have worn our *valenky*, tall felt boots because their felt soles would have instantly gotten wet. Thus, we wore *tapotchki*, which were basically home made slippers. Most of us couldn't afford to buy leather boots on the black market; instead we wore *tapotchki* made of scraps of felt with soles made from used worn out truck tires. Well it didn't take long for the *tapotchki* to get wet through and through, leading to our feet getting wet and extremely cold.

Upon reaching the workplace, we were given shovels and instructed where to move the dirt. The ground was made of clay and was wet. Everyone was slipping and falling. It was a miserable and very dangerous experience, even for young kids like Tolek and I. It was particularly dangerous since we were working on a side of a ravine where the creek ran and the dam was to be constructed. An unlucky slip and one could tumble all the way down, possibly into the creek.

Tolek and I worked as a team. We would load up a wheel barrel with the wet clay and then together push it to the unloading spot. This way we supported each other and diminished the chance of slipping. At noon all of us were given a ration of black bread and a bowl of soup. The hot soup was our savior. Tolek finagled a second bowl and shared it with me. This really made a difference.

As we were returning to the work place, a lady ahead of us slipped and fell down. We helped her up and later helped her along with the loading of the barrels. Her name was Schneider. I was totally unaware of who she was nor was I aware of the role she was to play in my personal future.

Boxing and Ania

As springtime progressed, many things started happening with great rapidity. The Soviet troops continued the offensive on the Byelorussian front. The Allies commenced daylight bombing of Berlin and aggressively pursued advances towards Rome on the Italian peninsula. This news made all of us very happy and allowed us to think in less serious directions. It probably was reflected by a greater activity in the "Polonia" boxing club.

Although it was allegedly a Polish club, the great majority of its membership was composed primarily of Jews from Poland or other countries west of Soviet Russia. We were busy preparing a major competition with the local Russian club, the "Dynamo." The work on Sundays, the *Voskresennik* has seriously cutting into our training time, which we needed since the fight was scheduled to occur soon.

We had spent every evening in the club, practicing and exercising. Soon, announcements of the boxing match were seen all over the city. After reading one I went into a panic. The Russians billed me as the former pre-war Polish flyweight-boxing champion. This was the epitome of Soviet propaganda and the "Big Lie" principle. Before the war, I was only eleven years old!

With much to live up to, we trained furiously. I was weighed in at the featherweight category and with the heavy exercise and limited food intake didn't worry of getting over the weight at the time of the weigh-in for the tournament.

So, our major preoccupation was boxing. This was my last year in the secondary school and in order to be admitted to the University I had to have very high grades. Boxing, however, was taking priority over everything--over the schoolwork and over Ada who was willing to be "understanding" and let me spend most of the evenings at the sport club in the practice ring. Actually, I think she enjoyed the fact that I was a boxer and could tag along with me to the practice fights. As for the schoolwork, it was quite late in the year to worry about. My grades were high throughout the years and I was certain that I would be graduating within the top 10% of the class, which should have been quite adequate for admission to the University.

My father who was the president of the club was quite supportive and Uncle Leon gave me all the opportunity to sell extra oil and make some money. Thus, things were looking good and I was looking forward to the night of the fight.

The match was to be fought at the facilities of the Dynamo club. The ring was moved to the basketball court because there was more space there for the fans. The tickets were sold out and there was a large crowd outside the club facilities trying to get in. My father was conferring with the manager of the Dynamo club. They returned to the room where we were changing and getting ready for the bouts and announced that the competition would begin with the feather fights and progress on to the other weight categories ending with the heavyweights. That meant that I would go first. The Dynamo officials came in to fetch me and accompany me to the weigh-in room.

Father and couple of Polonia officials were standing around the scales where a muscular man was being weighed. He looked at least five years older and appeared to be bigger or quite a bit more muscular than I. His face, a typical flat, broad one of a native Kazakh, appeared friendly and confident as he flashed a smile towards me.

His extra broad shoulders and muscular torso did not convey a good message to me. I could see that Father looked suspiciously at the scales.

After having stepped on the scale I waited until the attendant arranged the weights before looking. My heart skipped a beat; according to the scale, I was 113 pounds. My formal boxing weight division was junior flyweight and the maximum upper limits of this category was 108 pounds. By weighing 113 pounds, I moved into the bantamweight that would include fighters weighing up to 122 pounds. This could be devastating. Indeed my opponent's weight was 121 pounds.

Father took me aside and whispered, "The scale is being manipulated, your weight was exaggerated and your opponent's suppressed. He must weigh at least 130 pounds. There is very little we can do except to protest this, however, it will not do much for us. The Soviet team will laugh at you. We are on their turf; they can deny, fabricate and do anything they wish. You, on the other hand, can refuse to fight and by default, the victory will be declared for the opponent; or you can go out and fight a completely defensive fight just to protect yourself so you would not get hurt badly."

I was devastated by this development since I looked with great anticipation towards the competition and had sacrificed a great deal for it. Uncle Leon has provided me with extra food from the black market for which, I know, he had to pay dearly; I let my schoolwork suffer; Mother did a lot of housework that I normally would have done. Even Stella, my sister, was very helpful with the various chores although she was only eight years old. How could I give up without a fight?

For the past year, I had a reasonably good fight record. About 80% were winning fights and 5% were draws. I was agile but not very muscular. My strengths were speed, good footwork and long arms that gave me an advantage in the jabbing range. During our last encounter with the Russian junior team, I had no difficulties in handling my opponent who also was a Kazakh; however my wins were always on points. I never had a knock out punch.

This time the situation was in many ways different and very serious. Since I did not have a powerful punch, a weight difference would give the opponent an even greater advantage in respect to power and would reduce my speed advantage. However, I was not about to throw the fight despite Father's strong urging to do so.

As I sat in my corner, I still wondered what would be the right thing to do. Obviously, this was not the best frame of mind to enter the ring with. The introduction went by in a flash; I quickly touched my opponent's gloves and went back to my corner. When the gong sounded, I moved quickly to the center of the ring and started circling my opponent clockwise, peppering him with rapid left jabs. He was very cautious, bobbing away from my aggressive pursuit. Attempts to get close to me were effectively thwarted by my jabs and the first round ended with both of us sparring for a more advantageous position.

The second round was more difficult. He got closer to me on several occasions and pummeled me with body punches particularly to the sides of my rib cage. By the end of this round, I felt his punches and started getting tired. I was grateful that ours was only a three round bout and hoped that in the third round I would be able to out-punch him and even possibly get ahead on points.

I started the round by moving in quickly, hoping to score an uppercut followed be a couple jabs to the chin. While the first part of the plan worked well, my uppercut wasn't strong enough to cause much damage. Unfortunately, while executing it, I dropped my left arm giving him an opening for a right cross to my left rib cage. This hurt and caught my breath. At this instance, I was able to fully appreciate his powerful punch.

An attempt to jab my way out of this position was unsuccessful. He caught me with a straight left to the face and I could hear the crunch in my nose. Blood was running freely down my face and in the back of my throat.

I figured that there must be at least thirty seconds, a long time under these circumstances, to the end of the round. I brought up both cloves to protect my face and my elbows towards the abdomen and let him punch. He found my flanks unprotected and I could feel the full strength of his muscles there. Finally the bell!

I was still on my feet and barely finding my way to the stool in the corner. At least he wasn't able to knock me out. This was my primary concern and I succeeded in staying on my feet.

That night, our club was devastated. Only the heavyweight, a prewar seasoned, Jewish boxer from Poland had an easy victory. He knocked out his opponent in the first round. The rest either lost or fought to a draw.

My nose grew to the size of a large pear. Bleeding stopped but the dull pain was getting worse. Mother was placing cold compresses on my face. This greatly relieved the symptoms. However, the question was whether to see a doctor. The doctors that my parents knew at the plant and who were frequent guests for meals in our house were apparently not to be trusted medically for any help. They were at the plant primarily to write *spravka* (statements) in support of an individual's medical disability, or to attest to one's inability to go to work. Diagnoses or surgeries of the nose were far from their abilities and interest; I refused to see a doctor and that terminated the issue.

The following day my nose was still very swollen and painful. Below both eyes there was a purplish-yellow discoloration. That evening, when my father returned from the meeting of the Polish club, he gave me a large envelope full of papers that I was to deliver to a member of the club. He lived off Furmanova Street, about ten or twelve blocks north of us.

Since it was still fairly cold, the spring was coming slowly that year; I put on my *fufajka* (a very warm, quilted jacket) and ran up the street to deliver the papers. I had no problems finding the address Sedova 22, Apartment 2. It was just around the corner of Furmanova. I knocked at the door and a short, slim man opened it. I introduced myself and handed him the envelope explaining that my father asked me to deliver it. He smiled and asked me in. The apartment consisted of one fairly large room where one corner was partitioned by a curtain. There was a large table in the center of the opposite wall, with two long benches on each side. A sewing machine unit was located under the other window. The room was very clean, the wooden floor being well scrubbed most likely with a knife. I was a knowledgeable specialist on these matters since it was my responsibility in our house to scrub the floor using a huge knife. I never was able to maintain it that clean.

A nice looking, middle aged, black haired and dark eyed lady came over and said, "Come in, visit with us." At the table on one of the benches sat a girl with legs curled under her, obviously doing her homework. She had golden hair, huge blue eyes and the most beautiful face I had ever seen. She got up and said, "I am Ania." I awkwardly introduced myself and glancing at the open textbook asked, "Are you studying trigonometry?" Yes, she said. "Then," I remarked, "You must be in the 10th grade. We are the boy's school partnered with Desiatiletka Number 31."

"I am in Desiatiletka Number 31," she said.

"Well, how come we never met?" I asked.

"I know many girls from your school. One of them, Ada, is a good friend of mine."

"I know Ada," Ania responded. "She is one year behind me, in the 9th grade."

"It looks that you are using the same trigonometry textbook as we do, maybe sometimes we can study together. I will come by next week in case you have some questions; I like trigonometry." Ania smiled.

"I don't have too many problems with math; however, sometimes it may be easier to do some of the problems together."

I turned to her parents. "You must be from Poland," I asked.

"Yes, from Radom," her father responded.

"We lived in Trzebinia before the war, this is a small town near Krakow," I said, moving towards the door. It was time to go, having probably overstayed my welcome, I thought. I really felt like talking some more with Ania. Nevertheless I could hear myself saying as I turned towards Ania, "It has been very nice to meet you, hope to see you soon.". She smiled, "Certainly, we must do our trigonometry problems together."

I wished everyone a good night and left. On the way home I couldn't forget the way she sat on the bench by the table with her legs curled under. The more I thought about her, the more I felt like I had seen her before. Suddenly it dawned on me. She was the girl that Mother's patient introduced me to at the opera choir rehearsal as my "future wife." She did look different at that time, wearing very fancy high heel shoes and her hair was combed high off her forehead, but she certainly was the same girl.

I probably had blocked out from my mind that entire brief accident. I didn't think at that time or now that it was a great joke. Her mother, Mrs. Schneider, on second thought also looked familiar.

Wasn't she the lady that Tolek and I helped when she slipped and fell during the *Voskresennik* we worked at in the miserable rain and mud in the mountains? I promised myself to ask her about it when I visited them the next time.

Soviet Offensive.

In early spring of 1944 the Soviets started a serious offensive and moved with vengeance into Byelorussia where they captured its capital, Minsk. In May, the Germans surrendered in Crimea. Everyone was elated but there was a serious shortage in the work force behind the front since most of the adult men and many women were in the army.

As the weather was turning warmer, our diet was again going from bad to worse. The season for rhubarb we picked in the mountains was over. In Alma Ata, we had no garden like in Kargaly, thus, no vegetables. None were available on the black market either. Matter of fact, there was essentially no food of any kind at the black market.

Still, the news from the front was good. Radio provided very encouraging information concerning the advances of the Red Army and the progress of the Allies. The economy, however, was getting even worse than it been up to now. The food shortage was becoming extremely acute. Last fall, there were not enough workers on the farms to harvest the fields. When the fall rains came, the wheat and corn were still not harvested and were severely damaged. When the frost came the potatoes were still in the ground and they froze. Matter of fact when one could get potatoes on the black market they were wet and semi-rotten.

There was a great deal of discontent among people in respect to the way that problem was managed by the Kolkhoz bureaucrats. Apparently, people in neighboring towns and villages were willing to come in and harvest the potatoes to salvage the crop from freezing.

However, they wanted to keep most of the harvest for themselves. The bureaucrats refused their help; they would rather see the potatoes freeze and rot. While this was probably not the major underlying cause of the famine, it certainly was a contributing factor and also it had contributed an important psychological factor leading to the unhappiness with the system.

Despite this deterioration of living conditions, we continued our routines. I was in school every day; there were no changes in my study habits with Tolek. Also, we still would go to the movies or the opera, occasionally the theater with Ada and with Tolek who would usually bring his girl, Rifka. We looked forward to these outings despite growling, empty stomachs.

We were fortunate that the school started to provide some food during the lunch hour, usually cabbage soup but sometimes a muffin also. This was a lifesaver.

At that time I met a boy, Petya, one year older, who lived across the street. He was an avid chess player and this brought us together. When not with Tolek I would be with Petya playing chess or talking. He was a Russian Jew, intelligent, with a quick, agile and critical mind. He was attending a trade school to become an electrician.

In the Soviet Union, schooling was a bit different from that in Eastern Europe. In Poland I attended public school that lasted seven years (seven grades) and was compulsory. It was free and under total government control. Those who wished to continue their education had to take an entrance examination to Gymnasium after the sixth grade and would start the secondary education at this point. There were public and private gymnasia. Getting into public gymnasium was difficult because the exams were very tough. After four years of gymnasium, one attended the Lyceum for two years. Here one could emphasize certain areas of study, for example languages or science.

After the Lyceum one could take a comprehensive examination, the *Matura*, which was an extensive set of tests lasting several weeks during the summer vacations. This examination was compulsory for students who wished to continue their studies at a university. High grades at this examination entitled the student to enter any university without having to take an entrance examination. Thus, in the Soviet Union the entire pre-university educational program lasted ten years, while in Poland twelve years.

In the Soviet Union, after the seventh year the student had to decide whether to continue with academic courses or attend a technical school. If the decision was a technical school, the student would switch to a trade school for three years. Thus, the educational time period was the same, ten years, for both educational avenues.

I was surprised when Petya elected to attend a trade school, but it was his desire to be an electrician and work at a large electrical plant. This could have been a psychological response based on the desire to fully be a proletarian.

After we became very friendly I learned that he was also involved with gangs. Matter of fact he was a leader of a large gang in our neighborhood. Sometimes, Tolek and I would invite him to attend an opera or theater with us. He was more inclined to the theater and movies than to the opera. We not only liked his company but also felt secure having him with us when returning home late in the night. His gang was well known and respected by the other gangs and we were certain that this connection could serve as protection for us when the appropriate time would come. I would be faced with this issue on several occasions.

I soon found myself drawn to Ania's apartment. We indeed started doing trigonometry, at least once every couple of weeks together. But we did not go to parties or to the theater. Ada was still my girl. With Ania it was a matter of me assisting her with math, at least that what I thought. One evening, when I was coming to visit her, a tall, blond and handsome boy about my age stopped me at the entrance to the courtyard. "Are you here to visit Ania?" he asked. "Yes," I replied. "Well, don't," he said. "To make my advice to you stick, let me provide you with a constant reminder." Suddenly he punched me in the face. I was taken aback, but my boxer's instincts made me respond with a right hook to his face. This however, turned out to be an inadequate response because at that instant two Russian boys materialized behind me pinned my arms back and my assailant was free to work on my face at leisure.

"Let this be a constant remainder for you to keep away from this address, to never come back and to never see Ania again," he kept on saying, while hitting me over and over until I sank to the ground.

I was in no shape to visit Ania and I left. Instead of going home however, I went to see Petya. He was busy playing chess with himself. He was a real chess addict; any free moment he could find was filled with chess. He actually could play chess in his mind and keep the positions crystal clear so that at any moment he could recreate the game on a chess board and take off from there. When I walked in he instantly set up, moved to the board, set up the chess and invited me to take over the whites. He said, “At this moment the whites are in a much better strategic position. See what you can do with them. Who knows, you may even win!”

As he said it a broad grin brightened his face. I was in no mood for chess and I grunted. He looked up at me and his broad grin broadened even further. “Well, well, what do we have here? I thought that boxing was over until fall.” He said, as he started shaking with laughter. I was not amused and was almost ready to leave when common sense took over and I told him what happened. By the time I finished my brief account of the episode, he was totally beside himself with laughter. I got very angry and started punching him but he restrained my arms and said, “Emil, I am really sorry for what has happened to you and very sorry for my laughter. But your description of the fight and the sorry look on your face was so funny that I could not keep myself from laughing, forgive me.”

He went on: “Let’s take a look at this situation carefully. Obviously we cannot allow this fellow to push us around. Furthermore, he has to repay us for beating you up with the help of his cronies. First, let me find out what are his connections, particularly whether he is involved with a gang, if so which gang and how strong it is. We may have to contact your school buddy, Ivan Abossobayev, the son of the chief guy in Kazakhstan. He has the largest and the strongest gang around. Let’s take our time and do it carefully.”

I broke in, “what do you have in mind?” He responded with the usual smile on his face. “Well, we can not let him push our friends around and prevent them from visiting Anitchka.”

“Do you think we should respond with violence?” I asked.

“There is no way around it, particularly if we are dealing with a gang. They may hurt you badly, even permanently,” he responded, this time with a serious look on his face.

I said, “Do find out about the boy and in the meanwhile I will talk to Vania. Now, lets go back to chess and finish the game you started. I am not particularly eager to go home right now, particularly since I will have to explain the state of my face. Although I think that by now, Mother is accustomed to seeing all types of damage to my face.” At this point, we turned our attention to the chess.

While our family, because of Mother’s dental work and Leon’s connections, was partly protected from the economic disaster resulting in chronic starvation, the rest of the city did not fare as well. In the mornings, dead bodies, that accumulated during the night on the roadways, where removed by horse pulled wagons. To this day I do not understand why this mode of transportation, rather than trucks, was used.

Our life style continued unchanged. I was in school, also busy at home, being partly responsible for keeping the house clean, preparing most of the meals as well as going on the black market to sell or barter the oil supplied by Uncle Leon. Mother was very busy with her dental work from early morning until late afternoon and Father worked all day at the factory. Uncle Leon continued in charge of the transportation department and continued dealing heavily in various enterprises related to the interactions between their factory and other plants.

My school and personal life continued with its usual adventures. The episode with the blond fellow who had attacked me when I tried to visit Ania was dealt with rather quickly. Petya learned that he was a part of a small gang. Ivan's and Petya's gangs contacted the leader of that gang, suggested that an apology should be extended to me and that this fellow should simply forget about Ania and totally stop being involved with her life. I continued to visit Ania occasionally as if nothing has happened and was not molested in any form or fashion ever again.

The spring in Alma Ata was beautiful. Once the snows melted the trees turned slowly green and flowers, wild yellow tulips covered the foot hills of the towering, snow capped Ala Tau Mountains. The school year was to end soon. There were many school parties to celebrate the end of the school year. There was essentially no food at the parties but considerable amount of vodka. Why vodka was available for a rather small price while food was essentially impossible to get, was a mystery to me.

News from all of the fronts was good. That resulted in an upbeat frame of mind for the graduation from the 9th grade. I was ready for the summer. The weather was glorious, when not busy on the *Toltchok* or at home I did spent great deal of time with Ada or with Tolek.

Hunger and forced labor at the *Trudovaia Armia* or *Voskresennik* were still major problems, particularly since there was no school and they tried to take maximum time from us. Usually a weekend day and one or two afternoons a week satisfied their requirements. We also spent considerable time listening to the radio and discussing in great detail the news, particularly the military achievements of the Red Army.

The war was moving rapidly and the fronts were changing daily. All the Soviet Armies were on the offensive. The Allies were also very successful; they moved rapidly up the Italian peninsula and entered Rome in early June. This was followed by the opening of the second front in Europe--the invasion at Normandy. By the end of June the Soviets commenced a serious summer offensive resulting in the recapture of Minsk in Byelorussia and a rapid movement of the armies towards the west, towards Poland.

The black market business had improved markedly and it was not a major job for me to take care of all the bartering in a couple hours in the morning, leaving considerable time for other activities. While I still spent time with Ada and Tolek, I found myself more and more in the company of Ania. Our conversations, however, were usually quite serious and at a "higher plane." Was it because she was from Poland and Jewish or was it because she was quite different? I couldn't tell. I knew, however, that I enjoyed her company.

Nevertheless, Ada was my girl. We went for long walks in the hills, swam in the river, went dancing and kissed a lot. I wasn't about to leave her for no one.

Although, the school was closed for the summer we had to attend military classes, which consisted primarily of several physical fitness sessions and classes in military preparedness each week. In addition, we had to participate, twice weekly, in the Labor Army (*Trudovaia Armia*) activities. The Labor Army was a paramilitary organization that consisted of individuals who were not mobilized to the regular army because of health reasons or political "instability."

The *Trudovaia Armia* units were deployed just behind the front to perform various, primarily menial, tasks (digging trenches, construction work, etc). Also, students, university staff and other citizens could be assigned, part time (usually on weekends) when off regular work, to participate in the activities of these units throughout the country.

During the vacation time, after cleaning the house, dealing with the black market and doing the cooking, I still had considerable time left to do things with friends. There was a mountain stream, the Little Almaatinka, running through the City Park, where I spent a great amount of time with Ada. She loved the water. After a swim, we would hike into the hills, a great way of spending time.

On weekends there was a band playing in the park and there was a dance floor outdoors. Dancing was a real favorite activity for us. We usually would show up with a group of friends, Lapschin, Abossobayev, Tolek and a group of girls. Ivan Abossobayev, or Vania, as we called him, always showed up with their formal gang.

One particular night I was very happy that he used this precaution. As I was dancing with Ada, a hooligan came over accompanied by a group of friends, took Ada by hand and as he pulled her away from me he screamed, "no 'rzyd' (a derogatory term for a Jew) will dance with a nice Russian girl. I will paint your face so you will never forget this." To "paint" one's face was street jargon that meant to slice an opponent's face in several directions using a straight razor.

As he started the job and I felt the blade cutting into my nose, Ivan materialized with a group of his gang members. He apparently noted the encounter from distance and came running to prevent serious damage. The hooligan and his friends recognized Ivan's gang and instantly lost all interest in me.

In the meantime, blood was running down my face. The cut has opened the tip of my nose. However, there were no emergency rooms in the city to take care of such an injury. Few stitches would have been in order to close the wound. Since the wound wasn't closed, it did not heal well and I still have a scar on the tip of my nose.

****

The legal arm and the police organizations were not particularly interested in individual's safety; robberies and attacks on private individuals were common. That was why we needed gangs to protect us; otherwise, when it turned dark, it was dangerous to be any place but home.

It is of interest to observe that the state policy was to fight anti-Semitism; actually one could be indicted on felony charges for anti-Semitic activities. Nevertheless, there was a tremendous amount of grass roots anti-Semitism. Its origin is of interest since it presented frequently in a schizophrenic fashion. Most Russians who had contact with Jews commonly had at least one "good" Jew as a personal friend. Since some Jews were in the higher echelons of governmental hierarchy or on the upper rungs of industrial and trade bureaucracy, some Russians wished good relationships with them mostly for personal gains. Others, however felt especially hostile towards the Jews. Unquestionably, the proportion of Jews in high positions was higher than their numerical ratio to the general population.

The civilian law enforcement agencies and governmental agencies controlled to a great extend most of the overt anti-Semitic activities. The occult anti-Semitism, however, couldn't be controlled and it had surfaced violently later in the 20th and early 21st centuries, after the disintegration of the Soviet system. This suggests that the tolerance towards Jews during the "Jew-friendly" periods of time, during Soviet era, was based on the policies of the various law enforcement agencies at a given time period.

Tolek and Petya, my friend from across the street, were Jewish but all of my other friends were not. I, however, didn't feel that they had any anti-Semitic feelings in them. Matter of fact I don't believe that it ever occurred to them to consciously think about this issue. Nevertheless, anti-Semitism was real in Alma Ata, probably in the entire Soviet Union, and one had to be watchful.

In July, Igor and I visited with his father, Professor Litvinov, in his laboratory when he pulled out a July copy of *Pravda*, a leading Moscow newspaper, and showed us an article describing the liberation of Majdanek. At this time my friends, my relatives and I heard and knew very little of organized atrocities committed by Germans against the Jews. Back in 1939, while still in Lwow and shortly after Leon returned from the illegal venture to western Poland, there was considerable talk about Leon's reluctant attempts to convey the dire situation in Poland in the winter of 1939. His descriptions of Jews being shot in Trzebinia and children being killed by swinging them against a corner of a building were difficult to understand and accept as actions of people of a highly civilized country, Germany.

In the past three years, we had heard of the atrocities committed by the German soldiers against the Russian population. This was a substantial portion of the news all the time. However, we considered a great deal of this information to be Soviet propaganda. This article however, was blood curling. It described the liberation of a first "Death Camp." It talked about murder of tens of thousands of people using gas and then burning the bodies. It talked about total destruction of a group of people, the Jews. When I brought this article home and showed it to my family, there was total disbelief. There appeared to be a denial mechanism in effect. No one was able to accept this as a fact. Information obtained later clearly had shown that while this piece of news was true, there was also a great deal of news being managed from a political point of view. For example, the Polish Home Army uprising in August 1944 against the Nazis in Warsaw was not even reported. Matter of fact, the Soviet Army was close to Warsaw at that time, but no attempt was made to press the offense in order to relieve the Polish fighters in Warsaw. Warsaw was not liberated until January 1945. In Alma Ata, however, we were not aware of any of these happenings at the time.

The summer turned into fall. Tolek and I were busy with the studies in the tenth grade. We were happy that this was the final effort before graduation from secondary school. Tolek and I were doing quite well in school and this gave us a great deal of incentive to give it the last push in order to graduate with high grades.

The military situation clearly suggested that the Soviets and the Allies were winning the war and now it would only be a matter of time before the total victory. Uncle Leon "organized" a huge map that we hung on the wall and on it followed, in great detail, the advances of all the armies. The radio was quite exuberant and detailed when describing the military progress.

The weather of 1944 was turning cold signaling that the winter was coming. Uncle Leon made arrangements with a company that supplied Saksaul, for a large load of it to be delivered to us, obviously under a substantial barter agreement, "po blatu." Saksaul was the best wood for heating the house in winter. It burned almost like coal providing long burning coals and very high caloric mode of combustion. It was a highly desirable fuel. I asked Uncle Leon if we could provide Ania's parents with some of it in light of the rough winter that was developing. He smiled in his inimitable way and in a knowledgeable tone of voice asked, "What is this sudden interest in their well being? Could this have any thing to do with Ania?" I had no ready answer. I actually was not sure in my own mind why this sudden interest. Was it an honest attempt to help this family or was it a self-serving interest to ingratiate myself with Ania? I decided that there was no need to decide at this moment on my motivation. The question was whether Leon would do it. He again turned to me with an inscrutable smile on his face and said, "Let me see Ania's father, possibly we can do some business." I didn't respond, but I was eager to learn what business Uncle had in mind.

The winter break at school had come and we had time to go skiing. Since I was on the skiing team at school and like last year I again had access to school skis, arrangement was perfect.

I still had been seeing Ada but was spending more and more time with Ania. For whatever reason trigonometry became my obsession! One evening Tolek, Ania and I went to the theater. After the performance, on the way home, trudging through deep snow, the conversation touched upon skiing. I asked Ania whether she skied and whether she liked it. There was a slightly hesitant answer on her part, "I certainly ski and I love it." I pursued the issue inquiring whether she may like to go skiing the next weekend.

There was again a slight hesitation, but she did answer, "I'd love to go but I do not own skis and as you know one cannot rent them." This was music to my ears. "No problem," I heard myself saying, "I will get the skis for you, when would you like to go?" Again there was some hesitation in her answer but finally she asked, "How will Thursday morning suit you?"

I was delirious with expectations, "certainly, we will pick you up at eight o'clock." Words continued to tumble from my mouth. I couldn't stop talking, I was so very excited. I couldn't wait to go skiing with her, after all I was a pretty good skier and I wanted very much to show off. That night, on the way home, I thought about what happened and realized that I had behaved like a fool. I couldn't comprehend what had happened. Why was I this happy? Ada and I skied together a great deal, skiing with a girl was not a special event for me. There was no answer to this feeling. I know that I was counting hours to our venture on skis.

The very next morning I pulled Tolek out from his bed and together we went to school to check out the skis. We got our usual pairs picked out and very carefully selected a shorter pair for Ania.

We waxed them thoroughly and I still remember the loving care I lavished on her skis. I arranged for taking the skis home although we still had two days before our ski venture. I was very anxious and made sure that nothing would happen to the skis before Thursday.

Thursday arrived after heavy snow had fallen the night before, leaving the streets covered with fresh powder snow. It was very cold but the morning was cloudless. Tolek showed up at my house about eight o'clock and we set out to pick up Ania.

She was ready and waiting for us. She looked absolutely gorgeous. She wore a pair of black pants, high black boots, a black jacket with a beautiful light gray fur trim and a fur collar and a gray fur hat. I didn't realize that in the squalor we lived in anything this beautiful could exist. I looked at Tolek, Tolek looked at me and we were speechless. I felt quite embarrassed looking at my worn out *valenky*, a patched pair of old pants, a ripped and patched *fufajka* (a cotton quilt jacket), and a woolen military hat with earflaps. I certainly looked like a bum, particularly when compared to her outfit. I couldn't resist complimenting her and at the same time inquiring: "Where did you get this incredible outfit?" She responded in a matter of fact fashion, "my father is a tailor and a furrier, he was able to get some fabric and fur and he has made it for me."

Both Tolek and I were impressed and quietly went on towards the park. I carried Ania skis for her and we all were bantering about all and nothing. The park bordered some open fields that led to the foothills. We put on the skis in the park and trudged slowly through the deep powder towards the foothills.

I glanced at Ania who was ahead of me and wondered how this excursion would play out. According to the way she held herself on the skis, she obviously couldn't be an experienced skier. However, I was quite certain that she could ski reasonably well; at least, she did indicate this to me in a way.

As we traversed the park and moved into the fields, it became more and more apparent that Ania was having some difficulties walking on skis in this deep powder snow. She persevered, however, and kept on walking and did not fall even once. Although full of misgivings I exchanged a glance with Tolek and kept on going. Soon we reached an *aryk* (an irrigation ditch) that ran at the edge of the hills. It was empty at this time of year, partly filled with snow. I skied into it and the speed of the descent brought me up on the other side of the ditch. I hollered to Tolek to follow me in order to pack the snow a little to make it easier for Ania to execute this maneuver.

Tolek went down into the ditch and showed up on the other side with ease. Ania stood there a bit as if contemplating what to do and then suddenly let loose and came down into the ditch head first into the snow. Tolek and I skied quickly down into the ditch, first examining the skis, since it would have been a disaster if they broke, and then started laughing at Ania.

Her face was covered with snow, her boots came out of the primitive ski bindings, and she was waste deep in the snow and she kept on laughing. We couldn't stop her! Slowly she quieted a bit down but then we started laughing and couldn't stop. Soon, there were all three of us, waist deep in snow, roaring with laughter.

Later that afternoon, all three of us were sitting in Tolek's house. His mother made some tea but there was nothing to eat. Nevertheless we were having a great time drinking hot tea and reliving our skiing adventure, as I called it, our ski trip with Ania.

Well, the obvious truth came out, Ania did not know how to ski. This was her first time on skis! She wanted very much to come skiing with us but was afraid that if she would have indicated that she didn't know how to ski, we wouldn't have considered taking her with us.

We kidded her mercilessly; she took it like a trooper. I kept looking at her intently most of the time that evening. When I took her home, I put my arm around her and we just walked. I made myself a promise that I would have to do something about Ada.

February 1945 was an eventful month. Roosevelt and Churchill met with *batiushka* Stalin in Yalta. The radio and papers were full of the political activities in Crimea. Yalta was in all headlines. According to the press, *Tovaristch* Stalin was flying high while the capitalist leaders from Europe and America had to cave in to him. The Red Army was victorious, moving inexorably in its conquest of Eastern Europe. At the conference, the World Leaders proposed the establishment of a World Government, to be called United Nations.

A Declaration of Liberated Europe was accepted. Free Poland was established. The dismemberment of Germany was worked out in details. It was agreed that Germany should pay reparations. Also, numerous policies were hammered out concerning Japan, Asia, Africa and various parts of Europe. The analysts had a hay day trying to integrate the capitalist ideas into a palatable communist tapestry.

We were extremely excited. It felt as if the war was indeed coming to an end. If so what was to happen to us? There were numerous discussions among my parents, uncles and their friends. The paramount question on everybody's mind was whether the Soviets would let us go back to Poland or possibly give us the permission to emigrate and if so, how and where? Furthermore, will anyone have us?

After the big splash in the radio and newspapers concerning Majdanek, things quieted down. There were, however, rumors concerning liberation of other concentration camps. Shortly after the liberation of Warsaw in January, there was a rumor that the Soviets entered an even larger and more horrible death camp in the little town of Oswiecim in southwestern Poland. The town's German name was Auschwitz. This news was of personal interest to us but of no impact on the Soviet population. However, little was said about it and there were other, more important issues to deal with at that time.

The spring was again here. The weather was turning warm and there was more food than ever before. We still were hungry, but the black market was getting "fatter." One could actually buy several kinds of meat for an appropriate number of Rubles!

Since Mother and Leon were dealing with arrangements related to procurement of food, our situation was much rosier than it had been in the past two years. We were even able to procure some sugar. However, as the actual end of the war in Europe was getting closer, our anxieties were getting more severe. On April 21, the radio was full of news related to the fact that the Red Army reached Berlin.

There was a great debate in our family concerning the question: Would the Allies or our Army occupy Berlin? Well, we did and the Germans officially surrendered on May 7. The "Victory in Europe Day" (V-E Day) was proclaimed on May 8. We were in the mood to celebrate, but the emotions were subdued. Everyone was simply exhausted and hungry.

The war in the Pacific still wasn't over. The Americans, however, were on a great offensive and all the predictions suggested that this war would also be coming to an end soon.

While our personal living conditions improved, there was no improvement in the availability of food for the average worker. By the end of the war, the general living conditions actually deteriorated further. This should not have been a major surprise in light of the facts that even before the war, as we had experienced ourselves, the standard of living was quite poor, actually very low. We all felt that it may take quite some time before the living conditions would improve.

The Medical School

Tolek and I completed the *Desiatiletka* (High School) at the "ripe" age of sixteen with flying colors. This gave us the privilege to attend any university without having to pass entrance examinations. Tolek was thinking of medicine, while I was strongly considering physics, possibly under the influence of Igor whose father was a famous physicist working on fundamental problems dealing with splitting the atom. Igor was all set to enter the university to study physics. We spent a considerable amount of time in Dr. Litvinov's laboratory; the problems in the field of physics fascinated me. However, both of my parents were devastated by the idea of me pursuing studies in the field of physics. They felt strongly that I should become a dentist. They kept on trying to convince me to do so by bringing up current examples. Indeed if my parents, particularly my mother, would not have been a dentist, I had to admit that in Nuzy Yary we might have perished from starvation; even now her profession permitted at least some food to be on our table.

The discussions dealing with this issue became constant and very heated. I could see their point but the lure of physics had a very strong hold on me. Igor's mother was a Professor of Chemistry at the medical school. I talked to her frequently about my problem related to the difficulties in convincing my parents to let me study physics and concerning their fixation on dentistry. One day, with a conspirational smile on her face, she said: "I have a suggestion. How about medicine? You could study medicine to become a physician but then you could enter the field of research and have the same fun doing basic research in one of the biomedical fields as you would in physics." "Well," I responded, "this sounds interesting." I turned to my friend, Igor, "what do you say to this suggestion?" Igor just laughed. "You," he said continuing in his merriment, "will probably be unable to do much of anything but research, and however, you may indeed enjoy doing it in a biomedical discipline."

The next day I ran to see Tolek and tell him what Dr. Litvinov suggested. He was elated since it was his plan to enter medical school that year. "Well," he said, "we may continue to be classmates. This begins to sound better and better." We went to our house and I couldn't wait to talk to my parents. Father was at work but Mother was home seeing patients. I interrupted her bursting with excitement and brought up the idea of medicine. She immediately responded: "why didn't I think about this possibility when you so violently objected to study dentistry? Obviously medicine is great, and we will open an office for you and help you to establish a great practice. I can't wait to tell Father about your suggestion." She continued all excited. I also began to feel excited about this possibility. Tolek's mother was also very pleased with this possibility, hoping that Tolek and I would remain classmates and continue to study together.

I went to the University and applied for admission to the Medical Faculty (Medical School). While there I saw Igor's mother, Dr. Litvinov, and she had a huge smile on her face. "I will be seeing you in September. Get ready for some heavy studying, I will be very happy to see you and start the course work with you," she said. "Yes, Dr. Litvinov," I responded and thought to myself that it be great to have a good friend on the faculty in a new establishment.

While I was arranging for the admission to the University, history was being made. On August 6, the Americans dropped an atom bomb on Hiroshima in Japan. This was not broadcasted on the radio. But, the invasion of Manchuria by the Soviet Army and declaration of war on Japan was. Actually Father was the first to hear this news, and he came running incensed. "How do they dare to act this cowardly? Now that America has Japan on the ropes, the great Soviet Union declares a war against Japan and invades them?" This was pure politics to get in on the action and get a piece of Japan after America defeated them.

The Soviets were obviously concerned that unless they start moving against Japan rapidly, an American victory may prevent them from getting a piece of the pie. On August 9, the second atom bomb was dropped on Japan, and the city of Nagasaki was destroyed; on September 2, the Japanese signed a surrender agreement.

Soon I learned that I was admitted to the University, and so was Tolek. We were enjoying the last few weeks of freedom before the rigors of medical school. I was busy engaged in the various chores at home as well as spending time with Tolek, his friend Rifka and going places with Ada.

One evening Ada and I went to the opera where, as usual, we had great time. Ada was a positive influence on me in respect of appreciation of the opera- particularly since I already had the love for music, having seriously played the violin. She had a connection to the opera because of her older sister, Swetlana, who was a music student at the University studying voice. Swetlana had been performing in the opera for the past couple of years. Whenever Ada and I went to the opera, a rather frequent occurrence, this gave us the opportunity to get backstage, meet some of the performers and feel like a part of the action. On that night, we heard the premiere performance of the opera Chio Chio San, in the western world titled Madam Butterfly. This Puccini opera is a glance at a romantic interlude in China between a American Naval officer, Pinkerton, and a 15-year-old Chinese girl that, after having to give him up because of social and racial issues, commits hara-kiri.

Soviet Officialdom loved and backed this opera because, in their opinions, it exposed the discriminatory beliefs of the bourgeoisie society. Matter of fact, in classes on Marxism and Leninism in school, this opera was discussed as an example of class struggle between Marxism and Bourgeoisie society.

Nevertheless, during the performance of the opera our stomachs growled, I thought, louder than the orchestra, but the music was divine.

After taking Ada home, I slipped off the suit jacket and started on the way home, running as fast as I could. This was the only suit I owned. It was a gift from Uncle Leon who purchased it on the black market. The steel gray color of the suit looked beautiful on me, I loved it.

As I ran through the dark and empty streets, I realized how scared I was. But I had only a couple of blocks before reaching the house and the sensation of fear was nothing new. I was only a block away from the house. I could almost see its outline, when I tripped. As I was landing on the asphalt, I saw the foot that made me stumble and fall. A hand grabbed my suit jacket and a voice whispered, "Now, quietly take off your pants and hand them to me."

My heart stopped. I was petrified; not in fear for my life but in anticipation of the embarrassment following a scorning laugh of my uncle that I could already hear in my head. I could also hear the mocking question and the huge grin on his face. "Should we go to the *Toltchock* and get you another suit?" I knew that it would be financially a devastating setback. I could not face this happening.

Slowly I got up on my knees, and stood up. He was next to me holding a short club poised at my shoulder. While reaching at the waistband to start taking off my pants, I looked into his eyes. In the meager light of a single street lamp, I saw a set of cold blue irises with a twinkle of laughter in them. The guy was having fun with me; I was a good pick, a new suit, but also someone to make fun of while robbing him.

This sent my blood boiling. I turned slightly to the right, as if embarrassed to drop my pants in front of him, and at that moment grabbed the handle of my knife which always rested on my belt in a leather sheet on the inside of my pants. As he lifted his right arm to hit me with the club, I plunged the knife in the left side of his chest. He grunted and went limp. I pulled the knife out, grabbed my jacket from his hand and ran. It took me only a few minutes to get home. I closed the door and collapsed.

Mother and Father were awake. Leon wasn't home. I told them what happened and Mother almost fainted; Father, however, simply said, "let's wash the knife and put it with the other knifes in the drawer. Nothing happened, you came from the opera and read a book. We know nothing of any robbery or any knifing. Go to sleep."

So I did. Next morning I got up early and went back to the corner where I was attacked. There were a couple small blood smudges and a trail of dry blood droplets. He, most likely, must have fallen down and not gotten up before I disappeared in my house. I never learned what ultimately happened to him.

Return West

We, our family and acquaintances from Poland were in turmoil, the Polish club held almost daily meetings. Father had been attending all the discussions and was very actively involved. The big question was: "What will be happening to us?." Now that the victory is here, will we be able to leave the Soviet Union? If so under what conditions? And to what country? And when? My personal life was further complicated by the fact that I was on the verge of matriculating at the University and I wouldn't like to leave in the middle of the year or semester and face again a serious interruption in my schooling.

These concerns ultimately turned out to be mere details since in Soviet Russia the government was not worried about such issues. One couldn't simply plan, buy a ticket and go! In August we were called by the NKVD, interrogated and made to understand that it was possible to become a Soviet citizen and stay in Kazakhstan, or possibly in the Russian Republic. But if we wished to return to Poland it will be difficult and time consuming. We had numerous discussions within the family and with friends from the West, mostly Poland. One thing became crystal clear: we wanted to leave Soviet Russia the fastest possible way and this appeared to be possible only by going back to Poland.

Tolek and I were excited to start our studies at the University; we were looking with great anticipation towards the new experiences. On the first day, we were taken to a large classroom. The schedule of classes was written on a huge blackboard. We were directed to copy it in a great detail. This schedule was to run our lives for the next semester, until the New Year. Unfortunately, there was a serious shortage of writing paper; the school provided no typed schedules or any typed material dealing with the subjects and our classes. The students had to copy the information from the blackboard to whatever type of paper we could scrounge.

Again I was very fortunate. Uncle Leon got me several notebooks and a new fancy fountain pen. I shared the notebooks with Tolek and enjoyed the obviously envious glances from the other students who noted our notebooks and noted with great envy my fancy fountain pen. I think that this was the first fountain pen many of them had ever seen.

The first semester classes included anatomy, histology, inorganic chemistry and.... Marxism-Leninism! It became quite clear that the emphasis was to be placed on the subject of gross anatomy. This subject was to be thought throughout the first four semesters and was to include two daily one-hour lectures and a four-hour session in the dissection rooms. There we started our activities by learning how to handle the technical aspects of anatomical dissections of real human cadavers (human bodies preserved in formalin). Great deal of time was devoted in making us into good prosectors (individuals trained in the art and science of dissecting appropriately a human cadaver). There were six students assigned to each cadaver. The first of the four hours was devoted to a didactic discussion of the dissection techniques, procedures and issues we were expected to encounter during a specific dissection session.

The cadavers were well preserved at this point by having been injected with and then soaked for several months in a solution of formaldehyde. They were wrapped in white thin cotton sheets and kept in copper boxes on top of tables. The boxes had hinged upper covers that we could open and remove the cadaver. Then, we would close the hinged top, place the cadaver on top of the box and proceed with the dissections.

Every day after completing our work we would wrap the cadaver with the formalin soaked sheets. For the weekend or for vacations we would return the cadaver into the copper box and add some more formalin. Unquestionably, just the logistics of these procedures were complex, unpleasant and time-consuming.

Finally, the day came of our first dissection. Everyone was waiting impatiently for this moment. The prosector demonstrated the initial steps. With a grease pencil, he outlined on the skin of the cadaver lines where the skin incisions were to be made and showed which incisions were to be completed today. Subsequently he showed us how to dissect the skin away from the muscles, leaving all the underlying blood vessels and nerves intact. Then he pointed out that with the help of the anatomical atlases we should be able to identify and properly label each of these dissected structures. We were to start our work by dissecting the hand.

While being indoctrinated in the intricacies of anatomical dissections, we were also informed that the first part of gross anatomy is actually osteology, the study and the knowledge of the bony skeleton. Thus, in addition to learning the techniques of dissections, the minutia of arteries and nerves with their milliard of strange names, we also had to learn not just all the bones in the human body but the most miniscule bumps, indentation or holes in each. One of the skull bones, for example the sphenoid bone, had docents of holes, protrusions, spines etc., each with a foreign (Latin) tongue-twisting name. We would usually get done with the dissections by 5-6 PM, but then we would fetch our bone boxes and keep at it, boning up on osteology. We didn't have any hope to eat until 7-8 o'clock in the evening..

During the very first week in the Medical School, I noted Ania in the lecture hall. This was a pleasant surprise. I waved to her and she waved back visibly happy to meet someone she knew. After the lecture, Tolek and I went over to her and she was really glad to see both of us. "Its great," she said as we got together, "not only I will have company to study with, but you, Emil, live on my way home. I hope that I will be able to walk with you home. Often we finish late and I hate to walk home alone."

This was music to my ears. Ever since I started my university studies, things with Ada were cooling off. I usually spent all day at the Medical School, frequent evenings also. This left me very little time to socialize, particularly since Sundays were also spent usually in the school or on *Voskresennik*. Ania was a very bright and beautiful girl. I realized that I might indeed enjoy walking home with her and to study not only with Tolek but with her also. I recalled the feelings I had when being with her before.

That evening, all three of us walked home together. After walking about a kilometer, Tolek turned off towards his home. Ania and I continued. She lived only 5 blocks beyond our "house" (the converted soda kiosk), down Furmanova Street. From this time on, I almost always walked her home from the University. It quickly evolved from courtesy to pleasure.

Many times we were so engrossed in discussions that I would totally forget the fact that I was only to walk her home. Instead, we would go to the park, to hers or to my house and just kept on talking.

Soon I became almost a fixture in her house, and she a very frequent guest in ours.

The intensive schedule of our studies and the discussions related to our fate in Soviet Russia made the time fly and left us with very little time to ourselves, specifically to the development of personal involvement. We were just good friends. But as the winter progressed, we became more and more involved with each other. We would attend the opera, go to theaters, movies and concerts. Sometimes we would go to dances, but that usually with a group of friends.

Ania still had some boys that she liked to spend time with. At first I didn't object but gradually I started getting jealous. The reason for this jealousy, however, remained unclear. We, after all, were only good friends. Or, was that all? I wondered.

At this time, a store opened in the city that carried luxurious cakes and chocolates. It was the only store of its kind in the city. It existed in parallel to severe famine that still persisted despite the fact that war was over. One couldn't get bread in a government store for a reasonable price without coupons; one had to buy it on the black market at an exorbitant price. And here was a government store selling such delicacies.

Soon it became clear how this could exist. The government was selling these goods at prices that were as high as or higher than prices on the *Toltchok*. Since I had some extra money garnished from my black market dealings in edible oil, I was eying this store with great interest. The chocolates were the primary targets of my temptations. I had not had chocolate since we left Lwow.

Soon I also learned that the little two-inch squares, wrapped in silver foil with a red star on it, called "Moscovskaia Krasnaia Zwiezda," was an absolute paradise. Each would cost me almost the equivalent of an entire week of profits from my sales of oil on the black market. However, the temptation was too great; finally I gave in and bought one "Moscovskaia Krasnaia Zwiezda." I was not disappointed. Indeed the chocolate was a paradise on this earth. I divided the candy into four pieces and had a piece once a week for the subsequent four weeks.

As I was luxuriating in my candy paradise, the relationship with Ania was becoming closer and I started thinking about a surprise, a gift of these candies to her. I became obsessed with this idea. But, I felt that I should get her two pieces and this would cost me a fortune! After a great deal of deliberation, I decided to do it.

It was a beautiful evening; all three of us were on the way home from the School. Tolek turned off to go directly to his house. I continued with Ania. The streets were already clear of snow and one could feel the spring in the air.

I took out the two pieces of candy from my pocket and handed them to Ania. She looked at me with her huge blue eyes and a beautiful smile blossomed on her lips. "This can't be for me," she whispered. "I know these candies, I visited this store many times since it opened, I fantasized about getting one but obviously we couldn't afford it." She turned to the side and continued: "I can't accept this." I put my arm on her shoulder and implored, "but I want you to have it, I bought it for you, I want you to enjoy it." She looked at me again and said, "OK, but we will eat them together a small piece at a time." I was elated; I placed my hands on her shoulders and gave her a squeeze. Something warm went through my entire body and I dropped my arms quickly. After arriving to her house, I said goodbye quickly and I ran home.

As time went by, the family discussions became more heated. Father encouraged Leon to discuss our emigration problems with the director of the factory and pressed Mother to bring it up with some of her patients who had influence at the local NKVD office.

The issue was obvious, how to get out from Alma Ata? Was it possible to go directly abroad and if not, at least, back to Poland? The war was over and there were thousands of people who had these ideas. At this time, no one knew which way to turn. We couldn't simply buy a ticket at the railroad and go back to Poland. We needed appropriate documents for leaving the country, but also even buying a train ticket for travel between cities in the Soviet Union required NKVD permission.

Finally we learned that the NKVD established an office that processed requests for repatriation of people like us back to Poland. Father found out through the Polish club many more details and we all applied for this exit permit. The NKVD office provided no information concerning the timetable, the dates or the chances of our getting the permits.

Tolek's mother and Ania's parents also applied for the permits. We all were placed into a "waiting mode," hoping for quick results. As time went on I spent a greater amount of time with Ania. All three of us, Tolek, Ania and I, walked to and from school together, studied together and frequently went to the opera, the movies and the theater together. I noted, however, that as time went on, I tended to spend more time alone with Ania. We never talked about each other or about our feelings; the usual topics of discussion dealt with medical studies, literature or sometimes, politics. The latter, however, usually related to our chances of getting out of the Soviet Union and our fantasies about what will happen once we get out.

One evening, on the way home, I became somewhat romantic and began to fantasize about my ultimate plans to go to America. This was something I never talked about with Ania. We were not sufficiently close to be discussing our future plans particularly since the plans were pure imagination. Nevertheless, I realized that as I thought and talked about the future, subconsciously I have been including Ania into the scenarios.

That prompted me to ask her that evening if she thought that we would get together once we got to Poland. She turned her head towards me and I could see her huge beautiful eyes looking deeply into mine and I could here a whisper, "I really hope so." My heart skipped a beat. My tongue stopped responding. I felt paralyzed. The only thing I could do was hold her hand very, very tight as we walked briskly towards her house. When we reached her door I said "Good night," turned on the heel and ran home.

That night I couldn't fall asleep. Ania was always a good friend, a friend with whom I had a good time, a friend I could depend on, simply a friend. However, the feeling I had tonight was different. As we talked about getting back to Poland and discussed the ways we could find each other in Poland made me feel very uneasy. I realized that if we don't travel back together, we might have difficulties finding each other.

Then I realized that we might actually not be able to find each other. That made me cold all over. I sensed that I might not be able to go on not being able to talk to her, to study with her, to simply be with her. This was a very scary thought. This was a sensation of dependence for which I was neither prepared for nor ready for.

****

The studies were becoming harder, requiring more and more time. All three of us finished the osteology part of the anatomy course and passed the exams. This called for a celebration. Ania volunteered to organize a party and have it held in her house. Although the food situation was considered passable in all of the three families, it was not easy to "organize" the food for the party. I volunteered to get the vodka and herring; Tolek was to get the bread. The rest of the kids chipped in a variety of other foods.

Ania invited two of her girlfriends and we brought with us Vania Lapschin, our old friend from the high school. I don't know why but I was very anxious before this party. We were just friends, getting together to celebrate, why all this anxiety? Saturday rolled in. I was getting ready and by 5 PM I delivered the vodka and the herring to Ania's house. Ludka and Katia, her friends, were already there. I exchanged greetings with Ania and the girls and left. The party was not to start until 7 PM.

Tolek and Vania came to my house since I lived only few blocks away from Ania. Vania did not forget to bring his *garmoshka* and tried to persuade me to bring along my violin. I thought better of it and kidded him that I do not wish to compete with his *garmoshka.* I didn't think that my violin music would add to the party.

I was finishing getting ready and again I caught myself being very anxious. I tried to prepare myself in a very special way. After having pressed the only suit I owned, the steel gray beauty, I announced that I was ready, but it was still too early to go. As we sat, talking, Vania lowered his voice and in a conspirational tone said, "I have an idea, what do you say if we get the girls drunk and see how they behave, it may be fun." I was a bit uneasy with this idea, however Vania kept on pressing; it would be totally innocent, he insisted, there would be nothing improper attempted, just simple fun. We agreed to this little conspiracy and actually looked forward to the game. The time had come and we left for Ania's house in a great anticipation of the evening's fun.

As we entered the house I noted that Ania was behind a curtain drawn about the stove in one of the corners of the room. Nowhere did I notice her parents. The table was moved to the other side of the room where two of Ania's friends were busy setting things up. One was Ludka, who Tolek and I knew well, the other was Katia whom I met earlier that day. I introduced Vania to Ludka and both of the boys to Katia. I could sense an immediate attraction between Katia and Vania. Well, I thought, the party is beginning!

The table looked great; the centerpiece was a huge loaf of white bread. How Tolek organized this delicacy was a mystery to all of us. When we tried to find out how and where he got white bread, an almost unheard of delicacy, he just grinned. Next to the bread was a large bowl of pickles and next to it several sliced, salted herring. The *piece de resistance* was a huge bowl of steamed cabbage that Ania slaved upon in the kitchen when we walked in. Next to this cornucopia of delicacies were two bottles of vodka. The vodka was courtesy of Uncle Leon who was always able to get vodka easily.

The table was under the window and the two benches were pushed at right angles into the empty corner. This provided a good sitting arrangement and sufficient floor space for dancing. In the corner, where the two benches met, was a large potted plant. The entire arrangement looked good. It is remarkable how much space can be squeezed out for a party in one little room when the spirit and will are there.

Vania, with a look at Katiuscha, went over to the table opened a bottle of vodka poured it into a water glass, half full, and handed it to her. Then, he took the *garmoshka* and started playing "Talianotchka," a love song with a lively dance beat to it.

"Well," I cried, "let's have a party!" Tolek picked up the bottle and poured drinks, each consisting of a half a glass of vodka, for each one of us. We gathered all the courage that 16-year-old boys could muster to act like adults in respect to the vodka. We downed the half glass in one long swallow and tried to encourage the girls to do the same. Demurring, Katia, looking at Vania said, with a sweet smile on her face, "Give us some time, you just play; we love to hear you play 'Talianotchka.'" I walked over to Ania and asked her to dance. She put her glass with vodka down and I was surprised to see that most of the vodka was gone! This was almost a shock for me. I was not aware that she could drink this much. Actually I was a bit uncomfortable when Vladia suggested the little subterfuge, "the vodka stratagem," to make the girls a little more receptive.

First, I didn't think much about it, just a bit of innocent fun, but now realizing that the girls may actually drink all that vodka and probably get drunk, threw me in a little bit of panic. I don't think I bargained for that.

I took Ania into my arms and we started dancing. We had danced before at school dances with a great number of various friends around us. This time, somehow, it felt different. She felt different to me, lighter, more fragile, more precious. I wanted to bring her closer to me, hold her tighter, but the thought of vodka kept assaulting my brain. Am I taking advantage of this girl? Am I using vodka to do my bidding? Maybe it is I who needs a drink to develop a little more assurance?

After we danced for a little longer, I brought Ania back to the table and we had a bite of herring and pickles. She sat down on the bench while I refilled my glass with vodka. I noticed also that Vania had already refilled his glass and kept on talking to Katia while playing the *garmoshka*.

Ludka was engrossed in, what appeared to be, an earnest discussion with Tolek. She was a very serious girl and I wasn't surprised to see her act this way even at a party. As I looked around it became quite obvious that all of us were having a good time. However, I felt uncomfortable seeing Vania play the *garmoshka* so we could dance, while he had no chance to dance with Katia.

I got up and said: "I am going home to get my violin so Vania can dance also; it is just a few minutes walk. I turned and asked Ania, "Would you like to keep me company while I get the violin?" She readily agreed. I refilled my glass and took another sip of vodka; while doing so, I noted that her glass was empty.

We walked out together and ran all the way to my house. It took only a few minutes to get there. I picked up my violin and in no time we were back. This time there was almost no conversation between us; we just held tightly each other's hand.

On returning to the party, we were greeted with shouts and hand clapping. Vania was obviously delighted and we broke out together with the happy sounds of a "Kozatchok." This was a wild dance and in no time Vania put down his *garmoshka* and took Katia with him to do the "Kozatchok." They both were superb dancers. It was like a professional performance. Vania was obviously outdoing himself.

He would shoot up into the air, pirouette and go through incredible acrobatic jumps; he squatted, shooting his legs straight out from under and turned, with unbelievable speed, on the toes of one foot and fingers of one hand. There, he would perform a full somersault. How he managed it, with his long lanky body in the confines of the small room is still a mystery for me. Katia was pirouetting around him, almost in an ephemeral fashion, a representation of beauty, skill and fervor. It was a pure delight to play for them. I couldn't make myself stop and interrupt this incredible emotional, sensual and, yes, physical experience. Finally, they both stopped in pure exhaustion to thunderous shouts of all of us. Vania had another drink, Katia and Ludka's drinks were replenished while Tolek and I simply emptied our glasses.

The drinks were having an effect on us. The boys each had one and a half water size glasses of pure vodka. My head started feeling a bit light and I had troubles focusing and pronouncing some of the words. The girls' glasses were again empty. Vania with a glee in his eyes refilled them eagerly while throwing knowledgeable glances at me. Tolek danced, I think, once with Ludka. They, however, talked most of the time. Ania was busy behind the curtain where the *pietchka* (oven) was located. I went over to see what was happening and caught a wonderful aroma. She was preparing pancakes. That was why she wanted some oil from me. She got the potatoes and was making wonderful potato pancakes. Soon everyone was busy eating and...drinking some more. While the combination of pancakes and herring was considered a delicacy, the abundance of vodka had added the necessary touch.

I was still mystified; while it was obvious that the boys felt the effects of the vodka quite strongly, the girls were bright eyed, asking for more vodka. Tolek could care less, Vania however, was adamant. "We agreed on a plan," he whispered. "Let's stick to it."

He looked knowingly at the bottles of vodka then at the girls. I laughed, took a bottle off the table and started filling up the glasses, now, however, all the way to the top. The girls laughed and lifted the glasses. We took the vodka down at least one half of the glass. I looked up and the walls started moving, up and down, while turning around, faster and faster.

Next thing I knew I was waking up on a bed. Vania and Tolek were sleeping on a blanket spread on the floor. My tongue felt several sizes too large for my mouth and my head was several sizes too large for my neck. I had a large, 'economy size', splitting headache.

The girls were sitting by the table having pancakes. When they saw me wake up they burst out laughing. "Feeling better?" Ludka asked. "What happened?" I croaked. "Well," Ania answered, we got a bit suspicious when you guys brought all that vodka but decided to go alone with you to see who gets drunk first. You can see the outcome of this little contest." All three kept on laughing. I only shook my head, both, because of the cob webs in my head and because of the residual drowsiness and headache.

Slowly Tolek and Vania started waking up. We all felt embarrassed and did not know how to react. Finally I said, "Maybe we should call it quits and go home?" The girls got serious. "No," they said. "Let's have some tea. Vania, you play some nice songs and we all will sing." Tolek moved his head in agreement.

Vania started playing the most recent hit, "Tyornnayia Notch" (Dark Night), and everyone joined in singing. The tea tasted good. There were still a few potato pancakes left. We had a feast! Everyone was tired and by 2 o'clock we decided that the party was great but it was time to go home.

While walking home, my mind was full of impressions from the party. I was coming back, over and again to the same issue, the issue of getting drunk. I never drank enough to get really drunk. This time I did. What happened? Something didn't make sense. Was I so drunk that I missed something unusual and important? By the time I got home and quickly got ready for bed, trying not to wake up the rest of the family, I gave up trying to figure out why I got drunk at the party while none of the girls did.

The year was coming to an end and we were busy studying for exams. We completed osteology and myology (the study of muscles); also we completed inorganic chemistry, organic chemistry and physics. As the exams were looming just ahead of us, a serious issue came up. The NKVD finally responded positively to our request for a permit to go back to Poland. They told us that we would be permitted to repatriate but did not clarify whether we would need to purchase individual tickets on a train going to Poland or whether there would be trains organized by the government.

We were quite skeptical. In 1940, when we applied for a permit to leave the Soviet Union, instead we were sent to a Gulag! The possibility that this could repeat itself was frightening.

Father, however, was trying to allay our fears. His reasoning was simple. He said, "The Russians are now, in a way, friendly with the Western World since America and Great Britain indeed helped the Soviet Union during the war. Matter of fact without their help the possibility of winning the war with Germany was very tenuous. I don't think that the Soviet Union would make our repatriation an issue, particularly," Father continued, "since we will be going back to Poland, a country that is now developing a communist government that obviously will be very friendly with the Soviet Union."

In the meantime, a major meeting of the "Polish Society" was being organized. Ever since the boxing club had not done very well, Father was not very active in the Society. For this meeting, however, everyone, including me, went. The room where the meeting was held was relatively small, while the number of people trying to attend the meeting was large; probably several times more than the number usually attending these meetings.

I looked around and realized that with the exception of Ania's father, who had just walked in, I did not really known anyone there. When the level of noise in the room reached a crescendo, a man got up in the front of the room and spoke. After introducing himself as the president of the Society, he started by summarizing the current status and activities of the group and gave us information concerning our political status. First, he said, the Society conducted an informal survey and learned that the majority of those who were Polish citizens before the war wished to return to Poland. Secondly, he informed us that everyone wishing to repatriate must file appropriate papers with the NKVD and wait for the disposition of each individual case.

The first transport was due to leave Alma Ata for Poland in late April, which was only a few weeks away. This information led to flurry of activities. Mother got in touch with her friends in the NKVD, who were her former or current patients, to inquire about the actual status of our application. Also, we had to clarify the question of the logistics. The latter was clarified instantly. The NKVD organized trains that would take us to Poland. Apparently the president of the Polish society was correct. The first transport was to leave indeed by the end of April. The officials in the NKVD were to determine who would get on which train. We had to make a decision quickly.

I was unhappy since leaving at the end of April would not allow me to finish the first year of medical school. Father, however, was adamant. He felt we should leave as soon as possible. If it meant late April, so be it! He simply didn't trust the Soviets to keep their word. He wanted us out of the Soviet Union!

I had many discussions with Tolek and his mother concerning the trip back to Poland. Tolek's father was still held in prison by the NKVD for some imaginary "anti-government activities." They definitely were not willing to repatriate him.

Tolek and his mother were in a quandary. Tolek had an older sister who was an officer in the Kosciuszko Division, a Polish Army created in the Soviet Union in 1943 by Wanda Wasilewska. Tolek's sister survived the war in the military service and continued to serve in the Army after the war. She married a Polish Army officer and lived in Warsaw. Tolek and his mother wished very much to join her but felt devastated to leave his father in a Russian prison. There was no assurance that the Soviets would release him in the reasonable future, or possibly ever. They felt, however, that once in Poland, Tolek's sister and her husband, who was a high-ranking officer in the Polish Army, may be able to exert influence to have him released from jail. Tolek's mother had to make a decision fast, or to take a chance on a later transport.

I suggested that my mother try to talk to her friends in the NKVD concerning Tolek's family so we could possibly go back to Poland together. Indeed, a couple of days later we got notification that we were assigned to the first transport leaving Alma Ata on April 30, with Tolek and his family.

Unfortunately, Ania and her parents didn't get assigned to the first transport. At this point Ania and I were spending a great deal of time together. I began to panic. We definitely were not scheduled to return to Poland on the same transport. I had no address in Poland to give her. Neither did she have a Polish address. The only possible point of contact was her brother, Kuba. He lived in Poland and she gave me his address, but he apparently was also moving around at that time.

One evening, when coming back from the University, Ania and I started talking about what we would do after returning to Poland. I indicated that I would try to immigrate to America. At that point I took her by her hand and said impulsively: "I will take you with me to America, we will study and work together, and it will be wonderful." I also promised her that I would find her in Poland no matter what; she looked at me with a quizzical smile on her lips and said: "I hope so."

I had very conflicting feelings flooding my mind. On one hand, I wished to tell her that I cared for her very much and that I wished to kiss her. On the other hand, I felt it would be inappropriate and that she may feel offended. This made me pass on this idea.

To change the subject and lighten the mood, I asked her to tell me how during the party the girls managed to stay sober while we, the fellows, got drunk? I indicated also that if she told me the truth, I would also tell her about the ideas I had concerning our getting together in Poland and then going to America.

After the words escaped my mouth, I couldn't believe that I was brave enough to make such a presumptuous offer the second time. Firstly, I presumed that I would be able to go to America; secondly, I assumed that she would be interested in going to America; and thirdly I insinuated that she would like to do so with me! The enormity of this statement fell on me like a granite mountain. I didn't know what to say, how to exonerate myself from this situation. But Ania was not abashed. She looked at me with her beautiful wide opened eyes, a smile on her face, and said: "I would love to come." But after saying this she averted her eyes and dropped her head. Then, she looked up again and said: "As far as the drinking fun was concerned, it was simple. Do you remember the huge potted plant I placed in the corner where the two benches met? Well that's where the vodka that you plied us with ended up. We simply didn't drink. This was planned before the party. We decided to get you guys drunk while we would have fun watching you making fools of yourself. However, it wasn't that bad. You certainly did get drunk, but we had a lot of fun before you passed out!"

I looked at her with wonder in my eyes and put my arms around giving her a mighty squeeze, but I couldn't get myself to kiss her. Somehow, for reasons I couldn't understand, I felt that this would be taking an advantage of the girl.

With the day of departure rolling in with great speed, the entire family was thrown into a feverish activity. Our life in Alma Ata had to be liquidated. We got busy packing our meager belongings. The latter was a minor activity. We hoped that finally we would be able to get rid of the rags we owned and acquire more decent belongings. How mistaken we were! It took years!

Tolek and I went to the Medical School to inquire what documentation we would get from the University to attest to our standing in the Medical School. Here, Igor's mother, Professor Litvinov, was very helpful. She said that she probably could arrange for us to take the examinations in all the subjects early and if we passed them, have the school issue a certificate that we completed the first year.

That sounded great but despite having already started our studies in preparation for the final examinations, we were far from ready. We had planned to study 6-7 weeks prior to the final exam dates. "However," as Tolek would say, "to tell the truth" we had started our studies and were well ahead in our preparations. Despite the time necessary for packing and getting ready for the trip, we felt that we should be able to prepare for and pass the examinations also. We were extremely grateful to Professor Litvinov for making these arrangements and planned to take the examinations one week prior to the departure.

Suddenly it dawned on me that in a couple of weeks I would not see Ania for an indefinite period of time. She was to come to Poland on the subsequent transport but I did not know where in Poland she was going to stay. Now we were in school together. We saw each other and studied together every day. This actually made the upcoming parting much more acute. We found ourselves spending more time together; each putting up a brave face.

The time for the examinations came and went. Tolek and I took the test and passed them. Ania had to wait to take them at the regular time. Her transport wasn't even scheduled; it probably would not leave until the school year was well over.

Our last trip to the University was a sad experience. We picked up our school documents, said goodbye to our friends and spent a great deal of time with Igor's, mother. She was like our own mother. We promised to write her. And here came the saddest part of our parting. She asked us not to write her! She felt that it would be much too dangerous for them to receive mail from the west, particularly since Professor Litvinov, her husband, was engaged in a very sensitive area of research.

Uncle Leon performed his last important duty at the plant. He arranged for a truck to take our belongings to the railroad station at the time of departure. I was spending more and more time with Ania. I felt an unreal sensation of loss. There was nothing spoken between us. However, I felt as if a part of me was being torn off and left behind in Alma Ata. The reality of the situation was heightened by the fact that physically we, up to the last minute of my departure, behaved very proper towards each other; we hadn't even kissed.

The entire family, including myself, was totally consumed by the happiness of being able finally to go back home, to learn about the rest of the family, to start a new life outside of the Soviet Union. I was also dreaming of an exotic future in the Americas.

CHAPTER 13 Poland

The trip from Alma Ata to Poland was a blur. I vaguely remember going across the Ural Mountains and crossing the Volga River at Kuibyshev. Subsequently, we encountered a string of small, partly burned out railroad stations and almost completely destroyed large railroad stations. Food was still a problem. Except for the fact that we were free and excited because we were leaving the Soviet Union and going back home (?), the general flavor of the trip was depressingly similar to the trip east--to the Gulag--six years back. Whenever we arrived to a town, there was a sickly, smoke tinged odor in the air around the railroad stations, barely discernible, but definite.

The buildings around the railroad stations were, in many instances, in total disrepair and neglect and obviously no attempt was made to affect serious repairs. People walked in old, worn out clothing and there was tiredness, sadness and almost grayness in their drawn out faces. This was not a happy folk.

Tolek and his family were with us on the same train. We spent most of the time together. He was looking forward to seeing his sister who held an important position in the Polish Army. He was very excited and couldn't stop talking about her and her husband, the officer in the Polish Army. Whenever we stopped at a railroad station Tolek and I instantly disembarked trying to find out about the place, about possibly interesting things to see or possibly get some food. The major difference between this trip and the trip to the Gulag was the obvious fact that we were free to get off the train, but also that we now knew the Russian language. We conversed with no accent and particularly since we wore the same battered, Soviet-style clothing, the Russians would be hard put to guess that we were not natives.

Most of our forays, however, were not very successful. One of the major problems that plagued us here was the same problem we had on the train going to the Gulag, namely, most of the times we did not know when the train was going to leave the station; thus, any attempts to undertake an adventure outside the railroad station was usually not advisable. The train we were on was really a transport with modified cattle cars. Each had a built-in toilette, or better put, a facsimile of one and was equipped with bunks and mattresses. Most importantly, the doors could be kept open, weather permitting. The train had no fixed schedule and could pass through a station or be placed on a sidetrack for indefinite periods of time. This obviously slowed our trip markedly. It took us over three weeks to get from Alma Ata to Warsaw.

One late afternoon we stopped in an open field. This was the Polish border. Russian border police got on the train and inspected our documents very carefully, making sure that no undocumented person would slip out of the Soviet Union. During this procedure, they were proper and polite. After the inspection was completed, the train moved again only to stop in fifteen minutes this time in a little town. This was the Polish side of the border. The Polish border police came aboard and we went through a similar drill. Since it was getting dark the policemen had to shine flashlights into our faces to identify individuals. One turned to his companion and said with a derogatory smirk on his face, "wszystko zydy!" "They are all Jews!"

Tolek and I looked at each other with astonishment but didn't say a word. Tolek's sister was in the Polish Army fighting for Poland. I was thinking of Ania's brother who at that time was also in the Polish Army, an officer in an artillery company, who fought the German Army all the way through Russia into Poland, helped liberate Poland and then fought in Germany to deliver the decisive blow in Berlin that finished the war. We expected a somewhat warmer reception coming to what we thought to be our home. After looking at our documents at a perfunctory fashion, the border patrol left and the train resumed its slow journey.

This episode left us quite disturbed. In the Soviet Union, the government did not condone anti-Semitic activities, however, the grass roots anti-Semitism was widespread. There was obvious anti-Semitic activity on the part of the border police. I couldn't say if it was generally condoned or whether this was an isolated incident expressing individual and personal feelings. After the train started moving I tried to fall asleep but had difficulties, mulling over and over this incident in my mind.

Ultimately, I must have fallen asleep because when I woke up, with a start, the train was standing at a railroad station. I looked out the door and saw Tolek talking animatedly with Leon and Father. Leon was apparently off the train for some time and had been talking with some local people. I quickly ran over to them to take part in this impromptu little conference. Leon was obviously upset. Firstly, because he felt considerable hostility emanating from the people he talked to. They kept on emphasizing to him that the trains from Russia were filled primarily with Jews, and here they thought that Germans made the world essentially free of Jews. Apparently, they were quite disturbed by seeing "all these Jews." Also, they said that, and here he turned his voice down, in the suburbs of Lublin there was a *Katzet* (concentration camp) that also served as a *Vernichtungslager* (extermination camp). He couldn't get further details; most people were tight-lipped about it.

The camp apparently was accessible by a trolley car. Father definitely wanted to see the camp. The obvious question was, how long would we stay in Lublin? Josef, who was a ranking officer in the prewar Polish Army, took it upon himself to get more details from the railroad station management. He took off instantly to look for some station supervisors. We began to worry when over two hours went by and there was no Juzek in sight. Finally he showed up. He had difficulties talking to us. His face was ashen; there was a confused look on his face. Finally he spoke, "It was difficult to find anyone who had any information and who would be willing to share it. Finally," he said with a grin, "I forced my way into the office of the Station Superintendent and guess who was sitting there, Staszek, my old buddy, from a prewar army training camp. Well, this was a reunion. Ultimately, I got a chance to tell him briefly about us. Also,

I told him about the rumors we have heard in respect to the existence of a *Katzet* in Lublin.

When our conversation turned to this topic, Staszek became very pensive; he tried to switch our conversation to other topics, however, unsuccessfully. I told him that if there was such a camp, it was our desire to visit it. Finally, he relented. There was, however, great sadness in his face when he started talking."

He briefly summarized the story of Lublin during the war, its ghettos and its concentration camps. "Apparently," Staszek said, "Jews were locked up into ghettos by 1940-41, the largest in Lublin being Majdan-Tatarski, an entire section of the city. After the Germans attacked the Soviet Union in 1941, a camp for Soviet prisoners of war was built very close to the ghetto. It was named Majdanek. Originally it housed thousands of Russian war prisoners and some Polish political prisoners. Soon Jews from labor camps and ghettos in Lublin and the Warsaw areas and later from other labor camps were shipped to Majdanek also. In no time the camp became the primary extermination camp for this area of Poland. The Germans built gas chambers for rapid extermination of the camp's inmates and six crematoria for getting rid of the bodies."

Josef asked him if the people living in the city had any inkling of what was going on in the camp. Staszek responded very uncomfortably, "Yes, there was no way to prevent anyone walking or riding by from seeing the interior of the camp. The double barbwire fence surrounding Majdanek allowed for a clear view of the activities inside the camp. Matter of fact," he added, "the main road heading east, to Lwow and other eastern towns was running on the very border of the camp. Thus, it was impossible for anyone traveling this highway to miss observing the activities inside the camp."

Juzek also told us that Staszek was definitely assuring him that the train would not leave until evening. Everyone was shaken by the story of Majdanek. This was the first time that we were faced with definite indications of the unimaginable atrocities committed by the Germans.

My two uncles, Father, Tolek and I stood there looking at each other and not knowing how to react to this. Finally, Father broke the silence. "I want to go there," he said, "I want to see the camp with my own eyes." Both Juzek and Leon also indicated that they wanted to go. Uncle Leon raised the question of safety. Juzek said that he asked Staszek concerning the safety of Jews in the city and was told that it was O.K. However, he apparently said that there would no benefit in "advertising" that we are Jews. Since we spoke perfect Polish, our clothing was not different from the local attire and both uncles as well as my father did not look Jewish at all, with their blue eyes and blond hair, this was not a problem.

We returned to the railroad car and broke this horrific story to Mother. She started sobbing but at the same time repeating, "I was so afraid that this might be the case. I am so worried for my sisters and brothers. However," she said, "I feel that we must go to see the camp and I am coming with you."

Everyone's eyes turned to me, "We will be back in a couple hours," said my father.

"Oh, no!" I interrupted, "I am coming with you."

My mother looked at me with her huge sad eyes and said, "You really do not want to go with us."

"But I do," I responded. "I am not a child anymore. I am coming."

They realized that I was adamant and relented. Juzek knew from Staszek how to get to Majdanek and where the tramway station was. We started immediately. The city was in a horrible state. Many buildings were destroyed; there were mountains of loose brick from the destroyed buildings all over the streets. Restoration and repairs were proceeding slowly. Most storefronts were boarded up and most stores were closed. People on the streets were dressed like in Soviet Russia, in old clothing. The people on the tramcar looked shabby and tired. There was little conversation. We also didn't speak among ourselves not knowing what to expect. As for me, I was deep in thought. This return journey to Poland wasn't what I fantasized it to be. Maybe I expected the people to be happier, the country to be more prosperous and the repair of the war damages further advanced during the two years period of time.

The tram was passing through sparsely built up areas and in the distance we could see outlines of what appeared to be low laying groups of houses located on a huge almost flat field. There were no trees or other vegetation. The ground was dry and dusty. As we got off the tramcar and went closer to the barbwire fence, we could make out the entrance flanked by two square guard houses. Inside there were many rows of single-story high barracks; a barbwire fence separated each. In the distance I could see a tall, square brick chimney. As we got closer to it we realized that it was the chimney for the crematorium. Later when we got closer to it, we saw the gaping metal doors to the ovens in a crumbling brick structure. The barracks were long sheds made of wood planks. Inside there were constructed, on each side, three levels of shelves where the inmates slept.

It all looked unreal. We were unable to identify with the Jews who must have stayed there awaiting all forms of torture and ultimately death. Later we learned that a quarter of a million people were killed there; most were Jews. No one of us was crying… nothing was sinking in.

I looked at the barracks, the crematoria and the gas chambers and had the odd feeling of looking at it from somewhere outside, from an unearthly vantage point. Not that I wasn't exposed in the past to repression, to cruelty or to death. Images of swollen bodies of people lying dead on the streets of Alma Ata, people who died of starvation, kept on swimming in front of my eyes. However, this was different. This was totally unreal; it was not a result of a psychotic episode, an expression of a mechanism of war or a response to an economic calamity. This was a machinery of a psychopathic power that has gone berserk.

I did not feel that any of the scenario surrounding us had anything to do with reality or with us. Not a word passed between us. Everyone was consumed with his or her own thoughts. Ultimately we looked at each other and turned towards the gate. We quietly walked to the tram stop and made our way to the railroad station.

The trip to Majdanek was the first real direct blow administered to our psyche by Hitler. There was an inkling of this problem in the Soviet papers, but we thought that it was mostly war propaganda. There were some telltale signs of the existence of camps when we were passing the border patrol station entering Poland. This, however, was different. Hitler had waged a war against most of the civilized world, this was clear and exemplified by numerous precedents in the past. He had waged a savage war against us, the Jews. This I also knew ever since I could perceive the world around me while in Germany in the early thirties. However, wars raged regularly throughout our globe ever since the dawn of history and the Jews were persecuted with vengeance ever since the Romans destroyed the Second Temple, conquered the Jewish State in the Palestine area of Asia, and dispersed many of the Jews from their land in Israel into Diaspora throughout the world.

Majdanek however, was something different. Wars were waged against peoples who attacked you (militarily, economically or politically) or against people whose land you want to conquer. The Jews in Diaspora were persecuted primarily for religious reasons. For example the Inquisition wanted to see the Jews convert to Catholicism. Even Martin Luther during his livelong war against the Jews called primarily for conversions. Although it should be kept in mind that later in life his anti-Semitism became much more virulent and the "elimination" rhetoric in his violently anti-Semitic book, "On the Jews and Their Lies," could have served as an important factor in the evolution of Hitler's "extermination policy towards the Jews. In addition to these religious reasons, there were also other reasons that could be easily found and applied when convenient. Majdanek exemplified not only all of these reasons but also much more. It demonstrated the end results of the implementation of a policy of elimination of peoples by the simple expedience of physical annihilation.

This was nothing but pure evil; a sick, a pathological, subhuman instinct of destruction for the sake of destruction. Or was it also for the sake of pure, gut based hate? Or, at least in some instances, was it for the sake of material gains?

I was at loss thinking about it. I had no answers. How could a nation as cultured as the Germans face the real aspects of devising a system of annihilation of human masses? Questions, questions, questions! As the tram was winding its way to the railroad station, I developed a splitting headache. There was something in the back of my mind that tried to move to the forefront. I struggled to figure out what this thought was when suddenly it dawned on me. Not being able to face it, I must have been repressing it. I couldn't face this possibility; a possibility that the Poles were involved in some form or fashion in this senseless slaughter of innocent lives.

I could handle normally, and accept as inevitable, the emotional and physical aspects of Polish anti-Semitism, the anti-Semitism I experienced on a daily basis while living in Poland before the war. However, the thought of Poles, people I knew and lived with be, collaborating in these inhumane, atrocities committed in Majdanek was unthinkable.

I always believed that before the war, among the kids my age their basis of anti-Semitism was primarily religious. Later I realized that it was rooted also, to some extent, in jealousy related to the material and professional success of a segment, albeit small, of the Jewish population.

Father brought me back from my reveries into reality. "Let's get off the tram, we are at the railroad station," he said. The entire family followed him out and walked towards the train. No one uttered a word. We were totally absorbed in our own thoughts. At the train, we were barraged by questions. Answers consisted of monosyllables. Here I saw the birth of the "defense wall." During the decades to come, this psychological technique became a routine for the "survivors." I was reluctant even to discuss Majdanek with Tolek.

The trip to Warsaw took only a few hours. The train stopped at a siding off the main railroad station. This was as far as the transport train would take us. Tolek and his family were getting off there; his sister, Irka, was to pick them up. Their excitement was unbelievable. I was also excited because I had Ania's brother's address and hoped to look him up. Everyone was running somewhere. Arrangements had to be made for going to the final destinations.

There were several local Jews who came to meet the train. Most were members of Zionist organizations. They tried to provide advice and give us the "feel" of the current situation in Poland. The news was not very good. In general they indicated that while the current government was inclined positively towards the Jews, the general population was quite anti-Semitic, particularly in small towns. They suggested that those of us who lived before the war in small towns and wished to return there should go temporarily to a larger city in the vicinity of their town and from there investigate the question of safety in their hometowns. Most of the Zionists were young boys and were all eager to help in whatever way possible.

Tolek's sister did not know when the transport would arrive to Warsaw. The only way she could be informed was by going over personally to the address Tolek had.

I had Ania's brother, Kuba's, address and was happy to accompany Tolek and then have his sister help me in finding Kuba's house.

In view of the advice given to us earlier concerning going back to one's hometown, my family decided to go to Krakow. Father's family went to Krakow when the war started and Mother had several sisters and brothers living there. In view of this, they had to find out how to get tickets to Krakow.

No one had any objections to my going with Tolek and looking for Ania's brother. For reasons that I couldn't fathom after we came to Poland, particularly after we visited Majdanek, my parent's attitude toward me had changed. I was treated more like an adult rather than a "kid." Everyone listened to what I had to say and I was given a great deal more latitude than before. Possibly they transferred their attention towards Stella who was reaching eleven years of age and required more supervision and care than before.

Tolek came running. "Mother and Maryna want to go alone," he cried and added, "This is actually better. They may be able to find the address easier since they know the city while I have forgotten whatever little bit I remembered as a child from before the war." We walked along the railroad tracks towards the station. The buildings around the railroad lines were mostly destroyed. Once we got to the station, we found it to be almost destroyed. The huge steel spans over the main concourse connecting the vertical supports were still there but twisted into a series of curious shapes. The station's buildings were in ruin.

There were several trains in the station and a mob was milling on the station platforms. The shabby, damaged look and obvious disrepair of the station matched the general appearance of the clothing and demeanor of the crowd. It was a depressing sight.

Tolek's mother was with us; she knew the city very well. He claimed that he also remembered a lot. I had never been in Warsaw so I had to depend totally on them. There was a tramway stop a short distance from the station's exit. We decided to go first to Tolek's sister's apartment. Apparently we could get close to that address by taking the tram and then walking about twenty minutes.

The tram wound its way through narrow canyons dug out in the brick, cement fragments and steel debris of buildings that formerly lined the streets. The city was essentially destroyed. Before the war, there were many tall buildings in the center of the city. Now, only burned out skeletons remained reaching with jagged walls towards a clear blue sky. Mountains of loose, broken brick and large pieces of cement were piled up on the sidewalks and inside the gutted buildings. Some streets were still totally blocked by debris from the destroyed buildings. There were people on the streets working in this chaos of destruction. As we moved away from the center there were streets with smaller buildings that were only somewhat damaged. Old trees still lined sidewalks in some sections of the city as if in defiance to the insanity of the humans.

After getting off the tram, we continued on foot. The walk was actually very pleasant. We met very few people but we needed a little help in finding the address. Tolek's mother was quite familiar with this part of the city. Finally, we reached a nice, three-story tall apartment building with a well-maintained flower garden in the front. On the side of the entrance, there was a bronze plate with names and bell buttons. We found the correct name and rang the bell. There was no answer. After giving it a reasonable chance, and pressing the button repeatedly, we pressed a button of a neighbor. This was a lucky one. A window opened on the second floor, a lady leaned out and asked what we want. Here Tolek's mother took over and in no time Pani Szydlowska ran down, opened the front door and cordially invited us in.

She was a nice looking blond lady in her twenties who happened to be very friendly with Irka and her husband. She offered us a drink and suggested that we wait for Irka in her apartment. We talked to her for a while but ultimately decided to leave and ask her to tell Irka that the train was at a siding of the main railroad station and that we would wait there for her.

Our next destination was Kuba's apartment. We walked back to the tramcar stop and after a lengthy conference with the driver of the next car that came by, we decided on a strategy to find his apartment. This took us much longer since Tolek's mother was unfamiliar with that part of the city. Ultimately we got there; however, he wasn't home nor was any of his neighbors. I couldn't find any mailbox to leave a message. Nevertheless, I wrote a message and left it under the main gate.

We were very tired and hungry, but we had no money to buy a snack on the way to the railroad station. Even if we had, there was no place we could buy food. Upon our return, I was literally attacked by my parents and Leon. "We couldn't wait for you any more," cried Father. "The officials at the station wanted us out of the train cars. This is apparently the end of our journey on this train. Everyone was very rude; they also wanted us to get out of the station promptly."

Leon interrupted, "There is a train leaving in the evening for Krakow, I think we should get tickets to go there. It is close to Trzebinia, Jula had many sisters there, also we left Grandmother and Lola there. Maybe they survived the war and returned home. It's already more than a year since the war had ended here."

Everyone talked at the same time, but it appeared that Leon's suggestion was a reasonable one and soon he went with Father to get the tickets. While they were gone, there was a great excitement. Irka, Tolek's sister, found us. There was an unbelievable reunion. Everyone was crying. Irka came alone; her husband showed up later. He was making arrangements for the transport of Tolek's family belongings. We were obviously very happy for their reunion and hoped that when we got to Krakow we also would find at least some of our family there.

Tolek and I separated with heavy hearts not knowing where and when we would get together again. Our friendship was not only a very close one, but it also carried us through very rough parts of our lives. Despite the unbelievable travails, difficulties and lessons in simple survival, we also had great times together and found fun in every aspect of the experience. We promised to stay in touch and I admonished him to try and contact Kuba, Ania's brother, so he could also make contact with her.

Indeed we got tickets for Krakow and all six of us, my parents, uncles Juzek and Leon, Stella and I, as well as all of our earthly belongings loaded up into a compartment on the passenger train by early evening. This was a "local" train, which meant that it made scheduled stops at every single station. While a normal trip should have taken four to five hours, this train was to take the entire night to get to Krakow. We didn't arrive at the Central Station in Krakow until morning of the next day. There we unloaded and Mother and Uncle Leon went looking for any member of our family.

I looked around the station and then took Stella with me to look at the plaza in front of the station. It all looked very shabby but most of the buildings were intact. Whatever little we saw around the railroad station, it was nothing to compare with Warsaw which was in shambles. The reality of the situation had not yet registered with me.

I was in a semi-shock condition. Lublin and Majdanek were unreal. I heard of the atrocities, but before seeing Majdanek I had not intellectualized it. It was very remote and foreign to me. Now it became real and incomprehensible. Warsaw was a nightmare. It was composed of mountains of broken brick with people crawling between and on top of it.

The reaction of people was puzzling. Strangers were either blatantly or covertly hostile. Acquaintances, on the other hand, were excessively friendly. The reactions of the Polish people, that we had met thus far, were hostile, puzzling or ambivalent.

As I walked with Stella around the railroad station plaza, I spied a stand with *obvazanki*. My heart jumped with joy, since they were the same baked goods as we had before the war. Stella obviously didn't remember any of it and I wanted her to taste some. Unfortunately I had no money, a minor detail that had to be somehow corrected in the near future. We had to satisfy ourselves with inhaling the aroma of these incredible *obvazanki*.

Nearby, I could hear the excited voices of my mother and Leon as we sat, as usual, on top of our belongings at the railroad station. One look at their faces was enough to tell me that they had some bad news, but there was also great happiness.

They apparently found some survivors. Indeed, a young boy, two to three years older than me, two tall young women and an adult man were walking with them. My father jumped up and started hugging them. Everyone was talking. There were questions, responses, tears and laughter.

Stella and I were essentially on the side watching this happening. Ultimately, I learned that these were the three surviving children of two of my mother's sisters. They were my cousins; the adult man was a husband of the older girl. Upon liberation from the concentration camp by the Russians in 1945, they returned home to Krakow.

All of us were immediately invited to stay with them in the apartment house of one of mother's sisters, the mother of the young boy, Mendek. It was a four-story apartment house that originally housed a large factory manufacturing cotton thread on the ground floor. It belonged to Mendek's parents. Above there was an apartment housing my aunt's family that included eight children. Before the war, my aunt rented the upper three floors to different families. We were invited to stay on the ground floor, together with the rest of the family, as long as necessary to get things straightened out.

The ensuing week was like "Yom Kippur," the "Day of Atonement." Except for one sister who survived the concentration camps and was taken to Sweden after liberation, the rest of my mother's sisters who were in Europe during the war, all the brothers, and most of their families perished.

Hanka, the young women who came to the railroad station to see us, was my mother's niece and the man who came with her, Zdzich, was her new husband. They met immediately after being liberated from the concentration camps and married shortly after. The boy, Mendek, who also showed up to greet us at the railroad station was the surviving son of another of my mother's sisters. He also had a large number of siblings, unfortunately only one, Mendek's sister survived. Mendek and I, instantly became close, inseparable friends.

We were in the dark concerning the fate of the members of my father's family who were not with us in Russia or abroad. Father and the two uncles were eager to go to Trzebinia. They discussed the trip with our newly found family to a great extent. The consensus, however, was to wait. Apparently, the social climate was a threatening one. They, however, didn't want to wait. I also wanted to go but they were absolutely against it.

Soon thereafter, the three brothers left for Trzebinia. The trip was less than an hour by train. They were supposed to find out about Grandfather's apartment house and his businesses, the soda water factory and other enterprises, as well as the condition of our house, my parents' dental offices and laboratory, our belongings, particularly the art, furniture and equipment. Also, they were to find out about the farm belonging to Grandmother's family.

We didn't expect them back for at least a couple days. After all, they knew almost everyone in that community and expected to get a lot of information. To our great surprise, they showed up in the afternoon of the same day. We beleaguered them with questions. However it was difficult to get answers. They were evasive. They complained of feeling tired. They wanted to go to sleep. The very next day everyone wished to talk about Trzebinia.

Father looked the most distraught and most reluctant to talk. I had difficulties understanding the hesitancy on the part of all three of them to talk about Trzebinia. It was actually several decades until I finally fully understood their reactions. At the time, however, I had no inkling. To me it all sounded so straightforward. Yes, a lot of it was horrible, but I thought in very simple terms; one had to look at it and face it.

Finally, we learned that there were no Jews living in Trzebinia; none any more. Secondly, the Germans built an elevated highway in the front of Grandfather's house, blocking at the front of the house the view from many of the windows, thus making the house very unattractive to live in. Anyway, the City Hall started giving my father, who was the oldest of the three brothers, difficulties in respect to the establishment of ownership of this property. Furthermore, Father could not get into our house. There was a family living there. They were not willing to let Father in or to talk to him. My father and uncles knew most of the people in Trzebinia, a tiny town, by their first names. However, no one was eager to talk to them. Finally, an old friend of Leon's came over and explained quietly that it would be healthy for all three of them to leave the town and possibly return later when things may change.

All three brothers were visibly shaken, frustrated and very, very angry. Clearly they had not expected this type of reception from a group of people with whom they were very close for years; people who in innumerable ways benefited greatly from them before the war. But, maybe, they should have expected something of this nature, at least suspected that something like this might occur; however, why?

Well, for the past couple weeks, Mendek and I roamed the city and talked to many youngsters our age and older, both Jews and Christians. A disturbing bit of information came across from some of our gentile friends. Mendek and I couldn't establish the veracity of these stories thus we didn't even repeat them to anyone fearing of starting unfortunate rumors. Apparently the previous year (1945) on Saturday, August 11, a group of gentile Poles attacked Jews gathered in a synagogue. The story continued that the thirteen-year-old son of the janitor at the synagogue was paid by "someone" to smear himself with animal blood and come running from the synagogue screaming for help because he and other gentile children allegedly were being used to obtain blood for making Passover matzo. This ignited a pogrom with the people from the streets running into the synagogue to beat the Jews, and also catching Jews in the streets. Some of the beatings were assisted by army soldiers to the tunes of an army band playing nearby. Mendek and I were stunned and refused to believe these stories. We tried to put them aside as attempts by some of the kids to scare us by playing on our raw nerves as related to this topic. Unfortunately, later on we were able to confirm the veracity of these stories as related to this ignominious episode occurring just weeks after the defeat of Germany.

Our discussions with the gentile Polish kids also illustrated that there was a dichotomy in thinking and in acceptance by the general population of the current, poorly defined, political system and of the presence of Soviet military and political advisors everywhere. While I still remembered some of Poland's history from the grade school that I attended in Trzebinia before the war, I decided to read up a bit more on this topic to get some of the facts of Polish history into a better perspective.

It was essential for me to clearly understand the historical background, since the unbelievable atrocities committed, primarily by the Germans, against the Jews during the war years must have been met with, at least, tacit acceptance by the Polish population. This judgment I made on the basis of meager bits of information that we could glean from the responses of the young Poles we talked to.

However, the dynamics of the people's reactions leading to the situation in Poland during the war, I believed, had to have some basis in the past, in the history of Poland. The Poles, as a nation, had, for centuries, an exaggerated sense of patriotism and a visceral need for political freedom and personal independence. This need has not occurred at a whim or in a vacuum. Poland had a several centuries-old history of proud royal dynasties, basking in highly elaborate royal courts, cultural and educational institutions while at the same time depending economically throughout most of the history, until recent history, almost exclusively on agriculture, thus on the peasants, for survival. However, to provide for acceptable level of well being for the upper crust, in addition to agriculture, development of appropriate trade savvy and crafts became essential. This was recognized as far back as the time of the rule of Mieszko I, who established in Poland the first royal dynasty, the Piast dynasty in year 965.

Although Jewish traders traveled through the Piast's land prior to the establishment of the dynasty, it wasn't until after the dynasty was established and under the rule of dukes and kings like Boleslaw Pobozny and Kazimierz Wielki, that the Jews who were being persecuted in the West, were invited to Poland to establish trade and develop the crafts. In return they were guaranteed by the Royal Court full personal security, protection of their communities and of their property.

Under these arrangements the peasant became the "steel," the machinery of the Polish Royalty while the Jew its "oil," the lubricant that allowed the economic machinery to function and the trades and crafts to flourish. Most importantly, this system allowed the very thin upper crust of the Polish society of the Middle Ages, the *Szlachta* (nobility) and in more recent history, the *Inteligencia*, to harvest the fruits of the system and practice high level of cultural and artistic endeavors.

In the middle Ages, Poland indeed had culturally a highly advanced upper class. Poland had also been advancing politically. In 1791, it wrote the very first constitution in Europe. Unfortunately, by 1795, its three mighty neighbors attacked her and each annexed a third of her land.

Poland ceased to exist as an independent political entity. It remained partitioned until after the First Word War (1918). This century's long period of occupation was punctuated by a series of bloody revolutions, insurrections and national uprisings, all to no avail, until 1918.

It should be noted that despite the fact that during these centuries Jews were violently persecuted by the Polish population and later by the occupying powers, Russians, Ukrainians, Byelorussians, Latwians and Lithuanians, they had taken a formal and significant part in each of the uprisings against the occupying powers along the side of Polish revolutionaries. Colonel Berek Joselewicz formed a Jewish cavalry regiment that served with distinction under General Kosciuszko in the insurrection of 1794. Similarly, Jews actively participated in the November Insurrection (1830-1831), the January Insurrection (1863) and the revolutionary movement in 1905. And finally the Legions created after the First World War and commanded by General Pilsudski had a significant number of Jews in their ranks fighting again for Polish independence. After the First World War, the struggle was finally successful; Pilsudski became a Marshal and later the leader of the newly established country. He never forgot the Jews and until his death in 1935 kept the anti-Semitic drives of the Christian Poles under relative control. This situation had changed drastically after he died and the "colonels" took power. They established, to all practical purposes, a dictatorship with one of the colonels, Smigly-Rydz, being elevated to the rank of a Marshal and a leader of the country. At this point the anti-Semitism intensified and became, in many ways sanctioned by the government, thus paving the way and playing into the hands of the Germans after they occupied Poland in September 1939.

****

I had been spending a great amount of time with my newly found cousin, Mendek. We discussed at length the current situation in Poland and tried to explain the unthinkable as related to the war years and the Holocaust (at the time we were discussing these issues, the term "Holocaust," as coined later to denote the atrocities committed against peoples, particularly the Jews, during the Hitler's regime, did not exist).

We also indulged in ruminations into the Polish history. Unfortunately, Mendek had a five-year hiatus in his education. When the war started in 1939, he was in the 7th grade. Subsequently life in the ghetto and later a string of concentration camps precluded any further education. Now he was too old to enter high school and unprepared for admission to a university. However he was super intelligent. Matter of fact it was the intelligence that, most likely, gave him the chance to survive the concentration camps.

Mendek introduced me to parts of Krakow that I didn't know well, having only visited it occasionally before the war, while living in Trzebinia. We walked frequently to the River Wisla (Vistula) that was only some 150 meters from the house we lived in.

Since most of the apartment houses between our house and the river were bombed out and essentially flattened, we had direct access to the river walking next to the immense walls of the famous royal palace, Wawel. It has originally been a medieval castle, the seat of early Polish Royalty and the original capitol of Royal Poland.

We walked under the high flying buttresses of Wawel's defensive walls constructed on a hill overlooking the city and the River Wisla. We walked towards the river through a ring of parks, the "Planty" surrounding the "Old City" and the Wawel. Wawel bordered the river and between the palace's walls and the river there was a beautiful stretch of green filled with blooming acacia trees. There, under the imposing and, in this area, seemingly brooding Wawel walls, was the famous "Dragon Cave." According to the legend, the dragon required regular sacrifices of virgins to appease him and prevent the destruction of the castle.

Mendek and I felt that our people had sacrificed sufficiently to appease the dragon and we felt very comfortable to sit on the grass in front of the cave, in the little forest looking over the Wisla River to the other bank to the Krakow suburb of Praha. There was no street here, thus no traffic; usually there were very few people coming to this part of the river. We spent a great deal of time there, enjoying the peace of the surroundings, discussing the war, looking with trepidation at the current situation and trying to understand!

Mendek was a very sensitive fellow, at the same time he was extremely practical and clever. He could fix anything with his hands. At the same time he had a phenomenal memory, both photographic and co-relational. It was the memory that saved his life in the concentration camps. In Auschwitz, where he was sent after the ghetto in Krakow and camp in Plaszow, one of his supervisors noted his incredible memory and suggested that he be transferred to work in a camp supplying labor for German aircraft industry. He was transferred to Mauthausen were he was placed to work in stock rooms. He acted there as a human computer. Given a serial number of the part needed, he would provide instantly the exact location of the part, the building number, the floor, the room number, the cabinet number, the shelf number, the row and the bin number. This remarkable ability was his salvation. It gave him his life. Now, however, essentially alone, parents and siblings all murdered in the camps, he lost a great deal of will.

We spend hours going over these issues. He felt that he was too old to enter high school and too depressed to strike out alone to catch up with his formal education. The hiatus was just too great. He gave up. However, he continued searching for surviving members of his immediate family. One day a family acquaintance came over inquiring whether any members of Mendek's family survived. He received a letter from his cousin in the U.S.A. informing him that Mendek's sister survived the concentration camps. Shortly after liberation, she met a young man and unable to find other members of her family, she decided not to wait any longer but marry him and immigrate to America. She had written many times to her home address and to some of the relatives. The letters were being returned with notes "unknown" or "couldn't be delivered." The mailman must have decided that all of her immediate family was eliminated in the camps since people with other names were living in the apartment. He didn't bother to inquire any further assuming that people living under the address were some strangers. This callous, disinterested attitude of postal clerks towards the Jews after the war in Poland was not rare.

This news galvanized Mendek and obviously the rest of the family. Mendek immediately got in touch with his newly found sister in America and began an inquiry about the possibilities of emigrating to join his sister in America. An inquiry at the Polish State Department immediately doused him with a bucket of cold water. As we quickly found out from others who wished to emigrate, to obtain an exit visa from Poland was a drawn out, difficult and an almost impossible task. Furthermore, it was also very difficult to obtain an immigration visa for the U.S.A. There was a "Polish quota, which was very small and there was an established queue to get on the list for obtaining an application. One might have had to wait a couple years or more just to get an application. The picture was dismal.

My parents and uncles, as well as all the cousins with whom we lived, were very ambivalent about the direction of our immediate future and the question as to what steps to take next. Again the family had long discussions, meeting with friends and acquaintances, arguments, staying up nights being tormented again by the questions: "what to do next" and "how to do it."

Finally, our cousins made the first decision. Their parents owned a great deal of real estate in Krakow as well as businesses that were still active, although in hands of strangers, Poles, who took over the businesses during the war. In view of this, the cousins decided to stay in Krakow, hopefully for a short while, to dispose of these assets. Little did they know!

In the meanwhile my parents and uncles wrote to our relatives all over the world. Mother had a sister in New York who went there at the turn of his century as a little girl. Father had sisters in London, England, Zagreb, Yugoslavia and Melbourne, Australia. They lived there since before the war and were very happy to hear that we survived the war and were interested in leaving the continent.

Obviously the very first question was how to get an exit visa from Poland. At the moment no one had any good ideas. For me personally the question was even more complicated. I still did not know where Ania was. I was quite certain that they must have by now returned from Russia. However, I was unable to get in touch with her brother, Kuba. I had written him at the address Ania gave me but received no answer. I felt a great degree of sadness around me. The initial elation we basked in upon return from the Soviet Union to the land from which we left in such a hurry while escaping the horrors of war in 1939, a land were we left behind most of our families, was essentially gone.

Each member of the family was severely depressed. The reality was beginning to dawn on our cousins. The Germans and their minions murdered most of the immediate and more distant members of the families. There was nothing there in Poland to return to. A burned out, scarred land populated by the ghosts of our families and prewar friends. The trip to Trzebinia has essentially destroyed my father's equanimity and logical approach to life. He remembered the stately, busy and purposeful life before the war; the satisfactions and comforts he earned from hard study and later hard professional work of both Mother and him; the beautiful house and garden we owned; the family, grandparents, uncles, aunts and cousins, surrounding us with vibrant well being of their professional work or business. All of it was gone. The cold reality was beginning to dawn on him. It was also beginning to dawn on all of us. Mother started repeating: "I don't want to live in a cemetery."

The desire to further analyze the historical, psycho-social and economic factors that might have contributed during the war to the atrocious and inhumane behavior of the country and its Polish inhabitants towards its Polish inhabitants who also happened to be Jewish has died. I felt saddened and confused by the revelations concerning the behavior of Poland as a country and of Poles as people.

I thought that I could partly explain the current hostility of a large segment of the Polish population toward a small group of Jewish survivors on the basis of at least two factors: a. A guilt reaction for the behavior during the German occupation and b. Identification of the Jewish population in postwar Poland with communist sentiments not shared by many Poles. The hostility during the German occupation was much more difficult to explain. I felt confused and depressed. My depression was deepened further since I was entirely unsuccessful in locating Ania.

****

One day Leon came home all excited, he met one of his old friends who, before the war, was a partner in one of his businesses. The friend lived now in Wroclaw, formerly Breslau, were he claimed the business climate to be good and he wanted Leon to join him. Wroclaw was a large city in the western region of Poland, originally part of Germany that was annexed after the war with the Allied approval as reparation for the large hunk of eastern Poland taken over after WWII by the Soviet Union. Uncle Leon decided to visit Wroclaw. Upon return he bubbled with excitement. "The mood there," he was telling us, "is totally different. There is a large number of Jewish survivors of both the German camps and Soviet atrocities who live there. Living in Wroclaw they are away from their hometowns, the immediacy of the concentration camps and mass graves. This puts in their psyche a distance from the unthinkable; it allows them to concentrate more clearly on immediate problems, on earning a living and on planning for the future." He even inquired about the University and learned that the Medical School was open.

My parents didn't even stop to think. Mother asked instantly, "When can we go?" Father didn't even ask. He was ready to go and glad that she felt similarly. Mother realized that she lost most of her sisters who before the war lived in Krakow. She considered the city a cemetery. She wanted to get out as soon as possible.

Uncle Juzek, who was in touch by mail with my aunt, his sister, in Australia who was ready to do everything possible to get papers for him, also expressed the desire to go. His reasoning was that Wroclaw was closer to the border and he began to seriously contemplate the possibility of getting out of Poland by smuggling out through the borders since a legal exit visa was almost impossible to get.

The meager belongings we brought with from Russia consisted mainly of junk and most of it was discarded. Since we had no money, no new clothing items could be purchased. We traveled lightly!

The parting with the cousins was difficult; at that point, to our knowledge, they were the only few survivors of our huge European family who were not dead, victims of the Soviet or German camps. For me, the parting with Mendek was most difficult. In the few weeks we spent together, we became almost like brothers. He was set to do anything to join in America the only surviving member of the immediate family, his sister.

Ever since the years in Soviet Russia, I dreamed of going to America. We promised each other to meet there. We didn't even think how easy such promise was to make but how difficult it would be to carry it out. Actually neither one of us had any concrete plans how to achieve this goal. Not only did we not have any plans, we didn't even have the slightest idea how to go about making the plans.

Once the family decided to move, tickets were purchased, we got on the train and left Krakow forever. The train journey lasted only a few hours. Upon arrival in Wroclaw, Leon went looking for his friend. He had his friend's address but at that time, there were no functioning telephones. He had to find a way to get there. Fortunately there were already several tramway lines functioning in the city and he remembered his way to the friend's house from the last visit. He estimated that he would return in less than a couple hours. Three hours went by and there was no Leon.

Stella was crying, tired and hungry. All of us were hungry. There was no food on the train and during the brief stops at various stations we had trouble getting food. There were no food concessions at the small stations, and in most instances, the stations were either destroyed or severely damaged.

We had Leon's friend's address and Juzek was ready to go there with Father. Mother didn't like this idea being concerned about our safety during their absence. As we hotly debated the pros and cons of this move we noted Leon getting off the tramway car with another man. I let out a happy "war cry" and ran to meet them. Leon was walking with a handsome, fashionably dressed, young man. He introduced me to him. His name was Jan and he promptly informed me that he was a successful businessman dealing with arrangements for obtaining proper identification papers and for making arrangements for moving out of the country as well any necessary arrangements in courts and government offices.

By the time we joined the rest of the family I had already learned that Jan was Leon's friend from before the war in Krakow and that they were involved together in a variety of lucrative business ventures. This sounded intriguing.

As we listened to Jan, the mood of the family improved, particularly since he promptly invited us to stay with him until we could find suitable living quarters. He said that he lived alone in a three room, spacious apartment and our moving in temporary with him would be no hardship whatsoever.

Looking at our luggage he also said that we might be able to gather everything and take the tramway to his apartment. Between Father, Leon, Juzek and I, we had the luggage transported to Jan's apartment in no time.

With the necessary "pull" in the City Government offices exerted by Jan, we were assigned an apartment in no time. Actually we got two apartments, one for the uncles and one for our family. This was an unbelievable luxury. This was the first time since the war broke out seven years earlier on September 1, 1939, that we had a private apartment only for our family.

This was a "huge" apartment--two bedrooms, a living room, a kitchen and a huge closet that could be used as a storage room, although we didn't have anything to store. My parents stayed with Stella in a very nice size bedroom and I was relegated to the second, tiny bedroom. It was indeed tiny, housing a bed, a closet (in Europe one usually had a free-standing closet wardrobe) and a tiny desk with a chair. It was cramped, but this was the first time in my life that I had my own room. I was thrilled, I was happy and I wanted to stay in the room all hours of the day and night to savoir the newfound luxury and privacy. But, this wasn't all. The apartment was beautifully furnished. There was a handsome, blond wood, living room and a stately mahogany bedroom set. The kitchen housed modern, built-in white painted cabinets, an almost new gas range and a gleaming sink. This was unadulterated luxury. We all wallowed in it.

I learned later that these apartments belonged to German families who, under an agreement imposed by Russia and the Allies, were evicted or voluntary left for East Germany. This was irony. Our beautiful house, full of furniture, including expensive art, particularly paintings, was robbed by the Germans and taken to Germany in 1939. Now we had the opportunity to live in an apartment formerly occupied by Germans and enjoy their furniture. The difference being that we didn't rob or confiscate their furniture. We used it for a few months, taking good care of it during this time; and within three months, we left the apartment and Wroclaw. But this I will deal with later.

Looking out the window of my room I could see a good bit of Wroclaw, or what used to be Breslau. There were mountains of rubble piled up everywhere. Here and there were blocks of partly damaged three to five-story high apartment houses. Occasionally one could see intact houses like the one we lived in.

Once we settled in the apartment, I went to inquire about the Medical School. Indeed the Medical School was functioning under Polish management with Polish faculty. I explained my situation to the Registrar, provided her with my school documents from Alma Ata and was told to return within a week. The secretary also told me that there was a Jewish Student Union that I might wish to visit.

This was a good bit of information. I got the address and set myself on the way to the Union.

While walking there, I mused about the promptness of the secretary's diagnosis of my being Jewish, just looking at me. I was always told that I do not look particularly "Jewish." She apparently must have had a keen sense of identifying some specific diagnostic characteristics highly specific for the Jews!

Upon arriving at the address she gave me, I found a large, partly destroyed apartment house with a hand-lettered sign in front proclaiming: "Jewish Student Union." I eagerly walked in and found myself in a large unfurnished room full of young people, milling around, talking and jostling each other.

With astonishment and surprise, I spied, standing at the opposite wall, the tall frame of an old friend from Alma Ata, Staszek. The year we were departing from the Soviet Union, he was finishing Medical School in Alma Ata. I was very eager to talk to him since he was always full of information and good ideas. While I hurriedly made my way across the room to meet him, he noticed me, and came running to meet me. We hugged and laughed, obviously happy having met.

First, I asked about his wife, a beautiful, stately looking Russian girl with flaming red hair and the biggest blue eyes I had ever seen, actually bigger then Ania's. I knew very well because she was Mother's patient in Alma Ata, visiting frequently with her dental problems. His answers too were halting; apparently while Tania (Tatiana), his wife, was well and they decided to have a child, his entire immediate family was murdered in concentration camps. He was obviously upset and not happy to talk about it. Instead he tried to change the topic and tell me of his successes. He completed the course of medical studies in the Soviet Union and was informed that in Poland he would need to take qualifying exams to get a special certificate to allow him to take "Staz" a form of an internship in a hospital.

As we talked, a nice girl, a couple years older than I, came over. She was very nice looking and very friendly, constantly laughing and talking. Staszek introduced me to her. Her name was Duska. She was a student at the Medical Faculty. I told both of them about my visit to the University and was reassured that if problems arise, the Student Union may be able to help. This was good to hear. I got their addresses and promised to visit them.

The following week, upon returning to the University, I was informed that they would be willing to administer three one-hour examinations, one in organic chemistry, one in botany and one in osteology. If I passed these exams with grades above average in all of the three subjects I would be admitted to the second semester, currently in progress, and from that point on would be permitted to continue my studies in a normal fashion. I eagerly took on this challenge. It was to be an oral examination administered by professors from each of the respective disciplines. I was primarily concerned by the botany exam.

First, I disliked the subject and having a mind that rebelled against learning by rote memory, as required definitely for botany, I had to borrow a botany textbook and quickly try to review and memorize the hundreds of names of plants and their complex classifications. Still, it was a tough going. I am certain that I passed the exam only because of the kindness of the professor, a jolly rotund fellow who was more interested in learning how I survived the rigors of the Gulag in the Marijskaja Republic, rather than ascertaining the depths of my knowledge of botany.

I was not concerned about the other two examinations. I knew chemistry very well and osteology was a game I constantly played with Tolek. We quizzed each other on the knowledge of all the tubercles, foramina and other characteristics of the bones and betting, sometimes heavily on the replies. Indeed, I was quite self-assured when taking the two other examinations, although the Professor of Chemistry was quite pedantic and difficult to please. After completing all three examinations I was told to return to the Dean's office in one week to learn of the results of the examinations.

When I came home after the last examination, Leon was already waiting for me impatiently with news that totally swept me off my feet. Apparently, that morning he visited Walbrzych on some business, a town not far from Wroclaw. While walking down a street, he noticed Ania's father walking on the other side. They had a tumultuous reunion. Leon immediately started to agitate him to move to Wroclaw. He even promised to arrange for them a very nice apartment in the same house that we lived in. Ania's father listened to Leon's arguments very carefully. Apparently they were not very happy in Walbrzych and he promised Leon to discuss with his wife the possibility of a move to Wroclaw. Leon pursued the matter further by going to their house to talk to Ania's mother and try to persuade her. She apparently was delighted to see Leon. They enjoyed the reunion and by the time Leon was finish talking, and he was very good at it, Ania's parents were essentially convinced to move.

They were unable to "organize" a nice apartment in Walbrzych. The one they had was tiny and not on a very nice street. They had no friends in the neighborhood and had not found adequate jobs. The move to Wroclaw sounded to them very promising. I couldn't contain myself and finally blurted out, "How is Ania? Did you see her?"

"No," replied Leon, "I didn't see her, she wasn't home. I was told, however, that she is well and that she was also considering a visit to Wroclaw to investigate the possibility of entering the Medical School here." I was full of questions, impatient and all excited. Obviously I was ready to hop a train and go to Walbrzych right there and then. Leon restrained me. "Hold on," he said, "Ania's father will be here tomorrow to look around and I predict that they will move here within a week. Let me see if I can arrange for an apartment for them in our building. I noted that there are two vacant apartments."

I was speechless. I wanted to jump on the train and rush to Walbrzych. I wanted to see Ania right then. The obviously impetuous impatience was showing. It however, had to be tempered with the wishes of my parents, by the practicality of the venture, by logic and yes, by the costs. I decided to wait, see Mr. Schneider and learn how he may feel about the move and if positively, what would be his idea about the promptness of the move.

I didn't sleep well that night and got up very early. First I paced the room but later I went outside not to wake up the rest of the family. The sun was already well above the horizon painting pink the sharp edges of the ruins of buildings reaching for the sky. I walked among the broken bricks picking my way carefully and slowly, climbing up a mound of brick and rubble, all that remained of houses across the street from our building, one of four still standing essentially intact on our block. My thoughts were totally occupied by Ania. I tried to visualize how she looked. I worried that she could have forgotten me, or worse, found someone else. Obviously the worries were baseless. Or were they? How could I be so sure of myself?

After breakfast, I ran out to patrol the front of the house and wait for Ania's father. Soon Leon came out and joined me. "Go home," he said, laughing. "The train doesn't arrive at the railroad station until noon. At that time we will go to the station to meet him."

"I know about the noon arrival but there is an earlier train and there is a possibility that he could take it and arrive here early. I don't want him to miss our house," I said.

"Well," said Leon, "suit yourself, but I am certain that he will not arrive on the early train."

By eleven o'clock I started pestering Leon to get going to the railroad station. Finally he agreed to go. We arrived to the station by quarter to twelve. The train from Walbrzych didn't arrive until one thirty. From the distance, I could see Ania's father stepping out of the railroad carriage. Then--I couldn't believe my eyes--I saw Ania alighting from the train and following her father. She was wearing a beautiful dress with a pattern of green and blue leaves scattered throughout a white background, the same dress that she wore seeing me off at the railroad station in Alma Ata.

I didn't know how to behave or what to say. Should I give her a hug? I never kissed her before and although that was exactly what I wanted to do, obviously it would not be acceptable. Finally, I reached the spot they both stood. I pumped Ania's father's hand vigorously and immediately turned my attention to Ania who stood behind him. I looked into her round, ocean blue eyes, lingered over her golden hair swept up high off her forehead, her full, naturally red lips and the straight patrician nose. Yes, this was the face I loved and always kept before my eyes day and night ever since we parted. She came over and with a smile extended her hand to me. I took it, shook it and kept on holding it while grinning stupidly. Finally, I let go of her hand and tried to say something but couldn't get a word out of my throat.

In the meanwhile, Leon took their satchel and we walked out of the railroad station. I took Ania by the hand and followed them. We still had not said a word to each other. Finally, while still holding on to her hand I said very quietly, "it is so good to see you. I was unable to contact Kuba and was worried sick that I will never able to see you again."

Once I got this out it was as if a dam had spilled its water. I couldn't stop talking. I wanted to tell her in the next five minutes all that had happened since we parted. I am certain that the only thing I accomplished was to sound like an idiot and confuse her.

She didn't say much while I talked, she shook her head or nodded, occasionally she gave my hand a squeeze. Finally I stopped talking. She looked at me and in her even voice said, "Well, I don't have much to say. Upon arrival to Warsaw we found Kuba. The reason you couldn't locate him was because he changed his address after you left Alma Ata. Upon arrival to Poland we were told not to go back home to Radom. It was suggested that we go to Szczecin; I don't really know why we were directed to go there. Things, however, were not right in Szczecin. Father's former employee from before the war looked us up and suggested that we move to Walbrzych were he lived; we did. And here we are."

When we got home there was a real reunion. Everyone was happy to see Ania and her father. In no time Leon showed them the apartment located a floor below us. The apartment was very attractive, nicely furnished, clean and roomy. Ania's father was impressed. I couldn't tell if Ania really liked the entire idea. I told her that I was given the opportunity to take qualifying exams and had passed them, thus, I was to start my studies again in the Wroclaw Medical School in a week.

It was agreed that Ania and her father would stay with us overnight, return to Walbrzych the next morning and let us know later what the decision about moving would be. In the meanwhile, we initiated the necessary steps to obtain the apartment in our building for them.

That evening I took Ania to the Jewish Student Union. There were a lot of students but Staszek wasn't there. Soon I noticed my new acquaintance, Duska, talking to a tall student about her age. I felt a bit insecure to approach her, she was a bit older and looked to be very popular. I didn't want to impose.

However, I thought that Ania might wish to meet her. This gave me the courage to go over. As Ania and I approached them, Duska turned and noticed us. She beckoned to us and with a huge smile on her face that I learned later to be her trademark, introduced us to the fellow. His name was Genek and he was an advanced student in Pharmacology. Ania was visibly impressed that in the short period of time I managed to make some contacts and succeeded in getting into the Medical School. On the way home she was very quiet, obviously thinking about the new experiences. I didn't want to interrupt her thoughts and walked silently next to her, when I took her by her arm she didn't object to it.

The next day they departed.

The rest of the week dragged itself out; I couldn't find a bit of peace in myself anyplace. I was constantly thinking of Ania and dreading the possibility that they may decide not to come to Wroclaw. There were no means of communicating with Ania except by mail. A letter however, could take a week or even two to breach the "huge" distance between the two cities, probably some fifty miles apart! There was however, no remedy for this inconvenient fact. Luckily, Leon had to be in Walbrzych the next week on business, and I was convinced that he would visit the Schneiders, that's how I hoped to get some information!

Monday I went to the University. There I was directed to join the class dealing with the second half of organic chemistry, the class in physics, the "Practicum" (laboratory) in anatomy and lectures in anatomy. Myology was to be covered in the anatomy lectures during this last part of the second semester. I learned that the courses would not be easy and that they would take up most of my time.

One of the major problems was terminology; I took no Latin in Russia while my Polish classmates received solid grounding in this language while in the Gymnasium. This gave them a definite advantage over me in respect to learning new medical terminology. The second problem was the Polish language itself. While I knew spoken Polish, my knowledge of it was very primitive. I finished with the Polish language studies in the 5th grade. My classmates learned the literary Polish language and the fine aspects of grammar in the Gymnasium. Thus, I had to learn not only the medical and scientific subjects but also the languages. This, however, was a challenge and challenges I liked.

Leon returned from Walbrzych with good news. The business was quite successful and the Schneiders decided to move to Wroclaw.

They were to arrive by the end of the week. I busied myself with school until they arrived and then spent most of the time with them helping with the move.

They moved into the apartment a floor below us with no difficulties or surprises. It was a very nice apartment, beautifully furnished. I felt a little uneasy having Ania live just a few steps away. I must confess that I wanted to be with her all the time. This geographic condition made it easier but also made it much more difficult to stay apart!

Once Ania arrived, it became a burning issue to get her admitted to the University, particularly since she was even further behind into the semester. We had to mobilize all our "influence resources" to get her admitted. This time it took really a great deal of effort. Staszek fortunately had considerable influence, both in the Student Union and at the University. Between the forceful support of the Student Union and the inside influences of Staszek, Ania was given a chance to take exams and to qualify for admission. Passing the exams was no problem for her and soon we celebrated her admission to the school. Our lives returned to a routine on an even keel.

Uncle Leon was becoming more and more successful in his business while Juzek was more and more depressed and unhappy. My parents opened a little dental office in one of the rooms in the apartment and started practicing dentistry on a tiny scale. Both of them were getting more and more disenchanted with the opportunities and the emotional life in Poland. The murders of the family and friends during the war weighed on them heavily. Furthermore, it became clear that Poland, most probably, would not be granting exit visas, particularly not to those who did not have a definite entry visa into some country in this world.

This unsettling situation spurred further inquiries concerning illegal methods of getting out of Poland and for us these inquiries became a daily activity. We learned that smuggling across the border to Czechoslovakia was a viable possibility. One could make arrangements with a local peasant or have one of the Zionist groups organize the entire venture.

I became acquainted with the Zionist movement through the Jewish Student Union. The Union was a very busy place. There were always students milling throughout the building. There was good news, bad news, good information, bad information and gossip. There was always a lot of gossip. Gossip about the girls, the professors, the school, about love affairs, marital fights, essentially about everything and anything.

It was the exuberance of youth, particularly this youth that was finally presented with some freedom or probably even more so with hope, hope for a brighter future, an end to constant threats of death, torment or torture. There was always someone there who you wanted to talk to, to ask something or to give something. I became an intimate part of this living organism and literally lived there whenever I had free time. It was there that I learned about the active emigration to Palestine organized directly by groups of young people, all survivors of the war and prosecution by all kinds, types and shapes of peoples.

Boris was one of them. I knew him ever since I joined the Union. I simply was not aware of his work with the Zionists. Now that I became interested in the Zionist movement, we became very friendly. I attended with him some of the meetings of one of the Zionist groups in Wroclaw. I learned about the extent of the work of the Zionist groups in Europe at these meetings. I was absolutely amused by the ubiquitous presence of the organization throughout Europe, Africa and the Americas.

They had an extensive network assisting Jews to get out from Poland, make their way through Czechoslovakia and Austria to Germany where the Allies set up the "Displaced Persons" (D.P.) camps. In the camps, the Zionists frequently organized Aliyah's and led them, usually through Italy, to the British administered Palestinian Mandate, the ancient land of the Jews. I listened carefully about the ways of leaving Poland and talked about it with my parents and uncles. A plan for a possible run from Poland was germinating.

In the meanwhile, Ania and I were working hard to complete the second semester at the Medical Faculty. We would spend a great deal of time at the Medical School in the anatomy laboratory completing the dissections. We talked about everything--including the future. We agreed that there was no future for us in Europe that we should emigrate as soon as possible, and if at all possible go to America. While we talked nonchalantly about completing school, about acquiring knowledge and skills to contribute significantly to the advancement of humanity, about immigrating to America and starting a new life, we were talking about the future, about years.

While we were talking about the future, I was falling more and more in love, but I was trying to be a gentleman. On the other hand, however, I yearned to take Ania in my arms, and kiss her, and caress her, and hold and tell her how much I loved her! I still couldn't build up sufficient bravery to tell her about my love for her or, at least, kiss her.

On number of occasions I hugged her and held her very tightly, but in the last minute just before mustering enough valor to kiss her I would back off, afraid to kiss her, afraid that she may think that I may be taking advantage of her. Frequently on the way home from school, we would stop in a park that was partly destroyed during the war. In this park there were ruins of former Nazi meeting grounds with huge speaker stands, and spectator stone benches and walls around these structures, where Hitler would make speeches in front of huge audiences of Hitler Jugend (Hitler Youth) or other Nazi groups.

We would sit there, look at the ruins and muse at the futility of demagogues, at the insanity of some ideas and at the price some groups of people had paid for it. We were sad. But as I sat still and looked into Ania's eyes I knew that we had a different future ahead of us and was happy that I had her with me to face the road ahead.

If only I could muster enough bravery to tell her all this. Oh yes, we talked about the future, we indeed talked about our *futures*, but I never could get enough gumption to talk about our *future*.

The next time I came by the Union, I had a pleasant surprise. Inetka, a girl I knew well in Alma Ata, was there. She matriculated in the school and was studying chemistry. We had a long talk and I learned that her mother, little brother and stepfather were in Wroclaw, but they decided to go to Germany to a D.P. camp as soon as the semester would be over for Inetka. I also learned that once the school was over she was planning to go to Warsaw and visit her father.

This gave me an idea. I thought I might go with her and look in Warsaw for Tolek, since I lost track of him after leaving Russia. They were supposed to join his sister there.

While we talked, Ania came over and we had a great reunion further extended when Duska and Staszek joined us and we all went to get some coffee. A coffee shop was a great innovation in Wroclaw, a development that had just occurred. No coffee shops had opened since the end of the war.

That afternoon, while going home with Ania, I stumbled across an idea of how to broach my love for her. I decided that I would make a gold ring for her. First, a ring made of real gold was a first class, unheard of luxury. Secondly, I could get the gold from Mother who still had some dental gold and thirdly, I knew how to cast gold objects. I would cast it the way gold teeth are cast. Once the ring was completed, I could finish it and polish it on my parents' dental equipment.

The only thing I would need to pay for would be an engraving on the little golden square I was to fashion on the front part of the ring. I couldn't wait to broach this idea to my parents and find out if they would let me have the gold and let me have the use of the equipment.

Also, I had to be careful not to inadvertently let the secret out to Ania. I quickly said my goodnights to her at their apartment door and ran up to our place. I noted that Ania was put out at my quick departure. Usually I would linger, trying to delay the departure and trying to talk her into getting together after dinner.

Well, today was different. I was too excited and too impatient. I had to talk to my parents that moment. When I broached my idea to them, there was a sparkle in their eyes. They thought that it was a grand idea. Obviously they were happy to let me have the gold and obviously they would assist me all the way through with the manufacture of the ring.

I couldn't wait; I wanted to start the work on the ring right then and there. Father was laughing. "Come on," he said, "there is plenty of time, and we have to eat supper first. But, if you want to, you can start carving the ring now."

He gave me a piece of wax and asked me, "Do you know the size of her finger?"

I went white, "no," I said, "Do I have to?"

Father said, "Well, unless you know, how will you make the ring the size to fit her finger?" I didn't think of it, I started getting panicky, but he said, “Don’t worry, we will estimate, if necessary we will readjust later. “Here”, he said, handing me the wax and a carving knife, “start carving.” I deftly carved out a ring with a small square signet in front. Father looked at it and suggested to round up the edges of the square and carve little lines in the four corners of the square. In no time I was finished. Mother called for dinner. I ran, I wanted to be done with dinner as soon as possible to get back and continue working on the ring.

Stella, who was already eleven years old, heard everything and knew exactly what was going on. She laughed and was about to make a snide comment when Father took one look at her and she thought better than putting her nose where it didn’t belong.

Indeed I quickly finished eating and ran back to continue working. The next step was to prepare a bit of gypsum, pour it into a metal form and place the ring in it. Then I created a channel leading from the wax ring to the outside and the Gypsum was allowed to totally harden. At this point, the gypsum form with the wax ring in it was placed in water and boiled. The wax melted, ran out leaving a mold into I poured molten gold. Once the gold solidified, I broke the mold, removed it and polished it on the electric polisher that Father used for polishing gold teeth.

It was a simple job but I was really excited working on the ring. I couldn’t wait to have it engraved. There was an engravers’ shop about a thirty-minute walk from our apartment.

The next morning I told Ania that she should go to the University alone since I had an errand to run first and that I would meet her in the anatomy lab later.

That afternoon Ania’s parents were going with Leon to the market to sell a bedspread and I thought that would be a good time to give Ania the ring. I wanted to do it in privacy and in quiet. The apartment appealed to me as the perfect place.

The engraver was willing to do the job while I waited. This was great. I wanted him to engrave only two letters, an “A” intertwined with an “E.”

Once the morning classes finished, I suggested that we have a small lunch in a quaint little place close to our apartment. Ania smiled as she asked if I had made killing on the black market and what was the big occasion. We very rarely ate in restaurants. Our finances didn't favor such activities. I was, however, much to nervous and anxious to respond in a clever way. I rehearsed this lunch a hundred of times but was totally unable to say anything of consequence. All the way through the lunch, I tried to figure out how to get her inside their apartment, and once I would, what was I going to say.

As we were leaving the restaurant I reminded myself that I had forgotten my chemistry notebook at home and that I would stop to get it. She said it was fine because she also wanted to stop in her apartment to get a jacket. We agreed that I would pick her up in a few minutes.

After arriving home, I fell to my knees thanking God for this perfect turn of events. I checked on the ring that actually was in my pocket the entire time and ran down to Ania's apartment. She was at the door ready to leave when I asked her if I may come in. Giving me a surprise look, she said, "Sure," and opened the doors wider. I walked in but almost immediately lost my nerve; I felt like turning around and walking out into the hallway. With the last bits of will power, I forced myself not to turn around but to keep on moving to the couch where I sat down. I looked up at Ania and asked her to sit next to me. She smiled and while asking, "What do you want to tell me?" she sat down.

I averted her direct gaze and the sparkling smile and said, "I have something for you." She tilted her face and now laughing loudly, inquired playfully, "what is the big secret?" I still was ready to jump up and bolt out of the apartment when suddenly I felt her right hand over my left that was resting on the couch. It felt as if an electric shock had traversed through my body. A thought ran through my mind, it would be now or never.

I reached into the pocket and wordlessly handed her the ring. I had fantasies how I would hand her the ring while using the most beautiful words to tell her how much I love her. Then, take her in my arms and kiss her and sweep her off her feet. Even in my fantasies, however, the will power let me down. I couldn't even fantasize what should or would happen next.

Instead, I realized, that I simply handed her the ring and then stood stupidly next to her, paralyzed by a feeling of… what? Fear, love, insecurity, inadequacy? I didn't know what I felt. Suddenly, I felt her arms around me and felt her lips on mine. I was kissing her, holding her, feeling her entire body pressed tightly against mine. I felt dizzy, happy, elated and confused.

We walked to the University together for the afternoon session holding hands but not saying a word. While there, we didn't say a word to each other. My gaze would not stray, even for an instant from Ania's beautiful, pure face. I couldn't wait for the sessions to finish and be able to walk home with her holding hands.

That afternoon we went to the Student Union. The place was full as usual. Inetka came over all excited. "I decided to go to Warsaw," she cried over the din of student voices shouting all around us.

"When," I asked.

"Saturday," she answered. "Why don't you come along?"

I looked at Ania and asked. "Will you come?" She didn't answer immediately. Ultimately she said, "let's think about it. I don't know how my parents will feel about us taking off alone for such a long trip."

I smiled encouragingly although I had similar doubts. "Well," Inetka said, "the semester will be over this Friday and we will have time to do it."

We talked a bit about the trip, about the ending of the semester and about the general situation in Poland. Inetka told us that her parents were essentially convinced that they should try to smuggle across the border and go on to Germany. "It is only a matter of time before the Poles will get after the Jews again," she said.

I was less sanguine. Smiling, I suggested that she needed to have a bit more faith in humanity. We argued about this for a while and parted by promising each other to decide soon about the trip.

When I got home that evening, I found my parents, both uncles and Ania's parents deep in conversation concerning the possibility of leaving Poland. Leon was adamant in stating his case for staying in Poland. He felt that the business climate was good, since he had been doing very well the past couple months and didn't want to go now to a D.P. camp or to Israel. He had no fear of the Poles. He had excellent contacts locally and felt that the Poles could be fully trusted to behave humanely towards the Jews, particularly now, after what happened during the war.

Juzek was also adamant. He wanted to leave Poland. He was certain that once he was out of Poland he would get a visa to Australia with the help of Aunt Zosia, his sister, who lived there. He genuinely wanted to go there. Ania's and my parents were still ambivalent and I was too busy at this moment with Ania and with school to be worried about this issue.

I was more interested in getting my parents' permission to go to Warsaw. Since both parents were together, I broached the question to them of going to Warsaw with Ania and Inetka. As I brought it up, Ania walked in. She didn't find her parents home and figured that they may be visiting with us. She immediately supported my argument adding that we could leave Saturday and be back early the next week. Both sets of parents were a little reluctant. First, they were not swayed by Leon's arguments that Poles could be trusted not to turn against the Jews again, and they also worried that something bad could happen to us on the train.

Furthermore, I sensed that they were not entirely convinced that Ania and I should be permitted to travel alone for days with Inetka, a girl of almost our age and our good friend, as the only chaperon. I knew that we would not give a final answer that night, but Ania and I promised each other to lobby our respective parents to let us go and go that weekend.

When we got home on Friday, happy for having finished the semester, we couldn't stop discussing the final exams and speculating about the outcomes- hoping for high grades. Our parents joined us and informed us that they decided to let us go but they felt that we should go on a weekday. They felt that a weekday would be safer because there would be less of a chance for hooligans on the train during the workweek as compared to a weekend.

We were elated and set out immediately to see Inetka. When we arrived to Inetka's apartment, both of her parents were there. They were also a little weary in regard to the safety of this venture. However, ultimately they agreed to let us go.

We decided on a specific day of the next week and parted. On the way home, Ania and I had a long discussion concerning the trip. Actually, we had the same fears and concerns that troubled our parents. However, in our youthful exuberance and a taste for adventure we didn't take these concerns seriously or worry about them for a long time.

We hardly could wait for the day of departure. Uncle Leon was primarily concerned about our food on this trip. He told us that most likely we would not be able to get any food on the train and getting food at the railroad stations would be also problematic. The day before the departure, he showed up with a two-foot long salami and a beautiful round loaf of bread. Ania jumped and gave him an immense hug. Immediately he asked, "How many hugs for a loaf of bread. I will bring five, how many hugs do I get?" We all laughed and started packing.

We sat in the railroad car compartment with two middle-aged women and a young man. They obviously were Polish. We also could have easily passed for Polish kids; Ania with her bright blue eyes, golden hair and a small straight nose. Inetka had dark hair but also blue eyes and a slim tall figure; I had somewhat of a "Jewish" nose but my hair was auburn and eyes were gray-blue. We were not concerned.

Time was flying rapidly. Ania opened the basket with food and started making open face sandwiches. The aroma of the rye bread and salami was overpowering. We couldn't wait to sink our teeth into the salami.

However, before passing the sandwiches to all of us, Ania first offered some to the young fellow sitting with us in the compartment. We could see his eyes light up, however, he politely declined the offer. Ania with an encouraging smile insisted and he finally accepted it. In my mind, I was certain that he hoped for this outcome. Once he accepted the sandwich, the ice was broken and all four of us engaged in an animated conversation.

By morning the train pulled slowly into the Warsaw railroad station. The station by now was a familiar sight; I was there just several months back on the way from Russia. The station struck me to be much busier than I remembered; people were hurrying in all directions, pushing their way through the throngs, impressing me as being oblivious of the world around them. We said goodbyes to our new acquaintances at the train and disembarked rapidly.

The plan was to go first to Inetka father's address since this was the only address we were certain of at that time. Inetka was quite sure that she would be able to find her way there. After some inquiries from the tramway conductors, we took off and indeed found our way.

The meeting of Inetka and her father was very tumultuous. I never discussed with Inetka her family situation in respect to her father, stepfather and her mother. Ania and I elected to ignore it and left them for a little while to offer some privacy. They obviously were very happy to see each other. Inetka's father's apartment was, according to the prevailing standard, very spacious. It consisted of a living room, bedroom and a kitchen. There was also a private bathroom. This was an almost unheard of luxury.

He immediately invited us to stay with him, offering the bedroom to Inetka and Ania, and explained how I would share the living room with him. Ania and I, were very grateful to him and happily accepted the offer. Once this essential part of the household matters was resolved, we turned immediately towards the issue at hand. We had Kuba's address; it was only the matter of figuring out how to get there.

Inetka's father felt that Ania should have no problems finding the way to Kuba's address. However, to find Tolek was more complicated. There were no telephone books to consult. We decided to try again the address we had for him with the hope that the people living there may have had an idea where they moved.

This venture was a total fiasco. Not only was Tolek not at the address, as we expected, but also the people living there were totally oblivious of their names or whereabouts! Furthermore, other people living in these apartment houses, when learning of the names we were looking for, refused even to talk to us.

I was obviously disappointed not being able to contact Tolek, but we were looking forward to seeing Kuba and meet Bogna, his wife. Indeed we were very fortunate, at the very first trial we found the apartment and both of them, Kuba and Bogna, were home.

It was a great reunion for Ania. She loved and admired Kuba and immediately took to Bogna. I immensely enjoyed meeting Kuba in person. I knew of him only from Ania's tales. He turned out to be all and more that Ania was telling me. We spent a great afternoon together and promised to spend the next day together, before going back to Wroclaw.

Upon return to Wroclaw, we found the place in upheaval. We got in earlier than expected because we found a better connection from Warsaw and no one was meeting us at the railroad station. When we arrived by late afternoon, our apartment was full of people. Ania's parents were there, so were at least half a dozen of other friends including Inetka, her parents and her little brother. The Kielce pogrom was on everyone's lips.

I was particularly interested in this topic since the night before July 4, the day of the pogrom, we were traveling towards Warsaw and passing Kielce. Everyone was full of rumors. The only information that appeared to be fairly reliable was that a crowd of Poles attacked a group of Jews claiming that they tried to abduct and kill an eight-year-old Polish boy.

In this complex postwar atmosphere the event appeared to be a spontaneous anti-Semitic episode. It wasn't until much later that the information concerning this episode, "the Kielce Pogrom," was studied in great detail and a complex background of Soviet involvement in staging and provoking this and other anti-Semitic actions in Poland discovered. This involvement played an important role in the Soviet politics related to subjugation of Poland into the group of Soviet satellite countries. It was discovered later that these activities were also related in machinations designed to further Soviet influences in the Middle East.

All these complex political reasons for the pogroms were of no consequence for us at the moment. It was the naked fear and the impotent rage for what was being done to us after the years of murder and persecution. We only wanted some peace and an opportunity to live. This episode only strengthened our desire to leave and leave as soon as possible.

Uncle Leon, nevertheless, was very vociferous in his explanations. He felt strongly that he should stay and take advantage of the business climate to build up some financial advantages. Juzek, on the other hand, wanted to get out of Poland as rapidly as possible and to take advantage of the opportunity to go to Australia.

Father felt that we should leave Poland as soon as possible. He felt that there was nothing left for us here. Mother was still greatly upset with the loss of her family and friends. When looking around and being reminded by the environment of the murders committed on our close relatives as well as in general on our people, she couldn't find peace within herself. She also wanted to run. I easily could accept any decision made by my parents as long as it would include the Schneiders. I wasn't about to lose contact with Ania again.

As the discussions raged, two young men came in. They were active members of a Zionist organization. Leon invited them to tell us about their work. After a brief introduction, they promptly dove into the bare meat of the problem. The steady flow of illegal emigrants crossing the border from Poland to Czechoslovakia has been steadily increasing and after the Kielce pogrom reached alarming levels. In response, the Polish government beefed up the border patrols and promulgated a variety of rules to make it more difficult for the smugglers.

This made the job of the Zionists groups that made the contacts and paid most of the bribes, more difficult and much more expensive. Gilean, one of the boys, explained that until they got more money from the American Jewish organizations, all those who wished to cross the border would have to contribute to the cost. Zev, the other boy budged in, "we will, however, organize and fund the entire trip from Prague across the border to Austria and then to Germany."

Everyone speaking simultaneously tried to get detailed information from the two Zionists. It became clear that these boys were a godsend. They really had the contacts, the know-how to organize the escape and an organization capable of backing up this activity. We were convinced that this was the only viable solution to our problems. We formed a group of twelve, five from our family, three Schneiders and the four comprising Inetka's family. We were to leave by truck the following Saturday.

The best time to cross the border was on Saturday night when the border guards were least attentive and, if we were lucky, beginning to celebrate Sunday. I was amazed how rapidly everyone involved was able to make a decision because we had only a few short days to get ready.

Each person could take only one valise. Although we didn't own much and our possessions were meager, to decide what to put in one valise was extremely difficult.

Since Leon was staying behind, it was easier to take care of the belongings because he could sell what we could not take with us.

Actual packing took no time. The deciding took a little more time. Most of the time, however, was spent on saying goodbyes to those we were leaving behind and continually discussing the immediate and remote future.

We were told that the crossings became more difficult lately. There were, on several occasions, shootings resulting in serious injuries and even deaths. No one, however, was concerned about these possibilities. The worry was the unknown once we would get to Germany and the site of the ultimate destination. "Quo Vadis Domine?

During the several days prior to our departure, I spent a great deal of time with Ania. Whenever it was possible, we held each other tight; I kept on repeating how I would take care of her and how I would make sure that ultimately we would get to America.

America became the primary goal to strive for. It became the single overpowering desire and the ultimate ideal goal. I still don't understand how I developed the "chutzpa" to make such sweeping promises and why we made the United States our idealized goal. Nevertheless, it was perfectly clear in my mind that ultimately somewhere in this world I would finish my medical studies, that I would do all in my power to help Ania to do the same and that we would always be together.

CHAPTER 14 Crossing the Borders

Friday evening, after it turned totally dark, an indistinct panel truck pulled up at the back of the building. A middle-aged man with the appearance of a farmer jumped out and indicated to us to get into the truck. We quickly climbed in and he was off.

The last couple of hours we were obviously driving over a country road. The truck was gyrating widely when going over major size potholes. During the trip there was scarcely any conversation. We were forewarned by the driver, not in uncertain terms, to be as quiet as possible. Everyone was engrossed in their own thoughts. I was sitting next to Ania holding her hand tightly as if making sure that she will not disappear suddenly. Occasionally I whispered words of reassurance to her. I felt no fear or trepidation, just the opposite. I felt excited, I felt free, I felt as if we were flying off to a new and wonderful destination.

After the last sharp turn, the truck came to an abrupt stop. The back door opened and the driver said quietly: "Take your things and go to the barn. Try to be as quiet as possible. There is a barrel of water there and in the afternoon I will bring some food. When it turns dark, I will return and take you to the border. This will be a three to four hours walk depending on the situation in respect to the activities of the border patrols. Across the border my friend will meet you. He will take you to a small village where a panel truck will take you to Prague; there, the representatives of HIAS will meet you." There were no questions.

We all disembarked from the truck and entered the barn. It was small and filled with bundles of straw. Each one of us quickly acquired several bundles of straw and fixed some sitting arrangements. Mother unpacked some packages containing bread and sausages and soon we were busy devouring our food. Soon all of the people were eating.

It was still very early in the morning. Were we really this hungry? I wondered. I doubted that most of the people were actually that hungry. I think that they devoured the food to relieve the tension that had been building since we left Wroclaw.

Time just crept along. We whispered to each other to keep the noise level low. Inetka, Ania and I sat together. We were deeply involved in discussion concerning our immediate future. In our youthful optimism, we already jumped over the current obstacle--that is of staying alive now and of being able to escape to another country. We considered as our major concern the issue of whether we would be able to continue our studies and where? We had no idea where we may end up. However, it was reasonable to assume that it would be somewhere in Germany.

Inetka was a very serious student. She felt that chemistry was the basis of everything and she always made fun of those of us who studied medicine. We in turn felt that indeed chemistry is the basis of everything but medicine is the basis of life, thus it must be as important as chemistry. We fully appreciated how childish these arguments were, nevertheless, we enjoyed them since it was a fun way to pass time, particularly when the waiting was very stressful, as it was right then.

We couldn't wait for nightfall. Finally we heard steps. Everyone turned rigid in anticipation. The gate partly opened, a tall man squeezed himself into the barn. He was not our former driver. The man said in a soft voice, "It is time. We will walk out of the barn quietly, single file. I will lead, my son, who is waiting outside, will walk at the end forming the rear guard. All of you have to carry your own belongings. Please walk quietly, do not talk. We never know whom we may meet. It may be necessary to stop, and even under certain circumstances, to lie down on the ground. By midnight we should have crossed the border and be safely in Czechoslovakia, where a local person will meet us and take all of you to the next contact."

We left the barn in a single file. I was last except for the guide's son who closed our group at the very end. I asked Ania to walk just ahead of me. I wanted to have direct control of anything that may be happening to the two of us. As we left the barn the guide made a sharp left turn and entered a thick, dark forest, primarily pine trees. A thick layer of pine needles covered the ground; it felt as if we were walking on a cushion. It certainly was a nice surface to walk on, but more importantly, it kept the sound of our footsteps down except when one stepped on a dry branch that would crack when breaking. Our guide asked us to be careful and to avoid stepping on little branches when possible. Well the latter wasn't easy. It was pitch-black in the forest; we had difficulties seeing the person ahead of us. Fortunately we had an obviously experienced guide whom we followed in a single file. This made the task much easier. Otherwise, I am sure, we would be colliding with trees and anything in the way since we literally couldn't see anything.

My entire body was shaking with fear and anxiety, however, walking quietly through the forest brought to my mind the wonderful times I had during the vacations before the war when we walked through similar forests when similar aromas of the pine trees, mosses as well as patches of black berries attacked our ophthalmic senses. I was getting confused at times as we walked in the disorienting blackness and quiet. Where was I? Was I on vacations before the war or trying to illegally cross a border by walking through this forest?

My valise felt heavier and heavier by the minute. I could make out, ahead of me, Ania's silhouette barely walking and dragging her valise on the ground. Not wanting to make any sound I didn't say anything but took her valise from her hand and dragged on forward. Now with an almost impossible load, my progress was quite labored. However, I thought that by giving her a bit of rest she might be able to carry the valise later all by herself. Mercifully, the guide stopped and indicated that we could sit down but still not talk. I sat down next to Ania, put my arm around her and said into her ear in a barely audible whisper "I love you." She squeezed my fingers and placed her cheek against mine.

Suddenly the forest came alive with gunshots and screams of angry voices filling the air. The guide indicated to us with gestures to lie down and continue in absolute silence. All this must have been happening some distance from us since we couldn't see anything, not even lights from the shots. The guide didn't let us move for about one half of an hour after everything quieted down. Then he indicated that we were to get up and continue our trek through the forest.

Ania took her valise. I looked at my watch; it had phosphorescent numerals so I could make out the time. It was minutes after midnight. About thirty minutes later, he stopped and said to us, "Congratulations, you are in Czechoslovakia, please continue to be quiet. Wait here with my son; I will be back with our contact in a few minutes." Indeed in about twenty minutes he was back. "This is Vaclav," he said pointing to a shadowy figure next to him. "He will take you to a point on the highway to Prague where a truck will wait for you. Good luck, Go with God." "By the way," he said, "you can talk to each other, it's quite safe now. However, you will not be able to communicate with Vaclav unless you speak Czech. He, unfortunately, speaks only Czech. But this is OK, he will take you safely to the road; you will be there within one hour."

We took off barely dragging our valises but much relieved. I walked next to Ania helping her with her luggage. Although we were permitted to speak, no one engaged in conversation. We didn't feel that we were, as yet, "out of the woods," neither parenthetically nor literally speaking.

Suddenly we reached a clearing. The bright sunlight literally assaulted our eyes. About a hundred yards down the road I spied a small green military pickup truck with a green canvas top. Vaclav indicated that we should continue towards the truck. As we approached the truck two young men in khaki slacks and white shirts approached us with extended arms. The shouted "Shalom, Shalom" and started hugging us. They spoke Polish. The first thing they said to us was: "You do not need to be scared or concerned any more. You are safe here."

All of us started crying and kissing them and thanking them and telling them how happy and relieved we were to be there with them after the rather stressful months in Poland and the couple hair raising days while crossing the border.

They explained that we would be going by truck to Prague. There we would stay overnight in a hotel and subsequently continue to Vienna, Austria. In Vienna, we would go through a quick medical examination and after few days or weeks would be transported to Germany. In Germany, we would be placed in a Displaced Persons (D.P.) camp. Apparently they had it all well organized.

I had several questions: 1. "What are Displaced Persons? 2. Who organized the camps and for what purposes and….."

I obviously had many questions but when Father looked at me briefly but knowingly, I understood that I should stop. That I did although I did not get answers to most of my questions.

Matter of fact even later after we got to the D.P. camps, I didn't get answers to many of these questions. It wasn't until years later that I learned the details pertaining to D.P. camps. I feel that some of these details are of sufficient interest to be discussed here and now since they relate intimately to the entire D.P. camps situation and we indeed were on the way to one of these camps. The brief summary of our immediate future and of the itinerary as well as the terse reference to the D.P. camps induced a considerable level of anxiety, fear and ambivalence in all of us. I wished that we had had at that time the information about D.P. camps that I acquired much later. The information dealing with this period of time and with the "D.P. Camp phenomenon" did not become available to me until some decades later

By time we reached Prague, I stopped musing about the statements concerning the D.P. camps. It was dark when we entered Prague. The only thing I remember was a very wide street that we were told was the largest and central street. We drove on it for a very brief period. The truck then turned onto a small cross street and stopped in front of a building that looked like a school.

There we disembarked, went inside and were fed dinner. Afterwards we were brought back to the truck to continue our journey. The city reminded me a little of Krakow, although it was larger. There was also a large river, like the Wisla, that we crossed on a beautiful bridge all lined with monuments at both sides. Beautiful old buildings lined many streets. The city, similarly to Krakow and in contrast to Warsaw or Wroclaw, did not suffer severely from bombardment and destruction.

Within an hour we were speeding over a smooth highway towards Austria and Vienna. I slept through the border crossing, but apparently we went through it smoothly. The road was beautiful, winding through a hilly country and neat small towns populated by what looked to me like well-fed and quite happy looking people. Our guides said that we would not stop to eat but drive directly through to Vienna. Indeed by early morning we were entering a large city with beautiful four- and five-story houses, mostly not destroyed.

The truck drove through a gate into the internal yard of a large five-story building that turned out to be a former grade school. We disembarked and were led by our guides to a large room, which must have been formerly a large classroom, which was now occupied by several families and their belongings. The room was filled with beds that were positioned in square configurations, the size of the square depending on the number of beds creating the square, thus directly on the number of members of the family occupying it. Since two members of a family frequently occupied the same bed, many squares were composed of more than one family. The center of the square was utilized to store the belongings. There obviously was no privacy whatsoever. The bathrooms were in the hallways and we learned very quickly that one had to wait in a queue, particularly in the mornings, to get in to wash and take care of all the necessary functions.

We constructed a rather large square to accommodate our family that included Uncle Juzek, Ania and her parents and Inetka with her family. By now we were starved and went down to the large cafeteria-like restaurant on the ground floor, but no food was being served until noon. The two young men said their goodbyes, wished us good tidings and directed us to the administration floor were we could register.

The administration was on the third floor. The registration reception room was surprisingly small. We quickly learned why it was this small. The registration was actually a very long and complicated procedure. It was conducted, however, on one to one basis, thus it required many small rooms rather than one large registration area. The relatively small room where we started the registration procedure was actually a scheduling area where everyone was given the time and location to report for the "intake," rather than a "registration," procedure that also involved a medical examination and public health measures. We were duly registered and obtained appointments for the "intake" interviews. Every one of us had their interviews scheduled for totally different days except for me and Ania. Our interviews were to start the next day in the morning. I thought that this was great because it would give us coinciding time off, an opportunity to visit the city together.

I had a quick breakfast, coffee with sugar and bread and rushed to the third floor for the interview. I was led into a tiny room that housed a small table, one straight back chair behind the desk next to a tall, army green file cabinet and two stools in front of the desk. A middle-aged man stood up and with a broad smile extended his hand to me. "Now," he said, "please be totally relaxed, I need to get information about your background and your story of what happened to you during and after the war. He was actually quite thorough asking me repeatedly about items he found unclear but letting me talk spontaneously as long as I wished and on any of the topics we discussed. He explained that this information would be collected and ultimately studied in detail to get a clear picture of the happenings to the Jewish people during this period of time.

I found the interview quite pleasant and at the same time informative. He, however, cut me short when I tried to ask questions dealing with the current camp situation and the camp's plans for our immediate future. Apparently, a meeting was to be held where information dealing with that issue was to be presented and discussed. After about an hour, the interview was completed and I went to see the secretary to make an appointment for the medical examination and discussion of health issues. After a break for lunch, a bowl of split pea soup and two slices of bread, I was ready for the medical examination. It was carried out also on the third floor and didn't entail much discomfort. One item however merits a comment. In addition to being given some "shots" and another small pox vaccination, although we still had scars from our childhood small pox immunizations, we also were "deloused!" The procedure consisted of being dusted with DDT powder. Our clothing was dusted and each individual was dusted inside the clothing very thoroughly. We were grateful for this treatment. Ever since we entered Russia, infestation with lice was endemic. While personally we had this problem under reasonable control, it wasn't until this mass DDT treatment that the problem was totally conquered.

As I was skipping down the staircase on my way to our quarters on the first floor I met Inetka. She was also coming down. "I am trying to get everyone together for a meeting with one of the representatives of the Zionist youth organization. His name is Naftuli and he is one of the boys that helped us on the truck during our trip from Prague. We are to meet him at 4 PM in the dining hall," she said breathlessly. "Come along and help me," she added, as she ran down the stairs.

I followed her and we both started looking for others to tell them about the meeting. Soon we had our entire group together in the dining hall waiting. Naftuli showed up at four o'clock sharp. He couldn't have been much older than I, maybe eighteen or nineteen years old. His bearing and mode of addressing us was that of an adult and an experienced person. First he, welcomed us to this transition camp, the Beth Bialik camp, and reassured us that the worse is over and that from now on we were perfectly safe. Then he announced that the decision was made and places secured for us to be transported to Germany to a holding camp in Landshut, from where we would be assigned to a permanent D.P. camp. At that time, we would have the opportunity to ask for a specific geographic area for the assignment. But, he stressed, most likely, it would be impossible to satisfy everyone's requests. He also indicated that he would be traveling with us across the German border all the way to Landshut where the transition camp was located.

Apparently, as we were moving across the border from Poland to Germany, thousands of other Jews were escaping over similar routes. This swelled the Jewish population in the D.P. camps from the original of 5,000 concentration camp survivors in 1945 to a total of some 250, 000 souls by 1947. We were a part of this "Brihah," although, at that time we were totally unaware and insensitive to the global picture of this entire phenomenon. A phenomenon that obviously couldn't have been accomplished without the superb work and financial backing of the various organizations, and individuals from various groups, particularly Haganah, Jewish Brigade, Jewish Agency, JOINT, HIAS, UNRRA and others.

I was very impressed by Naftuli, his care for us and his kind and, at the same time, firm mode of leading and helping us. Furthermore,

I was totally unaware of the magnitude of the Salzburg operation. Later I inquired of Naftuli and was told that over two thousand refugees passed daily through Salzburg temporary camps on the way to permanent assignments. Apparently there were five temporary and three permanent camps in the Salzburg region. I was amazed and awed by these numbers.

As Naftuli finished his little "lecture," he was literally attacked almost by everyone with a million questions. They all boiled themselves down to two: where will we be going and secondly, when. He answered the first one by reiterating what we already knew, that we were being transported to Landshut. However, he had no answers to the many detailed inquiries, like "What major city is Landshut close to? What type of housing are we to expect? How long we should be there before being assigned to a permanent camp?" and other questions.

My understanding of the bottom line of his talk was simple, we are leaving within two to four days and this information was important to me because it helped me to schedule the plan of exploration of all the interesting highlights in the city. I should mention here that ever since we left Alma Ata I had a running feud with Mother concerning my desires for adventure, for exploring, for visiting and for enjoying the various places we traveled through. She felt that acting this way was *shvoiltug*, an idle activity fit for a "rich and a spoiled kid." She believed that I should be serious and introspect in respect to the dangers and difficulties we were being exposed to and should wait for more opportune times, somewhere in the indefinite future, to participate in such activities.

Fortunately, my father was always on my side. He kept on telling me, "Do it now, no matter how tough the situation may be, because tomorrow it may be worse." To this day I appreciate his thinking and his attitudes concerning these issues and whenever possible I still follow his advice. With this in mind, after supper, I talked to Ania and suggested that we go to town the following day. She was a little apprehensive but agreed. Later I talked to Inetka; she also was game for this idea.

Unfortunately, we didn't get a chance to see much of Vienna. We saw the Danube, visited the center of the city with its stately houses, many destroyed by bombing. We saw the famous classical

Gothic Cathedral, the Stephansdom on the Stephans Platz. It was also partly damaged, but we could go inside and see the structure of the incredible Gothic vault. I wanted to go to the famous Vienna Prater, allegedly the most famous entertainment center of the world with its renowned giant Ferris wheel. Unfortunately, we got lost on the tramways and never got there.

I also had the desire to visit the area of Prater and see the old Jewish district, the Leopoldstadt, which had become a ghetto of its own free will back in the 19th century. It was located on "Matzos (Jewish unleavened bread baked traditionally for the Passover holiday) Island" between the Danube River and the canal. Regrettably, we had no map, and none of us spoke adequately German. We barely found our way back to the transit camp.

We left Vienna on the following day and arrived in Salzburg in another transit camp in the evening. We registered, were given bed assignments and went promptly to sleep. As soon as we were done with breakfast the next day, we were ready to go and investigate Salzburg. It was a small town in comparison to Vienna, and we thought that we should be able to get around the town by foot. Stella noticed that all three of us were leaving, came running and demanded that we take her with us. I was not too eager to have her tag along. She was only eleven years old and I considered her a burden for such an excursion. I felt that she was too little to benefit from the sightseeing trip. However, she dug her heels in, started crying and calling for Mother. I knew that I lost and I responded to this blackmail with a resigned: "OK lets go, but you will have to keep up with us." The river of tears dried instantly and all four of us marched briskly out of the camp.

We didn't know where to go, nor did we know what to ask for as far as the directions were concerned. The city was essentially intact as if there was no war. The houses were beautiful, extremely well maintained, much better than anything I saw in Poland. As we kept on going, we spied what looked like a bridge in the distance. Indeed it was a bridge spanning over a rapidly flowing mountain stream. Later we learned that this was the famous Salzach River. The water was cascading over perfectly smooth stones, polished by the water flow probably for centuries. We stopped on the bridge looked at the lively stream, the hills around the city and the mountains. The mountains reminded me of my childhood years, the vacations in Szczyrk, trips to Zakopane, to Krynica, all in the impressive high mountains of Tatra in southwestern Poland.

Then I turned to Ania and Inetka, all three of us exclaimed at the same time: "like Alma Ata." Indeed in Alma Ata we lived at the foothills of the Ala Tau chain of Himalayan Mountains. While taller than the mountains here, they were similar in many ways. We all became engrossed in a discussion of how the beauty of nature can counteract physical adversity and how rapidly our minds forget the bad things while remembering the good ones. Finally, I had to interrupt the discussion pointing to a hill on the other side of the river with what appeared to be a mighty looking castle on its top.

It was getting close to lunchtime and the hunger level, after a breakfast consisting only of bread and black coffee, began to rise. We had to make a decision, either to go hungry and wait for food until suppertime or forego the excursion and start heading back to the camp for lunch. Better judgment prevailed. We turned around and headed back to the camp. We had the usual split pea soup but this time the soup contained sausage, which was a real treat. I hadn't had a sausage since Poland and there I had it only once. This was a good German sausage and with bread, it tasted heavenly. I also learned why the continuous split pea soups! Apparently, the Army provided the camps with a surplus of split pea soup powder. It came in one-gallon metal cans and I loved the soup. Thus, I was grateful to the U.S. Army and promised myself that next time I would see an American soldier, I would thank him for the soup. However, it dawned on me that this was probably impossible unless he spoke German or Polish; I didn't speak any English.

After lunch we again got together and marched to the city. This time we had a definite goal. We were going to the hill and hoped to get to the castle. It was about a one-hour walk. Soon by chance, we entered a large and most impressive street, the Getreidegasse, with stores on both sides lined by interesting buildings with Austrian motifs on them. The stores didn't show much of any merchandise and most of them were closed. As we got closer to the hill that towered some 400 feet over the city, we noted a funicular snaking up the hill towards the castle. We found our target! It was a booth where tickets were probably sold for the ride up the hill; we looked at each other and our hearts stopped. We had no Austrian money.

As we got closer to the booth we realized that it was closed, but the funicular was running. I looked closer at the booth and the signs on it, particularly the table showing prices. I prided myself for knowing German; actually my knowledge of the language was at the most rudimentary level. Most of the German language I learned as a child I had forgotten. Nevertheless, I was able to decipher the writing and understand it. I let out a yell and jumped up in the air with happiness. The sign said that one day a week, on a Wednesday, the funicular was free; today was Wednesday!

The ride up the hill was exciting, we were either among huge rocks or between luscious green leafs of stately trees. When we reached the top we stepped off on a cobblestone surfaced roof area of the castle. Everywhere we looked we could see Middle Age military artifacts. There were cannons scattered around and pyramids of iron cannon balls. A parapet surrounded the entire area.

As we walked to the parapet, the view of the surrounding city and the mountains in the distance became more and more magnificent. As we looked down, we could see the entire city with the silvery ribbon of Salzach River meandering through it. Almost at the center of the area, there were upper stories of the castle with a huge gate at one side. Next to it was a plaque describing the castle. This medieval castle was the Hohensalzburg Fortress; the largest, most fully preserved fortress in Central Europe. It was built originally in 1077 and enlarged to almost present size in 1519.

Although closing time was approaching, we still managed to squeeze in a small, free sightseeing tour of the fortress. Passing through the impressive entrance, we could see the corridors fanning in various directions. All of the interiors that we were able to see were covered by incredibly intricate woodcarvings. We visited the famous Golden Chamber and the Golden Hall. There, the walls were totally covered with superb paintings.

Our walk back to the camp was a very slow one. We were totally exhausted, not only by the sheer physical exertion, but also by the emotional impact of the castle, the views of the city and the mountains and the barbaric opulence of the interiors of the castle; all of this had sapped our energies. Also, we were getting really hungry.

The next day, Thursday, I got up early and took a walk. Returning from the walk, I met Naftuli. He greeted me cordially and fell in step with me. "Are you aware that you will be leaving for Landshut tomorrow morning?" he asked.

"No," I responded, "This is great, I am certain that all of us are looking forward to get going and settle, at least for a while, somewhere." He looked at me quizzically and asked: "where do you think your family will ultimately try to go to, any ideas?" I actually didn't know how to respond to this question. He continued, "While it may be difficult and dangerous, you should consider trying for an Aliyah, we need more 'oylem' in Eretz Israel." This was the first time anyone tried to talk us into going to Palestine. Actually, all of us were busy thinking what each day would bring and where we would have our next meal. No major discussions were devoted to the central issue of where and how we would get out from the D.P. camps. We reached the front door and Naftuli shook my hand and ran up the staircase. I went to our room.

Everyone was awake and in various stages of getting ready for the day. I went over to our group and told them the news. Everyone was excited, and as usual, full of questions. I explained that Naftuli didn't tell me much but that I was sure that he would call us together to provide the details. After all, he was our group leader.

True enough, Naftuli came over to the dining area where we had our breakfast and told us about tomorrow. He said that the trucks would be leaving by 6 PM and that we would be able to start loading at 5 PM. He said that we should arrive in Landshut by the following morning, but that it was difficult to predict how long it would take to cross the border.

This time the crossing was semi-legal, from the American Zone, American Army occupied Austria, to the American Zone in Germany. All the issues dealing with the border crossing had been cleared by the various international organizations and there should be no troubles. However, they preferred that the crossing would take place at night when there were fewer guards and less scrutiny.

Once again, he did all he could to reassure us. On the way out, he came over to me and said, "This evening, go up the hills around Salzburg, the view of the city at night is worth the trip. You will not see anything this stirring for a long while." I was amazed at his sensitivity and his ability, despite the mundane issues he had to deal with, to think of aesthetic issues and sense that I may be interested in devoting time and effort to them.

I walked over to the girls who were sitting at one of the tables and asked if any one was interested in another trip to town. Inetka had her medical examination that morning and a visit with the DDT team. Ania said that she had to spend time with her parents to get things repacked for tomorrow's trip, but would be interested to go to the city in the afternoon. In view of this, I took off alone and decided to investigate the route to the hills. Actually it wasn't that far from our camp to one of the hills. It took me about one hour, including the climb, to reach a glorious spot on the slope, at the edge of a forest overlooking the city. There was a wooden fence running up the hill separating something from something, both sides of the fence were fields covered with grass and occasional trees that looked the same to me. The fence stopped at the edge of the forest.

Sitting down on the end of the fence, I could gaze at the view in front of me and see the entire city. I was able to recognize the church steeples, the hill with the fortress, and the mighty mountains in the great distance behind the hill. As I was walking up the slope, my thoughts were preoccupied with many practical issues. Particularly issues dealing with the question "what to expect as far as medical school is concerned once we get to a D.P. camp?" The burning issue being the policy at the camp dealing with permission for the D.P.s to attend a university while being an inmate of the camp.

Obviously the second question dealt with the location of the university--will there be one within a reasonable distance from the camp? The third question was, will the university honor our credentials and let us attend the medical school? If we will have to live away from the camp, will the camp administrators allow it and how will we get funds to do it?

More and more questions were tumbling in my head including the question that was actually all the time there, worrying me no end. Even if I will be able to get to a university and be admitted, what about Ania?? This loomed over me as the most fundamental question. I actually was surprised at myself when I realized this truth. She actually assumed an image that was greater than the most important thoughts in my mind. This was getting little scary.

I reflected back on our friendship, lasting now several years. In my mind, it never assumed these dimensions. I thought that there were issues greater than Ania! Were there any? I went back in my mind to the time we were crossing the Czechoslovakian border illegally in the middle of the night, barely dragging our valises when shots where fired near us, I whispered to her "I love you." I never said these words to anyone and since that time never to her. She never said these words to me although she expressed herself in a variety of ways making me assume that she might harbor similar affection towards me. I was getting a headache from too much thinking, I was also confused and decided to go back to the camp. Having ran down the hill I reached some streets. There I walked on properly to the camp.

That afternoon all of us, including my parents and Uncle Josef, walked to the city. By now, I was the "expert." We walked to the river, looked at the fortress from a distance, and walked down the Getreidegasse. Then we meandered through various streets and ultimately came up on a beautiful building that looked like a theater with signs advertising concerts and shows. We learned from people in the building that this was the famous "Mozarteum" housing a concert hall and a school of music, all dedicated to Mozart who was born in Salzburg. Although this was off-season and there were no major activities in the building except for the Music School functions, my parents, who obviously spoke perfect German struck up a conversation with some of the people in the building and soon we were given a grand tour of the entire place.

On the way back to the camp, conversation turned back to our trip to Landshut. Everyone wanted to gaze into the crystal ball to guess what would happen next. Mother reminded the other ladies that we had to prepare some food for the trip because we would have no stops where we could eat, according to Naftuli.

After an incredible dinner consisting of goulash, a dish of beef cubes with potatoes and carrots in brown sauce, we felt like Turkish Pasha's after a feast. This type of a meal and this amount of food we had not had for weeks.

Everyone was in an extraordinarily good mood. Stories and jokes were told; people were laughing and feeling very happy. I asked Ania to come with me outside for a walk.

As we walked outside the camp, the skies were fire-red on the western horizon where the sun was setting behind the mountains. We walked slowly on a route by now well familiar to me, towards the hills. We didn't talk much. I held her hand as we walked. My mind was still full of thoughts from the afternoon. I wanted to tell her how I felt but I couldn't. My tongue was paralyzed. We walked in silence as the evening was turning into night and all was being enveloped by darkness. We reached the fence and walked toward its end on the hill, there we entered the forest.

Our feet sank in a thick layer of moss. I whispered to her. "Let's sit down." We sank into the luscious cushion of moss inhaling the fragrances of pine needles and pine sap as well as the mosses and berry plants. In front of us, we could see the entire valley of Salzburg. The evening lights were coming on and sparkling like stars in the sky. It was magic I looked at Ania and she turned her face towards me and looked straight into my eyes. I squirmed under her gaze and didn't know how to tell her how much I loved her and how much I wanted to kiss her. But again I felt as if I was paralyzed. I could barely comprehend the physical sensation of her arms around me, I wanted to put my arms around her and hold her tight, but I didn't dare.

However, at that moment I realized that my arms indeed were around her and that indeed I had held her tight against me and finally the realization came to me that I was kissing her face, her mouth, and her neck. I thought that I would pass out.

****

We began loading our belongings on the trucks at 5 PM sharp. I was constantly and furtively casting glances at Ania. I said to her, good morning but otherwise we didn't talk. By 6 PM, we were loaded on the trucks and ready to take off. I found a seat next to Ania. The truck was covered with a tarp that opened at the back. Thus, we could see only the road as we passed it. I was sitting fairly far to the back which gave me a reasonably good view of the countryside as we crossed it.

After several hours of driving, we were in the mountains and everyone wanted to see the views so I exchanged my seat with the Schneiders giving them the chance to see the "world". Ania went to the front of the truck with me and we sat down close to the cab behind some of the bundles. So far she hadn't talked to me at all during the entire trip, but she held on convulsively to my hand. We sat in the front of the truck some distance away from the rest of the people who were trying to get as close to the rear as possible to have a better few of the countryside.

I held Ania's hands and quietly whispered, "I love you very much." She whispered something back but I could not hear. Instead, I heard Mother calling both of us and asking if we wanted some food. This struck me very funny and I started roaring with laughter and hollering back, "yes, yes, we are famished." If it hadn't have been for the fact that as I hollered, everyone turned their heads to look at me, I would have grabbed Ania and kissed her over and over again. Instead, I only squeezed her hands and looked into her beautiful eyes. Gradually it turned dark; one by one, we all started falling asleep.

The mist was swirling and one couldn't see more than a few meters ahead of the trucks. The headlights, playing on the banks of fog, created an appearance of ghosts dancing round and round. Slowly the dawn was graying the sky. The trucks slowed down. I lifted the flap at the rear of our truck to look around and realized that we were driving over a narrow lane between rows of huge, military-looking tents. The truck stopped.

"Heads of families, please come out," a voice said in German. Most of the people didn't understand. My father translated. A handsome young officer, he couldn't have been more than twenty-two years old, wearing an unfamiliar khaki uniform, extended his hand to Mr. Weiss who was traveling with us and helped him climb down the back end of the truck. Slowly all the heads of families left the truck. We waited impatiently; both scared and excited to hear where we were to go next. The fog had lifted almost completely. The sun was partly out and it was nice and warm. We were in Landshut, a huge transit camp.

While in Vienna we were told that if all goes well, we might end up in Landshut. We might be detained only until ready to emigrate somewhere into a paradise, or, if not, shipped to one of the permanent D.P. camps. I turned to Inetka and said, "Let's stay here, your father knows his way around with the officials. He can arrange almost anything. I hope he also thinks this is a great place. Can you imagine, we can stay in these fabulous tents, this will be an adventure. Also, I know that we are close, several hours by train, to Munich. I always wanted to go to Munich; there we possibly could apply for admission to the university," I kept rattling.

"This is a great idea," she said. "As soon as Herbert gets back, I will ask him what can be done about this possibility." Ania listened carefully to our conversation. "I tend to agree with the idea of Munich," she said, "but, Landshut doesn't strike me as the place I would like to stay, even if we could easily get admitted to the University."

Herbert, Inetka's father, returned with a big grin on his face and interrupted our chatter. "Everyone stays on the truck," he cried. "We were assigned several tents and the driver will take us directly there, each family will get a separate tent."

Inetka and her family, Ania and her parents, my parents, my uncle Juzek who was with us, my sister and I, were all assigned to neighboring tents. We spent the day settling down and getting acquainted with the camp's layout. The toilettes, the dining area, the administration tents and the direction to town were the key points of interest. Everyone was in great hurry to learn all that could be learned.

No one knew, however, why this hurry, and where were we to go next? Days passed with astronomical speed. We really didn't know what to do first although all the necessities were provided for. The tents turned out to be great living quarters, particularly since it was still early fall and the weather was good. There was a very large dining tent in each of the "tent districts" that served some great food. Actually, as we moved progressively towards the west, from Russia to Poland, then to Czechoslovakia, Austria and finally to Germany, the food was becoming progressively better and the administrative personnel friendlier.

There were a number of officials quite willing to talk to us. They asked about our plans, particularly where we would like to be resettled. The Landshut camp was only a temporary facility. However, it was going to take a while to resettle the hundreds of thousands of people who survived concentration camps all over Europe and those who were running away from the eastern countries to Germany.

Jewish organizations like the JOINT and HIAS, the United Nations organization, the UNNRA, all with the help of the American occupation forces in Germany, were busy setting up many new permanent D.P. camps. In the interim, we settled in the "tent" city and our life became quite bearable. We learned where to get supplies and other necessities. Those who had some knowledge of German or English were recruited for various clerical positions. This was of major importance to all of us since those with positions in various offices had access to information of use to us.

Inetka, Ania and I made an excursion to Munich. The city was bombed out; however, the University was already made functional. We learned of the Munich Jewish Student Union, but were not ready to make any attempts to contact them or visit the University since we were totally unaware what the immediate future held in store for us as far as our long-term settlement destination. Time didn't stand still.

September was coming to an end and the weather was getting colder, sufficiently cold to worry our parents. Although we were in the south of Germany, the winters could be quite cold. The tents did not offer adequate protection from the cold weather. Many of our neighbors were assigned to various permanent camps. Ania's parents and my family wanted to be assigned to the same camp and this caused some assignment delays.

Soon we learned that Regensburg, a large city near us, an hour by train, had a large D.P. population. I went there with my father and uncle to visit and we found a number of cousins who survived concentration camps living there. It was a very emotional reunion. All of them however were from my mother's side. They promised to visit us in Landshut to see Mother. My father and Josef were very sad. So far they were unable to find any surviving members of their side of the family. All of my mother's cousins very granted emigration papers for the U.S.A., since they applied for the papers immediately after liberation in 1945.

Upon return to Landshut, we went to the camp director's office trying to expedite our processing for assignment to a permanent camp. We used the argument that all three families had children of college age and we needed to get a more permanent place soon because the college year had already started and if we waited any longer they would lose an entire year of schooling. We were promised quick action.

CHAPTER 15. Kassel

We were assigned to a D.P. camp in Muenchenberg, a suburb of Kassel, an industrial town in the heart of Germany. The camp was a group of tiny but nice, two-story apartments constructed around a small grassy park. The houses in most of the suburbs had escaped major damage from the bombing raids conducted by the Allies during the war. This, however, was not the case for the city of Kassel; the city was bombed severely, with a great deal of damage to the buildings. As we drove through the center of the city, we saw only ruins. Actually, the land was flat with mounds of brick and fragments of cement where houses must have stood. There was activity everywhere. People were cleaning bricks by hand, each brick individually, or clearing parcels of land probably for construction of future houses. Later we learned that the violent bombing by the Allies that resulted in this devastation was due to the attempt to destroy Germany's automotive industry. Kassel was the center for tank and truck production by the Henschel Company.

We were assigned an apartment consisting of one bedroom, a storage room, a living room and a small dining room-kitchen combination. This apartment was part of a large, two-story apartment house building.

After having experienced a variety of accommodations during and after the war years, it felt highly adequate. My parents and my eleven-year-old sister slept in the tiny bedroom. The living room accommodated me and my uncle Juzek. We felt at this point like royalty, with space to spare, since we also had a tiny kitchen and an indoor bathroom. The apartment had running water and electricity.

As usual, Mother set up the household and also unpacked her dental equipment, setting it up in the living room since Uncle and I didn't occupy it during the day time. My father, the perennial optimist, kept on repeating, "you see, all is working out OK, now we have to hurry to fill out the papers and go to America, England, Australia or Brazil." He contemplated emigration to occur in the matter of weeks. Mother, as always pragmatic, was concerned more with the immediate issues like food, clothing and funds rather than anything else. I did not feel any urgency of this nature. I had only two concerns, Ania and where we would go to school.

The first thing we did after moving into the apartment was to find out where the nearest universities and medical schools were located and see about admission since it was already October and we knew that the semester began in September.

While still in Landshut I visited Munich on several occasions. I felt very strange there; the Jewish Student Union was composed of much older kids. Ania and I were only seventeen years old. Most of the Jewish students were in their twenties, most in their late twenties. Apparently, our age group did not survive the Holocaust very well. Those between the ages of ten and fifteen surviving in hiding or in the Soviet Union were more susceptible to disease and hardship and more likely to perish than the more vigorous and more physically and emotionally fit kids who were fifteen to twenty years old during the war. In the final analysis, there was only a small number of us "youngsters" and we were not taken very seriously by our older peers who felt that we had plenty of time and could wait with the admission to the University.

Since we were moved to a D.P. camp in Kassel, quite a distance from Munich, Marburg or Frankfurt were the closest universities to be considered. My mother favored Frankfurt (am Main) and we made plans to make a trip to Frankfurt as soon as possible. November was almost here! Finally, we got enough money and obtained the necessary identity cards. Well-equipped, we boarded the train. The train was very crowded. Literally, there was no room to stand up, and one could forget about a place to sit down. On the way to Frankfurt we passed Marburg but, for reasons I still to this day do not know, we went on to the University in Frankfurt.

The train schedules during these years, even in Germany, were not very precise. We arrived in Frankfurt a/m after five hours. The trip actually could vary in duration by hours depending on the day. It was freezing cold in Frankfurt. By the end of October, the weather in Hessen could be biting cold and rainy. We had no friends or relatives in Frankfurt to stay with. Most of the hotels that were not bombed out were filled with American soldiers, civilian officials and their German girlfriends.

Anyway, we didn't have sufficient money to check into one of the precious few intact hotels. As we disembarked at the Haupt Bahnhoff, the railroad station, we were amazed how little destruction could be seen at the railway station and, after walking out of the station, how well the large apartment houses surrounding the Bahnhoff plaza were preserved.

The bombing raids essentially destroyed Kassel; only rubble remained in the center of the city. Frankfurt, on the other hand, looked entirely different in the vicinity of the railroad station. It looked intact. German civilians and American military personal were mobbing the station and the surrounding areas. People were constantly accosting us trying to sell cigarettes, cans of sardines or girls. The area of the railroad station was apparently quite popular with the black marketers. Since it was still early in the day, we elected to go directly to the University and try to accomplish as much as possible before noon in respect to the admission issue. The only information we had was the name of the University, the Johann Wolfgang Goethe University. My German was poor, Ania's essentially none. Only Mother spoke German flawlessly, with no foreign accent. Consequently, she took matters into her own hands, which she probably would have done anyway, regardless of the language situation. She quickly learned the address of the University. The public transportation was in operation. The electric trams were running since one of the first things the city did was to clean, where necessary, and restore the tracks to allow the tramways to operate.

After getting on one and venturing outside the railroad station plaza, we realized the enormity of the destruction. Most of the buildings outside the vicinity of the railroad station were flattened down to their foundations. Where, in the past, elegant buildings stood, now only mountains of brick and debris could be seen. As we traveled towards the Hauptwache, the destruction in this area of the city was essentially total. Finally we arrived at the University. Most of the University buildings were not destroyed although some showed considerable damage.

The entrance to the main building led through an imposing stone staircase towards the inner chambers. The building was impressive but the stone floors were worn and poorly kept up. Clearly, the walls also had not been taken care of for a while. Although, there was an obvious attempt to maintain the facility in a reasonable shape, the destruction wrought by the war, the obvious signs of lack of maintenance made the offices look gray, shabby and depressing.

Walking into the building, we quickly learned the location of the Herr Rector's (University President's) office and learned that we would have to deal with the Office of Foreign Student's Admissions, guarded strictly by Frau Schultz, the secretary. I was getting cold feet. Mother, however, wasn't deterred one bit. "Let me talk to her," she said. "I think that between explaining and convincing we have a chance to succeed," she added.

It turned out not to be this simple. First, we had to confront a clerk who guarded jealously the access to Frau Schultz. My mother explained to him politely the great importance that she, Frau Doctor Julia Steinberger, speaks to Frau Schultz in regards to the possibility of her children, Ania and Emil, being admitted to study at the University, and that she also had a small package to be passed on to Frau Schultz.

With this she handed him a small parcel. He said that Frau Schultz already left for the day but he would deliver the message and the package to her. She should be in the office tomorrow by 9 AM. My mother thanked him kindly but with an air of slight superiority and indicated that we would return in the morning by 9 AM sharp.

Leaving the office, we realized that it was getting dark. In Germany, the nights arrived early at this time of the year. We, however, had no place to stay for the night. As we were walking out of the dean's offices, on the way to the grand staircase, passing through a majestic stone colonnade while discussing our situation in Polish in a rather animated fashion, a young man stopped us. "I am sorry, but I couldn't help to overhear you, are you trying to gain admission to the University?" he asked looking at Ania and me. I answered, "yes, but right now we are primarily interested in finding a place to spend a night."." It was not only getting dark but also a cold rain was starting.

"I am Felix Sandberg," he said. "I started studies this year, 1946, actually the past September at the Faculty of Medicine [in Germany the designation for a school or college of medicine was Faculty of Medicine] and will be happy to talk to you about the situation here. We have a Jewish Student Union; its president is Erwin Gross. The Union has a small office right here, in this group of University buildings, building K, room 213. They are usually open three days a week. Today they are closed but you can try tomorrow. There is usually someone there after 3 PM. The president lives on Koenig Strasse 23 in apartment number 2. That address is in Sachsenhausen, the city district where the medical school is located. Unfortunately, I cannot offer you accommodations for the night because I live with a friend in a small room that we rent from a local German family. However, overnight accommodations are available for Displaced Persons free of charge in one of the bombed out schools, the Helderin Schule. One sleeps there in one large room with many people but it is warm and clean."

Overjoyed to get all this information, we literally attacked him with questions. "Wait with the questions," he said and added, "you look very tired and hungry, there is a good small Bier Stuebe nearby where students can get pretty good meals for a very reasonable price. Let's go there, have something to eat and then talk a bit. But first let's check at the school and get the accommodations for you." He added, "The school is within a walking distance from here."

This was a godsend chance for us. We were deeply moved by Felix's help and couldn't stop thanking him as we walked in the fine drizzle towards the school. The school building was a ramshackle; many windows were boarded up, but inside it was warm and reasonably clean. Indeed, a clerk told us that there were beds available but they did not have linens, thus we would have to sleep in our clothing, and if we wished, we can use their blankets. He assured us that the straw mattresses and the blankets were disinfected after each new user.

We had no choice and I should mention that this type of accommodations was considered to be quite good during the war, actually quite luxurious and enviable. We gratefully accepted the opportunity, signed our names and went to the restaurant to eat. The food selection was extremely limited. We ordered some potatoes and a small pork chop for the three of us and four beers. This was a small fortune in the occupation forces "Script." "Script" was the temporary German money printed by the occupation forces to replace the old German "Marks." The beer was great. It was dark and heavy with a bittersweet taste. The meal was certainly worth waiting for the entire day.

After we settled down and had a sip of beer, our newly acquired friend took the initiative in trying to summarize all the information he had. First, however, he was exposed to a barrage of questions from us: "Where you from? Where were you during the war? Where do you live now? Did anyone else survive in your family, what are your plans? What are your chances of going to America?"

He promised to give us all the answers to these questions, "But," I interrupted, "first there is an important issues to look at: What are the chances of getting accepted to the Medical School, particularly this late in a semester that started almost 8 weeks ago?"

He responded, "Well, you are really asking a number of questions, each having a different answer. Firstly, you are asking a general question concerning the chances of being admitted to medicine. Fortunately, I am a medical student, and thus I do have some information. There are, however, many factors that need to be explained. Number one, there is a major difference in the chances of being admitted depending whether you are applying for the first year, or for advanced standing. Secondly, it depends where you are from; thirdly it depends if there is an organization on campus, which may speak for you and help in the admission process, and obviously the most important question is, whom do you know?!"

I asked naively, "what about your grades, your academic standing in your former academic institution?" He looked at me for a moment and a big grin lit up his face, "baby," he said "wake up."

He certainly was much older than Ania or I; he looked like a mature man in comparison to our seventeen years. He probably was at least twenty years old, possibly twenty-one! However, calling me "baby" was a bit exaggerated. I began to object, when he interrupted, "OK, OK so you are not a baby, but you must face the facts of life. Obviously you have to have good grades, but this we assume. You must know that we have a student organization lead by our dear President Erwin Gross. He is a mature man finishing studies in dentistry. He has connections and is quite influential. He is your first stop, and probably also the last one in the court of appeals if initial attempts fail. Tomorrow you must contact him in the office of the Jewish Student Union and present your situation. The Jewish Student Union, (the *Juedische Studenten Verband*) consists of some twenty to thirty students and Erwin has pretty reasonable access to the clerk in the admission office. It probably will take a while to make all necessary connections, but in a week or two, you should have some idea what your chances might be. Most likely, if all works well, you will get an admission for the winter semester beginning in January 1947. Once you are admitted to the University, you will have the privilege of also becoming a member of the Jewish Student Union. This, in turn will give you the privilege to participate in the student life of the Jewish students in Frankfurt, the opportunity to obtain some portions of the CARE packages from America and possibly some informal help from the DP camp in Zeilsheim, a Displaced Persons camp in a suburb of Frankfurt where many of the Jewish students live. The organization will also give you some insight and familiarity with the University's bureaucracy. Our 'Herr President' is particularly adept in dealing with the bureaucracy."

My eyes began to close and the lids to stick together. It was almost impossible to keep them open. Having gotten up in the middle of the night to board the train, standing up most of the seven hours of the journey, then the stress in Frankfurt and finally this warm restaurant, a full belly and a glass of great beer, all of it was getting a bit too much. I was essentially passing out.

Felix noted it and quickly got up. "You must be very tired, lets go back to Helderin Schule were you will get some rest and we will see each other tomorrow," he said, helping me to get up.

"I will see you at the Student Union about five o'clock. By then my classes will be over and I will take a tramway from Sachsenhausen to meet you at the University," he added.

I felt, to all practical purposes, essentially dead. Helped, I think, by all three of them, I barely made it to our accommodations in the Helderin Schule and collapsed on the bed. Someone took my raincoat and the shoes off, but I was oblivious to everything.

At about seven o'clock, I woke up with an incredible thirst. I was lying on a straw filled mattress in a large bed covered by a thin, threadbare blanket and flanked on one side by my mother and on the other by Ania; they both were still asleep. All of us wore our street clothing. It was still dark outside and very cold in the room. I got up quietly and went out to the hallway looking for a bathroom. At the end of the passage, I found it. Actually, it was quite spacious and rather clean. There were no cups or glasses around. I got directly to the faucet and first quenched my camel size thirst. Then I went back to the room, found a towel, soap and a razor in our bag and returned to the bathroom.

In no time, I had the hot water running and luxuriated in the bathtub. Life was good! Upon my return, a gray light began to filter into the sleeping quarters. The morning was here. One could make out outlines of the room. I didn't realize that we were in a huge room; it must have previously been a classroom. Now it was literally filled with beds, few feet apart. Most were occupied with waking up people. Some were empty, some of the people were already up and gone.

I came over quietly to the bed, "wake up Mother, and wake up Ania," I whispered. That was quite ineffective. I had to raise my voice and shake them a bit to wake them from the deep sleep. Ania sat up, "where are we?" she asked, "Where did you sleep?"

"Well," I said, "all three of us slept together in this bad." By this time mother was also up. I pointed both of them to the direction of the bathrooms. However, since the other guests were also up it took Mother and Ania over an hour to wait in a line for the bathroom. This was a warning and a lesson for the next morning, if we were to stay there again.

Breakfast consisted of some bread and cheese that Mother brought with us from Kassel. We drank some Ersatz coffee in a small food store on the way to the University.

"I worry," said Ania to my mother. "Things appear very formal and not very friendly. "How are you planning to approach Mrs. Schultz?" she inquired.

"Don't worry" responded my mother with her usual optimistic smile. "I think I know how to handle Mrs. Schultz."

The electric tram stopped just a block down the street from the main University entrance. It was raining again, and it was cold and wet. We ran to the entrance, with all our belongings in tow, since it was unsafe to leave anything in the Helderin Schule. It meant that I was to drag a rather large valise with Mother's, Ania's and my clothing. Ania carried a bag with the provisions we brought from Kassel and Mother carried her purse that normally was the size of a small valise, but on this trip, it was bulging more than usual. It was full of chocolate, American cigarettes and roasted coffee beans. The coffee beans in particular were our currency. In the D.P. camps, the JOINT gave us rations of food shipped from America. The food included the above-mentioned items. We saved them and used them for barter. One could get literally almost anything, particularly for cigarettes and coffee beans.

We found the admission's office and the clerk who saw us yesterday. He appeared quite friendly and obviously remembered us. Although I was not a smoker, I asked the permission to smoke. He said, "certainly, if you wish, let me find you an ashtray." As he returned with the ashtray, I offered him a cigarette. I had a package of American cigarettes in my hand, a white and red package of Lucky Strike cigarettes. His hand trembled as he removed a cigarette from the package mumbling "thank you, thank you." American cigarettes were at that time in Germany a major treat. He obviously was very pleased. After removing the cigarette from the package he wrapped it carefully and commented, somewhat embarrassed, "if you don't mind, I will save this cigarette for after dinner tonight."

I responded, "well in this case, why don't you take few more, possibly your wife may also wish to join you," and I handed him four more cigarettes. This had to be a royal treat for him, since he didn't know how to thank me for it except to say, "thank you, my wife will be most appreciative." He said quickly, "I must find Mrs. Schultz so you wouldn't have to wait too long."

Well, the cigarettes worked. I was quite certain that the cigarettes would not to be smoked later that night, but instead would be used for barter. It didn't take more than a couple minutes for the clerk to return, "Frau Schultz just came in and will be happy to see you briefly, she will not be able spend much time with you because of a meeting she must attend shortly," he said. My mother thanked him and all three of us marched into the office of Frau Schultz.

It was a small room, with a desk and a chair, two guest chairs and a row of filing cabinets. Obviously, the war has taken a toll of the facilities, and noting was repaired as of yet. Frau Schultz was a pleasant looking middle age women, and she gestured for mother to sit down. She said, "setzen Sie sich bitter," in a pleasant tone of voice. Mother and Ania sat down while I remained standing. Mother opened the conversation in a perfect Hoch Deutch. Althoungh she has spent more than ten years out of Germany, her pronunciation was perfect. Mother's German startled Frau Schultz. She expected a foreign accent and was confronted with an obvious German person, at least a person who spoke impeccable German. An attempt for an appropriate but perfectly neutral interaction was becoming difficult for Frau Schultz. Her face reflected a degree of curiosity and she couldn't resist asking: "Sind Sie Deutch?"

My mother responded again in German, "oh yes, my family and I are from Kassel," and she added, "I got my doctoral degree from the Dresden University."

This bit of information clearly affected Frau Schultz in a curious fashion. To start with, she tried to convey an attitude of cool, proper, detached and superior person and expedite the business with us in an efficient and quick fashion. This now became difficult for her. My mother, while on one hand was very friendly and respectful of her, she also subtly conveyed the idea that it was she, not Frau Schultz, who had the Doctorate degree and that she expected some appropriate consideration in return.

Mother then deftly turned around the conversation to the topic of our visit, namely the possibility of our admission to the Medical Faculty (the medical school). She introduced me to Frau Schultz as her son and Ania as her daughter and simply summarized our educational background. She also assured her that we were excellent students and requested that we be admitted to the third semester of medical studies although we were almost two month late. Mother insisted that we would catch up with the rest of the class. We had official translations of our transcripts from medical schools in Russia and Poland and Mother handed the translations to Frau Schultz.

She was taken aback by the requests, started objecting and explaining how impossible this was. Mother interrupted her by reminding her how impossible the chances were for us to survive the war and even to keep up in some form and fashion with our studies and despite this impossibility here we were in Germany.

Frau Schultz clearly was shaken and found it difficult to respond. Looking at the documents she realized that Ania had a different last name from mine. "How come," she asked, "your son has different name from your daughters?" My mother didn't blink an eye responding, "She is from my second husband."

"But," she reasoned, "They were born the same year."

"This is true," Mother countered, "but eleven months apart. I divorced my first husband, then immediately remarried and instantly became pregnant." Frau Schultz didn't respond. She only looked at my mother and said that she would have to discuss this matter with her superiors and if we came next week she may possibly have some answers.

My mother looked straight into her eyes and said quietly, "Please try your best, you will not be sorry. They both will be good students and I am certain in the future they will contribute significantly to the field of medicine." At this point she opened her famous, giant-size purse, pulled out a bag of roasted coffee beans, about two pounds. A gift of this type was worth a king's ransom in this postwar Germany. She placed the bag on the desk and said, "I hope that you will be able to help. I must go back to Kassel tonight because I have no place to stay in Frankfurt. We will be back to see you in the late afternoon, about four o'clock, and I hope that we will hear some good news." She solemnly shook Frau Schultz's hand, Ania and I bowed politely and we left.

Later, thinking of the encounter, I wondered many times whether mother made the comment about our future contributions to the field of medicine because she thought that this might help us to be admitted to the school or that she actually believed it. I was speechless, "this certainly did not win us friends or influence strangers," I blurted out once we were some distance from the office, moving rapidly to the large stone staircase in the front of the building.

The rain clouds disappeared while we were in the office with Frau Schultz and the sun lit up the gray stones. Mother had a knowingly satisfied smile on her face. I actually felt warmer although I was certain that the temperature outside did not rise. It must have been the sun, the release of tension and the hope that all will turn out good.

We were hungry and exhausted but we were happy. The only thing we needed at that moment was a meal. "Let's go back to the railroad station; I saw a number of restaurants there. We should also be able to inquire about an evening train to Kassel for mother," I suggested. A tram took us swiftly to the plaza in front of the huge railroad station. The railroad schedule revealed that there were several trains leaving during the early evening hours in the direction of Kassel.

After a highly satisfactory meal, we returned to the University area hoping to find the office of the Jewish Student Union and get some additional information. The building K was actually an extension of the main building; we had no troubles finding it. It was much more difficult, however, to locate room 213. No one knew heard of it. Neither one heard of a *Juedische Studenten Verband*, or the Jewish Student Union. We, however, persevered. This met with success. Ultimately we indeed found room 213. The upper half of the entrance door was glass; we could look in before knocking on the door. It was a moderately sized room with two that we surmised to be, students, facing each other, engrossed in an animated conversation. A girl was part of the group, but she was only listening. The room was furnished with a large table and a number of chairs. There were several large cardboard boxes piled up by one of the walls. There was a bookcase with numerous books scattered in it.

We knocked on the door but there was no answer. After knocking several times we pushed the door. It was not locked. We entered and the girl turned her head toward us. "Are you looking for someone?" she asked.

I responded, "We are trying to gain admission to the Medical School at the University. We just talked to Ms. Schultz in the admission's office; she sounded quite optimistic about our chances."

One of the students, until now engrossed in a conversation, turned and looked at us. “This is quite impossible; you must first apply to the Jewish Student Union. We will check your credentials. If the review turns out to be satisfactory, we will make a recommendation to the University concerning your admission. You may start the process by making an appointment for an interview with our President.”

I was taken aback a little by the vehemence of his comments but responded calmly, “We are sorry, but we came to the University seeking admission to the Medical School and we were unaware of the Jewish Student Union. Instead of coming here first, we went directly to the admission’s office. However, we will be happy to meet with the President if you tell me who to see regarding the appointment.”

The boy turned around fully to face me. “Well,” he said, “it is difficult to see him, he is very busy man but Monika, who volunteers as a secretary to the President, may be able to make an appointment for you. She will be here tomorrow.” With this he turned back to the other students and resumed his conversation.

I addressed him again, “Is there a possibility to see him today? We have another appointment at the admission’s office later today and it would be nice to talk to someone concerning this matter before we see Ms. Schultz. He turned around again and reiterated that nothing could be done until tomorrow when the secretary was there.

Ania and I looked at each other, shook our heads slightly and headed for the doors. As we walked out, another student was coming down the hall apparently heading for the Student Union office. As we passed he looked at us, greeted us and asked, “Are you new students? I have not seen you here before.”

I eagerly responded, “Well, we are not students as of yet, but we hope to become students at the Medical School.” He smiled and asked, “Have you seen the President yet?” “No,” I responded, “but we hope to be able to make an appointment with him tomorrow.”

“That is good,” he said and introduced himself, “I am Henry, second year medical student,” adding, “If there is any thing I can help with, just ask.” This made us feel good. We again found someone who was wiling to talk to us and right now we badly needed that.

“Henry,” Ania addressed him, “do you have a little time to talk to us? We could use some information and advice. “Sure,” he said, "let's step out, there is a little inexpensive Bier Stuebe near by, there we can sit down and talk."

As we sat down, Henry with a big grin on his face said, "Zdzich is not a bad boy, he wasn't trying to be rude, he doesn't know any different, you will get used to him. He is second in command to Ervin, the president. As you will learn, their personalities reflect each other. Well, this puts the first issue to rest. Now tell me a bit about the two of you." We briefly summarized our background and the happenings on this trip including our meeting with Frau Schultz. Henry was roaring with laughter, "Now, this is the best story I heard for some time, I do hope that Frau Schultz will get you admitted with no assistance from 'Herr' President. It's time that someone shows him up. Don't get me wrong, he and the 'Board' are doing a good job but they are amusingly standoffish, and humorous. Ervin insists on being called 'Herr President' and makes a big fuss having appointments with the students that need to see him. He makes everything very formal. Don't take it very seriously. By the way, what are your plans?"

I responded that we hoped to hear today from Frau Schultz that we are admitted to the School and if so mother would return to Kassel and we would try to find a place to live in Frankfurt and get going with the school business.

"Well," he said, "If you stay then you shouldn't stay in Helderin School. I have a small apartment but you can stay with me or with some friends until you find a place of your own. I will be at the Student Union late this afternoon, after you are done with Frau Schultz come by and let's see what can be done."

Ania and I lost the use of our tongues. We were elated, we didn't know how to thank him, we didn't expect such generosity. The time was flying and the hour of our appointment with Frau Schultz was coming close. We got up, paid and scurried to pick up mother to go to the University.

Henry came with us, met Mother and then all four of us returned to the University. Henry went directly to the Student Union while the three of us went to see Frau Schultz.

We waited only a couple of minutes to be ushered into her office. Things obviously went well; we could read it off her face. She was genuinely pleased. She looked with a smile at Ania and me and announced proudly, “You both are now second year students at the Medical Faculty of the Johann W. Goethe University. The Dean thought, however, that under the circumstances of you enrolling late in the semester, and, obviously needing a little time to catch up, you will be better off starting with a combination of the first- and second-year status. The subjects during first semester include botany, zoology, organic and inorganic chemistry. For these subjects you will get full credit. Some of the other subjects, you will have to repeat with first-year students. Nevertheless, you will also be able to start on some second year subjects right away and at the end of the next spring semester, in 1947 you should be completing the second year and be eligible for the “Physicum”, the first essential medical examination . Come back tomorrow to the registrar’s office and bring with you a passport type of photograph. If you don’t have one, ask my secretary and she will direct you to a place near by; they will make one for you inexpensively when you tell them that you are a student at the University. Good luck to you, and in the future, if you need anything, call on me.”

We thanked her profusely. Ania even had tears in her eyes. Mother indicated that we should leave and she remained with Ms. Schultz for a few minutes. When she came out, she also had tears in her eyes. Later I asked what transpired in the office but mother was never willing to talk about it.

We got the address of the photographer; he took the photographs and told us to return tomorrow for the pictures. We then returned to the Student Union only to find Henry there. He was sitting and studying an anatomy textbook while waiting for us. When we told him the news, he barely could believe it. He was totally taken by Mother’s ability to “arrange” things. We told him that Mother wants to take an evening train back to Kassel and that we want to stay in Frankfurt a couple days to get the admission details finalized. Then, we want to go to Kassel for a day, pick up our things and return to Frankfurt. We would rent a room and start school. It all sounded so obvious, logical and simple. Henry volunteered to come with us to the railroad station, arrange for Mother’s train back home and then return with us to his apartment where we were to stay over night.

CHAPTER 16. Frankfurt

Everything worked as planned. After putting Mother on the train to Kassel, we went with Henry to his apartment. He rented one room from a German family. The room, however, was large, very comfortable with a large double bed, a handsome couch, closets and huge windows overlooking a little park with many trees. His landlady was an attractive middle-aged, dark haired lady with a very attractive seventeen–year-old daughter. The husband perished in the war.

After making the introductions, we went to the room and Henry offered to prepare some food for all three of us. I burst with laughter, when I saw him bring from the cabinet a gallon can of powdered green peas. Green pea soup! Vienna, here we come again! We explained to cause of our merriment and he joined us with some more hearty laughter.

Subsequently he explained that, while most of the students lived formally in a nearby D.P. camp where they got food rations from UNRRA and the JOINT, the Student Union was also a recipient of UNRRA food packages, and Care packages from the U.S. that were distributed to students. Green pea soup was a staple food that the entire student group received.

After we ate the soup, he turned with a mischievous smile. "Now, I bet," he said, "you will not be able to make fun of the food I serve you." He pulled out a tin can that he opened and emptied into a pan to warm it up. After it warmed up he served it. Indeed, he was right, we couldn't laugh. We never tasted anything like this before. It was pork in apple sauce! We would never dream of putting these two types of food together. While it appeared to taste good, we were not convinced that it was OK to place apple sauce together with meat. Well, it was a good subject for discussion before we went to sleep. Incidentally, Ania had royal accommodations on the couch, while I joined Henry in his large bed.

First thing in the morning, we went to the photo shop where we got the copies of our identification photographs. Then, the events, as they unfolded, left us absolutely amazed. We arrived to the registrar's office and gave them our names. They asked for our photographs and directed us to sit down and wait a few minutes. In about twenty minutes, our names were called and we were both handed handsome booklets, the "Studenten Buch" (a student record book).

Inside, on the first page, was our name and identifying data as well as the new photograph. On the subsequent pages all the courses we were to take were listed with special places reserved for professor's name, his signature, the grade, a space for comments and a place where the professor indicated the fee for the course and place for his signature indicating that the fee was paid to him.

This was true German precision, an amazing achievement for the few minutes we had been waiting, although I am sure that most of the material in the book was written in it already the day before. It was quite obvious that Frau Schultz had done a great deal of work for us in a very short period of time. Her work cut every knot on the way and ushered us, with neck breaking speed, into the ranks of students at the Johann Wolfgang Goethe University in Frankfurt. We were extremely pleased with the precision, speed and ease that we became matriculated at the University.

However, we totally forgot that, factually, we had lost a part of an academic year. In discussing this issue with Ania, I assumed a philosophical attitude, deciding that actually it was for the better. We would learn the language, become better students and ultimately, become better doctors. Most importantly, according to the lady that handed us the books, we could start attending the school that day!

Our first reflex was to run to the Jewish Student Union, try to become its members and look for someone to help us find the Medical School building and help us find a place to live. The Union's office was open and there was a young girl sitting at the table. We introduced ourselves and asked if the secretary was in. The girl indicated with a pleasant smile on her face that she was the president's secretary and asked us what she could do for us.

Still very excited, we told her how we arrived a couple days ago hoping to get admitted to the Medical School and how we saw the admissions officer, Frau Schultz. Our words were rushing tumbling, we mixed Polish with German and finally I looked at her and started laughing. "Please forgive us," I said, "we are very excited with this good news and are trying to spill it all out instantly to you or to any one who may wish to listen to us. We are admitted to the second year of the medical school (the "Medical Faculty") curriculum and we wish to talk to the proper person concerning joining the Jewish Student Union. How do we go about it?"

She shook her head, as if we indeed would have had lost our minds, and looked up at us from behind the table. "What do you mean that you just arrived and have been admitted to the University; this can't be so. You must first apply here, then we will evaluate your credentials and your fitness to be a student at this University, then we will make arrangements with the University concerning your admission. This will take a while; anyway, it is too late in the semester to be admitted this year. If at all, we will consider you for admission for the next semester, in January 1947."

She said this with finality and obviously with absolute conviction. I looked at Ania and she looked at me. I took her Student Book and, together with mine, handed them wordlessly to the secretary. She looked at them with surprise and quickly opened to the page with our photographs. She looked down at the photographs and up at us several times, shaking her head. She returned the books to us and said, "I do not understand this, there still is nothing I can do concerning your admission to the Student Union, you will have to see the president. He will not be here for a week or so. He is now very busy. Obviously you may wish to commence your studies and straighten things out here later."

I thanked her and said, "Before starting school we must go back to Kassel since we live there in a D.P. camp. Upon return with our belongings we will look for some housing and start the studies." She was still shaking her head, "How did you do it?" she asked. This time I also shook my head and responded, "This is a long story, when we will become members of the Union and we will have some extra time we will tell you!" We thanked her for everything and left.

The trip to Kassel went fast. We had a lot to talk about; obviously we were quite apprehensive, to be more precise, afraid of what will happen at school. Firstly, we were faced with a quite different educational system, facing a third system within one year. Secondly, my German was quite poor and Ania's actually non-existent. Thirdly, we were to enter the semester in its middle, thus to start already seriously behind the rest of the class. And finally, a few minor issues; for example we needed a place to live and food to eat.

The two of us swept into Kassel like a wind. It was hurry, hurry, and hurry. We didn't want to procrastinate a single day. We had to be back at the University as soon as possible. The year was progressing rapidly and we were falling further and further behind.

We wanted to tell our best friends about our luck with the admission process, about the skill of Mother's negotiations and the excitement of a new school. Both, Mietek and his wife Ania, our two best friends in the D.P. camp were happy for us but also sad that we were leaving. We tried to talk them into coming with us to Frankfurt and also enroll at the University but we were unsuccessful.

We got ready within a couple days and left for Frankfurt. This time we arrived in Frankfurt alone. It was scary. We knew really only one soul in the city, Henry. We took an overnight train to Frankfurt in order to arrive there as early as possible and start our search for housing. From the railroad station, we took a tram directly to the University.

The weather was turning colder, it was late fall and the fine rain added to the unpleasant humidity and chill in the air. The city was shrouded in fog that covered up, at least temporarily, the horrible scars left from the war. We were dragging with us large valises with all of our earthly belongings and hoped to be able to leave them temporary in the Jewish Student Union.

This time we had no problems to find room #213; we hoped that it would be open. We were lucky since there were several students sitting in the room by the table and talking. We walked in, explained who we were and asked if we could leave our belongings there for few hours. One of the students, Isaac, with a wise and kind face, who looked considerably older than us, said, "Sure, I have the key for the 'inner sanctum.' You can leave your belongings there. They will be as safe as our food rations stored there, that means pretty safe," he laughed. We dragged our belongings into the little room and were immediately surrounded by the rest of the fellows. They wanted to know where we came from, what were we doing at the University, were we planning to study and if yes, what? On and on went the questions. Isaac interrupted them by saying quietly, "Why don't you guys stop asking non-stop questions so that they could give you some answers."

Everyone started laughing but they wouldn't stop asking questions. Finally, I stepped in and in a loud voice started: "My mother," in the instant they heard this word, all questioning stopped and I could continue, "came with us few days ago, to Frankfurt; we went together to the admissions office, where she talked with Frau Schultz. The following day we picked up our Studenten Buch and were admitted to the Faculty of Medicine at the University."

Everyone around us, including Isaac, stood speechless with their jaws dropping. Finally one of them, a friend of Zdzich, looked at me shaking his head and said with a questioning tone in his voice, "yes, but this is impossible." Then he added, "No one of our people can be admitted to the University unless we have checked their credentials and the president has issued a formal approval for the admission of the applicant." Ania and I, silently took out our Student Books, opened them to the first pages with our pictures and placed them on the table.

A pandemonium broke out. Everyone wanted to see the books, and everyone was expressing their opinions in very loud voices. We were happy to see that despite the excitement and unruly behavior, they did not damage the books. Now their questions became more directed and pointed towards us. "How?" was the question on their lips. "All in good time," I said. "It will have to wait until we get together later, in a less rushed situation. I will be delighted to tell you, it is a long story."

Isaac picked up the books from the table and returned them to each of us. "Where are you staying tonight?" he asked. As I tried to tell him about Helderin Schule he interrupted, "No. No. You are staying with me. My landlady from whom I am renting a room will let me sleep over on the couch in the living room and you will have my room with a most comfortable bed in Frankfurt."

This was an unexpected offer. I looked at Ania, and she looked at me not knowing what to say. Finally, I turned towards him, afraid that my eyes would start tearing in response to his generosity, and gratefully accepted the offer.

At that moment, I also realized that he said that we would have the use of his private room with a "most comfortable bed in Frankfurt." Suddenly I went cold. He did say, "Bed," singular! The situation finally dawned on me. I had never stayed with Ania overnight in a private room with a single bed in it! This, however, wasn't the time or the place to discuss such an issue with Ania and I decided to go with the flow.

As the "where to sleep" drama had been unfolding between Isaac and us, the door opened and a short girl with dark hair and big smile on her lips walked in and came over to the table. She obviously knew everyone and after exchanging greetings with them turned to us. "You must be new, where you from?" she asked. As I was progressing quickly through a summary to answer her question, she instantly interrupted with a no nonsense tone in her voice, "well, so you are new students. Great, you will come and live in our neighborhood. I live in Fechenheim; another of our students, Arcik, lives there also. He studies dentistry. We will be able to travel together to the University by tram. Fechenheim is a very nice suburb of Frankfurt located on the River Main. It has withstood the war intact. I know of several rooms for rent there. Matter of fact there is a room for let in a small apartment house next to mine." I had troubles interjecting a word into the flow of her ideas. She was obviously excited about the possibility of our moving to Fechenheim, near her, and wanted to know much more about us. We, on the other hand, were excited about the possibility of renting a room, any room that would fit our needs.

Finally, I managed to interject and asked her when we could visit her to check on the availability of the rooms for lease. She said that she should be home tomorrow by 3 PM "By the way my name in Hanka. I will see you tomorrow," she exclaimed and left the room.

It was getting slowly dark, the rain continued. Isaac suggested that we start by taking our belongings with us to his place that could be reached from the vicinity of the University by tram. We were also told that the University's Medical School ("the Medical Faculty") is located in Sachsenhausen across the River Main. Thus, it would be nice if we could find a place to live in that vicinity. We were told, however, that it is difficult to find a place there and that this area of the city is very expensive. We were literally bombarded with information and ultimately developed a major headache. We were grateful to Isaac who kept on insisting that it was getting late and that we should get going to his place.

Reluctantly the students eased off their questions and let Isaac take charge of us. As we walked out of the Student Union we could still hear their excited voices discussing our temerity in going directly to the University admission's office and even more importantly our "chutzpa" to manage admission to the Medical School outside of the president's jurisdiction. We waved our goodbyes to them, dragged our valises to the tram and went on with Isaac to his apartment.

The house he lived in was substantial and entirely free of damage. When we walked into his apartment we were greeted by the landlady who was obviously waiting for him with dinner. He must have told her of his plans to invite us over because she did not act surprised; she greeted us cordially and tried to help with the valises. Isaac announced that he would stay overnight in the little sitting room while we will stay in his bedroom. He turned around towards us with a huge smile on his face and said, "I have the biggest bed in the entire province of Hessen with the best featherbed you could imagine."

I stole a glance at Ania who stood next to me obviously mortified in response to this announcement. Isaac, with a sweeping gesture of his arm indicated to follow him. He opened a door to a small room with a desk, a reading lamp, a desk chair, an easy reading chair, a bookcase and indeed the largest four poster bed I had ever seen. On top of the bed were two huge pillows and the thickest and fluffiest looking featherbed all encased in snow-white Damascus linen.

I grinned and started saying, "its great, but..." when Ania with a sweet smile on her face interrupted me saying, "Isaac, this is beautiful, I never have seen a bed or featherbed like this, it will be heaven to stay here, thank you so much!."

When I heard this, I almost fainted. Well, I thought this would be some mess to disentangle. I couldn't figure what Ania had on her mind but I went along with it. We left our valises by the French door leading to a tiny balcony and followed Isaac to the little dinning room. The table was set for four. It was a long and stressful day for me and I began to feel it. I was happy that we were ready to have dinner and some rest.

The first course was brought in, some kind of vegetable soup, and it was delicious. It was followed by a royal treat, pork chops with cabbage and mashed potatoes. I had not had a meal like that for months. Turning to Isaac, I commented with a smile on my face, "It looks like life treats you well!"

He responded laughing, "Well, at this moment life treats me quite well but the pork chops are in honor of your visit. They actually are a rarity. I had to give up two packages of cigarettes for them, good thing that I don't smoke. Incidentally, at the Student Union we get monthly rations consisting of some food but most importantly cigarettes and coffee beans. These two items are the real currency in Germany. You could buy anything for some cigarettes or coffee. We get a monthly supply of two cartons of cigarettes and a pound of coffee. This we trade or sell for local currency. It keeps us going economically. Furthermore, most of the students are also inmates of the Zeilsheim D.P. camp where they got some food rations and CARE packages from America.

"Since we could not work, these were the only means of support for us. And since some of the items, like coffee and cigarettes, could be sold, life indeed goes on.

He talked for a while but my lids began to feel like lead. Isaac noticing this immediately stopped the conversation with a pleasant, "children, it is time to go to sleep." We thanked the landlady and Isaac for the delicious dinner and went on to our room.

After closing the door I said to Ania, "well, I have some sweaters in my valise and between those and my overcoat I will fix a reasonable sleeping facility on the floor and you take the bed." She shook her head, placed her hands on my shoulders and said, looking deep into my eyes, "no, you come to bed, there will be no floor for you. We know each other long enough to know what we want, but this is not the time. You know that I am a virgin and I want you to know that I trust you." With this, she took her dress off and went to bed in her underwear, covering herself with the luxurious featherbed.

My mind was in turmoil. I clearly understood her comments but I wasn't sure that I could trust myself. We were never together and alone in a private room for any length of time. We kissed and hugged in the past, but this was different. I fantasized many times in how it would be to be alone with her but never dreamed of a situation like this. She simply left it in my hands but gave me an admonition that I couldn't ignore.

I must have slept through the night like a rock and awaken with a start. The daylight was filtering through the French doors leading to the balcony. Ania was gone. I quickly dressed and as I was putting on my jacket, there was a knock on the door. "Come in," I called out. Ania walked in closed the door, came over to me and without a word put her arms around me and gave me a big kiss on my lips. It was a peculiar kiss, a kiss of a lover but at the same time a kiss of a friend; a kiss of passion but also a kiss of gratefulness. I placed my arms around her and held her very tight against me. She whispered, "You were a perfect gentleman last night, but I don't think we should get ourselves in this predicament again, soon. It is much too difficult." I could see tears running down her face and I agreed.

We were supposed to meet Hanka in Fechenheim around 3 PM, thus we had a considerable amount of free time. Isaac had a class at 11 AM and he suggested that we come with him to the Medical School in Sachsenhausen. However, I reminded myself that the president of the Student Union also lived in Sachsenhausen. Turning to Isaac I asked, "Do you know the address of 'Herr President?' I understand that he lives in Sachsenhausen."

"I certainly do," responded Isaac. "Do you wish to visit him?" he asked. "Sure, if possible; do you think that he could be at home this morning?" Isaac thought for a second and slowly replied, "yeees, as I recall the dental students have this week off, for some funny reasons. He may very well be at home. "Well," I said, "why don't we all go to Sachsenhausen, you can show us where he lives, we can visit him, return here, pick up our valises and go to Hanka's."

This was agreeable to everyone and we took off. The address was near a tram station. It was raining and very cold. We ran the two blocks to Ervin's (the president) house. The house number was on a very handsome multi-apartment two-story high building, set off the street and surrounded by a small, well-tended garden, full of trees.

At the entrance, there was a list with names and apartment numbers of the occupants. We found Ervin's apartment on the second floor and ran up the staircase. I pressed the bell button and a female voice asked in German, "who is it?" I explained that we were a couple of new Jewish students at the Medical School and would like very much to meet Herr President. The women responded in an obviously irritated tone of voice, "Who sent you here? These is a private residence, go back to the president's office at the University and make an appointment, he may see you, but only there."

This response was quite arrogant and didn't sit well with me. I responded quietly, "well, I appreciate his desire for privacy but we have some issues we need to discuss with him very soon. At the office I was told that he most likely would not be in until sometime next week, the secretary actually couldn't tell me when. If he is not home at the moment we may wait for a little while. Our meeting should not take very long." I could hear a door chain coming off the hook and the door opened slightly. A young woman, obviously Jewish, peered through the narrow slit between the edge of the door and the doorframe. Ania and I bowed politely and I said good morning to her in Polish. She responded in German, "I told you that Herr President is not home, if you wish, you may wait for him here; I don't know when he will be back." With this, she slammed the door in front of our faces.

Ania and I were speechless; we looked at each other and burst out laughing. "There must be something wrong with Herr President's ideas of how to deal with his comrades and if this lady is his wife, her manners leave something to be desired; let's wait thirty to forty minutes if he doesn't show up let's go back for our luggage and find our way towards Fechenheim," I concluded.

We waited in the hallway for about thirty minutes, no one showed up. It was getting very cold. Finally I turned towards Ania and announced, rather angrily, "I had enough we both are freezing, lets go."

We were on the tram going to Fechenheim. There was only one other person, an elderly man, in the car. I talked quietly with Ania, both of us looking out the windows trying to discern the names of streets we were passing. We went by a huge industrial section extending for several blocks. Interestingly it was not damaged by the bombs. On one of the smoke stacks I saw a name painted, "I.G. Farben." "Well," I exclaimed to Ania, "the famous I.G. Farben, the largest chemical industry complex in the world, interestingly totally intact, how did this entire complex occupying many square blocks escape American bombing?" But, it wasn't until much later that I was given the answer to this question.

In the meanwhile, we were getting a little worried not knowing at which stop we should get off. Finally I walked over to the man sitting several rows ahead of us and in my best German asked whether he knew what stop we should get off for Schueshueten Strasse. He very properly replied that we need not to worry because Schueshueten Strasse was the last stop of the tram and we should be there in few minutes. He indeed was correct and in no time, we found Hanka's address.

Hanka was home already waiting for us. She lived in a beautiful corner room on the second floor of the apartment house with great windows overlooking the houses on both sides of the corner. But, the arresting sight in her room was an upright piano. This was an unheard of luxury. We immediately attacked her with questions about the piano. She answered simply, "I love to play piano. I played since I was a little girl. My parents had a piano teacher coming to the house every day, I learned quickly. They loved to listen to me play and spent at least an hour a day listening. When I was liberated from the camps and ultimately came here," as she progressed with the story her eyes began to fill with tears, "I became obsessed with the idea of getting a piano. Thank God for the coffee and cigarettes, although I smoke heavily and love coffee, I sacrificed, and for four pounds of coffee and five cartons of cigarettes, here is the piano!"

"You see," she continued, "my entire family was murdered, I was left alone. I practice very hard every day, but then I simply play, I play for my parents, I feel as if they would be sitting here and listening to me. This is very important, it keeps me going." When she finished, all three of us had tears in our eyes. I was thinking how lucky Ania and I were having both of our parents alive.

We started hugging and kissing each other trying also to make Hanka happier, but this was a difficult task. Finally I asked her where she was from in Poland. It turned out that she was from Radom, the same city that Ania came from. This coincidence was unbelievable. Hanka was two or three years older, this however was enough for her to have a clearer memory of Radom and it turned out that she heard of Ania's father and Ania thought she heard of her parents who were a prominent family in the city and one of the wealthiest. We were very happy getting to know her and recounting stories of the prewar life. This was a very common way of passing time and there was never an end to it. Interestingly, very little was discussed or reminisced about the war years. This period of time was usually kept very private and talked about only rarely.

Suddenly Hanka interrupted our merriment. "Let us get back to important issues. We have to go next door. There Frau Lange has a room for rent, I have never seen it, but it may be adequate for one of you."

We immediately put our coats on and went to the apartment house next door. Frau Lange lived on the first floor in a tiny apartment consisting of a tiny kitchen, a bedroom and a small sitting room with a couch, a table, a standing wardrobe and a little desk with a chair. Her husband was retired and the government was still unable to provide a pension. They were barely surviving and were hoping to rent this tiny room as soon as possible.

Frau Lange was a very pleasant gray-haired lady who, once she found out that Ania also needed a room, took us immediately to the second floor were Frau Braun also had a room for rent. It was a larger room with a substantial bed, a large table and a couple of chairs.

Frau Braun was single and she stayed in the apartment's large bedroom. There was a large kitchen that she offered to Ania to share with her. We didn't even discuss it. Ania nodded her head and I asked for the price, it turned out to be very reasonable. I took the room on the ground floor and Ania the one in Frau Braun's apartment. We brought our valises and unpacked while Hanka busied herself in her apartment with supper. We were admonished to move rapidly and return to her place within a half an hour so we could eat and spend more time together.

After dinner, Hanka played the piano and it was wonderful. We felt very happy and very fortunate. In this incredibly short period of time, we managed to get admitted to the University, make wonderful friends and find a place to live for each of us, most importantly in the same house.

It was still dark outside when I woke up. I couldn't sleep anymore, disorganized thoughts were racing through my mind, I couldn't concentrate on any one idea. I was thinking about Ania and at the same time I felt great anxiety about the school, a German Medical School; what I read about it filled me with great apprehension, going through such school was always described as a very though and exacting experience. This issue certainly was a huge unknown.

The questions of survival were also swirling through my head. Neither Ania nor I, nor our parents had tangible means of support. No jobs, no salaries. While in the camps, the basics, food and shelter, were provided. Here, however, we had to pay rent and other expenses, like tram fares, food when not home, etc. The big question was: where do we get cash? Our clothing was in tatters, to all practical purposes we had not bought clothing since the war started and I got one suit during this period of time and it was getting very small on me, I grew!

As I was trying to concentrate on a single issue and identify the most pressing problem, all of these different ideas where buzzing simultaneously through my head. I was making no progress in trying to place them in some order. And then, a new concerned came up in my mind. What about Frau Lange, my landlady or Frau Braun? Where they Nazis? How will our interactions develop?

It was really just a continuation of the environment of uncertainty, fight for survival and hope for future; a future that I had not thought about for some time. The present was moving with neck breaking speed, and every day was bringing up important issues requiring instant decisions that could influence our current situation, our lives in the future and our lives in general.

This was a new stage in the progress of our lives; could we be forced to stay here for months, years, indefinitely? There was no answer to these questions. We could have been given an opportunity to emigrate, but where and when? We committed ourselves here to a major undertaking, to attend Medical School, obviously with the goal of graduating, but we had no control of our destiny, specifically of the ability to stay here and finish the studies.

Then, the Pandora's Box of the current issues dealing with Ania opened up in my mind with enormous force. Our relationship was becoming very serious and some decisions had to be made. Even the mundane issues of daily living had to be decided upon. For example, should I call Ania and have breakfast with her or should she eat alone in her room and I could eat here? Little things like that would certainly be coming up in our interactions and would have to be settled. I knew what I would prefer, but was that what she would also like? All of it was really very confusing!

On that note, I decided to get up and get ready for the day. The issue of breakfast was resolved by Frau Lange. After getting ready, I went to the kitchen looking for her. She was obviously waiting for me. With a big smile on her face she informed me that she went up to Fräulein Ania and informed her that breakfast would be ready in twenty minutes and that she should come down to our place. "I trust that I did the right thing," she commented on her way to my room where she started setting up the table for breakfast.

I was speechless. Obviously, Frau Lange's willingness to fix breakfast for us would solve the breakfast issue admirably and to the highest of my expectations. I was very grateful; quickly and clearly I made these feelings known to her.

We took the tram to the Bahnhoff (railroad station). From there we had to walk. The tram connection to Sachsenhausen was still not fixed. We walked down the avenue to the bridge, crossed it and entered the Sachsenhausen District. The Medical School was to the right. Many of the buildings were damaged, some totally destroyed.

We walked by some clinic and hospital buildings just off the banks of the River Main. After asking for some directions, we found the main administrative building. There we were told that the most important subjects that semester would be physiology and anatomy taught right there. Lectures in the other subjects, like botany, were given at the main campus. We were to register for each and have the appropriate portions of the Studenten Buch filled in the respective offices.

We also learned something unique to German universities. We were to pay for the lectures on each subject directly to the professor's account at the time of registration. The amount was not very significant but we had to get the cash to pay. When we explained that we had no cash with us, the secretary allowed us to register with the promise that we would bring money the following day. Later we were told that all university payments were cancelled for students who were politically persecuted by the Nazi regime. As Jews, this included Ania and myself.

Anatomy was thought by Professor Stark while physiology by Professor Bethe. We went first to the anatomy pavilion and registered for the dissections. The dissection laboratories were almost full. Apparently this was a very well attended course. Actually one could work in this laboratory anytime between 8 AM and 5 PM.

We were assigned a cadaver number and went into the dissection room looking for our group. A group of eight students were assigned to a cadaver. At the station we were assigned to, there were only a total of five students. With us, it made for a group of seven. Three of the students were already there; we introduced ourselves and started getting acquainted.

Apparently the cadaver was by now totally dissected except for part of the head where the facial muscles were located. The muscles and the cranial nerves studies were also completed. The remaining portion of that semester and the next, the fourth semester were to be devoted to the neuro system, including the brain. The skull was to be cut open and the brain removed at the beginning of the next semester. Thus, the entire fourth semester was to be devoted to the brain anatomy and to a review of the entire anatomy for a major examination, the Physicum that was to include all the material learned in the Medical School up to that point.

Later in the afternoon, we registered in the section of histology that also was a part of the Anatomy Department. There, we met Professor Stark who signed the anatomy and histology pages of our Student Books. He was a tall, handsome man who looked to be a very strict but also a fair teacher. He was rather curt, but friendly.

This was our first contact with a German professor and it left an impression. We were also told that the payments to the professor were to be made when registering for the examinations. The examinations in Germany were oral and administered by the professor himself. This sounded rather scary and ominous. We were also informed that we would need to purchase our own microscopes for the histology laboratory. The school did not provide any. This sounded as a major blow to our economic situation. We thought that possibly the Student Union might have some ideas how to handle this issue or possibly Henry or Isaac knew more about it.

I was surprised that no one mentioned this to us, but our admission process was so unusual and so rapid that many things were apparently not touched upon by our newly acquired friends.

Finally, we finished with the formalities but I realized that we would not be able to attend histology laboratory until we secured two microscopes. Each student had to have a microscope, no sharing. Period!

I decided not to worry, and, instead, to concentrate on making sure that our credits for botany and the other courses would be properly recorded in our Student Books.

We walked slowly across the bridge busily talking about all the new information and the new impressions. It was scary. Ania's knowledge of the German language was essentially non-existent. My knowledge of the language was, at best, minimal. We were to start attending lectures the following day! Our anxiety level was making us crawl right out of our skin.

As we were getting off the bridge, on the right side of the street, we noted a *Bierstube* (a pub), so we decided to go in and have something to eat and drink. The dark beer was heavenly. We splurged and again had pork chops. "At this rate," I said to Ania, "whatever little money we have will be gone in a week." She agreed and told me that she had been talking to Frau Lange who informed her that she would be happy to cook dinners for us. This was good news. I told Ania that most likely we could get some food supplies from Kassel; also we could get some food from the Student Union. This should be quite sufficient for us and there should be enough to give Frau Lange some for her gracious offer.

I think that we were simply euphoric, all the experience, the warm Bierstube, the beer, oh yes the beer and all that talk made us happy, warm and high. Afterwards we barely were able to walk to the railroad station and take our tram to Fechenheim. We were planning to visit Hanka to tell her all the news, but by time we got home, the only thing we were capable of was to go to bed.

The week went by like lightning. We registered for the lectures in anatomy, histology, biochemistry and physiology. We got the credits approved for botany, zoology, organic and inorganic chemistry. Also, we got the hygiene course out of the way. In between these activities, we attended the dissection laboratory and the anatomy, physiology, biochemistry and histology lectures.

By the end of the week, we were 'brain dead'. I understood the German language by now well enough to make the lectures quite bearable. Unfortunately Ania was on a verge of mental breakdown. She tried so hard, but didn't understand enough German to appreciate what she was hearing during the lectures. The only consolation was that she began to communicate with our German colleagues. Her knowledge of Yiddish was quite helpful in deciphering German.

Friday evening we visited Hanka and had dinner with her while luxuriating in the tales of our adventures. She also introduced us to Arcik, the dental student she mentioned before. He was a very pleasant and an intelligent fellow. Both Ania and I developed an instant positive feeling towards him. I, however, became a little uneasy since I thought that I noticed great interest on his part towards Ania. This, however, I attributed ultimately towards understandable jealousy on my part. Ania was an extremely attractive girl, and I tried to think that I had, by definition, the right to feel jealous.

Meeting Arcik also had an immediate important influence on both of us. As we related our concerns in respect to the procurement of microscopes for the histology lab, he laughed, "Don't worry," he chuckled, I know a man who will get you all the microscopes you want, as long as you pay him. We can go tomorrow and see what he has available."

The evening was getting late and we were dead tired. I explained to Arcik the location of our apartment and we arranged to meet the next day to visit his acquaintance concerning the microscope.

Saturday Arcik walked to our place and together we went by tram to see the man about the microscope. Indeed he had two available. One was quite an old monocular scope; the other was a new, latest design, binocular microscope with phase optics. I couldn't believe it; the man wanted just two cartons of cigarettes and two pounds of coffee for the binocular and one carton of cigarettes and one pound of coffee for the binocular.

I told Arcik that we would like to buy the scopes but we had at this moment neither the coffee nor the cigarettes. He laughed, "Don't worry," he whispered to me, "I will pay him, and you can pay me back later when you will get your monthly 'supply." I was smitten by his generosity and camaraderie.

He didn't even want to hear my expressions of thankfulness. "I am sure that you would do same for me under similar circumstances," he remarked and indicated that we should go with him to his place to get the stuff. We were extremely relieved because this completed all the requirements for really getting going with the studies.

Our lives became routine. Getting up early in the morning when it was still dark to get the tram on time for the trip to the University. The dissections, lectures and, oh yes, the studies at home easily filled our days until midnight. Frau Lange would prepare dinner, most of the time, for both of us in her apartment. Occasionally Ania prepared food in Frau Braun's kitchen.

We saw Hanka at least once a week, Arcik less often. Our world, Ania's and mine, were limited basically to each other. We began to function almost as a single organism. We spent most of the day together, primarily studying, traveling or eating, always together. Since it was cold outside and I still didn't have a coat we spend most of the time indoors. Finally, we realized that we must go back to Kassel. Originally we planned to go back during Christmas vacation and this was only early December. Our food supply, however, and money were running out. The only means of communication with our parents was via mail and it was very slow.

We explored further the Jewish Student Union and submitted our application for membership. We still were unable to meet with the president, our schedules simply didn't allow it, and he apparently was an extremely busy person. The thought occurred to us that possibly he was not the best-suited person for the job, in light of his, what appeared to almost impossible schedule.

We visited the Student Union office at least once a week and talked about this issue with the secretary and the other students. The students only smirked while the secretary kept on repeating to us that there is very little that can be done until the president determines with certainty that we are legitimate students. This, she said, was, according to him, a highly improbable chance. She also informed us that, obviously, we are welcome to visit the Student Union; however, we must realize that we cannot expect any student benefits like C.A.R.E. packages, gifts of food, cigarettes or coffee until we formally become members.

As we were talking to the secretary, we could here a booming voice behind us exclaiming, "Here you are! Where were you hiding all these weeks? I looked for you everywhere, obviously, unsuccessfully." I turned around and literally fell into Henry's arms. He hugged me then turned to Ania with a big bear hug. We were very eager to give him a detailed account of our adventures, but the time was getting on and we had to get back to Sachsenhausen for our classes. When he heard this, his response was instant, "It's great, I have to go soon to the clinic also, thus, we can go together and on the way you can tell me the entire story."

He listened to us with great interest and when the story started bumping into the episodes related to our experiences, or the lack of any contact with Ervin, a wry smile crept on his face and he semi-whispered, "This is 'Herr President' for you." Then he continued in his smooth but booming voice, "Don't let this disturb you. This is his obnoxious way to behave, however, he is good politician and he knows how to get for us all kinds of benefits, particularly food, coffee and cigarettes. He must be upset that you encroached on his authority and his prerogatives by being admitted to school without his intervention. It must have touched his emotional crown. However, he will get over it, you are now legitimate students; he, not only will have to make you a member of the Student Union, but will also have to supply you with the benefits in a retroactive fashion. If he doesn't take care of this matter talk to me some more. I know how to get these things done. Now, I have to hurry, otherwise I will miss my clinic, I am already assigned to see patients and I better be there on time."

We shook hands and parted, he to the clinic us to the Anatomy Building. Henry was two years ahead of us which is why he was already assigned to the clinical areas. I was envious of him but at the same time proud and happy to have an upper classman as a friend.

The experiences with the empty cupboards and end of our money supply convinced us that we had to go to the camp to get some food and money. The week was coming to an end. We decided to take the Friday evening night train and spend the weekend in Muenchenberg. There was no way for us to warn our parents of the visit. Telephone would be too expensive. And anyway, they didn't have one and neither did we. Mail would not get there on time. We decided to simply show up Saturday morning on their doorsteps.

It was a true surprise, as expected; Mother started crying while Father and Josef kept on asking questions, nonstop. Ultimately, Mother dried her tears and asked me if I wanted to eat. I didn't think that she would ever ask. I was famished. Our last food was at breakfast a day earlier, and even at that time it was nothing to brag about. I couldn't believe it, but was pleasantly surprised when Mother brought out a sausage ring, a loaf of fresh white bread--white bread was still a delicacy, a rarity, ever since the begin of the war--and a cake. I started devouring these delicacies and, while doing so, I also realized how poor our diet was in Frankfurt and how rapidly we got accustomed to it!

The conversation quickly turned towards our studies and towards the conditions in Frankfurt. I dutifully reported all the details of our adventures in Frankfurt, particularly Mother's achievements in getting us admitted to the school and the astonishment of the students for being able to carry it out. I was particularly careful to detail the accolade of the students for this task. Subsequently I went into great details to summarize our food and money situation and brought up the loans of coffee and cigarettes extended to us by our friend, Arcik.

The family was very impressed by the warmth and help of our new friends in Frankfurt and Mother instantly started to figure what gifts she could gather for them. Father and Josef assured me that it would not be a major problem to supply me with food from the camp. Since I was a registered D.P. at the camp, they were collecting my food rations all the time and planned to continue to do so. The rations included cigarettes and coffee. Almost everyone, except Mother and Stella, was smoking. Stella was only twelve years old; nevertheless, she was receiving a full ration, including cigarettes and coffee. In addition, Mother started helping people with their dental problems; this work was usually bartered for cigarettes or coffee.

In final analysis, there was enough to provide us with money and goods to trade. This would allow me to survive in Frankfurt and attend school with no financial worries. Learning all this removed a major burden off my chest.

Once the issue concerning my economic situation in Frankfurt was resolved, the conversation moved on towards other matters that were also of major concern to all of us. The first topic was obviously our future. In this respect, there was a great deal to be talked about. We had to establish a permanent home somewhere; the "Displaced Persons" status had to end.

For us there were fundamentally three options. Since both of my parents were actually born in Kassel, although they did not live there long, both having moved to Berlin as children, an option to stay in Kassel had been considered. My parents visited the City Hall and once the officials learned that they lived in the D.P. camp, a commission was immediately set up to help them find a nice apartment in the city. The City Hall was even willing to set up a dental office for Mother, all of this as part of reparations (Wiedergutmachung) for the losses they suffered during the war.

This was a very tempting offer, I thought; however, parents were very skeptical, they neither fully trusted, as of yet, the German society nor were they emotionally ready to accept this offer. Although, at that time we had no idea of the full extent of the devastation afflicted by the Germans on the Jewish society, specifically the unthinkable number of Jews (6,000,000) who were murdered.

Mother continued to call Europe the "graveyard of the Jews" and was adamant that she could not live there. While this possibility was not totally discarded, we moved to the other options.

Emigration to Palestine was also a real possibility. Matter of fact I was to meet with Shmull, a nineteen-year-old boy from Poland who was an ardent Zionist. We were to discuss Aliyah Bet and my possible participation in this venture. The family, however, was never Zionist and at this moment, they didn't feel that they had the strength to move to a desert and fight for the establishment of a new country.

They were not "angry" people looking for some form of vengeance to repay the war years or for making a political statement; they, particularly Father, wanted to rest from the horrors of the war (this for him was the second World War of his lifetime; he fought in the First World War as a Corporal in the Austrian Army and was taken as a war prisoner by the Russians) and now he only wished to live a quiet and simple productive live. However, even if we would have elected to make the emigration to Palestine our priority, there was no clear way to accomplish it. The British established a naval blockade of Israel to intercept ships leased by the Jewish organizations to run the Aliyahs.

The way to get registered for passage was to travel illegally, in small groups, usually under the leadership of a young Zionist, to one of the port cities in Italy or to Croatia. We traveled in the past many times into an unknown situation; I was not certain that this would be a choice that we would be eager to repeat at the moment. We needed either something leading to a definite future or we needed to wait and rest. Anyway, I was to learn much more about this possibility when I was to meet Shmull the next day.

The most desirous solution was to emigrate to one of the Western countries outside of continental Europe. Juzek was in touch by mail with my aunt, Mother's sister, who lived in Australia for years. She promised to investigate the possibility of getting a visa for him to immigrate to Australia. She wrote, however, that she would be able, at this moment, to help only one person; the immigration laws in Australia were very tight. My aunt in London, Father's sister, didn't think that she could help to procure papers for our family to go to England. Mother was willing to let me go alone if I could get the papers but even this, she claimed, was impossible. The other possibility was the United States.

Actually, most displaced persons had hopes of emigrating to the U.S. or Canada. We had no relatives in Canada and did not consider this possibility. On the other hand, both of my parents had relatives in the United States. The relatives on Father's side were poorly known to him and he had no address or means to contact them. He didn't even know in what city they lived. Mother, on the other hand, was very close with her sister in New York who lived there most of her life and apparently was reasonably well to do.

The financial background of relatives in the U.S. was of paramount importance since to be able to support a visa application to the Immigration Service, the American relative had to guarantee that the immigrant would not fall on the government's dole. Thus, they had to reveal their fiscal background and show the willingness to support, if necessary, the relatives after their arrival to the USA.

Mother was absolutely convinced that her sister was sufficiently well off to satisfy the Immigration Service requirements and sufficiently motivated to do all that was necessary to get the permits. Mother was always a very good sister to my aunt. Although I wasn't privy to the details, I remembered my 'American' aunt and her boys, my cousins, visiting us in our house in Europe and spending their vacations with us.

Mother had been in contact with my aunt and discussed the emigration issues with her. I found out that several Jewish organizations had also undertaken to help the D.P.s by providing for some the necessary sponsorships. Primarily HIAS and JOINT were involved with these issues. Both Ania's and my parents applied to both organizations for assistance in getting immigration papers to the U.S.

There was, however, another aspect of the emigration issue. It was not sufficient to have a valid sponsor and all the necessary guarantees and papers. The United States had an annual quota for immigrants based on the place of birth, thus a "German quota," a "Polish quota," etc. This made the country of birth an important factor in the success and in the length of the waiting period required for the visa to be issued.

The largest quota was the German one, and, at the same time the percent of visa applicants born in Germany was the smallest. Thus, German born Jews had an easier and faster way to get the visa than, for example, Polish born Jews. To take this a little further, around 1946, there were approximately 1,000,000 D.P.s and of these less than 20% were Jews. The rest were primarily eastern Europeans, like Ukrainians, Latvians, Litvenians, Estonians, Poles, Russians and other nationalities. Thus, of all the annually available finite immigration spots to the United States, the Jewish D.P.s had only a chance of securing one fifth.

To place this in perspective, as partly discussed above, in Chapter 14, one has to realize that after the armistice in May of 1945 some 7 to 9,000,000 foreigners from all over Europe resided in Germany. Before the end of 1945 over 6,000,000 were repatriated to the home lands. Some 1.5 to 2 million remained in the D.P. camps, including about 50,000 Jews. Shortly after the establishment of the D.P. camps, the persecution of the Jews by the non-Jewish D.P. camp inmates became sufficiently severe to necessitate an intervention by the President of United States, Mr. Truman and by General Eisenhower to establish exclusively Jewish camps in order to prevent this unexpected and sick development. The horrible situation in the D.P. camps also prompted President Truman to exert pressure on the British to ease off their severe restrictions on immigration of the Jews from post war Europe to Palestine.

In response, the British appointed an Anglo-American Committee of Inquiry. The Committee recommended that Great Britain allow entry of 100,000 Jews into Palestine. Since 1945 and early 1946, there was about 50 to 100,000 Jews in the D.P. camps. This would have resolved the problem of the original Jewish D.P. population and saved all the countries in the world from having to accept some of the 100,000 Jewish immigrants. They would have to contend only with the immigration of the remaining approximate 800,000 non-Jewish D.P.s; this would not be neither insurmountable nor a distasteful task once the "Jewish" problem was solved.

Unfortunately, the British Prime Minister, Clement Atlee, rejected the recommendations of his committee and proclaimed again that the quota of 18,000 Jewish immigrants per year would stand. Great Britain feared repercussions from the Arab nations; they were particularly concerned with the possible squeeze by the Arabs on oil supplies and revenues from the Middle East. The British actually increased the severity of naval blockades of Palestine after the war trying to prevent the illegal Aliyah from functioning. These immigration numbers remained unchanged until 1948 when the State of Israel was established.

Inmates of the non-Jewish D.P. camps were a mixed bag. A substantial number, actually millions, were war prisoners, primarily Soviets; some were temporary laborers who moved voluntarily from eastern European countries to Germany to work in its war industry;

others were political prisoners. A relatively small segment of the general D.P. camp population was composed of former inmates of the concentration camps. A large segment was composed of German collaborators, particularly members of the military from Ukraine, where entire armies switched sides during the German invasion of Soviet Union. This group retreated from Russia with the Germans in response to the advances of the Soviet Army and by the end of the war found themselves in Germany.

Similarly, when the Soviets were pursuing the retreating German armies through the Baltic countries, some civilians from these countries also retreated to Germany. They were composed of a substantial number of civilians who didn't want to fall in the hands of the Soviets, afraid of repercussions for their collaboration with the Germans during occupation. Another group that joined the retreating German armies were the various concentration camp guards and other employees used for carrying on the concentration camp goals and participating in the mechanics of the "Final Solution" of the Jews. Ultimately, many of these groups ended up in D.P. camps.

After the war, the Allies tried to repatriate swiftly the foreigners who found themselves on the occupied Germany soil. Although during the first year approximately six to seven million people were repatriated--some forcibly because the Soviet Union demanded that all people who were born on Soviet Union soil before the onset of World War II must be returned to their homelands--many were not willing to return home.

Information filtering back from the Soviet Union suggested that even innocent prisoners of war (POWs) who by no fault of their own were captured by the Germans, they were treated harshly upon return to their homelands. This information as well as the fear of the various elements mentioned above influenced them to look for emigration rather than repatriation as the solution to the subsistence type of life in the D.P. camps. Consequently, the Jewish D.P.s had to compete for visas to the United States against their former torturers and murderers from the war years.

Finally, the greatest of the obstacles to emigration was the annual limit imposed by the United States Congress on the total number of immigrants who could enter the country. After the Harrison Report was submitted to President Truman in August of 1945 showing the miserable treatment afforded the D.P.s and specifically the Jewish D.P.s, Truman and General Eisenhower took energetic steps to reorganize the situation. The first step was to recognize the Jews as a distinct nationality and establish separate camps for the Jews. The fundamental issue, however, was to find a home for the Jews and for all of the other D.P.s. This was the world we were facing as D.P.s in 1946 with our lives Kassel and in Frankfurt.

Our parents applied to the American Council for a visa, and since Ania and I were underage, we automatically were included in the application. No one had any inkling how long the process might take. However, there was a rumor that those born in Germany would fall under the German immigration quota and have a good chance of getting visas much faster than those born in Poland. There were some D.P.s who applied for a U.S. visa shortly after the war and now, one and one half years later, they were not even called for the medical examination, a necessary prerequisite for issuance of a visa. Interestingly, this prerequisite later seriously influenced our personal emigration process. Thus, we were very early in the game of emigration and I was very happy that we didn't waste our time depending on hopes of getting to a permanent place very soon. Instead we grabbed every opportunity to further our education. In this context, a year lost not being in school would be a year difficult to regain in the future.

That weekend visiting our families in the Muenchenberg Displaced Persons camp was passing with speed of wind. We promised all our friends to spend time with them in a few weeks when we would come back home for the winter vacation. We did manage a few hours with our closest friends Mietek and Ania whose situation in the camp had not changed. They were a few years older and married to each other. As mentioned before, Ania and I tried to sway them to join us at the University but to no avail. They took the task that we had rejected - working very hard with the hope of getting visas as soon possible to emigrate either to the USA or to Australia. Mietek was in Muenchenberg with his older brother who also was married. His brother apparently had a good chance to get a visa for Australia.

In general, the people in the camp had a temporary type philosophy. Most friends of our age accepted the idea that it doesn't pay to start anything of consequence now, that we should wait until we get to a permanent place. Everyone was also hungry, both, for food and for material possessions. Years of war, camps, jails gulags, all had exacted their toll.

I think that this also explained the desire to deal on the black market that was alive and well at this time in Germany. The people in the camp settled into a reasonable and quiet life. Everyone was working on some scheme leading to emigration. The food, while monotonous, was adequate in volume. Clothing was available to stay warm, not necessarily fashionable. There was plenty of time to talk, play chess, visit and for those who felt need for it, be engaged in the black market.

The two days we spent in the camp were extremely important to us. Many family issues were hashed out and plans for future sketched out. It became clear to Ania and I, as well as to our parents, that from now on our plans definitely included both of us equally. Interestingly, this approach came through almost naturally, as if it was always considered an obvious fact. I was very pleased and grateful to my parents and Ania's parents for assuming this attitude.

It was getting colder and on many days snow was falling--nothing heavy but enough to let us know that winter was coming. I brought with me to Frankfurt my old winter coat and Ania brought her fur trimmed jacket and fur hat. Both had been custom-made in Alma Ata by her father. Seeing her the first time in these fur pieces in Alma Ata, I could think of nothing else but of a beautiful snow fairy Russian princess. She definitely looked ravishing in this outfit.

After returning to Frankfurt, I finally got a chance to meet Herr President. It happened in the Jewish Student Union office. By then, most of the students that frequently gathered in the Union room knew me. Many saw me in classes. I think that they all assumed that by now I was a member of the Union.

When I walked in, the room was full of students milling around. They were either discussing something loudly and vehemently, or standing in small groups whispering to each other. Occasionally there was an explosion of raucous laughter. I noticed my friend Henry by one of the bookcases lining the wall and walked over to him. He said excitedly, "Have you had a chance to talk to Erwin, 'Herr

President'? He is here, standing by the desk, next to the secretary. I will introduce you to him."

I said "OK, this should be fun." Henry admonished me, "Talk very loud so that the entire room will hear you. This will make him behave. If he doesn't he will be embarrassed in front of everyone." As we walked quickly towards the desk where he stood, many of the students noticed us and realized that something comical was about to happen.

Slowly, it became quiet in the room and most of the students directed their gaze at us. Erwin sensed this and looked up at us. Henry, with a twinkle in his eyes and a broad smile on his face, looked "Herr President" straight into his eyes as said, "Hello, Erwin, I want to introduce Emil to you. He was admitted to the University's Medical Faculty a few weeks back. I am certain you would like to recruit him to become a member of our organization. I hear that he is doing very well in osteology laboratory and is starting the dissections."

"Herr President" turned red first, then white. For a moment, he was speechless. Students were standing, watching and listening.

Finally, he started laughing and extending his hand to me. "Oh yes, I heard of you and Ania. Its wonderful to have you with us, we will be pleased to have both of you as our colleagues. Please have my secretary copy the information from your student books. Also, don't forget to pick up your food rations and care packages for this month. I hope to see you here frequently and if there is anything we can do for you just see me or mention it to the secretary." He kept on shaking my hand during this speech while I held on to his hand with a plastered stupid grin on my face.

As I started thanking him I could hear applause, some of the students came over, patted me on my back and murmured, "Good to have you with us." At this moment I comprehended why Erwin became a president, I also realized what it took in some circumstances to be a president. I also realized that this was not my "cup of tea."

****

Saturday morning. I was sitting in Frau Lange's kitchen having a cup of tea with her and her husband Dietrich. It was the first time she talked to me about the war and about her son. I think that up to now, topics related to the war were avoided. Probably neither of us wanted to create a situation that could be uncomfortable for either party. Frau Lange showed me a letter. It was from her son. He was a prisoner of war in the Soviet Union. The letter arrived in an envelope with no return address and the postal stamp revealed no name of the place from where it was mailed. She said that she found him through the Red Cross and that this was the second letter since the war ended a year and one half ago. The letter was very brief simply telling his parents that he was well and still in the prisoners of war camp near the Arctic Circle working in the forest.

She was crying. I well appreciated her son's predicament, since I also was in a Soviet camp, a gulag, near the Arctic Circle working in the forests--and I was not even a prisoner of war. I would have never seen that camp near the Arctic Circle or, matter of fact, Frau Lange's apartment, if it hadn't have been for the Nazis who chased us from our home in Berlin and later attacked Poland- causing the chain of events leading to this situation now.

I couldn't summon any pity for him or for Frau Lange. I was in no mood to reopen these issues. I had totally neutral feelings towards them and the Soviets. We were here; I felt, in transit, on the way to our permanent home, somewhere. This was the paramount thought in my mind.

Frau Lange obviously wanted to share her longing for her son, her feeling of unfairness for having to live his imprisonment as a prisoner of war. I sympathized with the feeling of generic rights of prisoners of war, rights that were being encroached upon by the Soviets. All prisoners of the Second World War should have been released by then. This was clear. However, specifically in respect this German soldier, I had no feelings.

Frau Lange, continued telling me what a wonderful son he was, how he sent her beautiful dresses when he was in France on the Western front and later when he was on the Eastern front how he saved his soldier's pay to buy and send her beautiful pieces of jewelry. She even remarked how inexpensive the jewelry must have been in the eastern countries because he was able to buy such beautiful pieces on a soldier's salary. I almost cried at this woman's ignorance and naiveté. I could visualize the necks, the wrists, the ears and the fingers of the Jewish women from whom this jewelry must have come. There was no "inexpensive" jewelry in eastern countries. It was actually very expensive. Jewish women usually paid for the privilege of having it robbed from them with their own lives. Obviously, Frau Lange had no idea how things were obtained by the German soldiers during the war. Herr Dietrich didn't say a word during our conversation.

As Frau Lange was spilling her heart to me, I could hear violin music. So as not to upset her I gently interrupted with a question, "who is playing the violin? She grinned and exclaimed, "Oh, this is Herr Lotz, he is a music teacher. He plays the violin beautifully."

"Where does he live?" I asked.

"On the other side of the hallway on the same floor, would you like to meet him?" she asked.

"I certainly would," I responded. "I do like the violin and have played a little before. I still have the instrument, matter of fact I have it here in Frankfurt."

"Well," she said with a grin on her face as she got up, her sadness disappearing instantly, "let's go and meet him." We walked across the floor to a perfectly varnished door with a large brass sign, Herr Lotz. Frau Lange knocked. The music stopped and the door opened framing a medium height, slim man in a white shirt and a bow tie holding a violin in his left hand.

"Oh, Frau Lange, please come in, what a pleasure, and who is the young man with you?"

Frau Lang turned towards me, extending her arm, and introduced me: "this is Herr Steinberger, my renter. He heard you play and enjoyed it immensely. He would like to meet you."

Herr Lotz invited us to come in and join him in the sitting room where he was playing his violin a few minutes back. There was a straight-backed chair with an upholstered seat standing next to an upright piano in front of a music stand.

I could see an open book of Kreutzer sonatas on the stand. "It is a pleasure to meet another violinist," he remarked, addressing me and pointing with an inviting gesture to a small couch facing the piano while he sat down on the chair.

I smiled and responded, "Thank you for your kindness, but I do not think I deserve to be described as a violinist. A more precise term would be a 'beginning student' who aspires to possibly become a violinist some time in the future."

At that point Frau Lange got up, smiled and turning to Herr Lotz remarked, "I think that two of you are getting along well, I shall go beck to the house and clean up the breakfast dishes." With this, she got up waved to us and left.

I had a pleasant conversation with Herr Lotz, learned that he was semi-retired but that he still played with the Frankfurt Chamber Music Orchestra, but most of the time he gave violin lessons. That gave me an idea.

"Will you be willing to also be my music teacher?" I asked.

He smiled at me and responded cheerfully, "It will be a pleasure and honor to do so. Bring your violin and let's see where we should begin."

I thanked him and ran back home to get my violin. I returned with trepidation, realizing that I had not played for some time and worried that I might not be good enough to be his student. With a smile in his eyes, he turned to me and asked, "What would you like to play? I will join you for company."

"Could we possibly play one of the Vivaldi violin concertos, any one?" I responded.

I liked Vivaldi. David and I used to play his works a great deal while still in the Gulag. Herr Lotz rummaged for an instant in a pile of sheet music and pulled one out. He opened it and stood it up on the music stand. It was Vivaldi's Violin Concerto in D Major, a favorite of mine. I felt quite confident, treading on familiar grounds. The music just poured out of my violin. Herr Lotz joined me, playing quietly after I started, but soon became entranced also by the music, and we just played.

After the first movement we stopped. I looked at him with expectation. "Well," he said, "it was not that bad. If you wish, I will be happy to take you on as a pupil." What will be the best days for you? I think that a weekly lesson should be adequate."

I was overjoyed but realized that I never, during the week, got home to Fechenheim before evening. I explained this dilemma to Herr Lotz and he grinned broadly, "Well, how about Saturdays, like today, at ten o'clock, for one hour?"

I was happy and I ran up to the second floor to tell Ania the good news. She was home alone because Frau Braun was visiting her sister for the day. We had the apartment to ourselves. I picked up Ania and danced with her all over the room, the hallway, all the way to the kitchen. She stopped our rejoicing and, breathlessly, kissed and hugged me. Then, she whispered, "How about a really nice lunch?"

I smiled and said, "Absolutely, but after…?"

Ania prepared lunch fit for a king. We didn't spare any of our food supplies. First I ran out to a nearby bakery to get some fresh bread; this wasn't the Soviet Union, one could indeed get some food in the stores; although many items, like butter, meat, sausage, cereals were still basically black market priced, and others, like American cigarettes, coffee, oranges etc. were simply not available in the stores. However, certain basics, like bread, beer and potatoes were usually available.

When I walked into Ania's apartment I could immediately detect that she was preparing my favorite food, food that we ate only sparingly because of its shortage.

She was frying canned meat that was frequently included in the C.A.R.E. packages. It came in small sealed tins and tasted heavenly. It had the name SPAM printed on the outside of the cans. Hanka, who knew English, read the details of label for us, apparently it was made in Argentina. Ania fried it with onions and served it with "kind of" scrambled eggs. The eggs were prepared from powdered eggs that were a part of the D.P. camp food rations. The powdered eggs didn't make the best scrambled eggs; however, we did not know how to prepare them in any other way. Actually when combined with the delicious fried meat and onions they added substantially to our luxurious breakfast. Obviously we didn't drink regular coffee, this was saved for barter. We were accustomed to "ersatz" (artificial) coffee particularly since we were lucky to have sugar; it was great! After the sumptuous breakfast we decided to stay home, study and enjoy each other.

The "Weihnachten," Christmas Holidays, were almost here. We were finishing the semester by boning up for the quizzes in anatomy. Only laboratory subjects had periodic quizzes. The major lecture courses only had a final examination at the end of a course and then, also, the big one, the "Physicum."

Physicum was a major examination! It was administered during the summer vacation after the first two years and it encompassed the lecture material provided during that period of time as well as all the material in textbooks the lecturer might have mentioned. At that time, we didn't wish to even think of Physicum. It loomed as a major threatening cloud in the future, a cloud that we didn't want to worry about.

The time immediately preceding the vacation was fun for many, as I learned; however, it was fun to look forward to primarily for students like us who were blessed with families and very close friends with whom they could spend time during the vacations. There were the others, like Hanka and Arcik that didn't have a soul to turn to. Some of the students developed very close friendships to at least partly replace families. Yes, vacations and holidays were a sad time for many of us. Ania and I couldn't wait to go back to the camp. We hadn't seen our parents, Stella and our friends for weeks.

Shortly before leaving for Kassel, we ran across Henry. He was elated. Apparently, he had a well to do relative in America in a city called Detroit. This was the place where Mr. Ford had his famous car factories. The relative was able to provide Henry with fabulous financial guarantee. This resulted in him getting a visa very rapidly.

He could barely articulate from the excitement when trying to tell us that early next year he will be probably departing for the "Promised Land."

We were not only jealous but also very happy for him. This was wonderful news. As we continued asking millions of questions, he suddenly stopped talking and held me by the shoulder exclaiming: "By the way are you aware that the German officials are issuing to all Jews a special certificate? It has a photograph, many stamps and a statement that we were *Verfolgte* (persecuted) people and we are granted the privilege of traveling on all state transportation systems (trains, trams or state-run buses) free and whenever there is a queue for any state provided items, like tickets, food, etc., we have the privilege of being served ahead of the others in the queue."

We were shocked, I personally couldn't believe it. This would be the first time as long as I remembered that being Jewish gave me a privilege rather than a disadvantage. Henry gave us the address of the office where he got his certificate and exclaimed, "Go now, I know how eager you are to get this document." We didn't waste a second to get on the way. We took with us the Identification Card issued by the D.P. camp administration; it actually was the only identification we possessed. We were in a foreign country, Germany, and being "Displaced Persons," we had no passports. Instead we carried with us copies of the D.P. photos, photos originally made for our Student Book. Thus, we figured that we had all the papers needed to get the certificates. Well, when we arrived at the office, the clerk listened, took a look our Identification Card, asked us for a photo and in few minutes the documents were ready for our signature. It was fast and easy. We couldn't believe our eyes when we looked at the handsome document typed on pink paper that was to give us such privileges! I couldn't wait to try it on the tram. We did almost immediately on our way home, and indeed, it worked!

This time we planned our trip to Kassel well ahead of time. This gave us the opportunity to write home and give them the date and exact time of arrival. We had a surprise in store. When we got off at the railroad station all members of both families as well as all our friends were there to greet us. It was a wonderful surprise. We hugged, we cried and we laughed. Everyone had a lot to tell and the din became unbelievable. Even Shmull was there. He finally got a chance to get closer to me and to whisper, "I must get together with you tomorrow, alone. Don't tell anyone about it. I will meet you in the center of the camp by the 'metzeive' (a wooden memorial in remembrance of the 6,000,000 Jews murdered by the Germans) at eleven o'clock" and he disappeared.

All of us took the tram to the outskirts of Muenchenberg and walked the rest of the way to our house. Mother had a reception for the entire group. Since it was already early winter, weather was not conducive to an outdoor party; it was too cold outdoors thus, all of us had to fit in the tiny apartment. It really was crowded but the company and the fabulous food Mother prepared compensated for this minor discomfort. Actually, I thought, crowding might not have been such a bad thing for our spirits.

CHAPTER 17. Aliyah

Ania asked me to come to her house the next morning. I told her that I would not be able to because of the eleven o'clock meeting with Shmull and his insistence that I come alone. She was a bit put out, but there was nothing I could do about it. I was actually very intrigued and curious to learn what Shmull had to say particularly since he made this meeting such a secretive event. I couldn't wait to see him.

He was already waiting for me by the "Metzeive"; his thin body in a beige trench coat etched itself against the black "Metzeive" with its white Hebrew and Latin lettering and the large number 6,000,000 clearly visible from here.

Noticing my approach he walked over towards me briskly, took me under the arm and literally propelled me down the road. "Let's walk to Muenchenberg, there is a little Bierstube there where we can sit down and talk. It's too cold to walk and talk outdoors," he said. I didn't say anything but walked alone with him.

After we arrived to the Bierstube, sat down and ordered our favorite "Dunkel Bier," he looked straight into my eyes and said in urgent voice. "I know how set you are on the medical school and I wouldn't ask you this favor if it wouldn't be very important. It also, however, should not interfere with your school. Today is December the 23rd, a day before Christmas; I know that you are not due back to school from the winter vacations until the second half of January. We have an Aliyah composed of people from the D.P. camps in Muenchenberg, Zeilsheim and near Marburg. We desperately need young men like you to help us lead them out of Germany to Naples, Italy. There another cell will take over, house them and hopefully help them to get on a ship that will become available in late January, then on to Eretz Israel.

Once the people are delivered to Naples, the *Shomers* (care takers) who traveled with them will be able to return to Germany, if they so desire. If you would be willing to help us, you would leave on January 2nd and be back by the 10th or 12th. You would do a great 'Mitzvah' (a good deed) and you would truly help us in a pinch.

Our people usually go all the way to Eretz Israel with the people they escort. Thus, they board with them the ships destined for Eretz Israel and frequently are able to return for another transport. Unfortunately the British are lately fairly successful in their blockade of Palestine. Many ships have to return, other are still wondering around the Mediterranean Sea and still others have been boarded by the British Navy and detained on the Island of Cypress.

We have lost a lot of young 'Kibbutznicks' who were doing this job and we must recruit some replacements to keep the Aliyah going. We need you. You have almost a week to think about it. I hope that your answer will be a positive one."

He indicated that he was finished and was ready to get up when I said, "Wait; there is a lot that you have to tell me before I could think about these issues. You know that I was never involved with Zionism or Aliyahs. Are you willing to answer a 'million' questions?"

He laughed, "Sure, shoot, I can stay here the entire day and talk to you but your parents will wonder and worry if you don't get back soon. How about me coming over tomorrow, early afternoon to pick you up for a little fun trip to Muenchenberg? We could arrange this little excursion to last few hours and during the time we can talk about all the issues, and your parents will not wonder where you are. Actually, you can ask Ania to come because if you decide to go, she has to be with us on this plan otherwise she will get very suspicious and will worry unnecessarily."

After the meeting with Shmull I ran over to Ania's apartment. Before I could say even a word to her, there was food on the table and her mother sat me down in front of all kinds of delicacies. Obviously, I couldn't resist. I knew, however, that this would interfere with my regular supper at home and suggested that possibly I should have dinner with them tonight, after getting clearance from my parents. I was ready to say anything to get Ania out of the house and be able to talk to her privately. She instantly read my mind and volunteered to go with me to convince my parents to let me have the dinner tonight in her house.

All that sounded reasonable to her parents and they let us go. Actually, we didn't have any privacy in my house either, thus the freezing outdoors was the only place we could talk. I tried to briefly summarize Shmull's proposal but Ania had too many questions to which I had no answers. We simply agreed to tell our parents that tomorrow afternoon we would be taking a little "adventure" trip with Shmull to Kassel and would be home for supper.

The three of us went to the same Bierstube I visited with Shmull the day before. He briefly summarized for Ania our conversation. However, before he was able to get going, I interrupted, "Shmull," I said, "we have been friends for some time. Please forgive me the rudeness of interrupting you but I know very little about the Aliyah and Ania knows probably even less. I remember, as a little ten-year-old boy, being dragged to Zionist meetings by my older friends. At the meetings there was a great deal of sound and fury about Zionism, Palestine, Kibbutzim, settlers, sand, sacrifice, Holy Land and many other slogans, words and ideas.

To be honest, most, if not all of it, went right over my head. Then the war came, we had other issues, problems and concepts to face and deal with. To start with it was the communism and the devastating Gulag; later, after having returned to Poland we had to face the totally mind blowing issue of the Jewish situation vis-à-vis Fascism, Nazism and, in Poland, blatant and naked anti-Semitism. At the same time we were facing the bewildered Nazi concentration camp survivors, our friends and relatives left after the meat grinder had finished with them. We had to accept the meaningless loss of most of our family members and accept the idea that 'life must go on.' True, a technique that gave us the chance to cope with this totally unbelievable and unacceptable reality. I am not certain that emotionally we are ready to deal with a fight in the deserts of Palestine or even the simple experience of Aliyah. This is why I would like you to give us a brief summary of the entire concept and history of Aliyah. Do you think you would be willing to do it?"

Shmull looked sadly at us and said, "I am more than ready to provide you with whatever meager information I have, particularly since I think that it will definitely help your thinking about this matter. Firstly, '*Aliyah*' is a complex concept with several meanings and implications. It is a Hebrew word that literally means '*ascent*' or '*going up.*' It actually implies the movement of Jews, as individuals or as a part of organized groups, from the *Diaspora* (dispersion in exile throughout the world), to their homeland, the Land of Israel, Eretz Israel

Those who '*go up'* or immigrate to the Land of Israel are called in the Bible '*Olim.*'" He stopped and looked tentatively at us with an inquiry in his eyes. "I really hate to bore you," he whispered, as if looking for encouragement. "Whenever you will feel that you had enough just interrupt me and we will change the topic."

I took a look at Ania, touched her hand and said to Shmull, "No, don't feel like this, we want you to go on. I am sure that Ania agrees with me that it is important for us to hear you out. Although we are familiar with some of these facts and have been exposed to many of these ideas, I don't think that we gave this topic a great deal of thought, thus, your interpretation of this issue is of great interest to us."

Shmull, visibly relieved continued with his exposition. "Well, I will not dwell on details of Aliyah's (the Hebrew plural of Aliyah is Aliyot) but will give you the two '*bookends*' that hold all the Aliyah's in between. You will be probably surprised, or reminded, that the first Aliyah was the return (the '*ascent*' as mentioned in the Books of Genesis and Numbers in the Torah) of the Israelites from Egypt to the Land of Canaan. The next major Aliyah occurred around five centuries B.C.E. It reflected the return of the Israelites from Babylon to the Land of Israel. These two major Aliyah's could serve as one, or the first, of the '*book ends.*'

Subsequently there was a variety of Aliyah's by individuals, small groups and groups of scholars and rabbis. The Aliyah's were not abandoned even with the destruction of the Second Temple. However, there is little known about the immigration to Israel after the birth of Islam in the fifth century and the subsequent Muslim Conquest of Palestine.

However, with the onset of the Crusades, Aliyah's recurred, particularly from North Africa due to renewed persecutions. It, however, diminished ultimately to a trickle due to fierce fighting between the Christians and Muslims in the Holy Land. With the Turkish conquest and the establishment of the Ottoman Empire, a complex patchwork of Aliyah's to the Holy Land evolved."

Here Shmull looked at us with keen eyes and asked, "Do you have enough?" We were so engrossed in his story that the question startled us and we almost jumped in our seats.

"No," we cried in unison, "you must go on, this really makes us understand the background leading to the current situation so much better" I interjected, "I thought that I clearly understood this part of our history but I was sadly mistaken, please go on, we need to hear the rest. You make it so clear and understandable."

Shmull was obviously again pleased and resumed with great enthusiasm. "The subsequent peaks in the Aliyah's were caused by various persecutory episodes in Europe, Africa and Asia. The more dramatic ones were the Spanish, later Portuguese persecutions related to the Inquisition. There were waves of '*Rabbinical,*' intellectual Aliyah's, followed by the highly organized '*Hassidic*' Aliyah's. The Hassidim, an orthodox Jewish sect, who made the Aliyah a fundamental part of their religious teaching and fundamental beliefs, established numerous schools of religious learning and a community in the Land of Israel.

At about the same time there were numerous individual and small Aliyah's from various countries in Europe and the Orient, North Africa, Iraq, Turkey, Middle East, Central Asia as well as Afghanistan and Southern Arabian Peninsula, Yemen.

The late nineteenth century witnessed a major resurgence of the '*Return*' to *Eretz Yisrael* activities. This time they were much more organized and under the guidance of the new Jewish nationalistic movement, "*Zionism*."

The First Aliyah at the end of the nineteenth century was inspired by the not very successful pre-Zionist Hibbat Zion and Bilu movements. It was followed by the 2nd, 3rd, 4th and 5th Aliyah's. Each wave of emigrations was the result of some calamity frequently associated with *pogroms* (massacres) in Russia.

The 5th Aliyah formally extending from 1929 to 1939 was stimulated to a great extent by the development of the Nazi state in Germany. This Aliyah resulted in immigration of close to a quarter million Jews. It exceeded greatly the British immigration quotas for this period of time, thus it was only partly legal; a large number indeed came to the Holy Land (British Mandate) illegally.

The immigration after the onset of the Second World War, the Aliyah Bet, was primarily illegal since the British had whittled down the quota to miniscule numbers. We still labor under this mini quota despite numerous appeals to expunge it. It looks that the Mufti of Jerusalem has greater influence on the British than the American Jews or the world's opinion. As an afterthought, I would like to add a comment to my summary of the Aliyah story. I wish to underline and emphasize the fact that the presence of Israelites in the Land of Israel, albeit in markedly fluctuating numbers, the fluctuations reflecting primarily the severity of foreign oppression episodes, deportation policies and the degree of enslavement, was almost continuous for close to 4,000 years. It lasted with minor and very short-lived interruptions from the days of Joshua bringing the Israelites back to the land of Canaan until now. This is the longest known continuous presence of the same 'People' on a 'Land' in the recorded history of mankind. Furthermore, I like to emphasize that after the conquest of Canaan about 1300 B.C., the Israelites experienced independence and autonomy usually under monarchal rule interspersed by episodes of foreign domination for a period of about 1,300 years, until the conquest by the Roman empire and destruction of the Second Temple in the first century of C.E. This is probably one among the longest lasting national, political, cultural and religious entities in the history of mankind.

After he stopped, we sat for a little while in silence. He looked at us, smiled and said, "This, I think, should be enough for today. Let's talk tomorrow some more about the Aliyah Bet in general. I would also like tell you about the Aliyah that I am to participate in shortly. This is the one I may wish to ask you to help us with." I got up shook hands with him and asked "how about a lunch tomorrow at our house, afterwards we may go for a walk?" His head shook in agreement and we left.

Ania was to join our family for supper that night and later we were supposed to visit with Mietek and his wife Ania. Although they were several years older, they were our closest friends and we always looked forward to spend time with them.

Our apartments were close to each other. However, I went to pick up Ania since by 7 PM it was already pitch black outside. As we walked to our house Ania was silent. She was obviously under the influence of Shmull's story. I interrupted her silence with a question: "would you participate in an Aliyah?" She didn't respond immediately and when she started responding "Why do you ask......?" the response has tailed off into a nervous laughter. "Sorry," I said, "let's talk about it later."

Mother had totally outdone herself. I couldn't remember a dinner like that since the times before the war. We had sweet fish and fantastic chicken soup with tiny pasta squares, sweet lima beans, a few slices of carrots and onions boiled in the soup; we had chopped liver, by itself a rare treat since actually it was not just chopped liver, but it was finely chopped goose liver (the French would call it, "Pate Foie Gras"); and after all of these delicacies we had the most delicious roasted goose. The latter was absolutely my most favorite dish.

Mother certainly had shown how much she loved us in a truly grand way by following the proverb: "Liebe gehts durch den Magen" (love goes through the stomach). Following this exclusive and sumptuous dinner, Mother made the most monumental sacrifice, she brewed real coffee. The coffee we drank after dinner could have bought us a suit, a microscope, two pairs of shoes, etc. To her, however, this was worth it. It completed the dinner properly; she delighted in making us feel good.

Afterwards the conversation turned towards the only topic worthy of discussion: emigration. This issue had been consuming everyone; it also was beginning to wear us out because, we "didn't see the light at the end of the tunnel."

Uncle Juzek was the only one with a promising future. Zosia, his sister from Australia, wrote that the visa application was apparently "progressing" through the bureaucracy of the immigration offices at a reasonable speed and she expected to see the visa being granted in the reasonable future, whatever "reasonable" meant.

The discussion then drifted to our visa application. There apparently was an office in the camp that was in contact with the various consulates, including the American Consulate. Father said that the office was able to trace our application that included parents, Stella and me and it apparently was "on its way." However, nothing specific could be gleaned from the trace.

Despite the wonderful meal, the mood was somewhat gloomy. I didn't have much to say about school, the emigration issue was "dead in the water" and in the camp itself, nothing of consequence had transpired. Basically there was boredom and lack of spirit.

I thought it to be prudent not to bring up at this time our conversation with Shmull. Finally I turned to Ania and asked her if she would like to visit Mietek and Ania. We got up thanked Mother again for the incredible meal and left.

Our friends were delighted to see us. We had a lot to talk about. I made the decision not to mention in their company our conversation with Shmull. Instead I engaged with them in my favorite sport; teasing about their lack of interest to join us at the Frankfurt University. They, however, were convinced that by worrying about the emigration issue and constantly badgering the people at the American Consulate they would be able to just pick up and go to America in the very near future! Well, it wasn't to be as simple as that.

As we argued and jousted in good faith, another friend of ours, Bolek, came to join us. "I heard that you just arrived from Frankfurt for a several weeks visit here. I stopped by your house, Emil, and was told by your uncle Juzek, with a 'knowing' grin in his face, that I will find 'the inseparable couple' at Mietek's house, so here, I am," he said patting me on my back.

Pleased to see him I shook hands and responded, "You are so right; I have to drag Ania with me wherever I go to protect her from all the sharks swimming in the calm waters." Everyone began laughing. Mietek, who knew that Bolek was trying to get himself into good graces with Ania, or to put it plainly, was chasing after her, stuck another needle into him. "Since you are this interested in Ania why you don't enroll at the University in Frankfurt, this will give you a better chance to see her more often."

He didn't respond immediately to Mietek's caustic comment, but after taking a long look at Ania he said, "Well Mietek, you may be right, I probably should do just that." Bolek was a very bright fellow, a bit older than Ania and I, but at that moment was totally disinterested in returning to school.

While Mietek was involved in some low intensity business deals, primarily at a local level, Bolek was flying high. He, like many others in the D.P. camps, was involved in dealing in food and clothing, primarily with other inmates of the various camps. This provided sufficient extra money to supplement the meager rations and allowed for some purchases of clothing for travel expenses.

I think that this business activity provided an outlet for the pent up energies that, because of the temporary living arrangements and totally unknown future, could not be directed into a more productive long range plans.

Everyone laughed and the conversation turned to the issue of emigration. I wasn't totally convinced that I should leave this remark unheeded. I just hoped that he would not follow up on his comment and complicate my life. I was quite satisfied with the situation with Ania and didn't look forward towards any complications.

The next day we had a great lunch at our house. Mother always enjoyed Shmull, "Such a nice boy," she would always say, "I love to listen to him talk; he is such a really good Jewish boy, so dedicated." I don't think that she would be this positive towards Shmull had she known of his efforts to convert me to Zionism and convince me to join an Aliyah.

I, however, also liked him and liked him indeed, in addition to all of the other positive characteristics, for his devotion to Zionism. The issue of Zionism, specifically the issue of emigration to Israel rather than to America had been a thorny, seldom discussed issue, within a large segment, possibly the majority of Jewish population that survived the Holocaust in Europe. There were two distinct major issues. One, dealing with the emigration to Israel, was usually discussed, at least to some extent, in response to the aggressive recruitment efforts by the young Zionists. The other one dealt with the issue of the concentration camps and general survival during the war. The latter was almost never addressed. Rarely did we ask each other about survival in a camp, which camp, or survival in hiding.

Occasionally a mention was made that some of us survived the war in Soviet Russia. I felt as if most of the people were too embarrassed to admit to anyone, particular to themselves, that they indeed survived these experiences. Guilt was probably the prevailing emotion related to the reluctance to discuss this issue to the situation but I don't think that we were ready to accept the presence of guilt either.

After lunch the three of us took off for a walk. The weather was perfect. The sun was shining; the temperature hovered around the freezing point. We were bundled up in coats and preceded on the road towards Kassel talking animatedly about the lunch. Soon the discussion turned towards the Aliyah issue. I made it clear to Shmull that both Ania's and my parents made a definite decision to do all they can to get a visa to the United States and we were planning to go with them. Shmull was visibly disappointed; however, he reassured us that he understood our position.

"Anyway," he said, "at this moment the transition camps in Naples and in the port cities in Italy are overcrowded with emigrants trying to make an Aliyah. The British apparently have redoubled the blockade efforts. In addition it is very difficult to procure ships and, in the recent months, most of the ships on the way to Eretz Israel were intercepted by the British; some were actually fired upon.

There is, however, a small group of students from Marburg and Heidelberg who will be moving on to Trieste, rather than Naples in the first week of January," he said, and he wondered if I could help him to round up the group and deliver them to Vienna, where they would probably be picked up by another group of workers and taken across the border to Trieste.

I indicated that I would be willing to do it but first would have to make arrangements to take the time off. Also, I didn't think that it would be wise to make this known to our parents or friends. "I understand that your vacation extends until the middle of January, you should be back from the trip by the end of the first week in January," he interjected. "OK," I said, "I should be able to clear my schedule within three days and will be in touch with you."

Our discussion turned towards local issues dealing with the food rations at the camp and the overcrowded trains. For the next couple of days I had extensive talks with Ania. The trip with Shmull was the central topic, however, the discussion spilled over to more personal issues. I shared with her my deepest thoughts dealing with our future. I think that it was the first time I elaborated on my long-range plans and her role in them. What it boiled down to was my asking her to come with me to America and later marry me.

I thought that we were too young at this time to make real commitments, but a tacit agreement was easily reached. We were dizzy just talking about it. I made a solemn promise to do everything humanly possible to bring her to America, apparently I was so sure that I would be able to emigrate that it didn't even occur to me to question this possibility. My only concern was that she might have troubles getting the visa. I really didn't think of the lack of logic in these conclusions. I must have simply enjoyed playing the protective male who would rescue his 'Princess' from any calamity.

Also, I explained to her that I don't want "just a wife." I saw in her a life companion in the quest of making medicine "better." Obviously for this purpose she must also complete her medical studies and again I made extravagant promises, how I would make sure that she would not only complete her studies successfully but also how I would assist her in achieving greatness in the medical field.

Maria Curie-Sklodowska, the great Polish scientist who moved to France where she discovered two new elements, Radium and Polonium, was Ania's role model. She would tell me how much she wanted to be a woman scientist, to make great discoveries for the benefit of mankind.

We were very young and very idealistic. Neither Stalin nor Hitler was able to suppress the fire burning in us, a fire to do things that may contribute to the well being of mankind. Obviously at that age, everything was painted on a huge canvas and through idealistic eyes. My idealism, however, did not encompass desires to struggle for political issues or deep philosophical concepts. We were more interested in simple scientific logic rather than in philosophical truths.

It was with these ideas in mind that we charted our ideal future and I took the liberty of taking the lead and promising Ania the ways and the means to achieve these goals. It was with the underpinning of these thoughts that we also discussed my involvement with Shmull and the Aliyah.

I felt that, although politics and political issues were not of interest to us, helping our friends and our people was. On that basis "we,"—yes, at this point we felt sufficiently committed to each other that it became a "we" issue—agreed that I should participate in the job with Shmull. It was decided to tell our parents that Ania and I, decided to return to Frankfurt immediately after the New Year in order to get some issues straighten out at the University. This would give me the opportunity to go with Shmull and no one would be aware of it.

After some discussions with Shmull, it was agreed that I would join him in Marburg on January 3rd in a house of one of the *Brihah* members. He gave me an address where to meet and the issue was closed. I felt very happy with this decision.

Brihah (Hebrew word for flight or escape) was a loosely woven organization composed of young Zionists from all over Europe. Originally they were not even a part of the Eretz Israel Zionist organization. *Brihah* had helped us immensely during our escape from Poland. They assisted with smuggling us across the borders from Poland all the way through Czechoslovakia, Austria and into Germany. They had friends at the 'way stations' throughout the path of the escape.

Now that I was able to, I was very happy to participate in their activities and at least in this minuscule fashion, repay them, at least partially, for their major effort in the past on our behalf.

Since the railroad route from Kassel to Frankfurt went through Marburg we bought ticket to Marburg with the idea that Ania would stop with me and when I would be ready to leave Marburg with the *Brihah* boys for our next destination, Ania would take the train to Frankfurt and wait there for my return in about a week's time, hopefully.

We found the address with no difficulty, but were absolutely amazed looking at the house. We expected either a group of crowded two story blocks like the ones in Muenchenberg or a run down tenement, like the ones in Vienna. Instead the address was an imposing two-story single house built out of stone located in a beautiful garden with trees and shrubs.

Nothing was damaged by the war or by the postwar economic want. There was even a functional electric bell that summoned, almost instantly, surprise, surprise, Shmull! We were not only pleasantly surprised but also relieved to see his friendly smiling face. He led us in and introduced us to Anciek and Fred, the other two members of *Brihah* group. I explained why Ania was with me and told them that there was a train to Frankfurt in two hours and that she planned to take it. Afterward I would be free to start the job with them.

Anciek suggested that we start walking slowly to the station. "There is a good restaurant there," he said. "We could have a meal, talk and put Ania in the train to Frankfurt." We all agree and took off.

I could see Anciek glancing at Ania from the corner of his eyes. He obviously was quite interested. I was getting jealous but tried to look at it from a practical point of view. He simply didn't have a chance in my opinion. Furthermore, Ania was leaving in couple of hours and the chances of him meeting with her in the near future were very slim. I tried to talk sense into myself, but only with little success. We spent the next two hours talking primarily about the current job we were to perform, about our backgrounds and our appreciation of the current political situation that was facing all of us. Neither Fred nor Anciek were particularly interested or curious specifically about our studies and our ultimate future. Except for Anciek's furtive glances at Ania, the talk was a straightforward discussion of logistics.

We were to play primarily a role of "baby sitters" for a frightened group of Polish Jews hoping to get to Eretz Israel by the sea via Trieste. Although, originally they were from Poland, they spent most of the war years in the Soviet Union, either on a *kolkhozes* (cooperative farms), *Sofhoses* (government farms), working in war factories, being a part of the *Trudovaya Armia* (Work Army) or being imprisoned in a Gulag (concentration or labor camps).

The *Brihah* boys, Anciek and Fried, were both from small Polish towns that apparently had rather strong Zionist organizations before the war. Since they were about three years older, they were teenagers before the war started, thus they were capable of thinking and acting more aggressively and acquiring skills related to Zionist activities with greater facility than nine to twelve years old boys. Anciek survived the war in hiding while Fred spent most of the war in Russia. They both spoke Hebrew, a result of prewar training in the Zionist camps in Poland.

As we were swapping stories, finishing our meal and enjoying our dark beer, time came to say goodbye to Ania since we could hear the train approaching. The railroad station was large but once the train pulled into it, the station filled with smoke that made my eyes tear. Was it the smoke? I wanted to think so! After a quick hug, I helped Ania up the high step on the train car and carried her valise inside. There wasn't much time, I wanted to give her a kiss but I was embarrassed and started turning away when she took me in her arms, kissed my lips and whispered "take good care of yourself, I love you."

Upon return to the apartment, I was apprised of the details. We were picking up a young couple and two young men in a camp near Marburg and driving with them south in a rented truck with a canvas cover over its back, similar to the one my family and I traveled in from Austria to Germany. In Regensburg we were to pick up three young couples and drive across the border to Salzburg, Austria, where we were supposed to pick up two more couples.

The border crossing from Germany to Austria was of no consequence. The *Brihah* boys had the necessary papers made out in all of the names in our group. In Salzburg, we were to be provided with a rented tourist bus on which we were to cross the Italian border as tourists who were to spend a week in Trieste. It all sounded simple.

The story suggested to me that the *Brihah* has done a careful and competent job and if the papers were reasonably good, I was quite confident that the scheme would work. Anciek spoke Italian quite well; he spent over a year around various ports in Italy working with the Aliyah's and learning Italian. He, however, was the only one speaking the language. We better not lose him, I thought to myself, particularly when he interjected with laughter, "The Italians on the route we are taking do not speak much German, definitely not Polish or Russian. In Trieste, I do not know anyone that speaks much German either." This piece of information didn't make me very happy. However, I understood that literally thousands of our people went this way and I was sure that we would also make it.

We thought that we would pick up the group from Marburg very early tomorrow morning. By the afternoon, we would arrive in Regensburg. The following day we'd pick up the group in Regensburg and drive to Salzburg.

On the third day, we would drive from Salzburg to Trieste. "Your job," Anciek added turning to me, "will be to make them comfortable and allay their fears. Tell them that you are a student at the University in Frankfurt that will make them more at ease and will relax them."

Once the plan was discussed in detail, the conversation turned to the experiences of the *Brihah* boys. They certainly had many stories to tell and it wasn't until midnight that we went to sleep. On the following morning we got up very early while it was still dark. The truck was parked on the grounds. As we drove into town, I realized that the house we stayed in was located in the medieval old town of Marburg. Under other circumstances I would have liked to spend more time there exploring the narrow streets and the ancient buildings. However, today this was not the case to be. The dawn was breaking; the sky was turning gray with a hint of pink in the east.

Fred, who appeared to be the intellectual in the group, called my attention to the right. There I could see, looming on a hill over the ancient town a huge structure, the Landgraves Schloss. Fred followed my gaze and with irony in his voice said, "this is the most famous place in Marburg. In the castle Martin Luther conducted his famous debates that resulted in the Reformation movement and ultimately resulted in Martin Luther becoming a rabid anti-Semite. I wonder," he continued, "What relation did this have to the ease of Hitler's rise to power that was significantly based on the philosophy of anti-Semitism."

I was not sufficiently knowledgeable in this topic or sufficiently erudite to enter with him into any kind of discussion. I was much more familiar with the theories of Marx, Engels and Lenin dealing with Socialism and Communism and with the murderous reality of its applications as administered by Stalin.

Shortly we arrived in the D.P. camp. The young couple was already waiting for us. They looked concerned and gazed at us with some suspicion. The man looked to be in his mid-twenties and his wife was obviously a teenager. I decided to take the lead and addressed them, "it's good to see you, we should have a nice day for the trip," I said as I extended my hand. The man took my hand eagerly and asked looking at his wife, "Do you think we will be safe? We are very tired to be constantly in this 'survival mode,' my wife is the only survivor in her family, and we would like to see some respite in our new country, Eretz Israel. Do you think that we will get there alive and once there stay alive? After six years of looking into the death's eye we would like some relief."

I wasn't prepared for this outburst; I was even less prepared to be the one addressed on this issue. My experience in responding to these types of questions was essentially nonexistent. Both Fred and Anciek heard our exchange, but it was Fred who intervened. In a sincere tone of voice, he responded to the man. "You can feel perfectly safe; the *Brihah* arranged every detail of this trip. We certainly will get to Trieste in three days without any mishaps, God willing. The sail, however, is a different issue. The British are getting more and more aggressive. There is a chance that we will be intercepted and forced back, or, as I lately hear be diverted to the island of Cypress where we may be temporarily interned.

No one can predict what will happen at sea. There we have no control whatsoever. The young girl took the man by hand and looking into his eyes said softly, "Don't worry Aaron, we will get there, I can feel it."

I was speechless, and had not a clue what to say or what to do. At that moment, two boys came running with satchels in their hands. "Sorry, we are late," one of them said, throwing his belongings into the truck. "You know how parents are, we didn't want them to come to the truck with us, they were crying. But now that we are here we are ready to go."

Fred was driving. I asked Anciek to join the people in the back of the truck while I moved with Fred for a while. I wasn't ready, at this time, to face the young man who was so distraught, probably having second thoughts about emigration to Eretz Israel. Placing myself into his shoes and Ania in the place of his young wife, I could clearly understand his turmoil and his concerns, particularly in light of his recent marriage to a young girl. I didn't think that I would have the guts or the bravery to do what he was doing.

Thoughts kept on assaulting my mind. Thoughts that were there before, thoughts that thought that they could actually live there; possibly forever? It was difficult to accept that only one and one half years after the cessation of a specific wholesale slaughter of Jews by the Germans and their accomplices, and the inhumanity committed towards them by Stalin, the situation in Europe in general, and in the D.P. camps in particular, was essentially intolerable. I kept on thinking again about the rigid enforcement by the British of their annual immigration quotas to Eretz Israel (about 18,000 souls). It should be noted that at the same time there also was a strict limit of similar magnitude on the quota for the immigration of Jews to the U.S. The U.S. quota did not change until after the state of Israel was proclaimed in May of 1948 and after it had opened its gates to all the Jews in the world. The relaxation of the quota limits to USA occurred only after strong intervention by President Truman. It should be also noted that while the minuscule immigration quotas to the U.S. were strictly enforced against the Jewish D.P.s, a large number of the non-Jewish D.P.s were arriving legally to the U.S. at the same time, ultimately encompassing hundreds of thousands. Who were the non-Jewish D.P.s? Well, in order to answer this question one needed to examine the more general question who were D.P.s?

After cessation of WWII, the Allied Forces occupying Germany and Austria soon learned that the majority of inmates of concentration or forced labor camps were originally from countries other than Germany or Austria. While some were Jewish, others originating from various Western and Eastern European countries were not.

Actually the Jewish population liberated from the camps was very small since the great majority was killed or died from disease and starvation before liberation or shortly after. All of those who survived, Jews and non-Jews, were classified as "Displaced Persons" (D.P.'s) and were placed into D.P. camps. The camp population, however, in addition to those who survived the concentration camps, consisted also of a huge number of Eastern Europeans who were not concentration camp inmates; they arrived to Germany or Austria after the onset of the war either in result of forced deportation to Germany, or to perform various types of labor or who moved voluntarily to Germany to function in the various areas of the German society. In addition, a very large segment of the D.P. population consisted of the

German collaborators from the various eastern lands that arrived to Germany with the retreating German Army.

This entire group of people had also fallen under the administrative rule of the Allied Occupation Forces and was designated as "Displaced Persons."

In 1945 there was approximately seven million peoples classified as D.P.s. The Allies considered the D.P. camps as a very temporary issue and hoped that the Army would be able to provide the necessary interim housing and food assistance until such time when repatriation of the D.P.s to their home lands could take place and automatically resolve the D.P. problem.

Indeed by the end of 1945 a majority had returned to their homelands in Western and Eastern Europe. As mentioned above, only about 1,000,000 still remained in the camps. Of this number, only about 50,000 were Jews. Attempts by the Army to induce repatriation of the Jews o their homelands were met with universal resistance. Since most of them were from Eastern Europe, they refused to return to lands where most of their families were massacred and were anti-Semitism was still rampant.

Unfortunately, various groups were originally housed together in the D.P. camps. This resulted in problems. The major problem being the vicious anti-Semitism directed against the few remaining Jews. Although somewhat less pronounced, there was also friction developing among the various non-Jewish ethnic groups. The Allied military administrators did not recognize in time the developing problems.

These not so friendly ethnic groups, with varying political and national elements, that included former native (Ukrainian, Byelorussian, Lithuanian and other) Nazis, as well as Nazi collaborators, were kept together in he various D.P. camps. In addition, some who ended up in D.P. camps were plain criminal element released from the concentration camps under political disguise.

The situation in the D.P. camps deteriorated rapidly, particularly since the camps housed an overwhelming majority of non-Jews from Eastern Europe who were not adverse to the practice anti-Semitism, making the life of the Jewish survivors difficult again.

The Jewish survivors organized rapidly. They called themselves "*She'erit ha Pletah*," a Hebrew term of biblical origin meaning "surviving remnant." With the help of American Army Jewish Chaplains, particularly Chaplain Abraham Klausner, the *She'erit ha Pletah* name gained wide acceptance. Since there were no army-recognized administrative bodies to represent the Jewish survivors, the *She'erit ha Pletah* represented by the U.S. Army Jewish Chaplains, tried to take some of these responsibilities.

Unfortunately, the interactions between the Jewish D.P.s and the army had deteriorated to a point that reverberations dealing with this problem reached Washington, D.C. Because of intensive publicity surrounding this issue, President Harry S. Truman appointed in August of 1945 the dean of the University of Pennsylvania Law School and the American envoy to the Inter-Governmental Committee on Refugees, Dr. Earl G. Harrison, to survey and investigate the conditions in the D.P. camps. His report was devastating. The Harrison report stated: "As matters now stand, we appear to be treating the Jews as the Nazis treated them except that we do not exterminate them. They are in concentration camps in large numbers under our military guard instead of S.S. troops." Harrison felt that the American military administration was responsible for this unbelievable state of affairs and expressed a strong opinion that the only solution to the problem is massive emigration of Jewish D.P.s to Palestine. He urged the British to issue 100,000 entry "certificates" not waiting for "solution of the "Palestine problem." The British did not heed this latter recommendation.

The report, however, created pandemonium in the United States and under the leadership of President Truman and General Dwight Eisenhower major changes in the policies dealing with Jewish D.P.s in the "American Zone" of occupation were instituted. Incidentally, no positive changes were made at that time in the "British Zone" where similar problems existed.

As a result of the policy changes, the Jewish D.P.s were recognized as a distinct ethnic group with specific needs. Also, they were given the privilege of living in separate camps, given broad autonomy and considerable latitude in self-governance. Their living conditions were improved and their desires to emigrate were recognized.

It is ironic to note, however, that recent studies of papers deposited in President Truman's presidential library have uncovered a presidential diary with entries made in 1947 that read: "The Jews, I find, are very selfish," also "...that Jews often expect special treatment and do not care how many other ethnic groups get murdered or mistreated (published in *Newsweek*, July 21, 2003, p.19).

After the Jewish survivors were separated from the others and began administering the camps by internally elected committees, they developed budgets with the help of UNRRA that soon was joined by a number of organizations that prominently included the JOINT (American JOINT DISTRIBUTION COMMITTEE). In February of 1946, the First Congress of *She'erit ha Pletah* elected The Central Committee of Liberated Jews in the American Zone with Zalman Greenberg and Samuel Grigauz as its official representatives.

In late 1944, after the Soviets liberated eastern Poland from under German occupation, a young Polish Zionist, partisan and poet, Abba Kovner, organized a group of Zionists that helped, after the end of the war, to smuggle Jews across the Polish border to Czechoslovakia and further west. Originally, they had no contact with the Zionists already in Palestine. However by the end of 1945 and early 1946 the group was augmented by officers of the "Jewish Brigade." The Jewish Brigade was a formal military unit composed of 5,000 Palestinian Zionists and recognized by the British as a distinct national unit within the British military forces.

The unit served on the Italian front under the command of a Canadian Jew, Brigadier Ernest Benjamin. After the war they became very much involved in the *Brihah* (Hebrew term for flight or escape), the illegal movement of Jews from Eastern Europe across numerous and different national borders to the D.P. camps and Palestine. They were joined in their efforts by members of Haganah, an Israeli military group, and were supported financially by various Jewish organizations, particularly the Joint and the Jewish Agency. This information I gained subsequently, while in Vienna. It explained the "magic" of our progress in 1946 across the various borders towards our goal, a D.P. camp.

Most of the one million D.P.s still in the camps by late 1946 refused to return to their homeland, many were afraid of repercussions from their native governments because of their collaboration with Nazis during the war. Matter of fact the Soviets strongly demanded that the Western Allies repatriate, if necessary by force, Russians and other Slavs found after the war in German or Austrian D.P. camps. This was done by the Soviets with the idea to look for collaborators among the returnees. It probably should be reiterated at this point that among the D.P.s there were indeed most of the German collaborators who retreated from their native land with the German army under the pressure of Soviet armed forces. One of the best known example of this element was the 30,000 to 40,000 strong army unit of the Ukrainian Kazak's who fought with the German Army and then retreated with the German Army to Germany. A similar group, composed of members of the O.U.N. (Organization of Ukrainian Nationalists), Ukrainians fighting for independence of Ukraine from Soviet Union and who during the war allied themselves with the German SS forces in mass murders of Poles and Jews in Ukraine, have also retreated with the Germans to Germany, ultimately ended up in D.P. camps and tried to immigrate to the States or Canada. They obviously refused repatriation to they homeland fearing legal action by the Soviet Government or as they claimed "political persecution."

In the case of the Kazak army, however, the Soviet Government forced the Allies to return this group to Russia, if necessary, by force to face punitive actions back home. It is ironic, but many of the D.P.s who were Nazi collaborators and were directly involved in murders of innocent civilians, particularly Jews, were able to emigrate ultimately to the U.S. or Canada as well as to other western countries.

Between 1946 and 1948 a large number of Jews from Eastern Europe, frequently with the help of *Brihah*, smuggled their way across the borders to the D.P. camps in Germany. Many, upon return after the war to their hometowns, found total desolation and usually the reality that most of their families were murdered by the Nazis or their collaborators. They also found a hostile atmosphere among their former local friends and neighbors. This is why most opted to escape to the West. By 1948, their numbers in D.P. camps swelled to about 200,000.

After waking up suddenly I realized that I was dreaming again about the D.P. situation, a situation that pervaded my waking and apparently my sleeping hours. Once I realized that I was fully awake I looked out the window and could see a river. Fred, noticing that I was awake commented, "This is the bridge over the Fulda River; once we pass Fulda we will be on our way, by the Fogelsberg Mountains route, to Bamberg. We should be there in less than two hours," he then added, "go back to sleep."

When I woke up the next time we were parked in front of a *Gasthof* (Inn), close to a river. Fred suggested that we have something to eat. Everyone piled out of the truck and we entered the Inn.

As we sat down for a meal Anciek said, "We are in Nuremberg, are you aware that the Allies have set up a tribunal in this town to try the German war officials for the war crimes they have committed? The trial has just begun." Except for Fred and Shmull, the rest of us looked at him with astonishment on our faces. I did not read German newspapers very often and I wasn't aware that anything like that was going on.

Shmull shook his head up and down and said, "Oh yes, this is a huge activity. Many important Nazi officials are held in jail and now will be tried here at the Nuremberg tribunal. There is a lot being said all around the world about this trial. A number of top generals, Nazi ministers and other officials were caught during and after the war, and they all will be tried here in Nuremberg in the Justice Palace.

After lunch, on the way to Regensburg, I will drive by it. After all, one of the defendants at the trial will be Hans Frank, the Governor of Poland from 1939 until the end of the war, and as you know during the war we called him 'the butcher.' Also, a number of other important German officials are awaiting this trial, I understand," he continued.

"They also caught Hermann Goering. We all knew that he was the second hand of Hitler. They also caught Rudolph Hess as well as and many others. I think that it is particularly important that Alfred Rosenberg was caught. As you probably know, he was Hitler's chief racial ideologue and theorist. He vowed to colonize the East of Europe and render it 'free of Jews.' He almost succeeded with the help of the rest of Hitler's clique. You realize that this trial is the first of its kind in the history of mankind. Attempts are made to define crimes 'against humanity,' crimes of 'genocide' and other legal issues to be the provenance of international legal bodies."

I listened to his erudite explanations with great interest since I was totally unaware of these issues. After what I considered to be a fiasco in my foray into political theories of communism, I devoted my energies and my thinking into two areas. The first was Ania, yes, probably a romantic overindulgence, and the other was medicine and biology. Matter of fact, I was beginning to develop ideas of going into research in medical sciences. The latter, however, was not crystallized in my mind. I still visualized myself as a doctor later in my life, a healer. Well, there was still plenty of time to wonder and I reminded myself not to forget my third concern, emigration to America!

As we drove through Nuremberg I was mostly impressed by the countless number of beautiful Gothic churches sprinkled all over the city. I thought that one of the most beautiful ones was the "Church of our Lady" on the Market Square. We continued our drive by the Palace of Justice, a huge gray building some four stories high, with a red roof, taking up a whole block.

After crossing the 900-year-old Ramparts surrounding the entire medieval city, we were again on the road, this time towards Regensburg. It was to take us less than two hours.

I moved to the back of the truck to strike up a conversation with the two young boys. They both were twenty years old, thus somewhat older than I, but we hit if off immediately. They both survived in Soviet Union in a fashion similar to my experience, Gulag and then a few years in Tashkent. I mentioned that our train on the way to Alma Ata went through Tashkent. At that time, they probably were not there yet, having arrived in Tashkent in the middle of winter.

I was curious to hear about their decision to go to Palestine. Apparently, their parents couldn't go with them. This Aliyah tried to recruit only very young people. The situation regarding the crossing of the Mediterranean Sea was difficult. The blockade was fierce. Some ships were turned around while other shelled; some were escorted to Cypress. The boys, however, did not sound concerned. They were excited and looking forward to the experience.

They were particularly interested in joining the Haganah and I could identify with them. Haganah was the underground military group organized by the Zionist movement back in 1920. They fought for the establishment of an independent Jewish State in Eretz Israel. I listened with a degree of envy to their excited talk about the new life in Palestine, about the adventures but not a word of fear, depression or uncertainty. They indeed felt that they knew what they were doing and they totally believed in the righteousness of their goals.

In contrast to them, the group of young people with whom I became closely associated was composed of students. They, while supportive of the idea, did not feel compelled to personally participate in the physical fight for the establishment of a State of Israel. However, talking to these two young fellows, experiencing their enthusiasm made me also anxious and ready to rethink my decision. I began to better understand Shmull's insistence that I join him on one of these trips. I think he felt that I deserved a direct contract with people who participated in the Aliyah and in the experience of Aliyah as such.

Approaching Regensburg I could see in the distance what looked like a gorge. Anciek said, "This is Danube, we shall be in town shortly." The city had a large "Old City," a real medieval town. The D.P. camp was located a little distance from there. As we arrived, it was getting dark; the long winter nights were with us.

We stopped in front of a structure that looked like an apartment house. Shmull was obviously familiar with the place and led us inside to a room where we were told to register. Shmull said that we were just in time for dinner, but we would go first to our quarters to leave our baggage there because it should be removed from the truck for safety. The room he led us to housed ten beds. Pointing with his hand he suggested that we select any of the beds, adding that we would need to sleep fast in order get up very early and start on the road before sunrise.

At dinner, we met two young couples who were to join us for the trip to Trieste. We didn't get much of a chance to talk since we had to hurry with the dinner to get to bed as soon as possible. I was in bed with the lights out going over in my mind the day's experiences. The meal was adequate in volume but nothing to crow about. The usual split pea soup prepared from the army surplus powdered split peas, *klops* (ground meat loaf) with a lot of bread and mashed potatoes in it, the latter also made from army surplus of powdered potatoes. We drank the "regulation drink," an artificial orange drink also prepared from an army surplus powdered concoction. Everyone, however, was happy. The meal satisfied our needs at that moment in every respect; it satisfied our hunger and thirst and was free! I was particularly happy with the drink since it tasted like oranges. I had not tasted an orange since 1939 when the war began; also, the drink was very, very sweet. Great!

As I started to think about the discussion I had with the two young men, however, my full stomach and the warmth must have taken precedence because the next thing I could remember was Shmull shaking me violently and screaming, "Up, up, everyone up. We must leave in half an hour. They are preparing breakfast for us in the dining room; see you there in ten minutes."

We all scrambled to get dressed. There was only one bathroom. This was a problem, but in ten minutes, all of us showed up in the dining room. We were fed hot oatmeal, again U.S. Army surplus, but, miracle of miracles! Delicacy of delicacies! It was served with real honey. I had not tasted honey, yes; I have to say again, since 1939. I wondered where they got these wondrous items!

I was so delighted with the reception in this camp and suggested that we write a thank you note to someone, but I didn't know who. Shmull thought it to be a good idea, so he "organized" a nice white sheet of paper and an envelope. My long hand was horrible, thus, I asked for help in rewriting the draft of my note on this nice, white sheet of paper. Shmull accepted the challenge; indeed, he had the most beautiful hand writing style. He also knew where to deliver the note. What a breakfast!

This time Anciek drove and Shmull sat with him in the cab. The rest of us piled up in the back of the truck. It was still very dark as the truck took off. Fred turned towards us and explained. "We will cross the border to Austria near a town named Passau. Fred has the documents for each one of us. It is perfectly legal to cross from Germany to Austria, however, the border patrols may check our documents in an attempt to prevent crossing of German Nazis to Austria, a no, no. Also, some patrols are not very happy to see a group of young Jews crossing the border. The British are trying to influence the Americans to prevent the movement of Jews south to Italy, where they may be able to get on a ship for Palestine. On this account, however, the Americans are not very cooperative with the British and usually there is no problem on the border. Just in case they stop us, let's remember that all of us are going to a big wedding of our friends or cousins in Lintz." We all shook our heads and smiled.

- "We will try to get there," he added, "at the daybreak, just before the change of the guards. This is the time when the guards who are getting of duty will be most tired and sleepy, while their replacement will be busy going over the night reports and will be kibitzing with the shift they are replacing. If the guards will decide to look at us we also should act tired and sleepy, definitely not anxious. We should be there within one or two hours, depending on the road conditions. As you notice we are in the mountains and at times we will have to go quite slow."

I planned to talk to the new arrivals but apparently I fell asleep. When I woke up, dawn was breaking; the truck was standing still and I could hear outside the murmurs of voices. Shmull had crossed his lips meaningfully with his finger and closed his eyes. We followed his request. The voices became somewhat louder and I could hear crunching of the gravel under the shoes moving closer to the back of the truck.

Suddenly it all stopped. I heard a loud OK. Then I heard the doors to the cab open and then shut. Shortly after that, we started moving again. Everyone was visibly relieved. Shmull was laughing, but I could sense that he was also relieved. "We encountered apparently a little problem; however, the boys were able to talk themselves out of it. They are an experienced pair," he commented.

Simultaneously, everyone in the truck started talking loudly; obviously it was a release response to the stress they were under. I felt, however, perfectly calm since I had nothing to lose, under the worse of circumstances they would have turned me back to Germany and I would go back to Frankfurt.

Our prospective *Halutzim* (immigrants to Eretz Israel, the fighters), however, had a great deal at stake. A delay of any kind could have cost them the opportunity to board the ship and could have exposed them to an indefinite period of waiting.

After seeing that everyone was calmed down, Shmull continued "the crossing of the border to Austria is child's play. The border guards aren't interested in our activities, nor do they care. The situation on the Italian border, however, is much more complicated. Firstly, the Italian border guards are guarding their borders against a variety of elements that try to cross illegally into Italy. Fortunately for us, they also are ambivalent in respect to Jews who are using their country, in defiance to the policy of Great Britain, to run an illegal immigration to Palestine.

We will be crossing the Italian border near the town of Villach. The town is a beautiful and popular resort. Although, it is not as popular in winter as it is in the summer, there are always people around, moving back and forth across the border. This makes it easier for us. The *Brihah* has made special arrangements. We will not be crossing through the regular checkpoint instead we will be taking a little country road that crosses the border outside of all the different settlements. Usually there is only one guard at each side of this checkpoint. The Austrian guard will be away having his coffee. The Italian guard knows that we are coming and will pay no attention to our truck as we cross the border and turn back to the main highway. If we are successful we should arrive in Trieste within about four to five hours. Let's hope that there will be no major snow storm on the border. A small storm will be actually desirable. A storm of any kind usually shuts down the activities of the guards on the border to the minimum."

I turned to Shmull and asked, "what if we are stopped?"

"Firstly, we will not be stopped," he spit out, "but, at the outside chance that we will, you do not need to worry. The guards will not do anything bad to us except for turning us back and making sure that the other guards are forewarned to prevent us from repeating the attempt."

I kept on asking these questions to dispel the fears of our charges. His logical and smooth answers went a long way towards this goal. I could see in their faces that my assumptions were correct.

"And now," Shmull continued, "you may as well relax and take a little snooze. We should be near the border in about four hours. The drive near the border should be quite exciting since we will be in the beautiful Carnic Alps."

We continued through the night and as predicted arrived at the border as dawn was breaking. We were in the mountains. It was snowing lightly; the white flakes were twirling in the light shining from a single lamp by a small guardhouse just off the road. A man in a military uniform came over to the cab. Fred handled him a stock of papers pointing to all of us in the back of the truck. The soldier smiled nodded his head and pointed towards the other side of the border. Apparently this was all for the documents inspection.

In a few minutes we stopped at another guardhouse, this was the Italian side. The guard came over to the truck, smiled and shook hands with both Anciek and Fred. We did it! We were in Italy. Shmull laughed, saying, "It usually doesn't work this smoothly. We were very lucky."

Sitting with our charges in the back of the truck I could feel their anxiety rising. Now that the trials and tribulation of crossing the borders were over, the next obstacle, Trieste, was obviously starting to loom large in their imagination inflamed by the stresses of the trip. I wanted to do something to allay their fears. After all this was my job. This ostensibly was the reason why I came along on this trip.

Prior to the journey, knowing that we would be going to Trieste--by itself a trip that was an experiment since this was a new route to take for the *Brihah* and the information available was, at best, only fragmentary--I contacted a Jewish captain in the U.S. occupation forces, an acquaintance I made while in Kassel. An acquaintance that, I hoped, was on the way of becoming a friendship, and asked him if he could get me some information about Trieste and the political situation there. He was very happy to do so. Matter of fact, he told me that was planning to collect the information anyway, for his own interest. He was planning to take a brief vacation there. He wished to experience the Adriatic coast as a tourist and see the ancient treasures of this area. Through military sources, he was able, indeed, to acquire some interesting information. I thought that to relay this information to our people in the truck would make them a bit less apprehensive about Trieste.

"What I will tell you about Trieste I learned from an American Army captain," I started, "Trieste has been a glorious city for centuries, a crossroad of commerce arriving from the Far East, the Byzantine Empire, from the Slavic countries, from the Germanic people and from the Italian inhabitants of the Italian peninsula. The mixed population of this entire province has faithfully reflected the influences of these various parts of Europe and Asia. Since early eighteenth century, Trieste became a free port and a major seaport of Austria, originally a landlocked country.

However, after World War I, Trieste became formally a part of Italy due to Austrian's unfortunate political alignment. After the Second World War, this time due to an unfortunate political alignment of Italy and the aggressive attitudes of Greater Yugoslavia, now a part of the Eastern Communist block, and due to a substantial Slavic minority in Trieste, Tito of Yugoslavia tried to annex Trieste, essentially by force.

The British and American Allies did not support this territorial grab and established two zones of influence. Zone A, encompassing the northern areas and northern Trieste and a Zone B, encompassing the southern areas. The Zone A was essentially under the rule of the American armed forces and it encompassed a great deal of the port facilities." I had my hopes that this explanation explaining the presence of Americans helped to reduce their fears, at least to a point. I continued, "The complete control of port facilities by American forces should make it more likely to get ships that would be willing to transport the emigrants to Palestine, albeit this activity was still formally illegal."

Up to now, the two young couples who joined us in Regensburg kept to themselves during most of the trip. After my little explanation they opened up, but they were obviously very concerned. Shmull's free and friendly attitude and my attempts to explain things apparently made a difference in their responses to the journey.

The two young boys joined the conversation and with infective smiles stimulated a positive atmosphere all around. Even the young couple, usually totally engrossed in each other, joined the conversation and the girl added her silvery laughter to what turned out to be a spontaneously cheerful conversation. Soon the two boys started singing Halutzim songs with the rest of the people joining in the fun.

Finally, Shmull had to quiet us down with a "Shh, we do not want to call any attention to our truck." It was getting dark. Anciek joined us in the back of the truck and explained, "We are approaching Trieste; I will drive to the Teresiano District, close to an old Jewish section of the city. There we will get on the Via Battisti and drive by the beautiful old synagogue on to the transit house. Since we are one of the earliest groups there, there will not be too many people there."

He turned towards me asking, "Do you want to stay in Trieste for a few days? there will be trucks returning north later on. You are welcome to stay."

I shook my head, "your offer is difficult to resist and I would love to stay and explore this fascinating city, unfortunately it will be impossible. I have to return to Frankfurt immediately, otherwise I will miss the commencement of the winter semester and this will be a problem. I understand that someone will take this truck tonight and drive back."

Shmull interjected, "yes, Heniek will drive up north tonight and I am going back with him, you are welcome to join us."

My response was prompt, "absolutely, you know I have to be back in school by the second of January. A lift to Regensburg will be great; from there I will take a train to Frankfurt."

Shmull nodded and added, "it's great, we will travel to Regensburg together. There I will take a train to Kassel and you will go on to Frankfurt."

Anciek remained in Trieste to help with the group of emigrants waiting for the opportunity to leave for Palestine while Fred was to drive the truck back. By ten o'clock we were ready to leave. It was going to be a difficult trip. All three of us squeezed into the cab and took off for Regensburg.

Two days later, dead tired, but alive I was in Frankfurt boarding the tram for Fechenheim. I must have looked like a ghost when Frau Langer opened the door for me. "Herr Steinberger," that how she always addressed me, "come in, come in, you look dreadful, what has been happening? Let me start heating some water so you could wash and let me call Fraulein Ania." I must have looked much worse than I felt.

Before I got my coat off Ania was already here. She threw herself at me as if seeing a dead man coming back to life; her face was wet with tears. She however controlled herself.

We had never shown intimacy in public and kissing would be considered "improper." She dried her tears and literally attacked me with questions. I promised to give her a precise account as soon as I wash and change my clothing.

CHAPTER 18. The Fourth Semester

It was January 1947 as we started the fourth semester. After we registered for the courses, the tempo of activities quickly reached a crescendo! We attended all of the lectures. This was not the style for the native, German students. Attendance was not required except for the laboratory exercises. There we had to complete the assigned experiments, provide the data to the instructor and take a weekly quiz.

The attendance at lectures varied greatly. The most popular were Professor's Stark lectures in anatomy. This was not a surprise; he had the most fantastic pedagogic skills, a "two fisted" drawing technique being his hallmark. He had just started a series of lectures on the anatomy of the brain that week and the first morning was devoted to a description of the major portions of the brain. Here he dazzled us with his "two fisted" drawing technique. Facing the blackboard he held a piece of chalk in each hand and simultaneously drew the two symmetrical parts of the brain. As he lectured on the various parts, he drew them at the same time in both brain hemispheres using both arms. The class was mesmerized. Not only was it the best bit of lecturing I ever experienced but also it was a bit of artistry and a bit of jingoism.

We were advised by the upper classmen to start reviewing the theoretical material as soon as possible and keep on slogging at current stuff since the amount of new material increased in volume and difficulty during the semester. In the previous semester, we took anatomy, embryology, physiology, biochemistry and general zoology, as well as respective laboratory courses. This semester we were to register for the last parts of anatomy, physiology and biochemistry as well as sports and work physiology, histology and general botany. This was to be accompanied by respective laboratory courses. It was an enormous load, particularly since Ania and I had less than perfect knowledge of the German language.

A couple weeks into the semester, we ran into Gienek, one of the pharmacology students who lived in Zeilsheim, a D.P. camp in Frankfurt's suburbs. In the course of our conversation, he mentioned a Doctor Piontek. Apparently, Dr. Piontek was a young German physician who volunteered as an instructor in the anatomy prosections. He was an assistant in the Department of Forensic Medicine but he was particularly interested in helping the Jewish students in their studies. Gienek offered to introduce us to him. Apparently Dr. Piontek was on the prosection floor. Gienek found him and introduced us.

Dr. Piontek was a very pleasant looking young man, a bit taller than I with much lighter blond hair and pure blue eyes. My eyes were blue-green. I do not know what prompted me to compare our physical characteristics, but I do know that I instantly took to him and the positive feeling must have been mutual. After a bit of conversation he suggested that we meet after the prosections and go to the Bierstube across the river, the one that we frequented on the way to the tram.

It was freezing cold and snowing as we ran across the bridge looking for the lights in the windows of the Bierstube. We literally ran into the place. The warm air that hit us as we entered, felt like paradise. The wind and snow were hitting us with vicious violence as we ran across the bridge and chilled us to our marrow. We certainly were frozen.

Dr. Piontek, incidentally I never addressed him any another way, steered us to the back of the room where he found a *gemuetlich* (cozy) corner. We took our coats and hats off hanging them on wooden pegs provided on the wall behind the table and beckoned the waiter.

Dr. Piontek immediately took over the ordering and suggested that we start with their delicious heavy dark beer and go on into"Kaessleriche Ribchen mit Kartoffeln Kloeser und Saure Kraut" (smoked pork ribs with potato dumplings and sauerkraut) while keeping our Steins full of beer. As time went on, Dr. Piontek looked progressively happier and insisted that we tell him our life stories and our reasons for studying medicine.

I noted that as time went on he looked more often at Ania than at me and obviously enjoyed the interaction with her. By then, I resigned myself to this fate. This situation was to repeat itself throughout my entire life.

It was getting late; we finished our meal long ago. I began to feel the effects of the beer. Dr. Piontek, I think, noted all this and suggested that we get going but I had to promise to look him up tomorrow. He said that there were some issues that he wanted to talk to us about.

On the way home, sitting on the tram for an hour, Ania and I had ample time to review our experiences with Dr. Piontek. Ania really liked him. Obviously he was very intelligent and knowledgeable. There was, however, something else about Dr. Piontek.

We kept on seeing Dr. Piontek in the dissection laboratory on a regular basis. The day after the dinner in the Bierstube we met as planned. He told us that he is looking forward to helping us in anatomy and histology or if we wish in the other subjects also. He would be happy to tutor us also. Furthermore, he indicated, that no remuneration would be accepted for his efforts. He felt strongly that it would be his pleasure to tutor us and he felt that by doing so he would be emotionally benefited.

We were very grateful to him and impressed by his kindness. The only help, however, we could use was a bit of inside information to make us understand better what to expect during the Physicum examinations and how to study for the oral examinations. The interaction between us evolved into a sort of friendship and we saw each other not only at the University, but also quite often socially. We talked mostly about schoolwork and sometimes he would take us to the Forensic Medicine Department where we would witness autopsies and roam through the forensic museum. We talked about everything. However, looking back I realize that we didn't talk politics, we didn't mention our trials and tribulations during the war, nor did we did we touch the taboo topic, the murder by the

Germans of millions of Jews only because they were Jews. Probably the sickest aspect of these murders, if there could be anything sicker than murder itself, was the fact that the Germans refused to kill Jews who were war prisoners or political prisoners as such. Instead, they were usually moved to Jewish sectors and murdered as Jews.

The spring was approaching and we were getting more frantic. It was school all day and study all evening, every evening. Isaac, our old friend, transferred to the University of Munich where he was to continue his medical studies. Henry, finally got his visa to the United States, and left for America. He left with us the address of his relatives in Detroit, Michigan.

The only close friends left in Frankfurt where Hanka and Arcik. We certainly knew a large number of students but very superficially. We were totally absorbed with the studies and with each other. In the morning, we would go together to the University, then return home together, eat dinner and then study together. The only time we were separated was at night when we slept in our respective apartments.

I have to admit that I frequently questioned the latter arrangement, however. I neither had the guts to breach this subject with Ania nor could I even imagine facing our parents with this dilemma. One had to deal with it philosophically. During the week, Frau Langer prepared supper for both of us. On the weekend, Ania would become the culinary whiz. She would make miracles out of a can of Spam and an onion and a bit of powdered peas.

Hanka, who lived next door to us, would frequently eat with us; she also was a very good cook and since she got provisions in Zeilsheim, she would occasionally have the opportunity to get fresh meat and butter. She and Ania would sometimes cook up a storm and we would have a feast. Sometimes the girls would invite Arcik who also lived in Fechenheim. He would get unusual delicacies and we would pig out in the afternoon and go to a movie house (there was one in Fechenheim) in the evening. In the spring of 1948 we saw probably the best movie of our lives, a new American film called "Gaslight" with Ingrid Bergman and Charles Boyer. However, luxuries like this, a good meal, a good movie were available only at rare intervals. Nevertheless we were very happy; life was good to us. I was particularly happy since I was in love.

Ice began to brake on the River Main. Soon Passover was coming. We decided to go home, to the D.P. camp for few days. We didn't think that we could be away from school for more than a few days, a weekend and a couple extra days. There was only a couple of months left prior to the examinations. We were to get the examinations schedule sometime in May. The examinations could drag on for many weeks during the summer. Actually, the way Piontek explained to us, my anatomy exams could be scheduled for the first week of June another subject in the middle of July and the rest of the subjects in August. Thus, he advised us to consider the summer shot! Particularly since Ania's examinations would most likely not be synchronized with mine, since the groups of four students taking the examination together might not include both of us.

The scheduling was an extremely complex issue. We didn't want to have the exams stretched throughout the summer vacations; on the other hand we didn't want them too frequently because each one of us wanted time for "last minute review." Some of us wanted more time for certain subjects while others wanted the extra time for other subjects. In other words, to satisfy most of the student's desires would be totally impossible. I was totally fatalistic on this issue, and anyway I wasn't big on cramming just before an exam. Thus, I tried to influence Ania to study as much as possible, but to forget the problems related to the exam schedules.

As time drew closer to vacation, we spent more and more time with Dr. Piontek. He was extremely helpful in reviewing the material with us particularly since he had a photographic memory and knew practically "everything." Also he was willing to give us an incredible amount of time. He was almost obsessed with the desire to help us. Sometimes, I felt uncomfortable accepting all of his time and effort. I wondered, at times, why he was doing it and couldn't come up with clear cut ideas. Occasionally our discussion would slide towards other Jewish students and since many lived in Zeilsheim, towards the topic of D.P. camps and from there sliding almost to the concentration camps. However, we always managed not to move towards the latter topic.

The lectures moved rapidly towards new areas. In biochemistry I was mesmerized by Professor Felix's lectures dealing with the intermediate carbohydrate metabolism and the fairly recently discovered Krebs cycle. When I mentioned these lectures to Dr. Piontek, he became very effusive and emotional in telling us the story of the Krebs cycle. First, he told us that Professor Krebs was a Jewish biochemist who developed the original data establishing the fundamental concepts dealing with the carbohydrate driven metabolic engine in the cells, the tricarboxylic acid cycle, named after him the "Krebs cycle."

Krebs made the initial discoveries while working with the Nobel laureate, Professor Otto Warburg, and later evolved at the University in Freiburg. With the ascent of the Nazis to power in 1933, he was thrown out of the University and forced to immigrate to Great Britain. Incidentally he was the Nobel Prize recipient for his work on carbohydrate metabolism in 1935.

We listened to these stories with opened mouths and Dr. Piontek continued with even greater vehemence. "The textbook you are using for biochemistry is by professor Lenartz. He was a professor at our university, the W.J. Goethe University, for years, a highly regarded academician. When Nazis came to power, those in the Department of Biochemistry who belonged to the party got together and physically threw professor Lenartz out of the window, killing him, so that a member of the party would take over the department."

As he was telling the story, tears were running down his face. We sat stunned, not so much in response to the story, since we knew of numerous episodes of similar nature, but in response to Dr. Piontek's reaction. (I should add at this point that I learned later that Dr. Piontek committed suicide shortly after the group of Jewish survivors who studied at the University with him had left Frankfurt.)

The semester was over. We got two weeks off prior to the commencement of the Physicum examinations. We decided to use a few days for a trip to Kassel and a visit with parents and friends but then a swift return to studies. Upon return to the D.P. camp, we were deluged with bad news. No one got any communications from the American Consulate concerning their applications for an entry visa to the U.S. My father was distraught, Juzek left for Australia and there was a letter from him rather glowing in content describing the wonderful reception he received from my aunt, his sister, and their entire family as well as from the Melbourne Jewish community. His letter exuded a very positive mood and sense of happiness. I thought it was wonderful. Juzek had lost his bride early in the war. He wedded her weeks before war's onset. He lost sisters and his parents, and he certainly deserved a bit of happiness. However, as Father said, so did we. I think Father was a little jealous of Juzek. Father would have also wished to see this chapter of our lives closed and a more positive, more optimistic one, preferably in America, opened.

I visited Ania's parents and they also had not heard from the American Consulate concerning their applications. Similar depressing news greeted us when we visited our friends, Ania and Mietek.

Shmull also came to see me as soon as he heard that we were in the camp. He was actually the only one I knew with some contacts and information. He told us in confidence that his sources in the Zionist party found out that President Truman had been pressuring the American Congress to pass a more liberal legislation specifically addressing the issue of Jewish immigration to America. Apparently, he felt that the strict quotas that applied to the Jews in D.P. camps should be relaxed and there was a good chance that such legislation would be reenacted.

My father's mood picked up immediately after he heard this bit of news. He was always a staunch supporter of American presidents and a believer in American fairness and justice. I was happy to see this change in his mental status.

Personally, I was too busy with school, exams and with Ania to be distracted by the reality of our precarious state of existence in the D.P. camp and in general in Germany. But, again, I always took my duties seriously and my life lightly.

****

Ania and I were walking briskly across the bridge over the River Main towards Sachsenhausen and the Medical Campus grounds after the return back to Frankfurt. By chance, Ania and I were placed in the same group for the anatomy examinations. I had an uneasy feeling that this did not happen totally by chance but that it was Dr. Piontek's doing. He knew that I wished to be placed with Ania in the same group for the exams and he was an instructor in the department. Well, I knew that I would not bring it to his attention.

We joined the two other students waiting in the hallway in front of Professor's Stark office. At ten o'clock sharp, the secretary came out and invited all four of us in. The exam was a four hours 'breeze'.

As we walked back across the bridge, I carried on a conversation with Ania in my usual paranoid way; complaining how poorly I did on the exam. She laughed, patted me on my hand grouchily disagreeing with me. Her reassurances, however, were not particularly firm. Her concern was further betrayed by the suggestion that we have some beer before having lunch in the Bierstube across the bridge.

After we were seated, I continued with my ranting. I was confused with the way the exam went. It ended up, I complained fuming, with Professor Stark asking one of the four students in the exam group a question and if he didn't know the answer, the Professor would ask the second student. If he also could not answer, the Professor would ask the second student then you and if you didn't know the answer he would invariably ask me to respond to the same question. Once I would respond properly he would keep on asking me additional questions until invariably I would get to a point that I also would fail to answer. Then he was satisfied! I almost screamed at Ania in the restaurant, completely frustrated. Dr. Piontek did not warn us of Professor Stark's examination techniques.

Our next exam wasn't scheduled for another couple of weeks. I actually began to get into the rhythm of this type of testing techniques and began to enjoy it. By the end of July, we finished all the examinations and were ready to go back to the D.P. camp in Muenchenberg.

We were actually looking forward to spending time with family and friends. However, before going back we invited Father to Frankfurt to spend a week there and see the city and the University. He never visited us before. Most of the city was actually in rubble. However, Fechenheim was intact; so was the huge I.G. Farben industry complex located between Fechenheim and the city that we saw each day we rode the tram to the city. The American Air Force had actually spared this huge chemical industry center probably for political-commercial reasons.

We greatly enjoyed Father's visit. A trip to the *Tiergarten* (the zoo) was memorable. The zoo was located not far from the Hauptwache that was almost totally destroyed, but the zoo was almost intact and the animals were doing OK. We also visited the University and showed Father the Medical School campus.

The air temperatures were great for a swim in the River Main and since the river was one block down the street, very close to us, everyday we would walk to the river for a swim. Father had no chance to swim since the war started. Thus, this was a treat for him. At the end of his visit, we took him to the railroad station and I made a promise to to come to Kassel in a week or two for a visit.

However, it didn't work out this way. The day after he left we started to organize our activities to obtain the necessary textbooks and notes to prepare for the next year, a very different year of studies that involved attending clinics and seeing patients. We were to embark on a very different style of study.

While visiting the Jewish Student Union to get some advice concerning the books for the next semester, we ran across one of our friends, Duska. She was all excited and obviously happy to have run into us. "I have an exciting bit of news. A friend of mine has connections in southern Germany, near the town of Berchtesgaden in the Bavarian Alps. You know, the place where Hitler had his villa, and she is willing to make arrangements for a group to stay there for a very reasonable price. I am organizing an excursion for a group of our students to visit this area. The place is supposed to be breathtaking. I thought we could take off for a week and go there by train. How about coming along? We will be leaving in five days."

I looked at Ania and said, "It sounds great; do you know how much it will cost?" I asked with concern. "You know we are very strapped for cash."

With her usual huge grin, she responded with a dismissive motion of her hand. "I was told that it will be rock bottom for the accommodations, we will take some food with us to help in this department and as you know we get free train tickets. Thus, the entire excursion should be almost free. Don't even consider not going!" she concluded with gusto and with an emphasis on the "don't."

This time Ania looked at me with a questioning but a very positive glance. "I agree with Duska," she said. "This is a fabulous opportunity. Let's go." I was taken a bit by surprise, as this was not the usual reaction I would expect from Ania. Usually she would not make a decision this rapidly and would be more conservative. I thought she really must want to go, and I definitely would jump at such an opportunity. I asked, "When do we need to get ready?"

"By Friday," she replied, "I will firm up our reservations. Let's get the train schedules and then meet on Wednesday, here at the Union. At that time, we should be able to make a final decision on which train to take. Let's consider going to Munich first because from what I understand, it is only three or four hours by train from Munich to Berchtesgaden." This sounded reasonable. We nodded and hugged. Her parting words were, "At noon here, on Wednesday."

Ania and I were supposed to leave for Kassel in about five days or a week. The trip to Bavaria would delay our return to the D.P. camp for at least ten days or maybe two weeks. We had to figure out how to ease the news to our parents. I was certain that they would have no objections to our excursion but, at the same time, we knew that they were already counting the days to our arrival. I let Ania compose letters to our parents. She was a much better diplomat than I.

CHAPTER 19 The Wonderlust.

Thinking back, I asked myself whether my "wanderlust," the irresistible desire to travel, was my "nature" or my "nurture." Was I born with it, or did childhood experiences of being constantly uprooted have a major influence on this aspect of my personality? Examples: Could my wanderlust be related to being expelled during early childhood from a comfortable life in Germany? This chilling experience was very vague in my mind. Other experiences that followed, rapidly and repeatedly, remained vivid in my memory. These were dislocations under progressively worsening conditions in Eastern Europe. Had all of these experiences made me so vulnerable to an opportunity to travel, that it was almost possible for me to refuse?

At that moment, I really did not care where a travel opportunity came from. I simply wanted to go to Berchtesgaden and it wasn't difficult to convince Ania to join me. On Wednesday, we picked up Hanka and Arcik went to the tram and by noon, showed up at the Student Union. Duska and her boyfriend, her sister, Zdzich and his wife, his friend, Szymczinski, with a girlfriend – were all waiting for us. With them was Fimek whom I did not know. Although he was a student, it was unclear to me, and I think to him, what he really wanted to study. Nevertheless, he was a spunky little guy who seemed to be a lot of fun and he was Szymczinski's "big friend". Ania and I immediately took a liking to him.

We learned that Zdzich had made an extensive study of railroad schedules. Duska announced that she had arranged accommodations for the entire group at a small bed-and-breakfast near Berchtesgaden--with incredibly low rates per night. Zdzich said that there was a train leaving early Friday morning for Munich with an excellent connection to Berchtesgaden. We would be in Munich before noon and board a train for a three-hour trip to our destination, arriving at 1 PM.

Everyone began speaking simultaneously, each having very important information that had to be shared instantly. It seemed that each person knew exactly what places of interest in the Bavarian Alps we should visit and in what sequence. Finally, Zdzich jumped up on a table and hollered, "Quiet! Unless we go about it in an organized fashion, we will never agree on anything nor will we manage to plan out the details of our trip. Firstly, let's all agree to get to the ticket windows about one and one half hours before the train's scheduled departure.

This proposal was seconded by all. Duska suggested we decide what to visit once we got there. This idea was also accepted and this way the major turmoil was averted. Friday was the day of the departure. We got to the station early trying to get seats on the train near each other, which was essentially impossible. The train was crowded, as expected, since the railroad was basically the only means of transportation for the civilians. I found a window seat and a seat for Ania also by the window facing me. This was great; we were close and we both could look out the window. The latter was a treat since we had not had a chance to travel much to see the country, except for the Frankfurt and Kassel route. We visited with each other, looked out the window and the time passed quickly.

We pulled into a huge structure of the Munich railroad station by noon and found the train for Berchtesgaden quickly. The Berchtesgaden railroad station was a major surprise. It was huge; the building was much too large and built much too impressively for a railroad station in a tiny town of several thousand's population. Later we learned why this disparity. With Hitler making his residence in Obersalzberg, near Berchtesgaden, where he built a *Berghaus* (a mountain house) at the Eagle's Nest, the station in the village continuously received delegations, diplomats, and a variety of high officials from Germany and from all over the world. Berchtesgaden was a very busy place and it indeed required a railroad station of the appropriate size and an important appearance to fulfill this role.

We stayed a few hundred yards from the center of a village in a small house that let some rooms. All the singles were divided by sex; males placed in one room, the females into the other. The married couples were given private rooms. We were crowded but happy.

The next morning, the first thing we wanted to see was the Eagle's Nest. When we walked over there we found that the U.S. military has barricaded the entire area and posted signs, "Entritt Verboten" (no entrance). However, the view of the mountains from that hill was breathtaking and we spent time walking around there and enjoying the view. Incidentally, in the early 1950s, the U.S. Military destroyed the *Berghaus*, the bunkers and all structures related to the Eagle's Nest to prevent it from ever becoming a shrine to the Fascist elements.

Once in the village, we were told that there were three places in the area that we should not miss visiting--the salt mine, the Chiemsee and the Koenigsee. We decided to spend the rest of the day in Berchtesgaden and go to the Koenigsee the following day.

We boarded a motor vessel on Koenigsee for a pleasure trip to its other end. The boat was powered by an electric motor; it was perfectly quiet and obviously did not pollute the beautiful waters of the lake. The lake was all that one could expect from a set of illustrations for a fairy tale. One breathtaking view would substitute another as the boat glided down the lake. The lake curves around the foot of the famous Watzmann Mountain whose rock faces dropped dramatically into the deep, green waters of the lake. All of us were excited, craning our necks with each turn of the boat to better see what came next.

As we sailed well into the lake, the boat started turning towards the shore where we could see the most picturesque church with white walls and red onion-domed towers. The boat had a scheduled stop there; we learned that the structure was the famous Romanesque St. Bartholomae Church.

Upon return we spent hours talking about our experiences, wallowing in the luxury of knowing that we now had the opportunity to experience such exquisite pleasures in such a short time since we were primarily concerned with the basics: how to survive, where to get food, how to stay alive!

The trip's experiences grew on me, particularly when I was alone and could meditate quietly at the enormity of this experience. We were literally yards away from the former center of the ultimate evil, Hitler's lair. The awe was further sharpened by the fact that we were able to visit this place, gawk at these incredible wonders of nature with Germans all around us, many behaving rather friendly towards us and sometimes even helpful. Only some twenty months back, we were considered by them an "Untermensch Rasse" (subhuman race). It indeed was confusing.

DID THEY CHANGE?

WERE THEY PRETENDING?

This part of the country was studded with mountain lakes. Some, like the Koenigsee, were very famous. Another beautiful and famous lake nearby was the Chiemsee. We decided to go there the following day.

The first day, however, we decided to spend time further investigating Berchtesgaden and later the famous salt mine. We were also told to walk down the road to the hospital; the view of the mountains from that vantage point was awesome, and snowcapped peaks literally towered in front of us. Then we were shown the road to take for a climb to the summit of Kneifelspitze, a steep mountain peak nearby. We decided to take the path. It indeed was steep and we were exhausted when we reached the summit; however, it was worth it, the views from the summit were absolutely breathtaking.

Upon return to the village, we took the walk to the salt mine. It was already early afternoon and we were hungry. However, there was no time to buy groceries for a picnic and we didn't have enough money to have both lunch and dinner in a restaurant. It was decided to skip lunch, go to the "Salzbergwerk" (salt mine), and worry about dinner later.

This was a good decision; the mine was worth the hunger discomfort. Luckily, we had enough money with us to pay the entrance fee and register for the next group. One couldn't just go in; we could visit the mine only with an organized group led by a guide.

While waiting at the entrance, we learned that the mine had been open since the fifteenth century and originally only highly important personalities were permitted to visit. Some people who were waiting with us had made this visit before and were very happy to give us a preview of "coming attractions." The entire group, composed primarily of Germans was very friendly and willing to interact with us with enthusiasm. Again an "unreal" feeling gripped me. We were in the heart of Hitler's country, next to his beloved *Berghaus*. I expected a different reaction from the Germans; I really didn't know what the reaction should have been.

Our guide arrived and called everyone. We were given what looked to be leather aprons. However, we quickly learned that these were not aprons but pieces of clothing to wear over our pants in the seat area. The efficacy of these odd pieces of clothing became clear shortly; first, however, we were taken to peculiar transportation equipment, basically a train composed of several "cars." These were about ten feet long and two feet wide. There were leather upholstered benches mounted lengthwise that we straddled sitting down. The entire contraption was riding on a narrow gauge railroad tracks. This explained some utility for the "leather aprons."

We quickly climbed on this peculiar "train" and straddled the center seat. The train rapidly departed into a dark tunnel, flying down through it, at what I perceived to be an enormous speed. Rocky outcrops felt as if they were almost grazing our heads. In a few minutes, we arrived in a large cave. Here I further understood the role of the mysterious leather aprons we had to cover the rear parts of our anatomy. We walked over to an opening through which one could see a cave some twenty yards below us. One could walk down a set of stairs or slide down a wooden structure resembling two banisters close to each other.

Here the essential utility of the leather pieces of clothing became further clarified. We were to mount this "banister," some six people at the time and simply slide down on our back-sides (protected by the leather aprons) into the cave below us.

I sat in front of the group, Ania behind me. As we let ourselves go, all the girls let out a scream. We were bending backward literally flying down the banisters and in a matter of seconds landed in the hall below that looked like something from a fantasy movie.

The columns of salt were translucent allowing varying color lights to diffuse through them creating this unreal fantasy world. The rest of the time was spent exploring deeper caves and more wonders of the salt world. We certainly became expert banister gliders because we took the glides whenever we could. The culmination was the last cave with a large lake filled with what looked like black water; we embarked on a flat raft that took us to the other shore of the lake by a sparkling spring at the brine-lifting machine.

That evening we broke up into groups for supper. The general "togetherness" was slowly getting the better of us. It was fun, but for change a bit of privacy was considered desirable. Ania and I had no chance of being alone and we definitely approved of an evening "off." Each got dressed in the best clothing we had and took off looking for a nice but a reasonably priced restaurant.

There were not too many within a short walking distance. Finally, we found what looked like a small Bierstube. They served a goulash, which was basically a beef stew with a heavy dose of paprika. We hadn't had it since before the war and happily ordered it with a stein of dark beer.

Just as we finished ordering, Zdzich showed up with his wife and a couple minutes later the two guys from Zeilsheim. Well, there simply were not too many restaurants in the neighborhood. We all laughed but decided to sit separately for some privacy and indeed we had some since we could talk privately to each other.

Ania's eyes were big and round with wonder and excitement. "We saw some beautiful things since we came here," she said. I looked at her with what I could feel to be love in my eyes and responded, "Yes, it is beautiful, majestic, impressive and awesome. I am so happy to be able to experience it with you. Sometimes I barely have the strength to refrain from putting my arms around you, hold you tight; tell you how much I love you when we witness together the miracles of nature, particularly the majesty of the mountains. On the other hand, I was laughing when you were screaming from fright when sliding down the banisters into the salt mine." She put her hand under the table, looked furtively around and squeezed my knee; there were sparkles of laughter in her eyes.

We awakened to sunshine and to a beautiful day. The skies were blue without a single cloud in them; it was a big day. We were to take a train to the "Markt Prien am Chiemsee," a beautiful little town on the western shores of Lake Chiemsee in southern Bavaria, near Salzburg. This town had special meaning to Ania and I, and we were looking forward to this excursion. The town was famous for its "picture book" appearance and the lake famous for the Herreninsel, a large island where in 1884 King Ludwig II of Bavaria built his last castle, the "Herren Chiemsee," a castle designed in the style of Versailles, the fabulous country palace built by Louis XIV of France.

We took the famous nineteenth century steam train for the couple kilometer's ride from Prien to the docks on the lake. There we bordered a boat that took us to the island. We learned that King Ludwig II ran out of funds and couldn't complete a replica of the entire Versailles; only the central portion was built. However, just this portion was unbelievable in its extent and beauty. The massive building was U-shaped, the front portion being almost 300 feet wide. The castle contained seventy rooms, of which only twenty were completed. Exquisite, formal French gardens with statues and fountains graced the front of the palace. Walking through the castle we were completely mesmerized. Never before had we seen such opulence and grandiosity. None of the Polish castles in Krakow or Warsaw could compare in sheer extravagance and artistic beauty. The enormity and the beauty of the castle was instantly stated when one entered the glittering Hall of Mirrors, an almost 300 foot long room with 44 enormous candelabras. The beautiful royal bedchamber was also amazing to see, especially since no one ever slept there and thirty hard working women labored for seven years just embroidering the bed cover.

****

The trip back to Chiemsee by boat and then to Frankfurt by train was uncharacteristically subdued. I do not know what everyone was thinking about. However, I suspected that all of us had somewhat similar thoughts. Guilt was eating away at me for the fact that I and my family survived the Holocaust, by the Germans and now I was enjoying the beauty created by the ancestors of our tormentors. The question, a burning question, was standing naked in front of me demanding an answer. Should I reject everything German? Should I refuse to acknowledge German culture, to study it, to learn about it and even to enjoy it where and when appropriate?

One example of the latter was this trip. Furthermore my parents, particularly my mother, were adamant about not staying in "their" homeland among "their" people, even though the city of Kassel offered to give my parents back their dental office, equipment, and apparently they were also willing to reimburse them for the furniture and paintings taken by the Nazis. Obviously we didn't know how far, if at all, this offer would hold if they indeed had accepted it. My parents flatly refused to deal with the German government on this issue. Was it right on their part? I couldn't come up with an answer. Neither could I decide on the question I had raised originally concerning this trip. The thoughts, however, placed a cloud over the enjoyment of this trip that by definition was fabulous.

Ania and I arrived back to Fechenheim totally exhausted. Frau Langer appeared to be genuinely happy to see us back in good health and in good spirits. Walking in I met Mr. Lotz in the hallway. He was also glad to see me back and immediately asked if I practiced my violin over vacation. When I told him that the violin wasn't with me, he was disappointed. "We will have to work twice as hard now that you back," he retorted.

Life was returning to the normal state. The food rations at the Student Union were delayed; however, we were to go to the D.P. camp for a while and did not worry.

****

The school year was about to start. A major change in the study styles and attitudes had to be developed. Part of our studies involved seeing patients at clinics. Oh yes, we had to register for all the courses, including courses dealing with the introduction to internal medicine, physical examination and pharmacology.

We embarked on the clinical part of our studies with great enthusiasm. Since there were relatively few students in medicine who were Jewish, I was always with Ania, attending classes together and registering for the same groups for clinical assignments. For all practical purposes we were always together in school and outside of school. The only time we were separate, as always, was when we went to our own apartments at night.

The 1947 Christmas vacations were spent again in the camp. I could sense that in Muenchenberg, everyone was depressed and the mood was low. Our friends, Mietek and Ania, still didn't hear from the American Consulate. Neither did any of our other friends. My parents did. I was surprised that they did while the others did not. Having been born in Germany, we fell under the German quota, while all our friends, including Ania and her parents, were born in Poland and were under the Polish quota. The German quota was moving much faster because it was apparently larger and there were fewer people applying. The Polish quota for the Polish Jews was bogged down.

The American President, Mr. Truman, apparently has submitted a bill to the Congress of United States to ease off this quota situation; at least these were the rumors we heard. In the meanwhile, my parents were told that they were to be interviewed at the Consulate in a couple weeks. Since Stella and I were underage, we were to be included in parent's visas and it wasn't necessary for us to see the consul. All four of us were to be given appointments for medial examinations after our parents passed the scrutiny.

Mother said that the Consulate informed us that her sister in New York provided an affidavit of financial guarantee for us and that the affidavit was approved by the American government. Thus the news was actually mixed; that dealing with us was positive, while that dealing with Ania and our friends was indefinite. Mietek's older brother who survived the war and stayed with them in our camp had just obtained a visa for Australia. He was to leave shortly to join his relatives there.

Returning to Frankfurt after the winter vacation, I got a letter from my parents that all of us were scheduled in Frankfurt's American Consulate for medical examinations in three weeks. This was good news. Both my parents and Stella were coming, so I planned to take time off from school and show them a bit of Frankfurt as well as the University.

Our school life was getting more hectic. Not only we had many lectures and laboratory sessions to attend, but now we also had clinics and patient interactions. This was very different from the theoretical part of the studies. We had to spend longer hours in these activities but the hours were in a way more interesting and, although more time had to be invested, in my mind they were less stressful than some of the theoretical sessions where one had to really strain one's brain.

Some of the clinical interactions were actually very funny although one had to keep the dignity of the situation in mind. In early spring, we were assigned to the obstetrical ward as clerks. That meant that we were assigned to a patient, in this case a pregnant female ready to deliver, and were supposed to follow the case until the delivery, regardless how long it would take. Sometimes, we were with a patient for an hour or two, she would deliver and we would go home. Other times we would stay with a patient who would not deliver for 24 hours or even longer. Thus, we had to miss some lectures and laboratories. This, however, was not a problem. We enjoyed the entire experience.

The family visit to the American Consulate for the medical examination was essentially a "non happening." The day after my parents arrived we went to the Consulate; there we were assigned a number, waited an hour and were called to see a doctor. My examination lasted no more than fifteen minutes; a chest x-ray was taken, I was given some immunization shots, a smallpox vaccination and a blood sample was taken. Later I was informed by the grapevine in the school that the blood test was to check for syphilis. And that was all.

We were sent home and instructed to wait for a report and for orders as what to do next. Stella and my parents spent a few days with us in Frankfurt. The weather was not very nice and we had no opportunity to do much, although there wasn't much to see in Frankfurt at that time except for mountains of debris from destroyed buildings.

School became very intense. The clinical experiences took a great deal of time, particularly if one was conscientious, as we were. Between school and my violin studies, there was no time for anything else.

Across the Main River from Fechenheim was Offenbach. A theater there staged operettas. Ania and I both loved the classical Austrian and Hungarian operettas and whenever we could spare the money, we would attend the theater.

Time continued to go by fast and uneventfully until early April. We got a letter from my parents that Father's chest x-ray showed the presence of a "shadow" that looked suspiciously like a Ghon's tubercle, meaning there was a possibility of a tubercular infection. Therefore, his visa was to be placed on hold for one year. During this time, he was to submit sputum for analysis at monthly intervals. If it would remain negative for twelve months, the visa would be reinstated. Otherwise his entry to the United States would be denied. We all had chest x-rays and sputum analyses in Soviet Russia and they were negative. This report caught us by surprise.

It was close to two years since we started the quest for America and now we had to wait another year and then we didn't know which way the situation would turn. Mother's response to this turn of events was to get me out of Germany. She contacted my aunt in London asking her to try and get a visa for me to go to London. The aunt didn't think that it was possible. She suggested that Mother appeal to the aunt in Australia.

Here I put my foot down. I did not want to go to Australia and leave my family and Ania in Germany. England, while not the best, in my opinion, was still different from Australia. Anyway, I was set on going to America. Didn't I promise Ania that we both would go there?

A friend of mine at the University knew a girl who worked in the American Consulate. She was a Hungarian and her name was Aliz. I asked him whether he could introduce us.

Within couple days, we were having a beer together in the Bierstube by the bridge. Aliz was three or four years older than I, a very pleasant and nice looking young lady. We instantly got along and were having a wonderful conversation. As we were jumping from one topic to another, I told her about our visa problem and Father's health examination findings. She laughed knowingly and said, "Yes, the visa problems. Everyone wants to go eventually to America, including myself."

She then asked some details about our case and asked my age. Looking at me with a smile on her face she said, "Most people still don't know that the United States Congress has passed a new legislation that was recently signed by President Truman. It not only increased the quota numbers but also contains some provisions that will make it easier for the Jews to be considered for immigration."

"But," she added, "You must obtain your own papers separately from your parents. Also it will be better that you do not get private papers with a financial guarantee from your aunt in America but get papers from the 'JOINT,' a Jewish aid organization highly familiar with these issues. This organization has large presence here in Germany."

I must have looked crestfallen. Separate papers, no involvement with the aunt, and, it looked like, no involvement even with my parents. "All by myself?" I asked. I was shocked and confused.

She looked at me with her big brown eyes in which I could see laughing specs of gold. She put her hand over mine resting on the table and said, "Let me help you. You will see it will work. I know people at 'Joint'; they will provide me with the application forms. Once they approve you and classify you as one of their registrants, I think I can get you a visa within a few weeks. There is really no reason why this couldn't be done because it is all legitimate, the only extraordinary thing will be my help in moving the application along the way."

I was dumfounded. I didn't know how to respond, how to thank her. She got up, walked over to me unperturbed, laughed and, looking straight at my face, gave me a big hug and a kiss and said, "Let's meet here tomorrow; I will have the application forms for you." She turned on her heels and walked away leaving me standing there in shock.

All the way home, while sitting on the tram, I was trying to figure out what had happened in the past couple hours. I simply couldn't understand the entire encounter and had real difficulties believing that it was all real. There were a number of serious issues to consider and I didn't even have an idea how to arrange them in the order of importance. Probably the most important issue was the decision whether I should even consider leaving for America alone, leaving my parents behind and leaving Ania here for an indefinite period of time. I had not thought of this possibility until now. Our separation in Poland after the return from Russia was sufficiently traumatic to stop me in my tracks just thinking about this repeating itself. It terrified me just to think about the possibility that I might have not found her at that time in Poland. Now, to leave her again struck me as an insane idea. I didn't think that I could handle it.

Leaving my parents behind created a somewhat similar problem. The more I delved into these thoughts the more dispirited I got. Suddenly it dawned on me that this entire scenario could be a hoax. What if Aliz simply had a bit of fun with me? What if she played a little innocent game? I couldn't disregard this possibility after I thought of motives. Why would she do this enormous favor for me? I decided to talk it over with Ania since I had no clue how to resolve this issue.

However, in final analysis, if Aliz would come through, regardless of the reasons, the motivations or whatever nefarious ideas she might have had, the situation remained unchanged in respect to me making up my mind concerning the acceptance of this entire issue of leaving alone for America. Exhausted I decided to put this issue aside until a discussion with Ania.

That evening after dinner I apprised Ania of my conversation with Aliz. She looked at me with suspicious eyes but a smile on her lips. "Well, 'Don Juan,' how did you charm this innocent maiden? Let's have the truth," she said slowly while the smile on her face grew and grew. I didn't know how to respond. Such a situation had never happened before. I could feel my palms growing moist and perspiration running down my armpits. I didn't know how serious she was. Was she upset? As she kept looking at me while trying to look stern, the smile on her face finally erupted into a golden twinkle of laughter. She jumped on me, kissed me square on my lips and whispered into my ear, "I love you."

After this display of some mirth and a lot of love, she sat down across from me and asked seriously, "What do you really think of this encounter? I like to believe that she took a sudden liking for you and sincerely wanted to help you. Does she know about 'us?'" she added.

I responded slowly, "I don't see how. Our encounter dealt exclusively with a brief summary of my past and Father's problem with the medical examination. Subsequently she immediately started discussing the approach of getting a visa for me. She was so assured, so confident and I must say, so forthright. She certainly took me by surprise with the kiss!" I finished lamely. Throughout my explanation of Aliz to Ania, she kept laughing. I didn't know what to make of it. Finally, I decided to take the bull by the horns. "Well," I said, "instead of laughing at me tell me what I should have done during the encounter with her and what do you thing I should do now?"

I think that Ania noted the edge in my voice. This was the first time I ever assumed this tone of voice with her. She sensed that I was getting really upset or more likely confused by not knowing how to act and what to do.

"I don't see what you could have done much different," she started, "matter of fact I don't see what you should have done that would have been different. I think Aliz is godsend help for you to get a visa rapidly and easily. We talked about this on numerous occasions and everyone, that means your parents, my parents and I, agrees that if you can go, you should. One never knows what difficulties may arise with time. Just go along with Aliz' advice and let's see what will happen." I looked into her eyes as I always did under similar circumstances. They were dark, the blue was clouded, she was very sad, also, I think, a little scared and I would have liked to think, a little bit jealous.

We sat close to each other for a long while, saying nothing, just holding on to each other very tight. I could feel that Ania was thinking of my going to America alone. This scared her, but thinking that she would have to stay behind not knowing when she would be able to join me was for both of us was an insurmountable thought for both of us.

Aliz was very precise; she brought the application forms and explained all the details of how to fill them out. The only problem was my birth certificate. I knew that I didn't have the original. However, I also knew that parents had to deal with this issue when they were filling out originally the visa forms for all four of us. After contacting them, I learned that indeed they traveled to Berlin in an attempt to get a copy of my birth certificate but were unable to get a copy of the original because it burned during the Allied bombing of the city. However, there were other documents suggesting indirectly that I was born in Berlin. Properly signed affidavits dealing with the assurances derived from these various documents were adequate for the American Consulate in lieu of the original birth certificate. I got copies of the affidavits, brought them to Aliz and she submitted the entire package for me to the Consulate.

We saw each other on numerous occasions during the time I worked on the documents. But once they were submitted she suggested that we wait until I hear from the Consul concerning the fate of my immigration application.

The spring vacation was around the corner and we decided to go to the camp for a week or so. With the first signs of blooming flowers and buds opening up on the trees the mood in the camp was much more optimistic than during our visit in December. There was an encouraging letter from Uncle Josef who left for Australia several months back. He was telling us how happy he was there, how the family and people he met in Melbourne were so nice. The big news concerned his meeting a lady he liked very much. We were very happy for him but at the same time, we wondered when we would finally find a place that we could call home.

The other big news was a letter from Uncle Leon, my hero, the man who probably was most important in our survival of the war, firstly getting us out in the last possible moment from under Hitler's power and then giving us the opportunity to survive Stalin. He simply informed us that he got married – with no details at that time. I was glad to hear that he got married at the same time somewhat amazed that it happened so rapidly after the termination of the war and before complete resolution of the many problems created by the war.

We were lucky to be at the camp at this time. The timing of our visit was very fortunate since it coincided with a general meeting of all the camp inmates. It was to deal with a discussion of the camp administration, the aid situation and the emigration issues. The meeting was to be held the next day at 2 PM. We were told that HIAS and JOINT representatives would also attend. Possibly, the final word wasn't heard as yet, but a representative of the American Embassy might also show up at the meeting.

That morning I met with Shmull, who was in town and very excited. "I am certain that you are well aware of the fact that the United Nations is debating and may soon propose the recommendation for creation of the State of Israel on the ancient lands of the Jews, in the general area of the Palestine Mandate. I think that the episode where the British attacked the ship "Exodus" with a load of D.P.s trying to reach Eretz Israel has tilted the opinion of many countries towards the establishment of a State of Israel."

Furthermore, Shmull was telling me in confidence, "the various Zionist organizations have redoubled their efforts to bring more Jews to Eretz Israel as rapidly as possible because the prevailing opinion was that the United Nations may vote for the establishment of Israel very soon and Jewish intelligence in Israel learned that the Arab countries would most likely attack the new State at the instant it is proclaimed. Matter of fact," he said, "the anti-Zionist activity on the part of the Arabs has markedly increased in the past several weeks, ironically under the protection of the British."

He also delicately commented on the possibility of my joining his Zionist group for another trip to Italy. I told him that regretfully I would not do it regardless of the outcome of the political maneuvering concerning the recognition of the State of Israel. I had thrown my lot with America. Furthermore, I told him, I may be getting a visa for America soon and may have to leave not waiting even for my parents or Ania.

The meeting in the afternoon was very well attended; there was standing room only but even standing room was barely available. Being in Frankfurt, and essentially removed from news dealing with D.P.s, I was eager to hear what new information the various representatives would share with us. Particularly I wanted to hear news about the immigration quotas.

For reasons that were totally unclear to me I felt very confident that Aliz would come through in respect to my visa. My concerns at this time were the regulations that may affect the visas of my parents and visas of Ania with her parents.

The full meeting hall was buzzing with conversations and excitement, which came to an abrupt stop when the representatives of the various organizations entered the speaker's area. I sat with my parents and Ania's family all the way in the back since we came only about one half of hour before two o'clock and by then most of the seats were already taken. The people were obviously eager to hear what was to be said.

Both the HIAS and JOINT (Joint Distribution Committee) representatives were very positive and optimistic. They made us understand that there were two primary issues to celebrate. The first dealt with the strong belief within the political community that a vote supporting the establishment of the State of Israel would pass in the United Nations and the second, with the new legislation by the United States Congress, the Displaced Persons Act of 1948 that was to significantly improve the odds for the Jewish D.P.s to be granted permanent entry visas to the United States.

There was a great deal of discussion between the representatives of JOINT and HIAS on one hand and our D.P. camp officials. The fundamental conclusions, however, didn't change the views on the two primary issues. Nevertheless the lengthy discussion with a very aggressive participation by the audience, was very beneficial to all of us. It was a form of catharsis that renewed our hope for the future and provided us with factual data confirmed in our presence by reliable officials.

After the meeting, the mood of the people exuded optimism and there was great deal of "thanksgiving" to President Truman for his courageous stand in fighting for increased immigration quotas for the Jews. In the eyes of the camp inmates, he was a real friend of the Jewish people, as many put it, "a real Mensch" (real human being). I could overhear bits of conversations, "not an anti-Semitic bone in his body," "a great, fair man with no anti-Semitic thoughts." People started looking at him now as they looked at President Roosevelt before, with awe.

Presidents Franklin D. Roosevelt and Harry Truman had an amazing ability to evoke strong feelings in their own favor, among Jewish Holocaust survivors in the D.P. camps. At that time it was very helpful to the survivors. It gave them a solid point of departure and a bright vision of the future, as well as the simple psychological benefit of "hero worship."

There is, however, another aspect of how these presidents may be judged by humanitarians in the future. Portraits of them change significantly when the historical and factual knowledge acquired and made public during the ensuing half of the twentieth century is plugged into the equation. Mr. Roosevelt's negative attitudes toward the Jews during the war have been well documented and do not need to be repeated or discussed here. Probably most damning was his disinterest in stemming the tide of Hitler's genocide by refusing to bomb the concentration camps. Nevertheless, the European survivors in the D.P. camps viewed this American hero as a friend and he certainly was my personal hero. Only much later, I learned that in many instances he acted against the general interest of the Jewish people.

The negative feelings of President Truman towards the Jews were apparently not known nor clearly understood for many years after his death. Matter of fact some of Mr. Truman's thoughts on this issue didn't surface until the discovery of a diary handwritten by him, found in 2003 at the Truman Presidential Library in Independence, Missouri. In this diary, Truman relates an episode dealing with the "Jewish ship," *Exodus*. It had been intercepted by the British Navy in 1947 and forced to return to Germany. The ship was carrying some 4,500 Jewish refugees who were trying to reach the Holy Land. The episode has been well documented in a book by Leon Uris that was used by Otto Preminger in 1960 to make a very successful movie. According to the entries in Truman's dairy, in July 1947 he was called by Henry Morgenthau who made an attempt to intercede for the Jews on the *Exodus*. Mr. Morgenthau, who served as the Secretary of Treasurer under President Roosevelt, at the time he was making the call, was the Chairman of the United Jewish Appeal. It was in the latter capacity that he felt an obligation to telephone the President and ask for intervention in respect to the *Exodus* and its human cargo.

According to the President's entries in the dairy, he was greatly annoyed by the call. "He had no business, whatever to call me," Truman wrote. He continued in this vain: "The Jews have no sense of proportion"; "The Jews I find are very selfish they care not how many Estonians, Latvians, Finns, Poles, Yugoslavs or Greeks get murdered or mistreated as long as the Jews get special treatment. Yet when they have power, physical, financial or political, neither Hitler nor Stalin has anything on them for cruelty or mistreatment of the under dog."

Apparently Truman had little factual appreciation of the plight of Europe's D.P.s. Firstly he assumed that the plight was the same for the various groups covered by this classification. He was not aware, and possibly didn't want to understand, as I discussed in great detail above, that many who after the war claimed a D.P. status were actually German collaborators from the various countries, like Ukraine, Latvia and others. Some of them even became members of the German military forces.

After the war, they found themselves on German territory since they escaped with the German Army that was retreating under pressure of the advancing Soviet Armies.

Truman apparently didn't appreciate the fact that the Jews, above and beyond the other groups, the Slavs, the Latvians, Estonians, Ukrainians and other nationalities, were indeed selected by the Germans for *"SPECIAL TREATMENT" (*annihilation*)*, a special treatment that was administered with German precision and efficiency.

The two presidents were icons in the eyes of the pre and postwar European Jewry. However, despite the publicly displayed positive attitudes of Mr. Roosevelt towards Jews, his actions were frequently negative. The most damning was probably his negative actions in respect to stemming the tide of genocide directed specifically against the Jews in highly selective and effective ways. Thus, the hero of the Jews, and during the D.P. camp days also, unquestionably, my personal hero, was a man who definitely did not act in a stereotypical fashion as an anti-Jewish person but acted many or possibly most of the times against the interests of Jews as people. It is telling to bring up an episode of Truman's trip to Chicago in April of 1943 to present a speech in support of the government's aid to the European Jews who were being exterminated by the Germans. During this speech, he implicitly criticized President Roosevelt for not doing enough.

The utterance of personal beliefs and the actions of President Truman are even more difficult to reconcile. The recently discovered personal writings strongly suggest that Truman had little personal, "gut" level liking for the Jews. However, it appears that his innate fairness and humanness did not allow his very personal feelings towards a group of people to affect his moral and ethical way of dealing with them as the President of the United States of America. His actions clearly and strongly support this conclusion. He was instrumental in getting the legislation on increasing the immigration quotas for the Jews in the D.P. camps. He lobbied strongly for the changes in the Displaced Persons Act to abolish the discrimination against the Jews and while at it against the Catholics also. One has to further applaud Truman for his deeds. He stood up against his cabinet and particularly against his Secretary of State, George Marshall, and threw the support of the United States in the United Nations towards the recognition of the State of Israel. He even outmaneuvered the Russians in the United Nations to get the U.S. on record of being the first nation to recognize the State of Israel on record. The Jews indeed respected and loved Truman in the D.P. camps. Despite the recent sensational revelations, personally I am still most grateful to this man and consider him an icon.

****

Upon return to Frankfurt, I had a letter from Aliz waiting for me. My application for a visa was approved. How she did it I don't know, but she arranged for JOINT to support my application and provide the guarantees. I had the medical examination for the visa scheduled for the next week. Good thing that I showed up back in Frankfurt on time, otherwise I would have missed the examination. Also, I was to show up at the JOINT offices to sign papers and get things straightened out with them. All of this caught me by surprise and left me breathless. At the same time, I had to start again the schoolwork and get the clinics, the laboratories as well as my lecture schedule squared away.

Despite the time pressure, I felt that the first thing on my schedule must be Aliz. In the final analysis she was the one who literally performed a miracle for me; a miracle that most likely would influence my entire life from then on. The next morning Ania and I took the tram to the city. Ania was to go to school and get oriented in respect to the schedules and I went to the American Consulate.

Luckily, Aliz was at the Consulate office. When she was told that I was in looking for her, she immediately came out to the waiting area to see me. She looked better than ever, in what appeared to be a new fancy dress. With her shiny black hair, she was radiating a good mood and fun.

As I opened my mouth to greet her, she laughed and put her hand over my lips. "Don't say anything come back at noon," she said, "We will go out for lunch and have a little conversation at that time," she added. I just whispered back, "Thank you" and left.

I didn't walk, I ran to catch the tram to the Haupt Bahnhoff (main railroad station) from where I walked across the bridge to the school. I had to find Ania fast to tell her what had transpired and to have enough time to get back to the Consulate by noon.

The most likely place to catch her, I thought, would be the clinic. However, once I got there she was already gone. Several of our friends were loitering in the nursing area. They looked up when I walked in and, without waiting for me to ask, announced, "She just left, probably to the biochemistry laboratory to register for the exercises. She already managed to get you signed up here as her partner for the clinical rotation. You got it made, Emil, you got a slave taking care of all you needs. Do you know a place where we could get one?" they asked. "Certainly," I responded, "take a walk to the Himalayan Mountains, you may find one there, I did!" We all laughed as I turned to the exit to continue my trot, this time to the biochemistry building. I walked directly to Dr. Rauen's office. He was a young professor of physiologic chemistry whom we befriended last semester. He offered to help us with the studies; somewhat reminiscent of the approach Dr. Piontek used offering to help us in the studies of anatomy and histology. Slowly a friendship developed between us and Dr. Rauen. It, however, was different from what we experienced with Dr. Piontek. Dr. Rauen was married; he impressed me as a much more stable but less sensitive person.

We did discuss with him the Nazi days in Germany. He claimed to always have opposed their philosophy, but never dwelled on any of the details or on the details of the genocidal policies of the Third Reich towards the Jews. I concluded, however, that he must have carried a burden of guilt that he tried to dissipate by helping us, the survivors. Again, the thought of revenge or "repayment" for the German atrocities never crossed our minds and Ania and I simply accepted their, both Piontek's and Rauen's, gestures of friendship and good will with pleasure and tried to make them understand our feelings and positions. Matter of fact, despite our marginal food situation, we tried to help them with the few "luxuries" we had, primarily coffee and cigarettes. They both smoked and both were coffee addicts as most of the Germans at that time, with true addiction-withdrawal symptoms. It wasn't until later, after I left Germany that Ania also learned of Piontek's morphine addiction.

I found Ania in Rauen's office. He was to be our instructor for the last part of the physiologic chemistry laboratory course. He signed our Student Books and we left obviously with a promise to see him the next day in class.

On the way to the departmental offices to get the schedules, I told Ania about my encounter with Aliz and my promise to have lunch with her. She was to provide me during the lunch with all the details of the subsequent steps hopefully leading to a visa for me. Ania took a long side glance at me but didn't say anything. I said it probably would be wise for her to go home now and I promised to do the same promptly after the lunch with Aliz.

We were finishing lunch in the Bierstube by the bridge on the river. Aliz sat next to me. She was sad. We just finished talking about ourselves. It was difficult for me. I didn't bargain for this load of emotional baggage. She was a real lady. She clearly understood the situation and accepted my obvious explanation of the situation. "This," she kept reassuring me "doesn't change anything, particularly my feelings towards you. I simply like you a lot. I made a commitment to see the issue with your visa through and this I will do. Maybe we will meet some day in America," she added smiling sadly at me. "And now let me tell you where we are standing in respect to your visa. I discussed your situation with the American Consul, as I mentioned in the letter to you, and he said that a visa cannot be granted on the strength of your parents documents since your father needs to be under medical observation by the consul's physician for at least one year before reconsidering granting his visa. The Consul also felt that the quickest and best way for you to be granted a visa would be to obtain the financial assurance documents from JOINT rather than from your parent's relatives in the U.S., particularly since you are 'underage' and must travel alone. In view of this information I contacted JOINT and told them that the American Consul *needs* to grant you a visa but in view of the fact that you are underage the Consulate needs an organization like JOINT to provide the necessary papers. Within a couple days I got a call from them requesting that you go to their offices immediately and they will provide you with all necessary documents within a few days."

I looked at Aliz with an open mouth and I don't think that I blinked once. I couldn't believe my ears. Nothing like that ever happened to me in the past and in my wildest dreams, I couldn't fantasize anything like this to ever happen to me in the future. I simply had no words; I didn't know what to do or what to say. I sat there paralyzed with tears streaming down my face.

I took her hands and kissed them. I looked into her eyes and could see tears in them, but only for a brief moment. Her eyes suddenly lit up again and the face became one big radiant smile. She embraced me and said quietly, "I am so happy that I could do this for you." After uttering these words, she returned to her usual quiet and warm demeanor. Now she acted again as a Consulate's official. She handed me an envelope that contained appointments for my medical examinations. As she was handing it to me, she started laughing again and said, "Well obviously one has to have a visa approved and to have the approval one needs the guarantee documents. Don't get concerned that we will get it done in an upside down fashion. It will all work, I promise. But don't forget to go to the JOINT tomorrow to get their part of work going. I already asked them to send the documents directly to me at the Consulate rather then to you. This will streamline the mechanics of the procedure. Furthermore, I think that they sensed that the Consulate would like to see all this expedited and JOINT is eager to cooperate and do us favors because this may work at times both ways. Come by and see me when you show up for the medical examination."

After her last sentence I thought that I lost my tongue. It must have gotten stuck to the roof of my mouth. I simply got up shook her hand and left. While going home my thoughts were in total disarray. I simply didn't understand what was happening. Knowing how difficult it was for a D.P. to get any information from the Consulate's offices and how long it could take for any action to be taken in respect to a D.P.'s case, I was totally confused as all these miracles were happening to me. Aliz was obviously behind the entire scenario.

But, if so, why was she doing it? The only logical conclusion I could arrive to was that her action was motivated by a very personal desire to assist me. She simply must have liked me very much and I didn't even dare to try to fathom her motives. Actually I was scared to do so. I had no idea how to characterize this and all of the other encounters with her. I thought of my relationship with Aliz in very innocent terms. However, maybe I was much too young to understand the nuances and the way of thinking of a much more experienced woman. I couldn't wait to talk about this with Ania.

After getting home, I had a violin lesson scheduled for the afternoon and postponed seeing Ania until that evening. It gave me a little time to get composed. Playing violin with Mr. Lotz was a great way to relax, particularly since he sensed my emotional turmoil and conducted the lesson to fit my mood. I didn't realize it at that time when I burdened him with my feelings of distress; however, some days later, thinking of that afternoon I did realize what he had done and how skillfully he carried it out.

I wished that I could have avoided a discussion with Ania about the encounter with Aliz. This, obviously, was impossible. After the music lesson I ran up to her apartment to see that she was already preparing supper with the anticipation that we would eat in her apartment and talk freely, not being cramped by Frau Lange's presence.

As I walked through the kitchen door she looked up at me from the stove where she stood and exclaimed with great satisfaction in her voice, "Frau Taub, [the landlady] is gone for the evening, we have the entire place to ourselves." With this she ran over, jumped up at me with her arms around my neck and legs around my waist kissing my mouth and repeating, "Can't wait to hear what has happened, tell me, tell me. Will she be able to move your application ahead of time at the Consulate?"

I knew who the "she" was and answered with reasonable degree of certainty in my voice, "I think so." She pressed, "Tell me more; I want to hear all the details." That was exactly the area I did not wish to delve into. However, I felt quite secure discussing the details of the technique used by Aliz in obtaining the visa. I was laughing when describing Aliz's approach in respect to JOINT and getting them to provide the guarantee for me in a matter of days by invoking the "Royal" powers of the American Consulate. I continued my tale by relating the clever way she acted as a secretary at the Consulate insinuating that it was the Consul's wish for JOINT to provide the guarantee documents while it was really her wish.

She, I indicated, has really handled the situation with sufficient cleverness to end up with a possibility of misinterpretation if a problem would have arisen. The "greasing of the wheel" to arrange for a prompt medical examination was apparently only a matter of her knowing everyone in the Consulate and having a good relationship with them. I assumed that she was able to pull it off because no one would suspect anything since she wasn't a relative of mine nor really even an acquaintance. And here again my mind started playing a trick. I felt like telling Ania about my suspicions of why Aliz was doing this for me. However, I really had no evidence for these suspicions and by bringing them up I probably would only begin to worry Ania. I bit my tongue in the last minute and let it go.

My visit to JOINT and later to the medical office at the Consulate went by like in a dream, I remember very little. While getting all this arranged, Ania and I had to manage a heavy schedule at the Medical School. Between the clinics, lectures, laboratories and weekly quizzes, we were totally exhausted.

In early May I was called to the Consulate for an interview. After completion of the interview, I was asked to place my hand over my heart and repeat an oath after the official administered it. It was the Pledge of Allegiance to the United States of America. I was granted a visa to enter the United States and to have the privilege of applying for citizenship in five years from the day of entry. Then I was asked to return to the Consulate on the following day.

The next day I was given all the documents and informed that I would be traveling to the United States on the steam ship SS *Marine Fletcher*, a U.S. Navy ship that would depart from the port Bremerhaven. I was to report to Bremen by June 10th and from there would be transported to the port of Bremerhaven.

Ania wasn't with me. She was in school taking a quiz. The schedule of my departure for the United States left me in shock. I was given less than a month to report to Bremen. A week would be required to finish my business in school and get the certificates and the signatures in the Student Book. First, I thought, it would be only proper to see Aliz now and thank her for the incredible effort she exerted on my behalf. I walked over to her office. She was there and eager to see me. I asked if we could have a lunch together. She looked at me with her "all knowing" wise eyes and said, "Sure, the same Bierstube at 12 o'clock?" I nodded.

I sat at a table in the corner. When she walked in, she came over and sat down across from me. I instantly started thanking her but she interrupted me by placing her fingers on my lips. "I appreciate and understand your need and desire to thank me, why don't you do it quickly and let's get over with it." I looked at her, said, "Thank you very much" and stopped right there.

She smiled her radiant huge smile and placed her hand on my hand resting on the table. "You welcome," she said continuing to smile and to press my hand, "and now let's just relax and talk to each other."

I started, "I just don't understand why you went through this much trouble to help me?" She raised her hand and started in a stern and even voice, "I learned to like you. Yes, I am older but I got to like you very much. I am very happy that I was able to help. I hope that your trip to 'paradise' will be safe and pleasant. I also wish you all the success in the New World, a land that you will have to face. Yesterday I learned about Ania. If she is your wish than I'd like to extend my hands to both of you. Sometime, in the coming years, you may think back to someone who helped you with your first steps towards a dream that you were just about to enter. I will be happy to know that I was a part of the solution to give you the opportunity to enter this dream. Good luck." She stood up. So did I. She embraced me, kissed me and left.

I sat at the table for a long while thinking how convoluted life can be. I had tears in my eyes. I knew that I would always be grateful to Aliz but I also felt that now I should forget her.

From the tram, I ran impatiently into my building and up to the second floor to tell Ania that I was to report to Bremen on June 10th. Breathlessly I banged on her door but there was no answer. Apparently, she wasn't home yet and Frau Taub was still at work. I went back to my apartment. Frau Lang was in and informed me that Ania still was not back from school. I couldn't hold back my feelings; I had to share my joy with someone. "Frau Lang," I called out, "Frau Lang, Ich moechte innen…" and I spilled all my pent up anxiety, happiness, fear and joy. As I was describing what has happened, semi-crying and semi-shouting, Ania walked in.

It was a bittersweet evening. We laughed, we cried, we were happy and at the same time very sad. We were forced again to face the cold reality. Ania was obviously happy for me, but at the same time she wished for a different scenario.

I was not happy, not happy at all. Matter of fact, and I didn't tell her that, I was seriously considering giving up the visa and waiting for everyone in order to go to America together. I was absolutely convinced that my family and Ania's family would ultimately get visas and go to America. This belief was strongly supported by the information I got from my greatest expert on the ongoing activities of the government of United States – Aliz! She told me that a new legislation was being crafted with the idea to help the Jewish D.P.s obtain visas. According to Aliz, this legislation was on its way for approval in the U.S. Congress.

My last train trip from Frankfurt to Kassel, loaded with both physical and emotional luggage, was sad. There was so much to tell Ania but I had no inner strength to talk about the various issues that floated in my mind. We sat close throughout the trip, holding each other as if not wanting to let go. Each time we would start a conversation it would stop almost automatically as we would increase the grip of our arms holding us together.

In Kassel the mood was almost festive. The word about improvement of the chances for getting visas became common knowledge and the camp was busy with rumors of people getting visas almost overnight. Letters were coming from the recent immigrants with good news. The JOINT apparently was very efficient in helping the newcomers with their immediate needs and in resettling them throughout United States. Although, according to the stories in the letters, most immigrants wanted to stay in New York, the port where most of the ships with emigrants were landing.

The activities in the house were running at a frantic rate. Mother was checking and rechecking the clothing I was to take with me. Father was looking into the possibility of buying somewhere two new shirts for me. Also, the "famous" gray suit I brought from Alma Ata not only was quite worn out but I also seemed to have outgrown it having gained some weight.

My parents decided to have a new suit tailored for me. In the camp, there was no shortage of tailors but the problem was getting the fabric. One had to obtain it on the black market, an expensive proposition!

Finally, the fabric was purchased and an elegant suit, black with a fine gray stripe, started taking shape; there was still a month before my departure, thus, adequate time for getting the suit completed.

On the morning of May 15, the camp was buzzing with excitement. Shmull was banging at the door. Mietek and Ania came over as the big news arrived. At midnight, on May 14, 1948, a provisional government declared the establishment of a State of Israel in the Holy Land. The United States of America was the first country to approve the declaration.

Celebrations began at the very instant the news became known, and continued for days. These were the happiest days for everyone in the camp. But, as could be expected, this happening spawned heated debates.

The youngsters were particularly happy and obviously partying the hardest. Matter of fact, someone suggested that we take off for a day and visit the famous "Riesenschloss" (the "Great Castle") in the Wilhelmhohe castle park near Kassel, and see the famous "Hercules." I thought that this should be a fitting place to celebrate. The construction of the castle commenced in 1701 and the structure was almost completed some sixteen years later, however, it was never used for living quarters.

We arrived at the 1,500-foot high wooded hill on which the castle was placed with great expectations. Looking up from the bottom of the hill, we could see the incredible structure on the top where an elaborate cascade built of stone blocks was starting and extending all the way to the bottom of the hill where we stood.

The cascade was dry today but I could imagine its beauty when water was flowing and cascading over the small waterfalls from the very roots of the castle down to the plane. The waterfalls cascading downward had rough-hewed stone steps on both sides to allow walking on the edges of the cascade. Outside of the steps was a thick forest of evergreens. We didn't walk; we raced up the steps almost 1,000 feet to the base of the castle. It was an imposing octagonal stone structure looking very barbaric to me. The first level had a huge arched entrance from where the cascade originated. It looked almost like an immense cave.

Inside the entrance were huge pedestals that we immediately climbed and assumed heroic poses to have pictures taken. In the center, there was an immense statue of a sitting Hercules. Its thighs were twice as thick as my waist. We immediately climbed into his lap and had pictures taken again. Really, we behaved like children. However, we had never been to a castle like this and all of us were in a hilarious mood for the reasons described before .

The second level had elaborate inner spaces with huge arched openings towards the outside. This was the main part of the structure. However, it didn't appear to ever been occupied by people. Nevertheless it was remarkable to see that there was no damage to the stone structures that I could see done during the intervening years by visitors, unless it was constantly being repaired. The latter I would doubt considering the history of the past several years.

From the second level, we climbed to the roof, a terrace. It had a roughly hewed stone balustrade around its perimeter and the famous 100-foot tall stone pyramid in its center. On top of the pyramid was the renowned copper sculpture of 30-foot tall Hercules crafted by Anthoni, a famous 18th century goldsmith from Augsburg.

The view from the terrace was breathtaking. We spent a great deal of time here, taking pictures and climbing wherever we could, like a bunch of kids that we actually still were.

****

The day arrived that I was to get ready for the eventful journey. I had very mixed feelings. To leave my entire family, parents and Stella behind; to leave Ania behind and to face a totally unknown world was frightening to me, although I wouldn't admit this to anyone. Probably an additional and paralyzing fright was the lack of the English language knowledge. Going to Russia was not frightening; there was some similarity between the Polish and Russian languages. Coming back to Germany was no major problem; the language came back to me rather fast. But, English? The only words I knew were "OK" and "Yes." I was certain that the extent of my proficiency in the English language was not going to get me very far. But, the decision was made.

Everyone came to the railroad station to see me off. I was given the medium sized prewar valise where I fit all my earthly possessions, including some medical school books and my new beautiful black striped suit.

Mother was crying Ania was smiling, and Father looked stern and kept on repeating: "we will see you soon." Stella was just standing there and crying. I took her in my arms and said quietly, "Take care of our parents; I will get everything ready for all of you in America." Mother dried her eyes and gave me some German money saying, "You may need this before you get on the ship." Then she also gave me her treasure, a twenty dollar bill. American money! "This," she said "should help you when you get to America."

I began to feel a little moisture on my cheeks, but when I looked at Ania, I still saw only a smile on her face. Her parents stood next to her. I walked over, shook their hands saying goodbye. They admonished me again to look up Ania's aunt as soon as possible, her mother's sister, and try to influence her to send the guarantee papers as soon as possible. I promised to do this promptly while looking at Ania who stood there still with a smile on her face.

I wanted very much to take her in my arms, and kiss her and keep on telling her over and again how much I loved her and how much I will miss her. The presence of both parents, however, had an obvious and fatal inhibitory influence on this desire. I gave Ania a quick hug saying, "see you soon," and turned around to board the train; the conductor was already waving his little round sign indicating departure. As the train started moving, I got to the window. The last thing I saw was a smile on Ania's face. She was a really brave little trooper.

In Bremen, I had no problem finding the place I was to report to. I showed the address to the conductor on the tram at the railroad station. He looked at it and with a smile explained to me which tram number to take. He obviously knew the address. I asked him and he shook his head affirmatively. "Oh yes, I know this address, many people," he said with a knowledgeable smile, "many people ask for this address."

For reasons I couldn't explain at that time, I wished to move away from him. I suddenly developed this burning desire to get out of Germany. I never felt this strongly before. Was it because this was the first time in my life that I was totally alone? Alone and not knowing when I would see my loved ones again?

The address turned out to be a large, several stories high, gray-beige building. I walked into a huge lobby full of people sitting on their suitcases or bundles. There was a long counter with a wooden top on the left side of the lobby. Several men were standing there filling out papers or talking to uniformed clerks. I joined them waiting for my turn to catch the attention of one of the staff.

As I stood waiting, a young girl walked in through a door behind the counter. She looked at the men busy who were either talking to each other or filling out forms. Finally her gaze rested on me. As she smiled at me, I couldn't help but notice a row of beautiful sparkling white teeth, and I smiled back at her.

"May I help you?" she asked in German. I pulled out my papers and handed them to her. She glanced at them and still with a friendly smile on her face remarked, "Oh yes, SS *Marine Flasher*, we will be losing you in few days. I have a room with three boys about your age in it, there is a fourth bed in there. Would you like to join them?"

I nodded and said, "why not?" She handed me a key, a slip of paper with the room number and my name and explained how to get there.

I dragged my valise to the second floor, found the room number and knocked at the door. Two voices answered in Polish, "come in." As I walked in I looked around the room. It was quite large with two large windows facing the street, four beds, one in each corner of the room, a wash basin, a chest of drawers and a standing wardrobe. Two boys were apparently talking to each other while sitting on the beds when I came in. They jumped up when I walked in and ran over to help me with the valise.

The taller one, who looked about five years older than I, stuck out his hand and announced in Polish, "I am Bolek and this is," he turned to the other boy who looked about the same age, "Staszek." I shook hands with him and with Staszek while introducing myself to both of them. "The young lady at the desk downstairs," I started, "Oh yes," interrupted Bolek, "Ryfka, she is quite a flirt, watch her." I continued, "informed me that both of you are going to America on SS *Marine Flasher*."

Their eyes lit up, "Oh, yes," they exclaimed in unison, "we sure are and can't wait to get to 'Ameritchka,' the very first day that we arrive, we will start picking up the gold off the streets and get instantly rich." They laughed, started hugging each other and hugging me. Soon we were rolling all over the beds and couldn't stop laughing. In the midst of this hilarity, the doors opened and a short, skinny looking fellow about my age imploded into the room collapsing on top of Bolek. He instantly sensed the state of hilarity we were in and not trying to figure out what, why or when, joined us.

After a while, exhaustion took over and we just simply laid there panting and looking at each other. Finally, the little fellow got up, walked over to me and said, "I am Romek, I am from Krakow. I am alone, everyone is dead but I am managing fine." Both, Bolek and Staszek jumped up, came over and put their arms around Romek saying, "He is a good fellow, little strange, but he has good reasons for it, the same reasons that the two of us have, except that he reacts to them a little differently, but don't mind him!" I also got up, put my arms around Romek and said, "It is good to meet you."

Soon all four of us sat on the bed and started really talking to each other. It turned out that all three of them were orphans, not only the parents but also the rest of their families perished in the war. They received special "orphan" visas from the American Consulate, they told me, and were to sail on the SS *Marine Flasher* to America. Apparently the boat was departing from the port in Bremerhaven in three days.

I gave them my brief story and we became friends. They apprised me of the routines at the camp. Yes, the building was considered to be a transitional D.P. camp. The people here were in transit, on their way to the United States. The building housed mostly families but there were also many singles like us.

There was a large dining room where breakfast, lunch and supper were served and I was quickly informed by my newly acquired friends that the food was very good and free. Although, they said, they like to roam the city, they also like to be back for the free meals and they advised me to do so also.

Soon I learned that Bolek and Staszek had advice and opinions about everything and they expected Romek and I, the two youngest in the group, to follow their suggestions. Since I was alone I was very happy to do just so.

We became a totally inseparable quartet. In no time, Bolek asked me how I liked the young girl working at the front desk in the lobby. I told him that I liked her very much, since she was pretty and pleasant. "But," I blurted, "she must be German, she talked German to me."

Bolek responded with a hilarious laughter, "no way, she is a nice Jewish girl originally from Krakow; she lives here, in Bremen with her parents who survived the war in hiding. They are waiting for visas. The mother has some medical difficulties, but they may get the visas within several months. I am trying to put the touch on her," he said with a mischievous smile, "so stay away from her."

I quietly responded, "I am not in the market, I have a girl and we are very serious."

He laughed again, and said, "Well, we will see how serious you are tonight."

The rest of the day was spent on the trams; the four of us rode all over the city, simply enjoying the freedom to do so. After the dinner, Bolek, apparently he worked himself up into a leadership position in our little group, turned to Staszek and asked, "how about it?" Staszek responded, "I am running out of money."

Bolek nodded sagely and with his mischievous smile on the lips said, "Well we will have no major expenses tomorrow and the day after we are leaving. Anyway, if you run out of money don't worry about it. I have plenty. Let's take the two youngsters with us, particularly the one deeply in love." As he said that, he turned towards me with a raucous laugh that infected the other two. Everyone was roaring with laughter. I turned beet red up to the roots of my hair, at least I thought so because my face turned fiery hot. This was the first time that anyone brought up my love towards Ania in this crass fashion, matter of fact in any fashion.

I was caught by surprise. Up to now no one, that included my parents and our friends, made any comments or remarks regarding the relationship between me and Ania. Only once, when he visited us in Frankfurt, Father sat down and talked to me seriously about Ania and his underlying concerns that I treat her in a gentlemanly fashion but he immediately added, "I am certain you would have done so without me reminding you about it."

Mother and Ania's parents usually just looked at us with happiness in their eyes and simply treated us as their own children. Here, I was rudely reminded of the reality and fragility of a relationship and was exposed to the brazen reactions of young men to this type of a situation. I wasn't prepared for it and didn't know how to respond to it. I probably shouldn't have taken this so seriously. They were friends, they were young and they obviously were having fun with me and with my "love for Ania."

After dinner, we left for the adventure. No one was willing to say where and what. Figuring my friends, I made an easy assumption. They were taking me to a "sex" show or a movie. Well I wasn't very far from the truth but I was not thinking big enough!

Sure enough when we got off the tram and walked a few blocks we ended up in a most unbelievable place. There were bars all around us with American jazz blaring; little "theaters" where for a few pennies one could see a sex show through a little hole in a wall. There were attractive but worn looking women enticing men with their "wares."

Bolek and Staszek were constantly accosted; Romek and I looking even younger than our actual ages were largely left alone except occasionally when a more matronly or motherly looking woman would come over and whisper nice words to us. I, obviously, had never been exposed to anything like this and really, I didn't know how to react to it and how to respond to the overtures but not be, at least in my opinion, rude to some of the rather aggressive women around me.

Bolek was in his element. He strutted, he joked with the girls, obviously was having "a time of his life." Although, first I felt uncomfortable, soon I joined the general levity and curiosity got the better of me.

Bolek was an obvious leader, he was the most experienced among us and the one with a pocket full of money. I commented that my finances were extremely meager and that I probably would not be able to keep up with them. Bolek only laughed. "Save your money, all of you are my guests. I closed a big deal on roasted coffee with a guy in Munich and made a lot of money. Tonight I want you to enjoy your last night out in Germany."

On this note he exclaimed, "lets step into this club," pointing at an entrance to a dimly lit place with a gorgeous semi-nude blonde welcoming all the newcomers at the door. "I know this joint, it has the best looking girls on the street," he added. Inside he handed some money to the waiter and we were seated at a table next to a little round stage occupied by a couple who were pretending or actually having a sexual intercourse.

As we walked out into the cool night, the blaring of the music, the smell of cheap perfume in the air, the almost naked bodies and the number of drinks I consumed made my head spin. I was convinced that I was deadly drunk and that I would simply collapse on the street.

Bolek and Staszek picked me up under my arms and walked me down the street. Bolek said while dragging me, "Now, a little walk will help. You heard it, you saw it and you smelled it, we will sober you up and have you do it!" he finished with his raucous laughter. We walked several blocks on a street lined with bars, clubs and various, what I interpreted to be, "entertainment places." Finally, we turned down a much quieter street. The houses here had, what appeared to be, plate glass storefronts. Inside the windows, lights were dim, however, when I managed to get my eyes in focus I could see behind each plate glass window a small room furnished with a couch, an overstuffed chair and a bed. There were scantily clad girls in many of the rooms; sitting, standing or reclining in a sexy pose on or next to one of the pieces of furniture.

To my inexperienced eyes the "places" looked actually attractive. The furniture was nice, the walls were wallpapered in an attractive way; in each room there was an attractive lamp on the night table, throwing a glow of light on the girls. From the distance I watched them, the girls, although barely dressed, looked neat and clean. And watching I did! I must have sobered up instantly. I never had seen anything like this. I never had seen dozens and dozens of attractive semi-clad girls smiling in a most friendly way trying to entice us to come in. I couldn't believe my eyes. The three boys apparently had the time of their lives, bending over with laughter, while watching me rather than the girls.

Finally, Bolek pointed to some of the windows asking, "Do you know why some windows are shut tight with a thick drape?"

I looked at him with, what must have looked like a professional drunkard's eyes, and responded in disdain, "What do you think; I am a nincompoop or a village simpleton? I certainly know! The ladies have probably a guest there and the drape assures them of some privacy."

"Well, well, well," quipped Bolek, "look at this educated 'Doctor.' Looks like that the medical school has indeed helped in broadening his horizons."

I was furious, "Don't you dare talk like this to me," but I was too drunk to continue. The words became slurred, everything started rotating in front of my eyes and I must have passed out because the next thing I knew we were back in our room when I regained consciousness. My tongue felt like an unfinished wooden board and I became violently nauseous.

The next day I didn't wake up until ten o'clock. The first thing I saw looking around were all three of my new friends sitting on the bed across from mine, each with a crestfallen face. It lit up like electric bulbs when I started moving around and tried to sit up. "Ah, he is alive," ejaculated Bolek jumping up and coming over to my bed. Staszek just sat there with deep concern on his face. Romek, the "kid," started laughing and choking on the words he tried to extricate from his dry throat, "I told you that he was all right, I told you not to worry."

All three of them climbed on my bed and started banging me on my back while laughing hysterically. I still felt hung over with a head that was several sizes too large for my shoulders. However, their laughter was infectious and in no time I joined them and we kept on to roar with laughter, ultimately rolling all over the floor until we simply stopped from exhaustion.

Finally, I washed up and since it was lunch time we marched to the dining room where I hoped to drink a gallon of water because my thirst was growing in the past half hour from severe to impossible. Bolek reassured me that this was a sign of a hangover and that once I would eat and drink, I would feel "like new." I really would have liked to believe him and even asked him if my headache would also go away; there was no headache medicine available in the camp.

The lunch consisted of, yes; you guessed it correctly, split pea soup and two slices of "Spam". I liked the soup, but left the salty

"Spam" alone. After the soup, I drank all the water that was available in the glass jars in the dining room. Miraculously, after eating the soup and drinking a gallon, or so, of water I started feeling quite good and was ready to join the fellows in their walk to the city.

First, however, we decided to check in the office concerning our departure. Sure enough, the SS *Marine Fletcher* was ready for departure and we were to be picked up the next morning to be taken to Bremerhaven. The four of us were assigned a berth next to each other.

As I looked to the left, to the right or up I saw an endless gray wall. I was standing on the pier holding onto my valise and looking at the hull of the ship. The four of us were about to board. The group of people ahead of us, as they walked up the steps of a gangway that snaked up diagonally on the side of the ship, reached the deck. There was one female, just ahead of me in line and she held in her hands two suitcases. My friends were lined up directly behind me single file. There was also a naval officer in a khaki uniform standing next to me at the foot of the gangway. Someone on the deck gave a hand signal and he turned to the women indicating that she should start across the gangway. Turning to me, he indicated that I should follow her. As she began to ascend, she tripped on the very first step and started falling. I dropped my valise and stepped over towards her, just being able to catch her before she fell. At that moment, I realized that she was a young, good-looking girl. She turned towards me and speaking in German thanked me profusely.

As we came up on the deck, I handed my boarding slip to one of the sailors stationed to help the passengers find their cabins. We were taken several levels below the deck into a huge hold. There were no windows or portholes here. Four-level bunks were lined up into many rows. Between the bunks, there were special areas constructed for our luggage in a manner that would prevent it from flying around when the boat got on the way. We were assigned bunks close to each other. Also, we were told that only two bunk layers were to be occupied since there would not be enough people to fill all four layers of the bunks. The space could have held 400-500 people; it was a huge room. Outside the bunk room there was a common bathroom area.

We dropped our belongings into the lockers and impatiently ran up several floors to the main deck using the metal ladders. As we moved to higher decks, we could see corridors lined with private cabins. These accommodations were for the returning soldiers, administrative, military personnel and their families. We didn't care, we were happy with our bunks as long as the boat would get us to America!

There were rumors flying. There were no leaders to inform us properly or to allay our anxieties. The main rumor was that we would be casting off in the early afternoon. That gave us time to roam around the boat and investigate.

The four of us were cut out for just such activity. We ran over to the front of the ship where we could see from our vantage point the work deck, one level below us, at the bow (front of the boat). This deck was closed to the passengers. It contained several monstrous winches, two with heavy chains leading to huge anchors fastened in the anchor wells outside of the hull. Other winches had lines or chains coiled on them leading outside the boat to the docks. There were two sailors working there among the various chains, lines and winches. It was fascinating and all of it looked very complicated to us.

To the back of us, there was a tall structure, some higher decks with an upper deck that was glass enclosed, probably housing the steering station. We took the metal ladder to the next level; it appeared to be occupied primarily by cabins. It had a deck running outside of the cabins all around the boat. From there we could see very well the embarkation process and the docks below us.

The dockworkers and the sailors were busy removing the gangway and the ladder; several sailors were busy with lines used for mooring the boat. The lines were gradually unfastened and the boat started moving slowly away from the dock.

Soon we were at sea. The weather was glorious. The sun was shining; there were small ripples on the water reflecting the sun's rays. Standing by the rail I could see the ship knifing its way through a sea of silver. I was totally mesmerized by the shimmering sea and the very slight motion of the boat. I think I fell asleep leaning against the rail, or was I in a twilight zone one experiences under the very special "wake-sleep" state?

I was rudely brought back to reality by Bolek who walked over from behind and playfully started choking me. First, I wasn't certain where I was or what was happening. Once I realized that it was one of Bolek's pranks, I punched him in the ribs and we started jostling with each other. Suddenly he exclaimed, "Take a look!" To the right of us, at a distance, one could see huge white cliffs rising from the sea. My rote memory of geography immediately told me: "the Dover cliffs." We ran to the bow of the ship to look on the left side. Indeed, in great distance we could see land shrouded by fog. I turned to Bolek and explained with excitement, "and this is France, I am sure; look, Bolek we are sailing between these two great countries, France and England, we will not have the opportunity to experience this again." We both were breathless; wonders like this are not to be encountered by many young boys who just barely survived with their lives during the past several years. This was excitement. This was luxury.

The main deck housed a dining room and several smaller rooms that we called the club rooms because they were furnished with wonderful overstuffed soft chairs, low coffee tables and tables with chess boards on them. The dining room was huge with many tables all covered with white tablecloths. The dining rooms looked like fancy restaurants. We were told that the ships were built to carry American troops during the war from the United States to Europe and Africa; however, except for the sleeping facilities that were Spartan, the rest of the boat looked surprisingly elegant to me. I looked at this environment through the eyes of one accustomed to the facilities of a Gulag and of Central Asia under the Soviet conditions.

During our first dinner aboard, we were still in the area of the Canal Da Mancha (the English Channel) and the seas were quiet, the boat was barely rocking. It was a festive night. For the first time since the war started, I was sitting in an elegant restaurant at a table covered with a snow-white tablecloth and set with glistening silverware and plates. There were waiters dressed in black with white towels over their forearms serving the first dish. The dinner progressed in an almost dream-like fashion. I don't remember what I ate but it was apparently very good since neither I nor any of my friends left any food on the plates. Looking around I noted that everyone was consuming their food at top speed as if being afraid that at any time someone may walk in and take it away from us. It was a memorable experience.

After the dinner, the four of us walked out on the deck towards the aft of the ship (the back of the boat). It was warm. The salty air felt good on our faces. The moon was throwing a silvery glow at the expanse of the sea lighting up brilliantly the wake that followed our ship in a perfectly straight line all the way to the horizon. The youngest of the four of us, Romek, looked up at me with his huge brown eyes and with wonder in his voice asked, "Is this America?" Bolek heard him and in his usual biting, cynical way commented, "enjoy it now; you will probably not have it this good again, at least not very soon, maybe never."

I squeezed Romek's hand and intervened, "Don't listen to this old grouch. Yes, I think this is America, but it may take us time and hard work to achieve something, but we will not give up, will we?"

While talking with conviction in my voice I wondered, indeed, how would it play out for Romek? He had no parents, no relatives and in America, he didn't know anyone. He was an orphan, and when he arrives in America he will be a single solitary soul there.

At this point Staszek went after Bolek, "don't be a 'sour-puss,' and leave Romek alone. The dinner was a great experience and I agree *this is* America! I enjoyed it; I was served a real fancy dinner. A dinner like this I have not experienced since before the war. I am looking forward to many more similar dinners in America. I started laughing, "this sounds great, I am getting excited and can't wait to get there and start doing all of the 'achieving' you mention, Staszek." On this note, we threw our arms on each other's shoulders and started dancing in a circle, while laughing wildly. As we kept on carrying on like this, I could almost feel a gaze on the back of my head; I stopped dancing and looked back. There, in a moon-cast shadow of the deck's upper structure, stood the girl I helped on the gangway; she was looking at us and laughing. Being in the hilarious mood that I was, I extended my arm towards her, took her hand and dragged her towards the circle where all five of us started dancing; circling faster and faster as we heard applause. We stopped dancing looked around and saw a group of men and women standing and applauding while laughing and trying to join us. Pretty soon a large “Hora” circle formed with people standing around the dancers singing and clapping their hands to the beat of the song.

I was breathless and so was the girl. I took her by the left hand and led her out of the circle of dancers. She was still laughing as we walked over to the rail at the edge of the deck. As she looked up at me, the moonlight formed dancing dots in her dark eyes. She must have been exactly my age.

“My name is Cornelia, Cornelia Euler Grebe,” she said. Then she placed her arms around me held me tight and kissed me on my mouth. Her mouth was soft, velvety, wide open and she was searching for my tongue. I was in shock. I didn’t know how to respond. I was surprised and taken aback, but at the same time pleased. Also, I noted that I was getting sexually aroused. She released her grip slightly moved her face a few inches away and looking at me with her dark eyes whispered, “I love you.” At this point, I thought I would faint. I never experienced this type of a situation. This encounter, in comparison to my past experiences, had compressed what has taken me under other circumstances months and years into minutes. She must have noted my consternation because she moved slightly away from me, breaking out in a laughter that sounded like many silver bells ringing in unison, and started talking. “Did I startle you?” she asked, continuing in German, “You must have a serious case of a ‘steady girlfriend,’ however, it doesn’t look that she is here, I didn’t see a female near you.”

I was again totally confused. She was beautiful, I was nineteen and we were on a ship in the middle of the Atlantic; I had to think very hard and very fast. As I started slightly distancing myself away from her, she tightened her arms around me, drew me closer and kissed me again, this time even harder. I instantly moved away hearing again the characteristic silver-bell laughter. Finally, I decided to take a different approach. I decided that maybe we should find out a little about each other before rudely rejecting her advances or unconditionally accepting them.

I started laughing, took her by the arm and led her towards one of the club rooms. “Let’s sit down in a comfortable chair,” I said, “and learn a bit about each other.” She followed me and with a happy smile on her face announced, “This is a great idea!”

We sat down across from each other and just looked. I broke the silence asking, "Do you know anything about people like me?" She lifted her face, looked me straight in the eyes and responded, with a very serious and somewhat sad look on her face, "I think it will be better that I tell you about myself first. I think that I do know about 'people' like you. Before the war started, I was a little girl. My father, a physician, practiced medicine, and my mother was a housewife. I have no siblings. We were reasonably well off, functioning quietly at the edge of the Nazi hysteria.

I began to realize at that time, that Father tried to stay away from politics, as far as possible. He managed to stay out of the Nazi party. Having had an old injury from World War I and being a physician kept him out of the military service. During the last year of the war, in order to stay out of Berlin that was being leveled by the bombing raids, we lived with some close relatives in a small town on the shores of the Baltic Sea. After the war, we returned to Berlin and at that time the real situation with my parents became clear to me. My father not only was not a Nazi activist, but he is actually a fair-minded individual who kept an enormous secret from me and from the world around him. He was a half Jew married to a gentile, my mother. If this would become known to the authorities he, undoubtedly would be taken to a death camp. Most likely the entire family, my mother and I would be imprisoned also. Fortunately the secret was kept and he survived.

Before the war was over I completed Gymnasium and having passed with high grades qualified for admission to the University. When we returned to Berlin, after the war, the universities started to function after the first few months. With Father's help I became involved in the work of some liberal organizations and became one of the founders of the, now very powerful and widespread, "Liberale Jugendbewegung" (Liberal Youth Movement).

Once the University opened its portals, I matriculated to study history and political sciences. I love my study area and in no time have succeeded in gaining sufficient recognition to land a job as a commentator with the Berlin radio, a guest columnist with newspapers and then as a student delegate at the Munich Student Conference and later as the German delegate to the World Student Conference in Zurich, Switzerland. Now I was selected as the first

German student to study at an American University, the University of North Carolina, and here I am."

I was dumfounded. My face must have looked absolutely stupid. My eyes must have been wide open like St. Florian's gate in Krakow, my brain was working with the speed of a lightning; still I had no idea how to respond to her. Was it all true? It was difficult to believe it, but for some reason I trusted her and accepted every word she uttered as a gospel. She looked up at me with her very dark gray eyes, a sad smile on her lips and took my hand in hers. After a while our hands separated we got up and went to our respective cabins.

When I woke up the next morning the boat was rocking a great deal. My three friends were gone, their bunks in violent disarray. I got up and went to the washroom. Many people were there, obviously seasick. This didn't help my morning state of mind nor my stomach. I ran up the several flights of stairs to the first deck and noted all three of my buddies by the rail. Periodically one or the other would get violently seasick.

I promised to have breakfast with Cornelia and tried to entice my friends to join us. They, however, couldn't even think of food without having their stomachs reach their throats. I left them at the rail with the admonishment that they probably would feel better by putting something into their stomachs. They promised to give my advice some consideration. Bolek remarked bitterly, "Go, and have a nice breakfast with your girlfriend." I laughed and ran towards the dining room feeling perfectly well. The seasickness had not caught up with me, yet.

The wind was very strong; I could barely open the door to the dining room. The room was almost empty. By the table at the window, looking out at the bow of the boat sat Cornelia. She looked mesmerized watching the huge Atlantic waves washing partly over the bow and sending sprays of water almost to the windows of the dining area. There was a great deal of noise around due to the spray hitting the windows.

She didn't hear me as I came up behind her chair and put my hands over her eyes. She was startled, as if waking up from a dream, but instantly she took my hands and kissed my fingers. I turned red and purple on my face and quickly sat across from her in a chair.

And again the silver bell of a giggle and again the mischievous look on her face!

She was laughing as she asked, "How do you like the weather? It is quite invigorating, wouldn't you say?"

I responded with a grumble, "I am not sure that I will survive it very long without getting seasick." She instantly replied, "My father admonished me to keep my stomach full to prevent seasickness and I am planning to follow his advice." At this moment, a waiter showed up. I was still unaccustomed to waiter service in a restaurant but I could tell that it didn't cramp Cornelia's style. The waiter spoke German; he announced the availability of bread, butter, ham, applesauce, preserves, coffee and eggs, boiled or fried. Cornelia looked at him and said quietly: "one of each, except 3 of the soft boiled eggs." Then added, "for each of us."

I was taken aback by this huge order but didn't say anything. Cornelia asked of my three friends and I told her about their vigil at the rail of the main deck. She laughed, shaking her head. "They should be here, it would cure their stomachs."

After breakfast, we went to the club room. There was no one there. She took me in her arms and we kissed while she whispered, "I wish we would have a private stateroom." I didn't reply. We sat down to play chess. She was a superb player. I was still pretty good after several years of very active chess playing in Alma Ata. However, I had troubles concentrating; I kept on loosing one game after the other.

By the afternoon, the weather got worse. The overstuffed chairs in the club room started sliding around. When walking on the deck, one could see it suddenly rear up only to slowly recede so that one had to start walking down as if walking downhill. Soon I learned that it was the down motion that created troubles for me. As the boat moved down, my entire digestive tract and its content started moving up. It took all the will power to fight the onset of real seasickness. The temperatures dropped and it was actually very cold on the decks. I had all my warm clothing packed and decided to stay inside to keep warm.

My friends would not get up from their bunks. They said that the only way to feel half decent was to keep ones body flat and the head down. I periodically brought them some water. They refused to go to the dining room to eat.

The weather didn't start moderating until we got close to the shores of the United States. During the last dinner, it was announced that we would be arriving in the New York harbor very early in the morning. We were given the documents that were kept in the American Embassy before our departure and the passports. I gave Cornelia my aunt's address and she gave me her uncle's address and telephone number. We didn't say goodbye to each other.

Early the next morning I awoke to the boat's siren. Getting dressed I ran up the staircase. The dawn was breaking. I could see behind us a light gray line in the sky. This line was rapidly followed by a golden-pink line that began to expand and fill the eastern sky. I was standing at the port rail and suddenly I saw it, an incredible sight, the Statue of Liberty glowing in the morning rays of gold and pink. My eyes filled with tears.

"Finally," I whispered. "Thank you," I said aloud. There were very few people on the decks; most were missing this meaningful and most sacred moment. It would transform me and open a new life for me; a moment that I will never forget.

These were my thoughts; however, the physical reality was heat. It was very hot and very humid. Never in my life had I experienced such heat and, particularly, such humidity. And this was only late June. Certainly, it was a contrast to the temperatures during the crossing of the Atlantic.

I was at the bow of the ship as we slowly approached the land facing the East River docks on Manhattan Island. I could see the imposing skyline of skyscrapers, but for this view I was prepared by pictures and magazine descriptions. What blew my mind was a highway, running along side Manhattan Island at the shore of the East River, which I later learned was East River Drive, absolutely packed with cars. I had never seen this many cars in my entire life as I saw on this stretch of road.

My mind drifted to the immediate future; will anyone be at the port to meet me? How will my family receive me in the States? Actually, I wasn't too worried because we were told that for those who had no families to provide immediate housing, the JOINT and the HIAS had rooms in a hotel to accommodate us. The major issue that hounded me was my inability to speak or understand English. I literally knew and understood two words only: "Yes" and "OK."

The boat was tied up to the pilings on the dock. The gangway was lowered and an official looking group of men boarded the boat. It was getting unbearably hot and confusion was reigning. I was informed that I would be in a group taken to a hotel by bus. The hotel was "Hotel Marseilles" on the corner of Broadway and 103rd Street.

I stood near the gangway in the company of my three new friends. All four of us were to be taken to the hotel. Looking over the rail, I saw a mass of people on the dock, milling and looking at us standing on the decks of the ship. Occasionally I could see a person waving frantically; apparently, they spied a familiar face on the boat. Most people on the boat, however, were standing there with their bundles and valises looking, but not recognizing a person or a face in the crowd on the dock. Beyond the crowd on the dock there was a highway with lines of cars zipping by at, what seemed to be, very high speed; beyond there was a forest of skyscrapers cluttering the firmament.

I was ready to start a new chapter in my life, but was I?

The End.

About the Author

Emil Steinberger was born in Berlin, and lived in Europe and Central Asia before and during the Second World War. He personally witnessed the Nazi triumphs in Germany and Poland as well as the rape of central Europe by the partnership of fascists and communists in the late thirties. Subsequent to immigration to the United States in 1948, he completed graduate and medical studies at the University of Iowa. Throughout his biomedical career, he focused primarily on academic medicine and research. He quickly rose to professorial ranks and became a departmental chairman. While in this capacity, he wrote over 400 scientific articles and book chapters and edited a number of scientific books. This book is his first venture outside the scientific publishing world. Currently he is retired and lives in Houston with his wife, also a retired professor of biomedical sciences.